SEARCHING FOR LILLY

Eagle Point Search & Rescue, Book 1

SUSAN STOKER

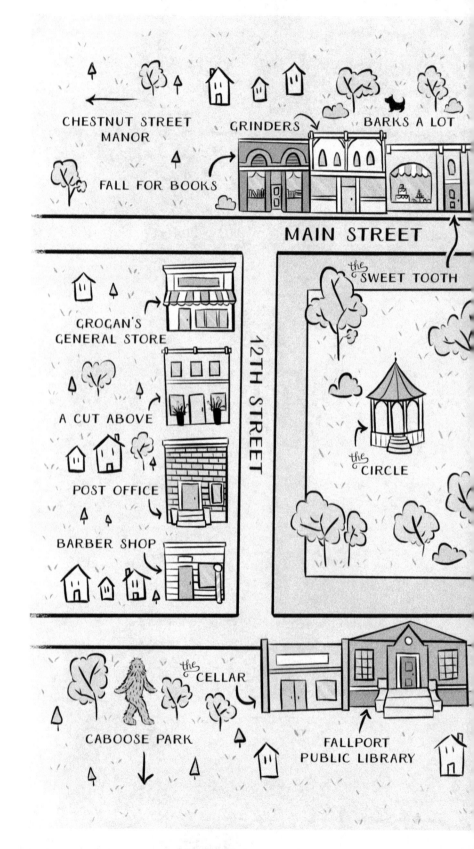

CHAPTER ONE

"If you've seen Bigfoot, raise your hand."

Lilly Ray refrained from snorting...barely.

If her dad or brothers could see her now, they'd totally be making fun of her. But a job was a job, and this one, as one of four camera operators for a brand-new show set to begin airing in the fall, was one of the better-paying gigs she'd had recently.

Though, when she'd signed on, she hadn't known exactly what the show was about. If she was honest with herself, however, she had to admit it wouldn't've made a difference. She'd needed a job, having quit her last one after the director wouldn't stop sexually harassing her. Female camera operators were becoming more common, but apparently not enough for some of the men she worked with to believe she took the job just as seriously as any male —and that she wasn't receptive to sex with anyone and everyone who expressed an interest.

Lilly wasn't a prude. She liked sex as much as the next person. Just not with conceited jerks who thought they were entitled to sleep with whomever they wanted.

So she'd quit, moving home to West Virginia to live with her dad and save money, as well as to regroup and figure out what she wanted to do with her life. At thirty-four, it felt weird to be living at home again, but her dad had been thrilled. And things were good for about a month, until she'd begun to feel stifled...and she remembered why she'd been so happy to move out when she'd finished high school.

Her dad was awesome. Supportive and encouraging. But he was also uber protective. He wanted to know where she was going and when she'd be back every time she stepped foot outside the house. The protective bubble had begun to smother her.

Her four older brothers were carbon copies of their dad. Lance was forty, Leon thirty-nine, Lucas thirty-seven, and Lincoln thirty-five. The "baby" of the family, and the only girl, Lilly had spent her life trying to prove she could take care of herself. Which was why returning home after her last gig had been a bitter pill to swallow.

So Lilly had taken the first job she could find, for a new show called *Paranormal Investigations*. It had sounded interesting, which was a bonus. She'd worked on plenty of shows that had bored her to tears.

Unfortunately, the gig would've been more attractive if every single thing portrayed on the show wasn't as fake as the boobs on every woman on the last reality show she'd filmed.

Lilly had been super intrigued when they'd gone down to Mexico to investigate the infamous Chupacabra, but after watching the producer—a slimy man by the name of Tucker Ward—and the four "investigators" set up and manipulate shot after shot to "prove" the infamous beast existed, she was quickly disillusioned and disgusted.

The trickery continued when they spent the night inside a supposedly haunted abandoned hotel in Nevada. The noises they'd heard and the piece of wood flying through the air had all been caused by one of the employees of the show.

They'd almost been arrested in Area 51 by the government, when they'd gotten too close to the famed research facility in the desert trying to prove the existence of aliens. And spending two weeks in Roswell, New Mexico, had been positively painful, as they'd visited the homes and sites of supposed alien abductions.

They'd even been to Point Pleasant, West Virginia, and "investigated" the existence of Mothman. Lilly had been embarrassed for her home state.

It wasn't that she didn't think there were things happening in the world that were unexplainable. She did. But after watching Tucker pay people to go on camera and retell their "experiences"—all totally made up—she'd become much more cynical.

But the paranormal was big business, and made a lot of money, which was why she currently had a job. There were countless productions about the paranormal, everything from shows like the one she worked on, to dramas like *The Walking Dead*, to blockbuster movies.

The setup for each episode of *Paranormal Investigations* was similar. Tucker and his three assistants traveled to the towns in advance, to scope things out. He'd arrange a location for the "town hall meeting," where they'd ask for stories from locals about whatever was being investigated. He'd then find a few people he could pay to *tell* said stories—the ones Tucker had already dreamed up. Then the cast and crew arrived, the town hall meeting would take place, and the "investigation" would begin.

Lilly was one of four camera operators, one for each investigator. Michelle Becker, Chris Carr, Trent Morrison, and Roger Kerr were the talent, chosen for their good looks...not because of any scientific experience they might have in the paranormal.

Trent was the backbone of the show's creation. Rumor had it that he and his friend, Joey Richards—one of the camera operators —had brainstormed the entire premise one night while drunk off their asses.

So, here they were in Fallport, Virginia. The small town was smack dab in the middle of the Appalachian Mountains in the southwestern part of the state. It was half an hour or so from Interstate 81, the main artery that went through Virginia. People didn't just accidentally show up in Fallport; the place was off the beaten path, so any visit was intentional.

It reminded Lilly a lot of the small town where she'd grown up. Quaint and old-fashioned...there was a Walmart, but it was on the outskirts of town, along I-480, near a Dollar Store and a Sonic restaurant, all staples of small towns in the south.

The setup for this particular town meeting had taken longer than normal. Tucker apparently had a difficult time finding people interested in lying on camera for money. With little wonder—this episode was all about Bigfoot. Despite the lack of interest from locals, Lilly had to admit, Tucker had picked a perfect place. It was likely anyone watching the show would believe Bigfoot might choose to hide in the densely forested area. There were hills and mountains all around them, the highest being Eagle Point, a majestic peak that gave the town a postcard-like appearance.

The high school gym was packed to the gills tonight. The townspeople might not be happy to have the show filmed there, but they were curious enough to want to find out exactly what was going on.

When Chris asked if anyone had seen Bigfoot, about half the hands in the room went up. Again, Lilly wasn't surprised. She'd seen this scene play out many times in the last few months.

Trent and Chris took turns choosing people, asking them to stand and tell their stories. The only people they picked, of course, were the ones Tucker had already paid ahead of time, but instead of rolling her eyes at the outlandish tales, Lilly kept her face a blank mask. As she'd been told many times by the producer, her job was merely to film. She wasn't supposed to bring any attention to herself whatsoever. She shouldn't make noise, ask questions, and never, ever, get involved in whatever was happening on the show.

That was easier said than done, especially when someone got hurt or was in a dangerous situation...which happened from time to time.

Just recently, Michelle had been interviewing someone in Roswell about aliens and they'd gone off on her out of the blue, shoving her hard enough that she'd fallen on her ass. Lilly's brothers had taught her how to defend herself—enough to possibly get out of a dangerous situation and get help—but she'd known if she attempted to help Michelle, Tucker would've lost his shit. He loved confrontation or when the talent got hurt. Said it made for better TV.

The hair on the back of Lilly's neck stood up—and suddenly she knew someone was watching her. It was an uncomfortable feeling; she didn't like not knowing who had her in their sights. She risked looking away from the viewfinder briefly, to see if she could figure out who was staring.

She was standing on one side of the room, and most of the townspeople were either looking at Roger, Trent, Chris, and Michelle—who were standing on a slightly raised platform at one end of the space—or at whoever was telling their Bigfoot story. Her eyes slowly roamed to the back of the room, where at least two dozen people stood watching the proceedings.

There was a man wearing a police badge, standing with his arms crossed and a frown on his face. To his left was another man, looking disheveled in a dirty shirt, ripped pants, scuffed shoes, and a baseball cap pulled low over his brow, his greasy, stringy, too-long black hair sticking out from under the hat. A flamboyant-looking woman probably in her mid-fifties, wearing a flowy black dress and about ten necklaces, had an amused grin on her face as she watched the proceedings.

There were several other men and women in the group, watching with interest...but it was the seven men standing nearest the door, slightly apart from the others, that caught Lilly's attention.

They were all fairly tall, well built, each with varying lengths of beard on their faces. Men who likely spent most of their time outdoors, who Lilly would describe as "rugged." She had no idea who they were, or what they might think of the proceedings...but a small shiver went through her at the sight of them.

Whoever they were, whatever they'd seen and done in the past, had marked them. They looked like hard men. Men who didn't care for bullshit. Who definitely wouldn't put up with the kind of shenanigans Tucker and the rest of the crew had brought to their town.

Lilly instinctively knew she didn't want to be on their bad side... but judging by the scowl one particularly handsome man was throwing her way, it looked like that was where she was, simply because she was associated with the show. The man had short black hair, with dark brown eyes that reminded her of the earthy bank of the river she and her dad liked to fish from. He had a square jaw, outlined by a mustache and trimmed beard. His brow was furrowed as he stared, as if trying to figure her out. She could make out a tattoo on his right bicep and inked words on his forearm.

A shiver ran through her, and out of self-preservation, Lilly turned her attention back to the camera. She focused on Michelle, who was now sharing some bullshit statistics that Tucker had probably made up.

Lilly's heart was beating fast, and she bit her lip as she stared through the lens. She wanted to look back at the man, to see if he was still watching her, but she forced herself to concentrate on what she was doing. Tucker would lose his mind if she screwed up the shot. The town hall meetings were the one thing they couldn't re-do if anything went wrong. He'd lectured her, Kate, Andre, and Joey, the other camera operators, over and over to pay attention and never, *ever* turn off their cameras, no matter what happened.

She had no idea why the man was staring at her. She hadn't done anything to bring attention to herself. All she'd done was stand off to the side and film. His expression hadn't been hostile...exactly. It had been more probing. As if he could somehow see through her and figure out her motivations for being there.

She practically snorted. Her motivation was a paycheck. She

was saving the money she earned on this job to get a place of her own once filming was over. She wanted a home base, somewhere she could come back to between jobs. She'd already decided she wasn't going back to California. Hollywood had sucked the life out of her. Yeah, she'd had steady jobs, but they weren't worth the toll the city had taken on her psyche. Not to mention having to dodge handsy men who believed every woman they saw was fair game.

Lilly wanted to believe in love, but with every year that passed, the dream of having her own family seemed less and less likely. She certainly hadn't found love in California. It seemed she may have to be content being Aunt Lilly to her brothers' children.

When Roger began his speech about the exciting days to come and how he and his fellow investigators appreciated everyone attending, Lilly knew that was her cue to pick up her camera. As the townspeople began to leave, she put the camera on her shoulder and headed toward Trent. She'd been assigned to him tonight. The talent would mingle with the townspeople and basically act like politicians...smiling and saying all the right things.

She stayed glued to Trent, aware the seven men at the back hadn't budged from their spots against the wall. They were observing to the very end of this meeting, apparently.

Trent worked his way toward the back of the room, and Lilly's stomach dropped. She didn't want to go near the men, especially the one who'd been intently watching her, but since that was where Trent was heading, she had to follow. She wasn't afraid the men would attack her or Trent or anything, but they definitely made her uneasy with their pointed attention.

Trent headed for Chris, who was shaking the police officer's hand.

"We appreciate you being here tonight," Chris said.

"I want to make sure I know what's going on in my town," the man replied without even a hint of a smile.

"This is Simon Hill, he's the police chief," Chris said as he introduced the man to Trent.

"It's good to meet you," Trent said with a smile.

"Have you decided where you're going to film this cockamamie show of yours yet?" the chief asked.

It took everything in Lilly not to grin. She liked this guy. He had the balls to say what she suspected a lot of people in the room tonight had been thinking.

Trent glanced at her and shook his head slightly. Lilly had been working with him long enough to know that meant she should put the camera down. She took it off her shoulder and stood nearby, somewhat awkwardly. She wanted to back off, to find something else to film, but remained glued to the spot.

Andre had dropped his camera too, but he didn't seem to have any problem with retreating from the somewhat tense scene.

"You might not believe in the paranormal, but I can assure you, after the things we've seen and experienced, it's real," Trent said.

Lilly couldn't stop herself from rolling her eyes. Luckily, she'd lowered her head and no one was looking at her.

Or so she'd thought. She glanced up and saw the man she'd noticed earlier, staring right at her. When their eyes met, his lips twitched. It was a slight movement, gone almost as soon as it happened. Had he been amused at her reaction?

She didn't dare look at him again after that.

Instead, she looked around the room for a distraction—and was surprised to note that everyone was gone. Everyone except for the police chief, the seven men, and the crew and talent for the show.

"Since it seems as if you're really going through with this ridiculous farce, I think I should introduce you to the men who will have to come find your asses when you get lost in our mountains," the chief said.

Tucker had joined them at that moment, and he said somewhat haughtily, "No one's getting lost."

A snort sounded from one of the men, and it took everything Lilly had not to smile.

"Right. That's what everyone says before they head off into the woods," the chief retorted. "These men are our local search and rescue team. They're the ones called when anyone goes missing. This is Ethan, Cohen, Zeke, Drew, Brock, Talon, and Raiden."

Ethan. That was the name of the man who'd been examining her so closely all night. His attention was focused on Tucker at the moment. "You need to leave a detailed account of where you're going to be filming," he said sternly.

Tucker shrugged. "I can give you a general area, but we go where the investigation leads us. Bigfoot isn't exactly predictable."

"I guarantee if you go tromping around in the forest without a plan, you're gonna get lost," Ethan warned.

"And we'll be called away from our jobs to come find your asses," the man next to him added. Lilly thought his name was Cohen.

"For the record, we don't mind getting called out when there's a real emergency, but if we have to go looking for you after you refuse to provide a well-thought-out plan of where you'll be...we won't be happy," Zeke said.

Lilly silently agreed. They were right. Of course they were. It also didn't help that Tucker preferred to do most of the investigations at night. It was easier to trick the audience and slink around perpetuating hoaxes in the dark, rather than in the daylight. But walking around a wilderness as vast as the Appalachian Mountains was very different from wandering in the deserts of the southwest or being confined inside a building.

She knew better than most, thanks to her dad and brothers drilling it into her head when they were hunting, how dangerous it was to go off trail. It was very easy to get turned around and lose your way...especially in the dark.

Tucker held up his hands in a conciliatory manner. "No one wants to get lost, not with creatures like Bigfoot out there. We'll be careful. And I'll be sure to look over the maps and let the chief know where we'll be hunting. The last thing we want, however, is someone to learn our location and come out to sabotage our search, or think they're funny by pretending to be Bigfoot."

"Oh, yeah, wouldn't want that," Raiden, the redhead with the matching bloodhound, said under his breath.

Lilly bit her lip to keep herself from laughing out loud.

"You really think you can find anything out there with just four people, plus four cameramen—sorry...cameramen *and* women—a sound guy, and a producer tromping around?" Brock asked.

"Maybe," Trent said, entering the conversation. "And while there'll be times when we'll have cameras following us, other times we'll use our handhelds, so it'll just be us investigators out there."

That was another lie. There wasn't one second when the camera operators weren't around. Tucker didn't trust the hosts of the show to get the best shots.

Ethan sighed. "Anyway, we aren't trying to be dicks," he said. "You'd be surprised how often we get called out to look for lost hikers. People who thought they were prepared, who knew the area. If you go off trail, you're gonna get lost. I'm not trying to scare you or stop you from doing whatever you're planning to do out there. I'm just urging you to use common sense. Cell phones don't work once you get on the trail, so you can't rely on them to save you if you can't find your way back to civilization."

"We have radios," Trent said, somewhat stiffly now.

"Which is good, except when they get out of range of each other," Drew replied.

"Look," Tucker said, obviously trying to be a peacemaker. "We'll be careful. We aren't stupid. Is there a reason you don't want us to find proof of Bigfoot?"

"Oh, good Lord," Raiden said with a shake of his head. "Come on, Duke. I'm sure you have to pee," he said to his bloodhound. The large dog stood up and shook himself, impressively sending a blob of drool flying across the room, before trotting after his owner.

"You might come across a black bear. Maybe even a bobcat, along with a shit ton of smaller mammals, but Bigfoot isn't in these mountains," Brock said.

Tucker didn't seem fazed by the skepticism. "That's what everyone says until we find proof. You'll be eating those words when you see our show."

Lilly was definitely uncomfortable at this point. Tucker was talking out his ass, just like always. He was a good producer. But he was also a scammer, which annoyed her.

She took a step backward, intending to extricate herself from the uncomfortable conversation and atmosphere.

"Don't move, Lilly," Tucker scolded harshly.

She inhaled sharply and nodded. She was well aware of the rule he'd pounded into her and the other camera operators. They weren't to turn off their cameras, ever. Even if they weren't holding them, Tucker wanted them running...just in case. He'd used someone's words—words they thought were off the record—against them in the past. So her camera was on, recording the entire conversation.

Since Andre had bailed before the conversation started, she was stuck.

Ethan took a step away from the wall at Tucker's tone. The look in his eyes said he was pissed off. Lilly held her breath, praying the men wouldn't come to blows.

"How long is this gonna take?" Ethan growled.

Tucker looked confused. "How long is what going to take?"

"This investigation? How long are y'all gonna be in town?" he clarified.

Tucker shrugged. "As long as it takes. I'm guessing it will take longer than the others, since there's so much ground to cover."

"Fuck," Talon muttered, then turned and headed for the door.

Lilly mentally sighed. She wasn't sure how much longer she could work on this show. It went against every moral she had. Lying, cheating, paying people off. It was nauseating...but the job paid well. She hated that she was putting money above her beliefs.

Even though she wasn't thrilled about her job, the little she'd seen of Fallport, she liked. The people were generally friendly, and while they were leery of newcomers, like residents of most small towns, they weren't hostile. Which she knew would change if they discovered what was really going on with this show.

"Just remember, it's not only your neck you're putting on the line," Ethan told Tucker. "You're endangering everyone who works on the show." With that, he gave the chief a small chin lift and turned to follow his friends.

The others didn't stick around either. They all followed Ethan out the door.

The second they were gone, Lilly let out the breath she'd been holding. She was both glad and disappointed the search and rescue team had left.

"I hope he's not going to be a problem," Tucker told the chief.

The older man shrugged. "They won't. And if something does happen out there," he gestured to the trees beyond the windows, "you'll be glad they're here."

"They're that good?" Tucker asked, sounding skeptical.

"Yes," the chief answered succinctly.

"I'm sure we'll be fine," he said. "Now if you'll excuse us, the team has some planning to do."

The chief of police nodded. "After you," he said, gesturing to the door.

Lilly took that as her cue to head to where she'd left her camera bag, so she could pack up. She was half afraid Ethan and his friends would be waiting for Tucker and the rest of them when they left, but the parking lot was empty.

"I'll call and let you know where to meet us tomorrow," Tucker told Lilly and the other camera operators. Per usual, the producer and the talent decided on the filming schedule. Lilly and the others just had to show up when and where they were needed. Which was good, because it always gave her some free time between shoots.

It was *bad* because she had no idea what they might be planning to do, in order to provide the "proof" the show needed to stay relevant and interesting.

Andre and Kate nodded and immediately headed toward the car Andre had rented. The two had gotten close over the course of the show and had no problem being left out of the day-to-day decisions about the program. Joey and Trent walked toward Trent's rental. They were best friends, and Lilly fully believed the rumor that they'd dreamed up the ridiculous show together.

Michelle, Chris, Roger, and Tucker, along with Brodie, the sound guy, all headed for the van one of them had rented. They tended to stick together when they traveled, which suited Lilly just fine. They all drank a little too much for her liking.

She wasn't close with any of the people from the show. They didn't have a lot in common. So little, in fact, Lilly had found separate living arrangements at the last few locations, apart from the rest of the crew. She preferred to find smaller independent places to stay. Bed and breakfasts that supported the local economy, rather than the larger chain hotels where the crew preferred to lodge.

She liked having time away from her co-workers, and unlike a lot of people, she enjoyed her own company. Maybe it was because she so rarely got time and space to herself when she was growing up. Her brothers had always wanted to know where she was, what she was doing, and who she was doing it with. She'd also loved hanging out with her brothers, but there were days she'd just wanted to be by herself. She hadn't had the opportunity often, surrounded by so many overprotective males.

She headed for her own rental car, put her camera on the back seat, then settled behind the wheel to drive back to the adorable B&B she'd found. It was called Chestnut Street Manor and was run by a sweet older woman, Whitney Crawford. Dinner tonight was going to be pot roast, and Lilly couldn't wait. It had been a long time since she'd had a homemade roast.

Trying her best to put thoughts of what she'd be doing in the upcoming week or so out of her mind—as well as the man named Ethan, who managed to make her feel both uncomfortable and alive at the same time—she pulled out of the school lot.

* * *

The man settled into his hotel room and sat on the bed, scowling as he stared blankly at the wall. Today had been frustrating. With every show they filmed, it was becoming crystal clear that nothing was going the way he'd planned.

Everyone had acted like idiots tonight, forgetting what they'd been told about the area and Bigfoot right before they went on air. Cameras were pointing in the wrong direction, stupid statements were made that would have to be edited out, and it had been almost impossible to get the sound right in the large auditorium. Not only that, but the townspeople seemed more skeptical here than any other place they'd been. They hadn't even found someone willing to lie on camera about seeing Bigfoot until right before the town hall meeting.

Yeah, it was safe to say he had a bad feeling about this shoot. They needed everything to go off without a hitch.

Nothing had turned out the way he'd wanted so far with the show, and given the local skepticism, this episode could make or break the entire season. He hadn't wanted to use Fallport as the location for the shoot, and it looked as though he'd been right. But had anyone listened to him? Of course not.

Idiots.

Changes would have to be made with how things were going... and if his demands weren't met, he'd make sure his involvement ended after the first season.

For a moment, he wondered if anyone would care. Then he clenched his teeth and pushed that thought to the back of his mind.

Of course they'd care. This show wouldn't exist without him.

Taking a deep breath, the man stood and began to unpack his suitcase. One week, give or take. Then they'd be done with this shoot and headed to Canada for the final episode.

After that, the *real* work would begin. Sifting through hundreds of hours of footage. Trying to make people sound smarter than they are. Cobbling together episodes and salvaging shitty sound.

If he didn't think he was on the verge of making it big in the industry, he would've turned around and left before now. But he believed in this project, and he'd do whatever it took to make it a success. Even if he had to lie, cheat, and steal.

Nothing and nobody would keep him from being famous.

CHAPTER TWO

Ethan "Chaos" Watson paced his living room in agitation. He wasn't sure why he was so unsettled by what had happened at the town hall meeting and the producer's unwillingness to listen to reason...but he was.

"They're gonna be a pain in our asses. Mark my words," he told his brother, Cohen "Rocky" Watson.

Rocky smirked. "Yup."

Ethan stopped mid-stride and glanced at his twin. They didn't look much alike, except for their height and brown eyes. Most people had no idea they were related, much less fraternal twins. But he and Rocky were as close as two people could be. They'd joined the Navy together, then made it through BUD/S and the rest of the training to be a SEAL. They weren't on the same team, but had frequently worked on joint missions.

When it was time to decide whether to stay in or get out, they'd made that decision together, as well. They'd come to Fallport, Virginia, eager to start a new life, one where they could still serve their community but in a safer context. Ethan had recruited others he'd either known from his time in the special forces community, or who had been recommended by his friend Tex, a former SEAL who seemed to know everyone and who Ethan trusted with his life.

"Why are you smiling?" Ethan asked Rocky. "There's nothing fucking funny about this."

Rocky shrugged. "Didn't you just tell me the other day that you were bored?" he asked.

Ethan sighed. He *had* said that. But he hadn't meant he wanted a team of Bigfoot investigators coming to town and announcing they'd be tromping all over *their* mountain, getting lost.

"The last time one of us said we were bored, we found the bodies of those two men who'd been tortured and killed by that serial killer, Andrew Ferry," Rocky said.

That hadn't been a good day. Hell, it hadn't been a good month. The murders and search for the killer had been the talk of the town for weeks. The only good thing to come out of the entire situation was that the locals had finally stopped treating the team as outsiders.

"It's just...there's something hinky about that Tucker guy and his show," Ethan told his brother.

"I agree," Rocky said.

"And we may have only lived here for five years, but if old man Richards actually saw Bigfoot on his property ten years ago, I'll dress up as a clown for the Fallport Fourth of July celebration."

Rocky laughed outright at that. "You hate clowns."

"I know, which is my point. There's not a chance in hell of that happening."

"You think that kid actually saw those tracks in the woods behind his house?" Rocky asked.

"Nope."

"So they were lying."

"Yup," Ethan said.

"Why?"

"That's the big question, isn't it? But since you asked, I'll tell you what I think," Ethan said. "I think this Tucker guy is as crooked as they come. He's a big shot Hollywood producer who's hoping to score ratings for his show. The only way he can get people to watch is if they actually find 'proof' of the creatures they're hunting."

"So old man Richards and the kid were paid? Like actors?" Rocky asked.

"That's what I think, yeah."

"It's not exactly criminal behavior," Rocky said.

"No, it's not. But if those assholes get lost tromping around the forest, *we* have to deal with them. You just got that job renovating that beautiful old house at the edge of town, and I've got my hands full with electrician work. Not to mention, it's a pain in the ass for the others to get called away from their own lives and jobs to find someone who got lost looking for fucking Bigfoot."

Rocky narrowed his eyes as he studied his twin. "What's *really* bothering you about this?" he asked. "Every summer we have to find plenty of people who come to town to tackle the hiking trails and get lost. Why is this any different?"

Ethan sighed and resumed his pacing. "I don't know."

Rocky rolled his eyes. "Bullshit. I know you, bro. We've faced down insurgents together. We practically share a brain. Talk to me."

Ethan turned to look at his brother. "I think it's because when the tourists head off into the wilderness without being prepared, they're putting themselves—and only themselves—in danger. That idiot's dragging a half dozen others in his wake."

"They could be just as bad as the producer," Rocky said reasonably.

Ethan knew his brother was playing devil's advocate. It was what they did when they were talking shit out. But for some reason, it really irritated him tonight.

"When that one woman lowered her camera, she didn't turn it off," Ethan admitted.

"Yeah, I noticed that," Rocky said with a nod.

Ethan wasn't surprised his brother knew who he was talking

about without having to ask. They'd always been able to follow each other's line of thinking. "And did you hear the way that asshole producer spoke to her?"

Rocky pressed his lips together and nodded again.

"Something's up with that show, and it's got my oh-shit meter pegged," Ethan said. "Mark my words, this isn't going to go well."

"You like her," Rocky said out of the blue.

"What?"

"The camera chick. You like her."

"Oh, come on. I just met her. Hell, not even. I didn't say two words to her," Ethan protested.

"I know...but don't think I didn't see how you couldn't keep your eyes off her."

Shit. That was the problem with being so close to someone else. It was almost impossible to keep a secret from his twin. "She seems different from the rest of those yahoos," Ethan said.

"In what way?"

Ethan didn't hear any disbelief or censure in his brother's tone. He was genuinely curious as to what he'd seen in her. "I saw her roll her eyes at something one of the hosts of the show said. She genuinely looked like she thought they were full of shit. And when she looked us over, she didn't see a bunch of backwater hicks. She saw...*us*." He knew he wasn't explaining his thoughts very well, and that ultimately he had no idea *what* the woman had been thinking, but Rocky seemed to understand.

"Yeah, I got that impression too," he agreed.

"Not only that, she's the only one of the crew who isn't staying at the chain hotel at the edge of town."

"How do you know *that*?" Rocky asked, clearly amused.

"I overheard Otto and Art talking tonight before filming started."

Rocky laughed. "I swear, those two are better than the Emergency Alert System. Throw in Silas, and nothing in this town is a secret."

Ethan had to agree. The three older men took it upon themselves to know everything they deemed important that went on in the town. "Very true. In this case, they said she was staying at Whitney's B&B."

"And?" Rocky asked. "What does her not staying with the others tell you?"

"I don't know," Ethan admitted.

"And that drives you crazy."

"You have to admit that it's weird. Why would she not be staying in the same place as the rest of the cast and crew? She didn't seem as buddy-buddy with the others though. Maybe that has something to do with it."

"Maybe she's new. This could be her first shoot with them."

Ethan shrugged. "Don't know. It just...it made her stand out."

"Whitney could use the business," Rocky said.

"I know. And she's probably thrilled to have someone to talk to," Ethan agreed.

"So...what? You're upset that she seems pretty cool, yet she's involved in this farce of a show?" Rocky asked.

Ethan did his best to sift through his feelings. "Yeah. Pretty much."

"You know, since she's staying over at Whitney's place, you could always go talk to her without the other asshats around," Rocky suggested.

Ethan wanted to dismiss his brother's suggestion...but he couldn't ignore the spark of excitement that lit deep within him when he thought about it.

Rocky smiled.

"What? I didn't say a word," Ethan said.

"You didn't have to. I know you. Look, I'm all for you pursuing someone. It's been so long since any of us have had anything close to a relationship that I'm totally rooting for you. But more than that, getting to know her better, even if it's just on a friendly level and nothing more, means that we might get some insight into exactly what's going on with the damn show. If we can keep those yahoos safe while they're wandering around the forest, in the dark, the better off we'll all be. And if you get some in the process...lucky you."

Ethan couldn't help but chuckle. "Dude, she's here for what, a week? We're not gonna decide we're soul mates and move in together in that amount of time."

"That's not what I said," Rocky told him with a smirk. "But if you're thinking about living the rest of your life with her already..."

"Whatever," Ethan said with a roll of his eyes.

"Hey, we aren't getting any younger—"

"Thirty-five isn't exactly old," Ethan interrupted.

"It's not, but you know Mom and Dad met and got married when they were in their early twenties. And they worked out. Hell, Mom never looked at another guy, even after Dad died. I'm pretty sure she thinks we're hopeless and that we're gonna be alone for the rest of our lives," Rocky said.

"We won't be alone. We've got each other," Ethan said without hesitation. It was what they always told their mom when she got all sentimental and emotional about their love lives—or lack thereof— when they went home for the holidays.

"All I'm saying is that a woman has piqued your interest for the first time in ages. We both know there isn't exactly a plethora of women in Fallport for us to choose from. You don't have to pledge eternal life, but getting to know her, and maybe having a little fun in the process, wouldn't be a bad thing. You've been pretty grumpy lately."

"It's not because of a lack of sex," Ethan grumbled. "The mayor's been pissing me off."

"He's been pissing us *all* off," Rocky countered. "That's nothing new. The prick feels as if he's better than everyone...and hates that he has no control over our team. Look, I don't care if you have a fling or not, I'll love and respect you no matter what. But seriously, I haven't seen you this worked up in a long time. You saw something in her that interested you. And maybe she's good at hiding her true thoughts and she's really a bitch. But then again, maybe she's not. If there's a possibility that she thinks this entire show is bullshit, and she got a room away from the cast and crew because she doesn't want to be associated with them, then you'll kick yourself if you don't at least try to get to know her."

"Fine," Ethan said. He might be pretending to be irritated with his brother, but deep down, he was relieved to have his blessing. "I'll talk to her tomorrow. See if she knows where the searches will be taking place so we know where to start if they all get lost."

"Do you know if they'll start filming tomorrow?" Rocky asked.

"No. But I bet everything I have that if I stop by the post office, Silas or one of the others will know, and I can get them to tell me without much effort."

"Not taking that bet," Rocky muttered. "You good now?"

Ethan smiled. His brother had followed him home just to check on him. He hadn't even had to say anything for Rocky to know he'd been worked up about something. "I'm good," he said.

"I'll be headed home then," he said.

"Let me know when you need me to swing by the house and get started on rewiring the electrical system," Ethan said.

"I will. With any luck, we won't see each other for a search before I need your help," Rocky said.

Ethan nodded. He hoped that would be the case, but he had a gut feeling the group from Hollywood would make that impossible.

Rocky gave his brother a chin lift and headed out.

Ethan locked the door behind him and sighed. Then he went back to pacing.

His apartment wasn't very big, so it didn't take many steps to get from one side of the living room to the other. The place was on the shabby side; the only lure of living here was the fact that his brother had an apartment in the same complex. They might not want to live together anymore, but Ethan couldn't even think about not being in the same city.

His thoughts turned back to the town hall meeting, and for the first time, he realized he didn't know the full name of the woman he couldn't stop thinking about. Though it wouldn't be hard to find out. He grinned and shook his head. The gossip network in this town was better than some of the intelligence he'd gotten in the Navy.

Tomorrow, he'd find out not only her name, but see if the hunch he had about her was correct.

He hoped it was. He really, *really* hoped he was right. Because there was something about the woman that had captured his attention. It wasn't really her looks, though she was pretty enough. Average height, around five foot eight, with dirty-blonde hair that she'd worn in a simple, unfussy bun. Blue eyes that seemed to twinkle with humor...when she let down her guard enough to let her feelings show. He thought she might have some curves, but it was hard to tell in the cargo pants and oversize T-shirt she'd been wearing. The boots on her feet were sturdy and appropriate for the area and the job she was doing.

All in all, everything about her was understated...so Ethan couldn't figure out why he couldn't stop thinking about her.

No, that was a lie. He knew why. It was because when she'd studied him and the rest of the Eagle Point Search and Rescue Team hanging out at the back of the room, despite looking slightly uneasy for some reason, she also seemed...intrigued? Maybe it was because they were all tall and muscular, and looked a bit intimidating. Or it could just be that they weren't hard on the eyes. At least according to other women they'd met.

Whatever the case, Ethan was intrigued. The others on the show didn't seem to notice much going on around them, too engrossed in what they were doing.

But the camera lady, Lilly, had taken one look at them and somehow instinctively known they were more than they seemed. It was just something in her body language, the look on her face, that made him think she realized they weren't just a bunch of bearded, small-town good ol' boys.

And she'd be right. Ethan and Rocky had been SEALs. Zeke had been a Green Beret. Drew had been a member of the Virginia State Police. Brock had worked for US Customs and Border Protection, and Talon had been a member of the Special Boat Service in the United Kingdom, which was a special forces unit in England's Royal Navy. Raiden had been a Coast Guard dog handler. They each had their own particular skills that helped make the SAR team one of the best in the state...and possibly the entire East Coast.

Anyway, the woman intrigued Ethan, and that hadn't happened for a while. So tomorrow, he'd do what his brother suggested to assuage his curiosity.

Most likely she'd be busy anyway, filming the yahoos who were going to be searching for Bigfoot. Or she'd look down her nose at him because of where he lived and what he did for a living. Or she'd just want to do her job and get the hell out of Fallport. It wasn't exactly a big city...which was why Ethan and his teammates liked it.

Frustrated that he couldn't stop thinking about the woman, Ethan stomped into his small kitchen. It wasn't gourmet by any stretch. The countertops were Formica, the appliances plain white, not the stainless steel that was all the rage. The floor under his feet was covered in cheap vinyl tiles...but none of that mattered. He was a simple man who didn't care much about home decorating. He was just happy to have a safe place to lay his head.

He pulled a carton of milk out of the fridge, filling a glass to the rim before chugging the entire thing. He wiped his mouth with his sleeve and grinned. Rocky made fun of him all the time for actually using a glass, especially since he lived alone. He could drink out of the carton if he wanted. It wasn't as if anyone was there to complain about it.

But their mom had drilled manners into him from a young age. And even now, though he hadn't lived at home for a long time,

Ethan couldn't bring himself to do something as uncouth as drink straight from the carton.

He put his glass in the sink and headed for his living room, grabbing his laptop along the way. He needed to check his messages and see what jobs were on his schedule for the upcoming week. Work had been slow, and for once, Ethan was grateful. He'd have plenty of time to track down the camera lady, maybe even offer his services as a guide.

The idea appealed to him. He could spend more time with Lilly and hopefully learn more about the show—and where they'd be searching—in the process.

It wasn't exactly a lame excuse either, he really *did* want to make sure no one got lost while filming in the forest. And Rocky was right. It *had* been a damn long time since anyone had caught his attention. Tomorrow, he'd see if he was simply losing his mind, or if she was someone worth knowing...like he suspected she may be.

CHAPTER THREE

Lilly sat at Whitney Crawford's small kitchen table the next morning and stared at the spread in front of her in disbelief. She was the only guest at the B&B at the moment, but Whitney had made waffles, scrambled eggs, hash browns, cinnamon rolls, banana bread, as well as bacon and sausage. There were so many dishes on the tabletop, there almost wasn't room for the plate the older woman had put down in front of Lilly after she sat down.

"I wasn't sure what you might like, so I made a bit of everything," Whitney said with a huge smile.

Lilly smiled back. She had a feeling when the B&B owner was younger, she probably turned a lot of heads. She was still a lovely woman, with light brown hair and gray eyes that seemed to twinkle all the time. Her face was full of laugh lines—no surprise, since she laughed easily and a lot—and she was a bit on the plump side. She was kind and friendly, and had made Lilly feel right at home from the first moment she'd talked to her on the phone when making reservations for the room.

After getting a text that said she wouldn't be needed until after lunch, Lilly had slept in that morning. The bed was ridiculously comfortable and the crickets chirping outside had reminded her of being home in West Virginia. The shower offered amazing water pressure, so Lilly had stood under the hot spray for way too long. Then she'd checked her emails, sending notes to each of her brothers and her father, letting them know she was in Fallport, safe and sound, and that filming should start later today. She was well aware that if she didn't keep in contact with them, they'd worry—and possibly show up in person to make sure she was all right.

Being the baby of the family, and the only female, was a pain in her ass at times, but it also felt good to know how much she was loved. She was extremely close to her family, and Lilly wouldn't have it any other way. She'd never missed having a mother growing up because her dad had done a wonderful job raising her, making sure a day never went by without her knowing how important and special she was.

She could've very easily ended up spoiled rotten, but her brothers made sure she didn't get too big for her britches. Lilly had spent most of her childhood following along behind them, wanting to do everything they did...which meant she'd learned to hunt, shoot, change a tire, and fix stuff that broke around the house. She watched war movies, loved sports, and generally enjoyed being one of the guys.

"Is something wrong?" Whitney asked, the worry clear in her tone.

"Oh, no. It all looks delicious," Lilly said quickly. "I was just thinking about my family."

"You miss them?" Whitney asked.

"Every day," Lilly said. "But all it usually takes is a day in their presence and I wonder why in the world I missed them so much."

The other woman laughed. "Yeah, I get that. I had eight brothers and sisters."

"Wow, I thought I had it bad with four," Lilly said with a smile.

As Lilly served herself a little bit of everything, Whitney went on to tell her about her own family. They were scattered all over the country, with families of their own, and they didn't stay in touch too often, but it was easy to see the older woman still loved them all.

Lilly ate her breakfast, stuffing herself so much that she knew she wouldn't have to eat lunch, otherwise she'd puke while trying to lug around her camera, following whichever host she'd be assigned that day. Just as she finished, a knock sounded on the kitchen door. Whitney stood and went to open it.

Turning, Lilly blinked in surprise at the man who entered.

Ethan. The man who'd caught her eye the night before. The one who seemed to look straight through her.

The one who'd made it clear he wasn't impressed with Tucker or his show and didn't exactly want any of them in his town and forest.

It wasn't *his* forest, but Lilly had a feeling if anyone pointed it out, he'd definitely set them straight.

"Look who's here!" Whitney said, beaming. "I don't know if you two have met yet. Ethan, this is Lilly Ray. Lilly, this is Ethan Watson. She's here filming that paranormal show," the older woman told him.

"I know."

His voice was deep and raspy—and it was all Lilly could do not to melt into a puddle right there in her chair at the sound of it. She stood and held her hand out to him.

"We saw each other last night at the meet-and-greet," Lilly told Whitney. "But it's nice to officially meet you, Ethan."

When his fingers wrapped around her own, tingles shot down her arm. Lilly could only stand there, staring at him.

"It's good to meet you too," he said. "I'm sorry if I'm interrupting."

He hadn't let go of her hand yet, and Lilly couldn't bring herself to pull it back. They stared at each other for a long moment. She had no idea what he was looking for, or what he saw when he gazed into her eyes, but he finally squeezed her hand gently and let go.

His fingers brushed against her palm as he did so, sending another quiver through Lilly.

His lips twitched as if he knew how he affected her. And why wouldn't he? Lilly had a feeling this man didn't miss much, which made him more...dangerous to be around.

Maybe that wasn't the right word, but generally, people didn't notice her while she was filming. Which was by design, really; it wasn't her job to stand out. She also preferred it. She could roll her eyes, or curl her lip, or grin at something someone said on set, and no one ever noticed. She was safe hiding behind her camera.

But Ethan Watson wouldn't miss a thing—and that made him dangerous to her peace of mind. She'd have to be on her toes while he was around. The last thing she wanted was Tucker, or *anyone* she worked with, to realize how little respect she had for them. She'd be out of a job faster than she could blink.

"Are you hungry, Ethan?" Whitney asked, breaking the strange connection between him and Lilly. "I made a bit too much this morning."

He chuckled. It was a free and easy sound. "I'm thinking that's an understatement. But I'd love to join you, if it's not too much trouble."

"Of course it's not," Whitney said. "I'll just grab you a plate."

While the older woman went over to the cabinet, Lilly stood there awkwardly, not knowing what to say. Luckily, her host returned quickly and Ethan began to fill his plate.

They all sat down around the table and Lilly did her best to engage in small talk. She'd never been the best conversationalist, and definitely not around people she didn't really know. Her family teased her for being a blabbermouth, and they weren't exactly wrong. It was as if she bottled up all the words she didn't feel comfortable saying in her everyday life, saving them for when she was around the men she loved and trusted most in the world, then they all came pouring out.

"So, filming begins today?" Ethan asked.

Lilly nodded.

His lips twitched again, as if he found her amusing but was controlling himself from commenting on her lack of enthusiasm to talk about her job.

"How did you get started as a camera operator?" he asked.

Lilly wished she hadn't already finished eating. At least then she could concentrate on something other than Ethan. But since Whitney had already taken her empty plate to the sink, she had nothing to distract her. "I kind of just fell into it," she told him honestly. "I've always been more comfortable behind the camera, and when I was in college, one of my friends was in the AV club and convinced me to come to a meeting. I found that I liked watching plays and shows come together from behind the scenes...and the rest is history."

While she was speaking, Ethan's gaze was locked on hers. As if she was the most important person in the world at that moment. As if he hung on every word she said. It was intense...and very flattering at the same time. She couldn't remember anyone, ever, paying that much attention to her when she spoke.

"I bet you've seen some wild things," Whitney said.

Lilly forced herself to look away from Ethan's brown gaze and nodded.

"Rumor has it you just came from filming in Nevada," Ethan said.

Lilly nodded again.

"The Goldfield Hotel?"

She really didn't want to talk about her job, but she didn't want to be rude either. "Yeah."

"What's that?" Whitney asked.

Ethan turned to the B&B host and explained. "Goldfield, Nevada, was a mining boomtown in the early twentieth century. The Goldfield Hotel was the centerpiece of the town. It's now abandoned, and considered to be one of the most haunted buildings in the country. There have been many people who've filmed shows there over the years, trying to prove that ghosts are real and to catch some of the hauntings on camera."

"Oh my goodness," Whitney said, her body almost quivering with excitement as she turned to Lilly. "Did you see any ghosts?"

Shit. Lilly didn't know what to say. Even though they'd been there for several nights, they hadn't caught anything on camera. That wasn't to say Lilly didn't feel extremely uncomfortable the whole time she was there. She did. The feeling of being watched didn't go away until they'd left the town. She didn't get a malevolent feel from the hotel, more of a sad vibe. Especially in room 109. The room where a woman named Elizabeth was supposedly chained to a radiator and forced to stay until she gave birth to the hotel owner's baby, which he didn't want. The stories varied about what happened, whether she'd died in childbirth or the owner had killed her. But either way, Lilly definitely felt the presence of *something* in that room.

Of course, just *feeling* something didn't make for exciting TV. So Tucker had Brodie play a clip of a baby crying down the hall, behind a closed door. It sounded eerie and haunting from inside room 109, which was what he was going for. And Roger, Trent, Chris, and Michelle overacted the scene, looking shocked and pretending to be scared out of their minds.

The next night, trying to replicate the footage another, very popular investigative TV show had filmed, Tucker had Joey throw a board toward Trent and Michelle when they were standing in the basement. He'd misjudged his strength, though, and hit Michelle in the shin, leaving a bloody gash on her leg.

Tucker, of course, had loved it and was practically giddy with the footage.

With those incidents in mind, Lilly wasn't sure how to answer Whitney. Did she see any ghosts? No. Did she feel them there? Yes.

Knowing she'd taken too long to answer, she gave the sweet older woman a small smile. "I've signed a nondisclosure agreement, so I can't discuss what happens behind the scenes on the show. But

I *can* tell you that there's no way I'd want to spend the night by myself in that building."

Whitney beamed. "Ooooh, I can't wait to watch the show!"

Lilly managed not to grimace. Barely. Her gaze shifted from her host to Ethan, and she wasn't surprised to see him studying her closely.

"You filming in the woods today?" he asked.

Glad he wasn't going to comment on her belief in ghosts or press her for more information about the hotel, Lilly shrugged. She really *had* signed an NDA, and while she hated how fake everything was on the show, she couldn't talk about it without risking being sued by the production company. "I'm not sure. I haven't heard from Tucker yet about today's schedule. Usually, we first interview the people whose stories we're going to highlight. Then we'll go to the locations where they said they saw something. The talent will all get together to investigate, and we try to catch something on film."

"There are four camera operators? That seems like a lot," Ethan said.

"It's not, really," Lilly told him. "Sometimes we're each assigned to one of the talent, but usually someone is in charge of getting wide shots, someone will be off getting scenery snippets that will be used to fill the segment, and someone else will be getting close-ups. It all depends on where we are and what kind of shoot we're on."

Ethan nodded. "Has the show filmed in the forest before?"

Lilly shook her head. "No. So far we've been inside buildings, or within a limited area, like a cemetery. We've done outdoor shoots, but in wide-open spaces in Nevada and New Mexico."

"Let me guess...aliens?" Ethan asked.

It was easy to hear the skepticism in his tone. Feeling defensive, even though she'd gotten more cynical about the show as time went on, Lilly stiffened. But she didn't get a chance to answer before Whitney spoke.

"Aliens? Oh my!"

Her excited tone made Lilly smile. She tried to tell herself that what Tucker did wasn't illegal. No, the paranormal beings they filmed weren't real...but they were making a show to entertain people. If he made up stories and paid people to share fake sightings, they weren't really hurting anyone. Watching the show would be a nice break from reality for many people.

Ethan pushed his now empty plate away and rested his elbows on the table, his gaze boring into hers. "You need to be careful. Trust me, you don't want to get lost in the wilderness."

"I know," she said softly.

"I'm happy to meet with Tucker and go over the best trails to use," he offered.

Lilly pressed her lips together. There was no way Tucker would take suggestions from a local on where he should film. He was arrogant and conceited, and even though he'd never been in Fallport and definitely wasn't an outdoorsy kind of guy, he'd still think he knew best. Besides, he wouldn't want anyone to know where they'd be filming, so they couldn't sneak out there and watch him being deceitful. Lilly wouldn't put it past him, or any of the talent, to have a full-size Bigfoot suit stashed in their luggage somewhere.

"Right. He's not going to want my advice," Ethan concluded without Lilly having to say a word. "Is anyone on the cast or crew an experienced outdoorsman?"

"Just me," Lilly said honestly.

His brow rose. "You?"

Lilly huffed out an irritated breath. "Yeah, me. And it's *outdoorsperson*, not man."

Ethan nodded his head in acknowledgement. "What makes you experienced?"

"I have four older brothers. We grew up in a small town in West Virginia similar to Fallport. We didn't have cable or anything, so we entertained ourselves by playing in the woods. I followed my brothers around from the moment I could walk. I wasn't allowed to join the Boy Scouts, since I was a girl, but I did everything they did while they were earning their merit badges. I even went hunting with them, learning to shoot when I was eight. I don't like killing animals though. I just enjoyed spending time with my dad and brothers as we sat in the forest, waiting for a buck to walk by.

"Camping was also one of our favorite things to do as a family. I can start a fire with a flint and a few sticks, can recognize the tracks of most animals in this area, and can use the stars as a rudimentary map if I have to. One summer, we even hiked part of the Appalachian Trail. It's been a while since I've had the pleasure of camping, but I haven't forgotten what poison ivy or poison oak looks like, and in a pinch, I'm sure I could probably make a halfway decent shelter."

Lilly couldn't believe she'd word vomited all that, but she'd been irritated by his skepticism. She hated that some people didn't think women were just as capable as men in many areas of life. She loved proving them wrong.

Ethan nodded, and Lilly swore she saw a bit of respect in his eyes. But instead of further grilling her on where she thought Tucker might want to film, or delving deeper into how exactly they were planning on finding Bigfoot, he asked, "Did your mom like outdoor stuff too?"

"My mom left right after I was born."

He blinked and grimaced. "I'm sorry."

Lilly shrugged. "Don't be. I had an awesome childhood. My dad is amazing. I wouldn't change one thing about how I grew up."

"And you shouldn't," Ethan agreed quietly.

Lilly stared at the large man sitting next to her, at a loss for words.

She had the sudden urge to confide in him. Tell him what an ass she thought Tucker was. How she hated the show she was working on. That she agreed with him; taking the show into the forest with a bunch of people who had no idea what they were doing in a setting like that was a bad idea. But instead, she just sat there and stared at him like a complete dork.

"Well...don't mind me. I'm just gonna pack up some of the leftovers," Whitney said as she stood from the table with a small smile.

For some reason, Lilly blushed. She hadn't realized she and Ethan had been staring at each other for as long as they had.

"You seen much of Fallport yet?" Ethan asked.

Lilly shook her head.

"You want a tour sometime? I mean, I'm assuming you get some time off from the shooting schedule?"

"I do. Once we start, things get pretty intense, but Tucker isn't allowed to work us twenty-four hours a day. There are rules about that sort of thing."

"So?" he asked.

"So...what?" Lilly asked in confusion.

He grinned. "You want a tour?"

"Oh! Sorry. Um...I don't have to work every hour of the day, but I also don't know when I'll get time off. It changes depending on the filming schedule."

"Ethan's work is flexible," Whitney piped up from where she was standing at the counter with her back to them. She was putting the leftover bacon into a Tupperware container. "He's an electrician. A darn good one too. He works when people need him, so he can adjust his schedule to yours."

Ethan shook his head and his grin widened at her words. "She's right. I'll give you my number, and you can let me know when you have time."

They were exchanging phone numbers? Lilly silently squealed a little inside. Things like this didn't happen to her. She was plain ol' Lilly Ray. No one ever looked twice at her. But then again, Ethan wasn't actually asking her on a date. He probably just wanted to keep an eye, and ear, on what was going on with the show. Wanted to make sure no one got lost in his forest.

"Um...okay."

"You should totally take her to Grinders. Oh! And The Sweet Tooth. You like pastries, right, Lilly?" Whitney asked.

"Who doesn't?" Lilly asked.

"You'd be surprised," Ethan muttered.

"No one I want to know," Whitney replied, ignoring Ethan's comment. "And the Sunny Side Up Diner looks like a complete dive, but it's one of the best places to eat in this county. You have to take her there too, Ethan."

"We'll see," he said diplomatically. "But no one's meatloaf is better than yours, Whit."

The older woman blushed. "Oh, go on, you. And I'm sure Zeke would like to see you guys in his bar too."

Ethan looked at Lilly. "You met Zeke yesterday. He owns the local pub, On the Rocks."

"Cute name," Lilly said.

"Yeah."

The amusement was easy to see in Ethan's eyes.

Lilly wasn't sure what was happening. Last night, she'd gotten the impression that this man and his friends didn't like her, or *anyone* who had anything to do with the show. And even when he'd first arrived this morning, she'd kind of gotten the same vibe. But now he was sitting there, smiling at her, planning on giving her a tour of Fallport—which, to be honest, wouldn't really take very long, as it wasn't that big of a place.

From what she'd seen, there was the downtown area, where a courthouse and most of the locally owned shops were located, situated around a town square—a huge grassy area, complete with a gazebo. Main Street ran along one side of the square, connecting downtown to the more well-known franchises—hotels and fast food restaurants—closer to I-480. That was the road that led to the interstate, thirty miles to the east of town.

As she struggled to come up with something else to say, her phone rang. She leaned to the side to pull it out of her pocket. It was Tucker.

"If you'll excuse me, I need to take this," she told Ethan.

He nodded.

Lilly stood and headed out of the kitchen into the formal dining room. Whitney had told her yesterday that this was where guests usually ate, but since it was just the two of them, she'd asked if it would be all right for them to eat less formally in the kitchen. Lilly had wholeheartedly agreed. She'd always choose casual over formal any day of the week.

She stood at the window on the far side of the room, looking out at the backyard and the trees that seemed to go on forever beyond. The Chestnut Street Manor backed up to the forest and was extremely peaceful. Lilly had a feeling she'd need the relaxed ambiance to help her get through the shoot.

"Hello?" she said after clicking on Tucker's name.

"I need you at the gazebo at the center of town at eleven-thirty. We're gonna head over to the kid's house first, film him telling his story again, then go to the old guy's place. We'll do the same there, then get some shots of the team discussing strategy."

Lilly had gotten used to Tucker's blunt way of speaking. He never asked her how she was doing or if she'd slept all right. She knew he was somewhat irritated that she insisted on staying in local bed and breakfasts where possible, instead of at the same hotel as the rest of the crew, but since she paid for the difference in price when there was one, he never put up too much of a stink about it.

"All right. Are we headed into the forest today?"

"Why?"

Lilly blinked at his curt tone. "I was just wondering what kind of clothes I need to wear."

"What does *that* matter?"

The question was just another that proved how ill-prepared he was for this shoot. And Lilly wasn't about to go into why she'd want to wear slacks and boots and layer her clothing if they were going into the forest. That would just annoy Tucker and make him think she was trying to tell him something he didn't already know. "I was just curious," she said instead.

"We're going to play things by ear. We might take an

exploratory hike to get some shots during the day. We also need to reenact what our witnesses saw, and we have to do most of those in a forest-like setting."

Lilly knew that meant they wouldn't actually film where the so-called witnesses claimed they saw Bigfoot. Tucker would film whichever he deemed the best locations. "Right."

"Eleven-thirty. Don't be late," Tucker said, then hung up.

Lilly scowled at her phone. When was the last time she was late? Never, that was when.

The longer the filming for the show went on, the more Lilly lost respect for not only Tucker, but also the four cast members. Individually, Roger, Trent, Chris, and Michelle were all right. But they were all hoping for this show to be their "big break." They wanted to be huge stars...and were willing to set aside their morals to make it happen.

"Everything all right?"

Lilly jumped at the sound of Ethan's deep voice and turned to see him leaning against the doorjamb that led into the kitchen.

She slipped her phone back into her pocket and nodded. "Yeah. I need to be at the gazebo at eleven-thirty."

"We call it The Circle."

Lilly nodded. That made sense. It was a beautifully and elaborately designed circular gazebo. "I bet there have been lots of weddings there," she commented inanely.

He nodded. "Yeah. So...you headed into the forest today?"

It was obvious he'd overheard her half of the conversation with Tucker. "It's undecided. Which means I need to be prepared for anything."

"Hiking boots, cargo pants, and jacket over a T-shirt, over a tank top, then, huh?"

Lilly couldn't help but laugh. "Yeah. If we were just doing local shots, I could get away with wearing a pair of shorts and my sneakers, but if we go into the forest, I definitely want to be wearing clothes that cover me. Many times we have to back into bushes and stuff to get the best shots."

"Right. So...your number?" Ethan asked as he pulled out his phone.

Lilly suddenly felt unsure. She was only going to be there for the duration of the shoot, then she was leaving. Luckily, there was only one more episode scheduled for the first season of the show. Then she'd have to decide whether to return to West Virginia or not, and the next job to take.

Admittedly, she wanted to settle down. Find a nice town like Fallport, someplace not too far from her family, and build a life there. As for her job...that was something she'd have to think about. She'd been doing the camera operator gig since she graduated from college, but she couldn't deny it no longer held the appeal and excitement it once did. Though she had no idea what else she'd do for work.

"Lilly?" Ethan asked. "If you're uncomfortable giving me your number, you can just stop by On the Rocks and let Zeke know you're looking for me. He can get a hold of me. Or, hell, Whitney has my number. I've rewired most of the electrical system in this house. She can call me."

"No, it's fine," Lilly said quickly. She was just giving her number to the man, not agreeing to move in with him or anything. She blushed at the thought.

"Do I want to know what that blush is about?" Ethan asked with a small smile.

Shit. She'd already forgotten how observant he was. Most people wouldn't even notice, or they'd politely refrain from bringing it up...but not Ethan.

"No," she said, knowing she was blushing even harder.

Now he stared at her with a huge grin on his face.

Shit, was he really waiting for her to tell him what she was thinking? There was no way Lilly was going to admit the thought of moving in with him wasn't exactly repugnant.

"As much as I wish I was, I'm not a mind reader, Lil. Your number?"

Oh! He was waiting for her to tell him her number. Lilly rolled her eyes at herself. Jeez, she was such a weirdo. She quickly rattled off her digits and watched him program them in.

"Got it," he said as he pushed off the wall and came toward her.

Lilly lifted her chin as he got closer. He was the perfect height for her...not that she was thinking about him in *that* way.

Aw hell, who was she kidding? She totally was. The man was ridiculously handsome.

He stared down at her for a beat, then nodded as if he'd found whatever he was looking for in her eyes. "Be careful today. I wasn't kidding last night when I said it was easy to get turned around and lost in the woods."

"I didn't think you were. I've got my GPS, so I should be good."

Ethan blinked. "You have a GPS?"

"Of course. When I found out we'd be looking for Bigfoot, I didn't think we'd be searching the city streets of New York for him."

Ethan looked relieved at her words. "Good. That makes me feel better."

"Me too," Lilly said. "I don't know how things are gonna go once we get in the forest, but I'm guessing the talent's not gonna pay any attention to where they're going. They're gonna hear something and rush off willy-nilly, leaving us camera operators to follow them as best we can."

Ethan's lips twitched.

"Although, if they get lost, that'll just make for better TV," Lilly felt obligated to warn.

All amusement fled from Ethan's face. "They'd do it on purpose? Worry the townspeople, force my team and me to give up a day or more of work, simply because it's good TV?"

Lilly winced. "Um..."

"Don't answer that. You don't have to."

"It's just that, while I may have a GPS, I'm not allowed to inter-fere in anything that happens while the cameras are rolling. I'd be fired on the spot if I did anything that made the viewers realize the talent isn't walking around in the woods by themselves."

"That's ridiculous," Ethan said in disgust.

"Which part? That we aren't allowed to help or say anything, or that anyone watching the show might think there weren't four camera operators, a producer, and a sound guy walking right along-side the cast members?"

"Yes," Ethan said firmly.

Lilly couldn't help it. She laughed. "Well, that's kind of how every reality show works. I don't like it, but I knew what I was signing up for when I came on board."

"How about this—if those yahoos get lost, you use your GPS, mark the spot, and get your ass out of there. Come find me. We'll let them stew for a while before we go bail them out. Deal?"

"Deal," Lilly said with a smile.

"You aren't what I thought you'd be," Ethan said out of the blue.

"I know," Lilly said seriously. She'd heard that kind of thing all her life. People always expected her to be different than she was. More outgoing. More interesting. More feminine.

"You're so much better," Ethan said, almost to himself. Then he took a step back and nodded. "I'll send you a text later to see how things went today. You get a dinner break?"

It took Lilly a second to focus on what he was asking. She was stuck on the "better" thing. "I don't know."

He frowned. "You don't know if you'll get a break to eat?"

"Well, sometimes, if filming is going really well, we'll work through dinner. It's not a big deal."

"It is," Ethan insisted. "But all right. How about you text me when you have a moment? I can call Sandra—she owns Sunny Side Up—and get a to-go meal and bring it to you if you aren't going to get a break."

Lilly tilted her head, studying him.

41

"What?" he asked.

"Why are you being so nice?" she asked, genuinely curious.

"I don't know," he said.

Lilly couldn't help but grin at that. His answer had been so honest. So blunt.

"I came over here today to give you another warning, in the hopes I could get you to talk to Tucker. There's no fucking Bigfoot in these mountains. Trust me, I've walked many, *many* miles and haven't seen or heard anything out of the ordinary. There are bears, bobcats, and moonshiners who don't take kindly to strangers sticking their noses into their business. But no Bigfoots. Or Bigfeet. What's the plural of Bigfoot, anyway?"

Lilly shrugged. "I have no idea."

"Anyway, I'm guessing finding nothing doesn't make for exciting TV, and since I'm one hundred percent sure the talent, as you call them, aren't gonna come across the carcass of a dead Bigfoot, that means there will probably be some games afoot. And you probably know all about what those games are, and are probably involved...hence the NDA you had to sign. So really, I came by to try to intimidate you and pass along word that if my team and I have to come searching for anyone, we aren't gonna be happy."

Lilly swallowed hard. This man was smart. He'd seen right through Tucker and hadn't bought into his bullshit. She didn't like being lumped in with Tucker and everyone else, but the bottom line was that she *was* involved.

"But warning aside...I'm intrigued by you. You're a complex woman, and something about you has piqued my interest," Ethan finished.

"I'm not complex," she blurted. "What you see is what you get."

"We'll see," he said mysteriously.

"Seriously, Ethan."

"All right."

"And I'm leaving as soon as the show is finished taping."

At that, his brow furrowed. "I know. But that doesn't make me want to get to know you any less."

Lilly was baffled. She wanted to tell him he was being ridiculous. That she wasn't the kind of woman to have a fling. She wanted to settle down...have a family, kids, a home. But instead, she blurted, "You're confusing."

He grinned. "I know. Give me enough time and you'll figure me out." Then Ethan nodded at her again and turned to go back into the kitchen.

Lilly remained where she was. She heard him thank Whitney for breakfast and say goodbye. The kitchen door opened and shut, and still Lilly stood there.

She had things to do. She had to change and make sure all her camera equipment was good to go for the day's filming, but instead she was standing there wondering what the hell had just happened.

Whitney stuck her head into the dining room and chuckled. "The Eagle Point men have that effect on everyone," she said, seeing the semi-dazed look in Lilly's eyes.

"So they're players?" Lilly blurted, needing more information on Ethan Watson before she did something stupid—like fall head over heels for him.

"Not even close," Whitney told her. "As far as I know, they haven't dated anyone in town since they arrived five years ago."

Lilly's eyes widened. "No one?"

"Nope. But that doesn't mean they haven't had offers. They're good men," Whitney went on. "It took a while for the town to accept them, but after all the people they've helped, both towns-people and strangers alike, it would be awful for us to treat them as outsiders."

Lilly nodded. She understood how small towns worked. You usually had to be born in them to be considered a local. Her dad had lived in her hometown for over forty years and a few people still referred to him as a newcomer.

"They're all former military," Whitney whispered, as if afraid the house was bugged and someone might hear her. "Except for Drew, he was a police officer here in Virginia. But they've all seen some pretty intense things in their lives. They came here for a slower pace. To not have to watch their backs all the time."

"How do you know all this?" Lilly asked.

Whitney chuckled. "The information network in this town is better than anything the government might set up in their fancy CIA or FBI offices," she said. "I'll give you a head's up—if you meet a man named Otto, Silas, or Art, don't tell them *anything* you don't want every citizen of this town to know."

Lilly took her new friend's words to heart. There was a group of gossipmongers in her own hometown, except they were women. They delighted in passing along any scrap of information they heard, even if it was completely false.

"Anyway, all's I'm saying is that you couldn't do better than Ethan Watson."

"I'm not looking to date anyone," Lilly said. "I'm here for a job, and that's it."

"Um-hmm," Whitney said with a nod. "But love doesn't care about a person's plans. It happens when it happens, and if you're smart, you'll not turn your back on the possibility."

It felt as if Whitney was reprimanding her, though Lilly hadn't done anything wrong.

"If nothing else, he'll be a good friend," Whitney said. "You want me to pack you a lunch?"

"No. Thank you, though." She patted her belly. "I've eaten enough to last me for quite a while."

"You say that now, but when you're standing in the heat with that heavy camera on your shoulder, you'll feel differently. I'll pack you a snack, at least."

Whitney started to head back into the kitchen, but stopped and turned around once more. "He's a good man," she said softly. "Reminds me a lot of my late husband. You could do worse. A lot worse." And with that, she disappeared into the kitchen.

Lilly let out a long breath. She'd forgotten how nosey people in small towns were, but she really didn't mind. She and Ethan weren't going to end up together. She wouldn't be in town long enough for them to form any kind of attachment. But that didn't mean she couldn't take him up on his offer to show her around. She liked what she'd seen of the town so far, and was curious to see the places Whitney mentioned. What could be the harm in having Ethan be her tour guide?

With that decided, Lilly headed down the hall to her room. She didn't want to be late and set off Tucker's infamous bad temper. It would make the long shoot even longer. She needed to check her cameras and get to the center of town well before eleven-thirty. Maybe she could get more information out of Kate or Michelle as to what the plan was for the day.

She did her best to put Ethan Watson—and the way he made her feel as if she was the only woman in the world when he looked at her—out of her mind. She was here for a job. Nothing less. Nothing more.

CHAPTER FOUR

She should've taken Whitney up on her offer to make her lunch. Lilly had long since consumed the snack her kind host had made for her. The cast had split up, with Roger and Trent going to the boy's house, and Chris and Michelle heading to the older man's property. Lilly had been assigned to Chris for the day, and it had taken everything she had in her not to laugh out loud at the over-the-top acting by both the talent and the local man who'd embellished the fantastical story about the night Bigfoot came into his yard, snatched up his dog, and disappeared back into the forest.

The entire crew had met back at the parking area for Barker Mill Trail, a popular hike that led up and into the forest, after the interviews were over. They had about an hour left of daylight and Tucker wanted to get started with filming tonight.

He'd just explained the agenda when Roger shook his head. "It's too late."

Tucker glared at him. "I *know* you're not contradicting me," he warned.

Lilly braced. It was obvious Tucker wasn't in a good mood, and

Roger wasn't helping the situation...even if she totally agreed with him.

"You know as well as I do that the night shoots are way more complicated than the ones in the daytime. We all need to change anyway, we can't be wearing the same clothes we did today. We can use tomorrow to look at the maps and figure out the best places to film."

"I've already looked at the maps," Tucker said acidly. "You think I'd just have us walk around without a plan?"

Lilly did her best to keep the snort of disbelief from escaping. That was exactly what Tucker usually did. He was the king of winging it when it came to the schedule.

"Maybe we can just check things out for a little bit tonight," Trent said.

He was the suck-up out of the four hosts. Lilly didn't care much for any of them, but Trent was always the first to kowtow to Tucker. It was probably why he got a lot of the prime shots in the show... like in Nevada. He was the one who "saw" the lights in the sky. He'd pouted when Michelle had been the one chosen to be hit by the flying board at the Goldfield Hotel, but Tucker placated him by saying it would be better for a woman to be injured. The audience would feel more sympathy for her.

"See? Trent's in, why can't you be like him?" Tucker asked Roger.

Lilly held her breath, waiting for Roger's reaction.

"Because he's willing to do whatever you say no matter how ridiculous in order to stay on your good side. We all know he's your favorite."

Tucker crossed his arms over his chest and glared at Roger. "You got a problem?"

"Yeah, I do," he replied without hesitation.

Looking around, Lilly was glad they were the only ones in the parking lot. The last thing anyone needed was someone overhearing or watching this confrontation. The show hadn't aired yet, but it wouldn't be good for their dirty laundry to become common knowledge.

Roger was the oldest of the four hosts at twenty-seven. He was six feet tall with brown hair and hazel eyes. They were all uncommonly good-looking. Michelle was twenty-two, petite, blonde, very busty, and as slender as a model. Her main role was to smile a lot, wear low-cut shirts, and fawn all over the three male hosts.

Chris was twenty-five, six foot two, stocky, had a fairly bushy brown beard, and played the skeptic of the bunch. He was the one tasked with throwing around alternative reasons for the things they saw and heard, but of course at the end of each episode, he "admitted" that he couldn't explain what he'd seen.

Trent was twenty-four, only a little taller than Lilly at five-nine, had black hair and brown eyes, high cheekbones, dimples, and was always joking around on camera. He was the buddy, the one the locals were always drawn to because of his easygoing nature.

Of course, that was all a show. Lilly had seen him lose his shit on more than one occasion...when he didn't get a first-class seat on an airplane, when the rental car he wanted wasn't available. He treated people well when it suited him, but really didn't give a second thought to those he thought beneath him. He never thanked any of the camera operators or Brodie, and in fact, as filming progressed, treated them more and more like crap.

Roger was the only one of the four hosts who'd been on television before. Granted, it was a short-lived show about competitive eating. He was the host, and while the show had received horrible ratings, he thought he knew better than everyone because of his experience.

Tucker, in his mid-forties, was the oldest. He had a paunch that stuck out over the waistband of his pants and a receding hairline— and Lilly was sure he didn't like anything about his job. She had no idea why he'd been hired in the first place; his only claim to fame was a grandfather who'd been a famous director back in the day. She figured someone had been paid to let Tucker have control of the series.

He stepped closer to Roger and they faced off in the parking lot. Kate, Andre, and Joey, the other camera operators, stayed silent as they watched the showdown.

"You think you know better than me?" Tucker asked.

"As a matter of fact, yeah, I do," Roger said, not backing down.

"It would serve all of you right if I walked away right now. Left you to your own devices."

Whatever was going on between the two men, it seemed as if it was about more than just the decision of whether to keep filming tonight or not. But since Lilly wasn't privy to what the rest of the cast and crew talked about in their down time, purposely separating herself from them, she had no idea what the issue might be.

Roger rolled his eyes and ran a hair through his perfectly coiffed hair. Lilly resisted the urge to smooth her own locks. She'd thrown it up into a messy bun earlier today when she'd gotten hot, and she was positive she probably looked like something the cat dragged in by now.

"It wouldn't be a bad idea to do some preliminary shots tonight," Michelle tentatively suggested.

"Yeah, we could get some clips of us walking, the trees, the moon, things like that," Chris agreed.

Roger blew out a breath and stepped away from Tucker. "Fine. Whatever."

"Good, now that that's settled, we can get to fucking work," Tucker grumbled. "We'll head out tonight and get a few preliminary shots and scope out the area. Kate and Andre, you guys are in charge of getting shots tomorrow of the town. We can splice them into the final cut. Joey, you and Lilly have tomorrow afternoon off, but will work the night shift. We'll head into the forest in the evening and stay as long as it takes to get some sort of usable footage."

Lilly had no idea why everything paranormal had to happen at night. As if Bigfoot was strictly nocturnal. Along with ghosts, and aliens, and everything else they'd filmed. She wasn't a night person, but she wasn't going to disagree with Tucker.

Andre was the oldest and most experienced camera operator—and the only one with the guts to ask, "What's the schedule? How long will we be in town?"

"As long as it takes," Tucker said without pause. Then he added, "We'll spend a few nights with the whole cast, then we'll split up and film them in pairs. They'll pretend to talk to each other on the radios, we'll do some knocks, and they'll hear some returned. Then we'll do some calls, and again, will hear some back. We'll ramp things up with finding some unexplainable footprints and maybe a shadow moving in the trees."

Lilly sighed. She hated the subterfuge. Undoubtedly the tracks would be made by one of the crew, same for the knocks on trees and anything the team might hear. She just hoped Tucker hadn't invested in a freaking Bigfoot costume. That would be going too damn far.

"Tuck, I was thinking, what if we switched things up and one of us spent the night out here in the forest? We could use a handheld and be out here by ourselves," Trent said. "We could buy a tent at Walmart and set it up and record all sorts of spooky shit happening at night."

"Dude, that's what that other Bigfoot show does. We're already pushing our luck by having the town hall meetings and shit like they do. If we do a solo mission, it'll be even more of a blatant copycat situation," Joey said with a shake of his head.

Joey and Trent were close, which was why Lilly figured he felt comfortable speaking up. But despite being such good friends, he was always disagreeing with anything Tucker wanted to do, throwing in his own suggestions as to how a scene should go.

"No, I think it's a good idea," Tucker said. "And since you suggested it, you can do it. Make it two nights."

Trent grinned. It was obvious he'd hoped to be chosen for the solo filming.

Tucker turned to Lilly. "Since you have tomorrow off, you can go to the store and get the tent and other stuff. But don't go overboard. Buy the cheap shit."

Lilly bit her tongue. She wanted to protest that she was a camera operator and not a personal shopper, but instead she simply nodded. It wasn't worth getting pissed off about, and it wasn't as if this was the first time he'd sent one of the crew off on an errand.

"*He* got to do the overnight thing in Nevada," Michelle whined.

"You want to be by yourself, in the woods, in the middle of the night?" Chris asked wryly. "Dude, you're scared of freaking spiders. No one who watches this show, and sees the way you screamed when you saw that bug in Mexico, is gonna believe you spent the entire night outside by yourself."

Everyone chuckled, including Lilly. Michelle's reaction *had* been pretty funny.

"Shut up, asshole," she mumbled.

"Kate, you can get the handheld ready for Trent," Tucker ordered.

The other camerawoman nodded.

"All right, so tomorrow night, we'll get some shots of all four of you guys walking around and doing Bigfoot searching, then, Trent, you can head off into the forest for two nights by yourself. We'll get more footage of the rest of you three walking around and making discoveries."

"Wait, you mean he'll really be camping?" Brodie asked.

"Yeah. Why?"

"The sound's gonna be shit," Brodie complained.

"It'll be more authentic if he's not all wired for sound. The handheld will be good enough, and those wood knocks will sound even spookier on the shitty microphone."

Brodie shrugged, not convinced.

"The chances of him getting lost are even greater if he's out there by himself," Lilly felt compelled to say.

"He'll be fine," Tucker said, dismissing her concern out of hand.

"So we'll be working throughout the night for the next few days?" Chris asked.

"Yeah."

"I hate staying up all night," Michelle complained.

"We'll make it *look* like we're out all night, but we'll probably be done by one or two in the morning," Tucker said, used to Michelle's bitching. "The faster you all nail the shots, the quicker we'll be done each night. Andre, since you're the tallest, you get to be Bigfoot," Tucker informed him.

"Oh, joy," the cameraman deadpanned. "Wait—I thought I was working tomorrow during the day and had the night off."

"You do. We'll do the shots of Bigfoot in the forest the night after," Tucker said.

"Please tell me I don't have to put on a fucking costume," Andre muttered.

"I couldn't find one that looked authentic," Tucker admitted. "So you'll need to dress in black and we'll get you walking in the distance in the dark. It'll be fine."

Lilly wasn't exactly convinced. The other shows had heat sensors and specialized equipment. They had none of that. She wasn't sure anyone watching was going to believe Roger, Trent, Chris, and Michelle actually saw Bigfoot when no one else on any other show had, but whatever. That wasn't her problem. Her job was to point the camera and film what was happening. Period.

As if he could read her mind, Tucker said sternly to the group in general, "Remember, you've all signed NDAs. If I hear one word leaked about what happens on set, your asses are gonna be sued. Got it?"

Everyone mumbled their agreement.

"Good. If we're done fucking around, we have some work to do," he added, before turning and heading for the trail entrance.

Lilly snuck a look at her watch. There was no telling how long Tucker was going to keep them all tromping through the woods tonight.

"This sucks," Kate muttered as she fell in line behind Lilly and they all headed into the forest.

Lilly gave her a quick grin, letting the other woman know she shared her thoughts, then she reached down and reset the GPS she had hooked onto her belt loop. She hadn't noticed anyone else carrying one, but at least Tucker did seem to have a trail map in his hand. She'd be surprised if he knew how to read it properly, but she wasn't about to ask. If Tucker got them all lost, she'd have her GPS, with the trail marked and the parking lot waypointed. She'd be able to get them out of the forest so they wouldn't have to call for help.

Thinking about the men who'd be sent to find them had her mind turning to Ethan. The guy had popped into her thoughts throughout the day, which was unusual for Lilly. But given his blunt honesty earlier that morning, she was intrigued. It was impossible to push him completely to the back of her mind.

She hadn't had a chance to text him today, and she really could've used whatever meal he'd planned to bring her from the local diner. They'd stopped for a break, as required by the Screen Actors Guild, but she'd made do with Whitney's snack. She hadn't wanted to eat too much, assuming she'd be hiking through the woods way before now. Instead, she'd been dealing with temperamental hosts, a producer stretched too thin while trying to run two separate shoots at the same time, and watching painful overacting by the townspeople.

Ethan confused her. Kind of scared her too. But she had to admit she hadn't felt this excited to get to know someone in a long while. Even after tripping over a root in the path because she was thinking about him, almost falling on her face—and nearly breaking the very expensive camera she was carrying—she *still* couldn't keep her thoughts off the man.

But it didn't matter how intriguing he was. She was going to be here a week, maybe a little more, and that was it. That wasn't enough time to start a relationship. She'd be friendly to Ethan, but that was all.

The thought that she'd lost something before she'd ever really had it hit Lilly hard, but she shook it off. She was too old to have one-night stands, and Ethan was obviously very happy in Fallport. He had friends, a great job, and he provided a service that was very much needed by both the townspeople and tourists alike. He wasn't leaving, and she couldn't stay. So that was that.

However, a small part of her, deep down, insisted on reminding her she wasn't happy with *her* job anymore. That she wasn't getting any younger and her chance to have children was quickly coming to an end. That if she didn't start getting serious about finding someone to spend the rest of her life with, she'd end up alone and bitter.

"Lilly! Run ahead and get some shots of the team walking toward you. Everyone else, off the trail so you're out of the shot!" Tucker yelled.

Lilly was thankful for the interruption, because no matter how much she told herself to stop thinking about Ethan, she wasn't able to do it. Concentrating on getting the shots Tucker wanted was a surefire way to not only occupy her full attention, but also to get them out of the forest faster.

* * *

Five hours later, the cast and crew emerged from the forest trail, tired, cranky, and not speaking to each other. The walk down the trail to the parking lot was done in almost complete silence, which was unusual. Someone was always joking with someone else, or planning the next shot, or talking about the next day's filming schedule.

Apparently walking around in the dark, in the forest, was much more stressful on everyone than being in a building or the defined space of a cemetery, or even out in the open desert. Everyone had fallen at least once, and the mosquitos that came out just before it got completely dark had driven everyone crazy.

Tucker had been overbearing—more so than usual. Joey and Andre had been sullen. Even the talent had a hard time being convincing on camera. Lilly wasn't sure any of the shots they'd taken tonight would be usable, but she kept her mouth shut. Point and shoot. That was her job.

She was never more relieved to be staying at a separate hotel than everyone else as she was right that moment. Everyone drove off without saying goodbye, which was fine with Lilly.

She sighed and pulled her phone out of her pocket. No messages. Weird, considering she always had at least one email or text from her family. Then she noticed that she had no bars. The reception was nonexistent, as Ethan had warned.

And just like that, thoughts of the man she'd managed to push to the back of her mind were at the forefront once again.

Shaking her head, she turned on the engine and headed toward town. She contemplated stopping at the diner to grab something to tide her over until morning, but decided against it. She was sweaty and felt gross, probably looked like some sort of paranormal monster herself at that moment. The last thing she wanted to do was become the subject of the next day's gossip. Besides, this wasn't the city; Sunny Side Up was probably closed by now.

So she drove back to Chestnut Street Manor, trying to ignore the way her stomach rumbled. She didn't think Whitney would mind her raiding the fridge for a snack. Her host had insisted that she make the house her home for as long as she was there.

She'd just pulled into a parking spot at the back of the house when her phone suddenly began dinging with notifications. Turning off the engine, Lilly picked up the phone and smiled. Yeah, she was definitely back in the land of cell phone reception because she had three emails—two from her brothers and one from her dad—a voice mail from a scammer claiming her social security number

55

had been suspended, and a text from a number she didn't recognize.

Too tired to move right that second, she sat in her car and read the notes from her family. Nothing was wrong, they were all just checking in and chitchatting. Then she clicked on the text, preparing to dismiss it and head inside.

But instead, she saw it was from Ethan. And there wasn't just one. He'd sent several texts over the last few hours. And suddenly she wasn't as tired as she was before.

Unknown: Hey, It's Ethan. Just checking in like I said I would. You hungry? I was serious when I said I'd bring something from Sunny Side Up to you.

Unknown: I'm hoping I didn't hear from you because you're somewhere out of range and not just ignoring me. Let me know when you get this.

Unknown: It's a good thing I know you're filming in the woods tonight, otherwise I'd be worried. And before you ask how I know that…you're in Fallport. There's always someone who knows what's going on and is more than willing to gossip about it. Will you let me know when you get to the B&B? Just so I know you're not lost in the forest and in a Donner party kind of situation. :)

Lilly couldn't help but laugh out loud at that. Without hesitation, and with a huge smile still on her face, her thumbs raced over her screen as she replied.

Lilly: First, it's spring, not the middle of winter. Second, if you think I'm gonna eat any of the people I work with, you're insane. If the level of crankiness that abounded tonight was any indication, they'd taste bitter and would be full of gristle.

. . .

She hit enter before realizing that it was almost midnight. Shoot. She probably shouldn't have texted so late, even if he *did* ask her to.

When she saw three dots dancing at the bottom of the screen, she felt a little less guilty.

Unknown: I'd ask how tonight's shoot went, but I think your answer told me quite clearly. You eat?

Lilly stared at his text for a long moment. She wasn't sure how to feel about it.

No, that was a lie. His concern felt good. Really good.

Realizing she was unexpectedly on the verge of tears, she took a moment to program Ethan's number into her phone. It had been a crappy day, at least the second part of it, and his concern for her, a stranger, was almost more than she could take right this second. When she had her emotions under control, Lilly slowly typed out a response, doing her best to keep her sarcasm to a minimum.

Lilly: I thought about digging some grubs out of the dirt when we were walking in freaking circles as Tucker tried to find the perfect spot to do a three-minute piece where the talent was discussing the interviews they'd done today, but decided I'd hold out for whatever Whitney had in her fridge.

Ethan: Don't blame you. Whit's an amazing cook and I'm sure she's got plenty of leftovers you can pilfer. You still want a tour tomorrow? Or did your schedule get changed?

Lilly: I'm off tomorrow afternoon, but I work in the evening and into the night...and probably will for the next several days. Why is it that Bigfoot can only be found in the dark?

Ethan: It's easier to hide the shenanigans that go along with the search. How about if I stop by around the same time I did this morning? It'll give you time to sleep in a bit.

. . .

Lilly stared at her phone. Was this guy for real? He was funny, considerate, and he seemed so eager to hang out with her. She honestly didn't understand why.

Lilly: That might not be the best idea. I need to go to the store and pick up some stuff for the shoot. And since I'll be working nights for the foreseeable future, I should probably take a nap before work.

She held her breath when it didn't seem as if he'd respond. Then the three dots appeared.

Ethan: I've been thinking about you today.
  Ethan: And I don't do that. Ever.
  Ethan: When I meet someone who I know is just in town to go hiking, or on vacation, I immediately dismiss them. That sounds bad, but it's true.
  Ethan: I love Fallport. I worked my ass off to protect my country and our freedoms so I could live the rest of my life in a sleepy town just like this one.
  Ethan: I haven't had a real relationship in years because this is where I want to be and most women can't wait to get out of here. But you're the first woman I've met who I haven't been able to get out of my mind. I know you're only here for a job. I know you're leaving. I just can't seem to make myself care.
  Ethan: Just a few hours, Lil. Let me show you Fallport. If nothing else, maybe you can use what you learn on that damn show.

Lilly took a deep breath and closed her eyes. She could picture Ethan quickly typing all that out. Hitting return, not caring that he was sending multiple texts. He'd laid it all out there. Blunt and straightforward.

Her thumb was moving before she realized she'd made her decision.

Lilly: Ok.

Ethan: Thank you. I'll see you tomorrow then. We can get your errands done, then I'll give you a tour. I'm sure Whitney will make a huge breakfast like she did today, so we'll have a late lunch. That will help tide you over for work, and it'll mean fewer people to stare at us while we're eating. I'll even get you back to the B&B so you can take a nap before you have to go to work. Where are you right now?

Wow, that was an abrupt change of topic. But Lilly wasn't sure she wanted to think about being the center of Fallport's attention and people staring at her while she ate, so she went with it.

Lilly: At the B&B, in my car. I checked my messages when I pulled in because my phone went crazy with notifications after getting back to civilization.

Ethan: lol. Hearing Fallport described as civilization is funny. But I understand what you meant. This isn't the city, but we do have crime here, believe it or not. Go inside, Lil. Grab a snack, get some sleep. I'll see you tomorrow.

There he went with the concern thing again, making Lilly's toes curl.

Lilly: Okay. I'm sorry I texted so late.

Ethan: I'm not. I was worried. Besides, I was up anyway.
Lilly: You all right?
Ethan: Yeah. Sometimes I just can't sleep. Too many demons in my head.

Lilly frowned. For some reason she didn't like that. And she knew nothing about Ethan. Not his age, how he'd come to be in Fallport, or what might've caused those demons. Although his earlier comment about working his ass off to protect his country and freedoms confirmed what Whitney had told her that morning. She wasn't surprised he'd been in the military. She could easily see that in him...and his friends, for that matter.

Ethan: Lil?
Lilly: I'm sorry about the demons.
Ethan: Thanks. Every day gets easier. Now, go inside before I have to drive over there and make sure you're safe and sound.
Lilly: My brothers taught me how to protect myself. I'm good.
Ethan: Glad to hear that, but still...I'll feel much better when I know you're behind closed doors.
Lilly: I'm going, I'm going. Ethan?
Ethan: Yeah?
Lilly: Thanks for making my crappy night less crappy.
Ethan: Any time. Good night.
Lilly: Night.

Lilly was smiling as she climbed out of the rental car, got her camera bag from the back seat, and tiptoed into the house. She was still grinning as she carried a plate up to her room that Whitney had put in the refrigerator with a sticky note attached that said, *Lilly, put this in the microwave for two minutes. Enjoy.*

The casserole was delicious and filled the empty spot in her gut.

Lilly showered, changed for bed, brushed her teeth, then climbed under the sheets. She had a tough week ahead of her, what with all the night shifts and dealing with a cast and crew that was clearly feeling the stress of their current filming schedule and location, if today was any indication.

Though admittedly, that had started a couple weeks ago. The excitement of a new show, and new co-workers, had faded and personalities were definitely clashing.

Despite all that, Lilly couldn't stop smiling as she thought about the next day...and getting to know Ethan. Things between them couldn't go very far. He had no desire to leave Fallport and Lilly's job took her all over the country. But that wasn't going to stop her from hanging out with him tomorrow. It might be a mistake...but to hell with it.

She was going to take one day at a time and simply enjoy getting to know an interesting man who made her smile. Whatever happened, happened.

With that thought in mind, Lilly fell into a deep, dreamless sleep, feeling excited about the next day for the first time in months.

* * *

The longer he worked on this show, the more unhappy he got. The lack of respect he was shown was ridiculous. No one listened to him...anything he suggested was dismissed out of hand. As if he was stupid or something.

Well, he wasn't going to stand for that. Something had to change. He didn't know what, but he'd stay on his toes to exploit any mistake anyone made. This show was supposed to be his big break, and so far, it was nothing but trash.

It was up to him to shake things up. To make it a show people couldn't resist watching. A show they'd be talking about on social media. He'd do whatever it took to make it go viral.

Anything.

He just had to be ready to make his move when the time was right.

Feeling better about his decision, even if he didn't know exactly what he was going to do, he relaxed a bit. Over his dead body would anyone take away this opportunity for him to *be* someone.

CHAPTER FIVE

Ethan glanced over at Lilly while he drove toward the Walmart on the outskirts of town. He'd woken up early, despite having gone to sleep later than usual. He'd thought about Lilly way too much...then an unsettling nightmare interrupted his rest. But he didn't want to think about that at the moment.

Fallport wasn't most people's idea of a great place to settle down, but he loved it. Loved how most people knew each other. How there weren't many secrets. Everyone felt as if they were family. Sometimes annoying, but when push came to shove, when someone needed help, the entire town banded together.

He'd seen it over and over again when Eagle Point SAR was called out. The townspeople rallied around the family and friends of the missing, bringing them meals, taking turns sitting with them while the search was on, and if the outcome wasn't positive, which unfortunately was the case sometimes, they raised money for funeral costs and anything else that might be needed. And all that happened if the missing person was a local or not.

Ethan and his brother—hell, all of the members of the search and rescue team—deserved Fallport after everything they'd seen and done. They'd settled into their everyday jobs, and yet still nurtured the part of themselves that urged them to be of service. The city paid them for the time they spent on searches, but it was merely a stipend. Nothing they could live on, but combined with their other jobs, no one was in danger of starving or being home-less. He and his team were all more than content with that, and with Fallport.

Lilly was his polar opposite. She had a job that took her all over the United States. She'd be gone in a week or so, as soon as the episode was done filming.

Ethan knew that, but he didn't care. There was something about her that he couldn't resist. It was possible she'd turn out to be a raging bitch...but he didn't think so. Over the years, he'd honed his ability to read people quickly. And what he saw in Lilly, he couldn't resist.

For starters, she didn't take herself too seriously. He hadn't missed the way she'd rolled her eyes at some of the ridiculous things being said about Bigfoot sightings in the town hall meeting. She also seemed annoyed at Tucker when he was abrupt and rude to not only the men and women who were working for him, but the townspeople too. She was close to her family, as he was to his, and was thankful to Whitney for her hospitability. Which might not seem like a big deal, but he'd seen the older woman get taken advantage of more than once by ungrateful guests.

A part of Ethan was actually hoping that by hanging out with her more, he'd find something that would turn him off. Something that would make it easier to say goodbye when she left. He was aware that made him kind of a dick, but then again, he'd never been in this kind of situation before. Wanting to know a woman, but scared to death that he'd like her *too* much, getting hurt when he was left behind.

"Thanks for doing this," she said quietly in the lengthening silence in the car.

"Of course."

"I know I could've gone to the general store I saw downtown, but Tucker's kind of a tight-wad when it comes to the budget, and I'm guessing that the camping gear there would be more expensive than at Walmart."

"I'm sure you're right. Old man Grogan has some good prices on everyday items and groceries, because that's what the townspeople buy most. But anything that a tourist might be interested in, he hikes the price up," Ethan said with a shrug.

"That's actually pretty smart. It's like going to a store in an airport. Or at a resort. People are gonna buy what they want no matter the price simply because it's convenient," Lilly said with a smile.

"Exactly. So...camping gear?" Ethan asked. He hadn't wanted to pry and ask what she needed to purchase, in case it was something like feminine hygiene products that she'd be embarrassed talking about. But since she brought it up, he figured it was all right to ask.

She wrinkled her nose, and Ethan smiled at the cute expression.

"Yeah. Trent had the great idea to spend the night in the forest by himself, to see what kind of Bigfoot evidence he could find. He said something about the beast being curious and coming closer to check him out if it's just him and not a big group, or some such ridiculousness. As if there haven't been thousands of people who've camped in the Appalachian Mountains already, who *haven't* had a curious Bigfoot come to their campsite to visit. Anyway, so Trent needs a tent and a sleeping bag and other basic stuff."

"Don't take this the wrong way, but he doesn't seem like an outdoor kind of guy," Ethan said.

Lilly laughed, and it was all Ethan could do not to run off the road. She was so darn pretty with that smile on her face.

"Yeah, he's really not. You should see him with his anti-bacterial wipes. He's obsessed with the things. At the shoot at the Goldfield Hotel, he refused to touch anything because of all the dust and dirt everywhere. Andre, one of the other camera guys, didn't help when he told him what's found in dust. That it's sloughed-off skin cells, dust mites, bits of dead bugs, clothing fibers, bacteria. Then he mused out loud about whether the dust in the building could be from people who'd been dead for decades. The look on Trent's face was priceless."

It was Ethan's turn to laugh. "Sounds like I'm gonna have to dust when I get home later," he said after a moment.

That made Lilly chuckle again, and Ethan had a feeling he might become obsessed with making her laugh in the future.

"Anyway, so yeah, I've been instructed to buy the cheapest stuff I can, because we all know it won't get used again. Wait, is there anyone around here who could use the camping gear? I can try to get Tucker to donate it when we're done using it."

"Absolutely. I can think of a couple people off the top of my head who would love that," Ethan said.

"Great. My plan is to get a tent, sleeping bag, a cooler, a camp chair, and a lantern, because it'll look cool on camera, I think. We've got plenty of headlamps and flashlights, so I don't need to get any of those."

"Sleeping pad? Pillow? Mallet for hammering in the tent stakes? Ice for the cooler? Plates and cutlery so he can eat? Does he have the proper clothes for camping? Like moisture-wicking shirts and stuff? It's supposed to rain a few days from now. Oh, and toilet paper."

"So, at risk of making you think I'm heartless...no to most of that. One, Tucker would kick my butt if I bought too much stuff. Two, I'm betting Trent will take one of the pillows from the hotel out with him, which is a shitty thing to do, but that's his speed. Someone can get ice later. If I get it now, it'll just melt. I'm sure he'll grab fast food before he heads out for the night, or he can grab sandwiches or something. He doesn't need cutlery or plates for that, and I'm pretty sure he wouldn't want me choosing his food anyway.

"I have no clue about his clothes, but that's also not my issue. Hell, as Tucker always says, suffering on film makes for good TV, so if he's in the rain and cold, all the better for ratings. And I'll remind him about the TP. Again, he'll probably take some from the hotel."

Ethan didn't comment. He wasn't all that surprised at her answer.

"Everyone thinks this show is gonna be a huge hit," Lilly said quietly.

Something about her tone had Ethan glancing at her before returning his attention to the road. "You don't?"

"I know I'm supposed to be supportive and upbeat about the shows I work on...but this one is a disaster. All of the paranormal things being investigated have already had multiple shows about them. There are like, four Bigfoot shows on right now...and those are *specifically* about Bigfoot, not paranormal things in general. Same with the shows about ghosts. We aren't focusing on one thing, and I think that's a mistake. Not to mention, we aren't doing anything different from anyone else out there, and we have no specialized equipment. We're tromping around in the dark pretending to see and hear stuff that isn't there."

She sighed. "Shoot. Forget I said that last part. I could get in big trouble for saying that out loud."

"My lips are sealed. You can talk to me about anything and I'd never tell a soul. Besides, you never know," Ethan said diplomatically. "This show might resonate with viewers."

"Maybe," Lilly said with a shrug as he pulled into the lot of the big box store.

Ethan pulled into a parking spot and shut off the engine. "Come on, let's go get this stuff for your guy, then I'll show you the town."

She gave him a small smile. "You mean there's more than what I've already seen?"

He chuckled. "No. But I'm guessing you haven't been inside all the stores. There are a lot of amazing people who live in this town, and I'm thinking they'll be thrilled to meet you."

"Me?" Lilly shook her head. "I'm sure they'd rather meet Roger or one of the others. They're the ones who have a shot at being famous."

"Nope. I mean, sure, they wouldn't mind meeting them, but I'm guessing with how the rest of the cast and crew keeps to themselves at the hotel here at the end of town, they aren't too interested in getting to know the townspeople. You've already piqued their interest by staying at Whit's place."

"I like supporting local businesses," Lilly admitted.

"Which is why they'll probably want to meet you, and not the others," Ethan told her. Then he turned and climbed out of the car. Lilly met him at the back and they walked side by side toward the entrance.

"Don't be surprised if people look at me funny," Ethan warned.

"Why would they do that?" Lilly asked.

"One, I don't shop here often. Two, I'm never in the company of a pretty woman. And three, they'll probably be shocked you're hanging out with me."

"Whatever," Lilly said with a small laugh.

He hadn't been kidding, but Ethan let it go. He wasn't the most gregarious of his teammates. That would be Drew. His former job as a state police officer made him the ideal person to talk to the press and reassure the townspeople when needed. Or Zeke. As the owner of On the Rocks, he knew just about everyone. Well, those who came in for a drink at the bar. He was also more personable.

Lilly made quick work of her shopping list. She didn't linger or go to any section in the store other than the camping area. She got what she needed and headed for the checkout lanes. Ethan nodded to a few people he knew, and like he'd thought, they did a double-take when they saw who he was with. When he was out and about, he was either alone or with one of his teammates. The sight of him with a woman was definitely something different. He had a feeling by the time they got back to town, everyone would already know he was hanging out with Lilly.

As he pushed the cart with the camping supplies out to his car, Lilly said, "Thanks again for taking the time to do this with me."

"Of course. You need to drop this stuff off anywhere?"

"No. I'll just bring it tonight when we meet up."

"Cool." Ethan put the things she bought in the back of his Subaru Outback, then went to the passenger side of the car. He held the door open for her, shutting it once she was settled. Then he wheeled the cart to the corral in the parking lot and headed back to the car. When he sat down, Lilly was looking at him with an odd expression on her face. "What?" he asked.

She shook her head. "Nothing."

"Seriously, what? Don't be afraid to talk to me," he ordered.

"I could've put the cart away," she said.

"I'm sure you could've," he told her. "But I wasn't about to stand there while you did so. Or even worse, sit in the car and wait for you. That would've been rude. And not something that'll ever happen as long as I'm around."

"That's...nice."

"I'm guessing the men you've been with haven't bothered to be gentlemanly in the past, huh?" he asked as he started the engine.

To his surprise, she chuckled. "My brothers used to say things like 'last one to the car has to put the cart back,' and of course, since I was the shortest and youngest, I was always last. As I got older, I wanted to do everything my brothers did, and that meant not being a diva and having people wait on me."

Ethan smiled. "What about men you've dated?" he pressed. He couldn't deny he was curious.

"No. Not them either. You have to understand, in the circles I'm in, I'm in the background. No one looks twice at the camera operators. We're just...there. The few times I've attempted to date recently, it's been a disaster. Besides, I can take care of myself. My dad and brothers taught me well. I guess when you can change the oil in your car, rebuild porch steps, and chop your own firewood, it turns some men off. Or makes them think it's not necessary to do polite things like open doors or stick up for you when someone makes a rude remark."

There was so much in her statement that Ethan wanted to comment on. He decided to break it down. "You were the first person I noticed at that town hall meeting," he told her honestly.

She looked at him in surprise.

"The stars of the show were at the front of the room, but they're all so young, and the way they seemed to be talking down to everyone annoyed me. So my gaze began to wander—and I saw you rolling your eyes at something one of them said. You did it subtly, but I caught it. And it intrigued me enough to look twice...and I have to say, I liked what I saw. A woman comfortable in her own skin. Which is way sexier than someone who tries too hard by caking on makeup and pouring herself into tight clothes."

Lilly simply stared at him, so Ethan went on. It was probably good that he was driving, so he didn't freak her out with his intensity. His mom constantly told him he needed to chill out. To not be so serious all the time, but he was who he was.

"And if your dates were disasters, it was on *them*, not you. I think it's awesome that you can look after yourself. I can't think of anything less appealing than having to be responsible for every traditional 'male' thing that goes along with a relationship. Though I'd prefer to work side by side when it comes to things like working on a car or chopping wood, it's definitely not a turn-off that you can do such things. There's also no correlation between you being able to take care of yourself, and me being a gentleman.

"Lastly, we aren't really dating, but I'd never let anyone bully someone I'm with, regardless. I don't care if they're a man, woman, or child. If a man you're dating doesn't immediately stand up for you if someone's being rude, you don't need to be with him. But I can't imagine what in the world someone could possibly have a problem with you about."

"Hollywood's a tough place to live," she said in lieu of an answer.

Ethan gave her time to elaborate, and when she didn't, asked, "And?"

Lilly blew out a breath. "I was like a bull in a china shop. Everyone was always worried about their looks and weight and persona, but I couldn't be bothered with any of that. I'm not petite, never will be. I like to eat, and while I try to be healthy, sometimes that's just not possible when I'm working.

"I was with a man once—I think it was like our fourth date or something, so we weren't exactly new, but we also weren't sleeping together or anything. We were in a coffee shop and I ordered a doughnut. I'd just gotten off a twelve-hour shift and was exhausted, but the guy really wanted to see me. So I agreed to meet him for a coffee before I went home and crashed. Anyway, the girl behind the counter smirked and made some crack about how I'd be better off skipping the pastry. Then she proceeded to flirt with my date until our coffees were ready. He not only didn't call her out for her rude remark, he flirted back."

"Asshole," Ethan said. "I hope you kicked him to the curb."

"Of course I did," Lilly said. "I mean, I know I shouldn't have eaten that doughnut, but I hadn't eaten since breakfast and I was starving."

"Fuck that. I don't care if you'd just eaten a four-course meal, you want a doughnut, it's nobody's business but your own. And for the record, there's nothing wrong with your shape. Not at all." Ethan couldn't help but let his eyes stray down her body for a moment. She wasn't stick thin, but neither was she obese. She was...normal. Which he liked a hell of a lot.

"And the fact that he stood there and let her flirt with him after insulting you was fucked up. I hope you know that."

Lilly nodded. "I do. But really, I'm used to it. It feels as if guys are always looking for the next best thing. Someone smarter, who makes more money, who's prettier. Honestly, it's just easier being single."

"You just haven't met the right kind of men," Ethan told her.

She stared at him briefly, but didn't comment.

Ethan wanted to reassure her that *he* was the right kind of man, but he had a feeling things were already getting too intense between them. He'd known her for two-point-three seconds. She wouldn't trust him yet, and she shouldn't.

Vowing to prove to her, even if she was only in town for a week, that there were men in the world who could appreciate a woman like her, Ethan changed the topic.

"I'm guessing you aren't hungry yet, since Whitney made another huge brunch for you before you left the house, so I thought we could walk around the square and I could introduce you to people, show you the charm of Fallport."

"You'd be right, and I'd like that. Seeing the stores and stuff from the car isn't the same as going inside. Talking to people and making connections."

Ethan saw her visibly relax in her seat, now that they weren't talking about her anymore. That was one more thing that made her stand out from other women he'd known. Most had loved to talk about themselves. But not Lilly.

They were silent as they made their way into town. They passed the only car service shop, where Brock worked. A few houses, a couple other businesses, before entering the town square. There were streets and buildings along all four sides, with a large park in the middle. The gazebo, which the locals called The Circle, was the pride and joy of the town, with most of the residents having helped raise funds to build it. The Fourth of July and Christmas parades were the highlight of the year, ending at the square, with floats made by local organizations and the high school kids. There were a few festivals held in the park and even the occasional concert. Not with any famous bands, but rather singers and groups from southwest Virginia who made the rounds in their attempt to gain fans.

There were parking lots tucked behind the buildings, but Ethan was lucky to find a spot right in front of the post office. He smiled when he saw Fallport's favorite gossip trio in their usual spot, playing chess on the sidewalk under the large awning in front of the building.

"You ready to meet the biggest busybodies in Fallport?" he asked as he shut off his engine.

She grinned. "Ready."

"Do me a favor?" he asked.

"Sure."

"Sit there and let me come around to open your door. I know you're perfectly capable of opening it yourself, but if I don't, I'll *never* hear the end of it from Art and his crew."

She laughed. "Right. I can do that."

"'Preciate it," Ethan told her. He quickly opened his door, well aware three pairs of eyes were glued on him, and walked around to the passenger side. He opened the door for Lilly and she graciously held up her hand so he could help her out.

"Nice touch," he muttered, and her lips twitched as he led her over to the men who weren't even trying to hide the fact they were watching.

"Otto. Silas. Art," Ethan said, greeting each of the men and nodding. "This is Lilly Ray. She's in town working on that Bigfoot show."

"I heard Harry's already ordered T-shirts and hats that say 'Fallport, Home of Bigfoot' on them," Silas grumbled in response.

"If we get overrun by people wanting to see Bigfoot for themselves, I'm gonna put in a complaint with the mayor," Otto threw in.

"I think it'll be a good thing. We need more pretty women in this town," Art said with a wink in Lilly's direction.

"Why would you want that? It's not as if your tallywacker works anymore," Silas groused.

"I might be older than you, but there's nothin' wrong with lookin," Art fired back. "Maybe if you weren't such a stick in the mud, you'd appreciate a pretty girl like I do."

Ethan risked a glance at Lilly and saw she was doing all she could not to burst into laughter.

Since the day he'd met the three best friends, they'd always argued. Art was the oldest at ninety-one and never missed a chance to let the others know that he considered himself the wisest of the bunch. He had brown hair that he rarely seemed to comb, so at the moment, it was blowing around his head in the breeze. He wore a pair of overalls and the same slippers he always had on his feet.

At sixty-nine, Silas was the youngest, who constantly got shit from the other two about his inexperience in one area or another. He was completely bald, wearing the same baseball cap he'd had on every day since Ethan had moved to town. He was at least a hundred pounds overweight, but took pride in the fact that he could still compete with the younger participants in the hotdog eating contest every July 4th. His shirt was wrinkled and worn, but he didn't care. He was completely comfortable in his own skin.

Otto usually played peacekeeper, since he was between the other two in age, at eighty. He was as skinny as Silas was overweight. But Ethan knew it wasn't because the man starved himself. He'd seen him eat more food than he and his teammates could consume in a single sitting. Lines covered his earth-brown face, making it obvious he'd spent a lot of time in the sun in his lifetime. In contrast to his dark skin, his hair was as white as a sheet and always meticulously groomed. If it was a windy day, like today, he'd have a comb on him so he could make sure his hair didn't get messed up.

The three men were best friends. They'd all grown up in Fallport, left, got married and, after their wives passed away, made their way back to the small town they'd missed since leaving. They each owned houses near downtown, and every morning, they made their way into town after breakfast and sat in front of the post office playing chess, finding out all the town gossip from people walking by. They'd wander over to the diner for lunch, then make their way home around five when the post office closed.

"It's very nice to meet you," Lilly told the three men.

"Why? We haven't even said three words to you," Otto said bluntly.

"Don't be rude," Art chided before looking at Lilly. "It's nice to meet you too. You believe in Bigfoot?"

Silas made a weird noise in the back of his throat. "You can't ask her that."

"Why not?" Art asked with a tilt of his head.

"Because! She works on the show. If she says no, it'll make the show look bad."

"What if she says yes?" Otto asked.

Silas looked confused for a second, before sitting up straighter and saying, "Then she'd be lying."

Lilly burst out laughing, and Ethan couldn't help but chuckle right along with her.

"You've got a nice smile," Silas told her.

Of course, that made her self-conscious, and the smile the older man was admiring faded. "Um...thanks."

"What are you doing with Ethan?" Art asked.

"Well, he offered to show me around," Lilly said.

"Not much to see," Otto said with a frown.

"Oh, I don't believe that. Besides, if he hadn't, I wouldn't have gotten to meet you three," Lilly said diplomatically.

"That's true," Silas said. "Hey, you want to eat lunch with us? Heard Sandra's got fried chicken on special today."

"Oh, um..." Lilly said uncertainly, looking at Ethan to save her.

He had no problem bailing her out, especially since he wasn't ready to share her just yet. That thought alone should've convinced him that he was already in over his head when it came to this woman, but he refused to acknowledge it. "Sorry, guys, but we've got a lot of people yet to meet. Lilly also needs to take a nap, since she's working through the night on the show...not to mention, Whitney made one of her infamous brunches again this morning for her guest."

All three men nodded, and Ethan knew it was that last fact that convinced them.

"Wish she'd go to work for Sandra," Art said.

"Damn good cook," Otto added.

"You're gonna regret missing the chicken," Silas muttered under his breath.

Ethan heard Lilly once more muffling a snort. "You ready for the tour?" he asked.

"Yup."

"Don't let Harry talk you into buyin' one of those Godawful Bigfoot shirts," Silas warned.

"She can buy whatever she wants," Art scolded his friend.

"It's a moot point because Harry doesn't even have those dang shirts yet," Otto said. "Can we get back to the game?"

Chess was a game for two people, but that didn't prevent the three friends from somehow managing to play a game between the three of them. Ethan had no idea what the rules were for their version of three-way chess, but if they were content, he wasn't going to say a word about it.

Lilly gave the men a little wave, then looked up at him.

Ethan held out his elbow. "Shall we?"

Her eyes twinkled as she wrapped her arm around his. "Lead on."

For a second, Ethan was paralyzed. Her touch made him shiver, and he loved the look of excitement, curiosity and, yes, attraction, he saw in her eyes. It made him want to skip the tour and take her to one of his favorite lookouts in the forest. The one he'd named the search and rescue team after. The one far away from any civilization, where they could be alone...and he could maybe get her out of his system.

He was sure this was some passing fancy. She'd come to town at a time when he was feeling lonely. His sister had just had a baby and his mom had been bugging him to find someone to settle down with. He liked his solitary life, but he also felt as if he was at a crossroads. If he didn't find a woman soon, one he could imagine living with for the next forty years or so, he had a feeling he never would. He'd end up just like Otto, Silas, and Art...playing chess in front of the Fallport post office with one or more of his teammates, who were more like him than they cared to admit.

"Ethan?" Lilly said with a small frown as she looked up at him.

Mentally shaking his head, Ethan pushed the thought of kissing this woman out of his head. He once more reminded himself that she was only going to be in town for a week or so, and this would probably be the only time he'd get to spend with her, since she'd be working nights. "Sorry, just thinking. Let's start on this side of the square and work our way around. That work?"

"Of course. You're the tour guide."

Ethan had himself under control until she squeezed his arm, then began to slide her hand away. He brought his other hand up quickly and kept it in place. They stood like that for a heartbeat, staring into each other's eyes.

"Not much of a tour if you just stand there," Art observed unhelpfully.

"*Shhhh*. Can't you see they're flirtin'?" Silas said in a stage whisper.

"Weirdest flirtin' I've ever seen," Otto mumbled.

Lilly smiled at him, and the spell Ethan had been under was broken. He turned and led her down the sidewalk toward the hair salon on the square. There were bound to be locals to introduce her to in there, and Ethan had a feeling it would be in his best interest to surround himself with as many people as possible.

Otherwise, the urge to kiss Lilly, to see if she was feeling the same pull toward him as he was to her, would overwhelm him, and he'd find himself offering to take her to the Eagle Point lookout, regardless of whether or not it was smart.

CHAPTER SIX

Lilly's head was spinning with all the names of the people Ethan had introduced her to. With each business they visited, she fell a little more in love with Fallport and its citizens. It was a quaint little town, where nearly everyone was down to earth and genuinely friendly. About half the people she'd met seemed interested in the show. The other half were skeptical of the premise.

They'd stopped into A Cut Above, the hair salon; Grogan's General Store, where she met old man Grogan and listened to him talk about the awesome design he'd had his grandson do for the Bigfoot apparel he'd ordered. Then he'd taken her to Fall For Books, the used bookstore, and pointed out Knock 'Em Down, the bowling alley, before mentioning The Cellar...which apparently was a pool hall frequented by some of the not-so-wholesome residents of Fallport. He warned her never to go there by herself, which Lilly had no problem promising.

He'd bought her a coffee at Grinders, the coffee shop Whitney had mentioned, and Lilly fell in love with the quirky shop. Instead of a plain ol' boring paint job, there were quotes from books all over the walls. Some of the quotes Lilly recognized, but most she didn't. And almost all of them had something to do with drinking coffee.

Then he'd insisted on getting her a cinnamon roll from the Sweet Tooth, the bakery next door. Lilly couldn't help but moan in ecstasy after her first bite. It was one of the best things she'd ever eaten. Store-bought doughnuts would never compare to that delicacy.

When Ethan made a strange noise at her moan, she looked at him in confusion. The spark of desire in his eyes almost caused her to choke on her cinnamon roll. She hadn't purposely made sex noises while eating the sweet treat, but she quickly realized how she probably looked and sounded.

Afterward, they continued around the square, and Ethan introduced her to probably the friendliest homeless man she'd ever met in her life. Davis Woolford looked to be in his late thirties, and had no problem telling her that he'd ended up in Fallport by accident. Just got off at the wrong bus stop and never left.

After Davis had wandered away, Ethan leaned down and said, "He's a former Marine. Has PTSD pretty bad. The whole town watches out for him. When it gets cold, we make sure he has a warm place to sleep. Most of the shop owners are pretty cool and give him leftover food they'd otherwise throw away. He gets his hair cut for free, and Zeke lets him hang out at On the Rocks as long as he doesn't cause any trouble."

"That's all awesome, but why doesn't someone offer him a job? Help him get off the streets for good?" Lilly asked.

"He looks happy, but he's deeply troubled," Ethan said. "He can't hold a job. And believe it or not, he's kind of Fallport's watch-dog. When old man Grogan had a heart attack in his store, Davis was the first to find him. He did CPR until the paramedics arrived. Saved his life. When a little girl slipped away from her mother's watchful eye while playing in the square, Davis grabbed her just as she was about to step into the street in front of a truck. My team and I have tried to get him a room...nothing fancy, but somewhere he can go to get off the streets, but he says he prefers being out in the open, not being confined."

Lilly's respect for the man in front of her, and the town, increased. She hated to think of anyone going without basic necessities like food, water, and shelter, but it sounded as if Davis was at least content with his life.

"You ready for something to eat?" Ethan asked after he showed her the dog park. It sat behind a row of buildings on one side of the square.

She wasn't, but Lilly nodded anyway. She didn't want this day to end. She was enjoying getting to know the people of Fallport...and spending time with Ethan.

"Do you care if some of the guys on my team join us?"

Lilly wasn't sure about that; she usually wasn't the greatest with new people. She found herself wanting to impress Ethan...and if one of his friends disliked her for any reason, that wasn't how she'd want the day to end. But she nodded anyway.

Being astute, Ethan stepped closer, making her feel as if they were the only two people in the world, even though they were standing on a public sidewalk in the middle of town, probably being watched by curious eyes in all the shops. "You can say no," he reassured her in a quiet tone.

"No, it's fine," Lilly said, forcing herself to smile. "Why wouldn't it be?"

"Well, as much as I like my friends, I'm tempted to tell them lunch plans are off. I'm enjoying having you all to myself."

"You gonna stand there all afternoon or finally feed that girl?" Otto called out from across the square, back in his seat in front of the post office.

Both Ethan and Lilly chuckled.

"Guess that's my cue," Ethan said, holding his arm out to her once more.

Lilly wrapped her hand around his elbow and smiled as he led her toward the diner.

"The library is over there," Ethan said, motioning to the side of the square they hadn't gotten to yet. "Raiden works there. He's the redhead with the bloodhound. Talon is a barber, and his shop is on the corner. Drew is an accountant, but he works from home. Zeke owns On the Rocks, Brock works at the auto shop down the road, and my brother has his own construction company."

"Wait—your brother? Like, your *real* brother?"

Ethan chuckled. "Is there such a thing as a fake brother?" he asked.

Lilly shrugged. "I just thought it was a figure of speech."

"Well, all the guys are my brothers, in that sense, but Cohen—who goes by Rocky—is my real brother. We're twins, actually."

Lilly looked surprised. "You guys don't look alike."

He smiled as if he'd heard that many times in the past. "I know. We're fraternal twins. But if you want proof, I'm sure I can dig up our birth certificates to show you."

Lilly blushed. "No, no, no, I'm sorry. I just...I had no idea."

"We were in the military together, got out, and a friend of ours —a former SEAL we know—told us about how Fallport was looking for a search and rescue team. I'm not sure either of us would know what to do without having the other close."

"I can understand that. I miss my brothers like crazy, but I'm sure it would be even worse if I had a twin."

Ethan nodded. "It's not something we can explain, but I think it would feel as if we'd lost a part of ourselves if we didn't live near each other. Anyway, Raid said he'd come to lunch today. Tal and Zeke too. I hope that's okay. The others were disappointed they couldn't make it, but are interested in hanging out with you another day."

"That's fine, but..." Lilly bit her lip as they continued their stroll toward the diner. "I'm not sure why they're interested in meeting me."

"Because they're curious about the show. Because they've never met a professional camera operator before. Because they want to see if you'll share what the plans are for filming, so they can figure out if we're gonna have to go into the forest to find anyone. And because it's been a very long time since I've shown an interest in anyone...so they're curious."

Lilly glanced up at him at that last part. She had no idea what to say. It was nice to know she wasn't the only who felt some sort of weird connection, but she wasn't sure what to do about it, since she'd be leaving as soon as filming was over.

"Here we are," Ethan said, seemingly oblivious to the turmoil his words had caused within her. He held open the door to the diner and gestured for her to precede him.

The second Lilly stepped inside, her stomach growled. She hadn't thought she'd be hungry after the large meal Whitney had served, then the cinnamon roll, but the smell of garlic and baking bread was too much to resist.

Ethan's lips twitched. "I swear every time I come in here, I say I'm not going to overdo it, but then I can't help myself. Everything tastes as good as it smells. Promise."

Lilly didn't get a chance to respond before a woman headed toward them.

"Ethan! It's so good to see you! You haven't been here in what, three days or so?" she asked with a smile. She was probably in her mid-forties and could've easily starred on a runway in Paris...she was that beautiful. She had a short and tight afro, which perfectly framed a face with flawless chestnut skin, and Lilly found herself smiling as she watched Ethan interact with the woman. She was tall and slender, and she wore three-inch heels, making her the same height as Ethan as she gave him a brief hug.

This was a woman who was comfortable in her own skin, and it showed.

Ethan returned the embrace, then turned to Lilly. "Sandra, I'd like you to meet Lilly Ray. She's here working on that TV show. She's one of the camera operators. Lilly, this is Sandra Hain. She owns Sunny Side Up and is responsible for me losing the svelte shape I had when I moved here."

Sandra laughed uproariously, and Lilly discovered even that was beautiful.

"It's nice to meet you," Sandra said, holding out her hand.

Lilly shook it, feeling self-conscious about the calluses on her palms from lugging around cameras all the time.

"I heard you're staying at Chestnut Street Manor...you couldn't have chosen a better B&B. And I know you're eating right, because Whitney can't resist feeding her guests. Usually they're so satisfied, they never make their way here."

It was obvious Sandra was friends with Whitney. There was no animosity in her tone and the huge smile on her face seemed genuine.

"You aren't wrong," Lilly said. "I ate so much this morning that I swore I wasn't going to be able to eat again until tomorrow, but the second I walked in here, my stomach decided it was completely empty and if I didn't fill it with whatever you're baking, it was going to revolt."

Sandra laughed again, and Lilly couldn't help but smile.

"You're sweet," she said. Then turned to Ethan and repeated, "She's sweet."

"She is," Ethan agreed.

"Well, as you can see, we aren't that busy right now, so sit wherever you want. The specials aren't quite ready for dinner yet, but if you're lookin' for suggestions, the chicken-fried steak is amazing today. We're just finishing up the first batch of garlic-parmesan pretzels we're tryin' out for a new appetizer. Y'all can let me know what you think...if we need more garlic or parmesan or whatever. And by the time you're done eating, I'm sure the first batch of volcano cakes will be done."

Lilly's mouth was watering by the time the woman had finished speaking. "Yes," she blurted.

Sandra grinned. "Yes to what?" she asked.

"All of it. Just yes."

"I remember the last woman you brought in here," Sandra said, turning to Ethan with a raised brow. "It was, what, three years ago or so? Anyway, she ordered a salad. A *salad*," she emphasized, as if the word offended her. "And if I remember correctly, that was the day I made my grandma's lasagna for the special." Sandra shook her head in disgust. "I like this one."

Lilly wasn't offended Sandra was talking about her as if she wasn't standing right there. She was used to people doing the same at home. She supposed small towns were similar, no matter where they were located.

"Me too," Ethan agreed good-naturedly. "We'll take the chicken-fried steak and pretzels, and definitely the lava cake. Raid, Tal, and Zeke should be here any moment. You got enough for them too?"

Sandra rolled her eyes. "Does the sun rise in the east? I run a diner, kid. Of course I have enough food. Jeez. Raid bringing his mongrel dog?"

"I'd assume so, yes, since he doesn't go anywhere without him," Ethan said.

"Fine. I'll see if I can rustle up a bone for him too then. We're in between shifts right now, but Karen's around somewhere. She'll bring you plates and such. Water for you, right, Ethan?"

"Yes, ma'am."

"And for you?" Sandra asked, looking at Lilly.

"Water's fine. Thank you."

"Easy to please too. So far so good," she said with another meaningful look at Ethan before turning to head back to what Lilly assumed was the kitchen.

"Don't mind her," Ethan said as he put his hand on the small of her back, leading her to a table along a side wall.

His hand was warm and heavy on her back, and Lilly liked the feel of it. He pulled out a chair and she sat, pleased when he took the seat right next to her. Their backs were to the wall, so they could see the entire dining room. It wasn't a huge space, and there were only a couple other occupied tables. It had a homey and relaxing atmosphere. Lilly hoped the food tasted as good as it smelled.

"I grew up in a town a lot like this one," she reassured Ethan. "It was so frustrating when I couldn't ever get away with anything. Someone always tattled to my dad."

Ethan smiled. "You get in trouble a lot?"

"No. I was a good girl. But the few times I did try to have some fun, I was always ratted out."

"Like for what?" Ethan asked.

"Like the time my friends and I wanted to try cow-tipping."

Ethan burst out laughing.

"Seriously. We'd learned about it from other kids at school. Even my brothers had done it. I'd heard them talking about it. So we went to the Allen farm to see what it was all about. Of course, we'd been drinking beforehand, so that didn't help. We made a crap-ton of noise and there was no way we were sneaking up on any cow. We tried to approach a few, but they weren't asleep, and they just ran off before we could get close. We traipsed all over the field, trying to find a cow that would cooperate. We finally found one that didn't seem to care there were a bunch of giggling, tipsy girls approaching it. On the count of three, we pushed as hard as we could—and the stupid cow just turned and mooed at us before walking off."

She waited until Ethan stopped laughing before she continued. "So, we were disillusioned and left. Cara was driving—she hadn't been drinking, just so you know; we weren't stupid enough to drive in the mountains of West Virginia while drunk. Anyway, we were hungry, so we stopped at an all-night diner a lot like this one, and proceeded to track cow shit all over the floor. Not to mention, it was all over Cara's car too. Our sneaky night ended up being the talk of the town for the next few days. My dad was pissed, the farmer was pissed, and I was grounded for three weeks. So, yeah...I know all about how small towns work."

Ethan wasn't even trying to hide his amusement, and Lilly loved that she could make him laugh. For some reason, she had a feeling he didn't smile or laugh a lot.

"Here's your water," a woman said, making Lilly jump in surprise.

"Thanks, Karen," Ethan replied.

The waitress didn't even glance at Lilly. "You're welcome. Hey, there's something wrong with the lights in my bedroom. They're constantly flickering. You think you can come take a look sometime?"

"Sure," Ethan told her.

"I'm off tonight around nine. You could come over then," she said, smiling suggestively. It took everything within Lilly not to roll her eyes at how blatant the woman was being.

"Sorry, I don't work in the evenings," Ethan replied, then turned back to Lilly without introducing her. "You've got four brothers, right?" he asked.

Karen might be desperate for Ethan's attention, but she wasn't dumb. She got the hint and turned away, heading for the kitchen.

Lilly did her best to hide her smile, but knew she hadn't succeeded when Ethan sighed.

"She won't get the hint," he said quietly. "I don't want to hurt her feelings, because she's actually a nice woman most of the time, but I'm just not interested."

"I'm guessing there aren't a lot of eligible men in Fallport," Lilly said. "And even if there were, you're probably one of the best options. You're good-looking, smart, and seem like a nice man. It doesn't surprise me she's doing her best to catch your eye."

"She was rude to say that in front of you," Ethan replied, frowning.

"It's okay," Lilly said.

"It's *not*," he insisted.

Lilly wasn't about to share all the times women had hit on men she'd dated in the past. She hadn't been in love with any of those men, and it took too much energy to get offended. Even when working on a show with a full crew, most of whom were usually men, women hit on her co-workers as if she wasn't there. She was used to being dismissed.

"To answer your question, yes. I have four brothers. Lance, Leon, Lucas, and Lincoln. Lance is six years older than me, and the others fall between us."

"Let me guess, your dad's name starts with an L too?" Ethan asked with a smile.

"Nope. It's Mark."

Ethan blinked, then chuckled. "Right."

"My mom's name was Lisa. She was the one who thought it would be cute to give us names all starting with the same letter. Of course, she didn't stick around long enough to deal with the amount of teasing we got as a result."

"I'm sorry."

Lilly shrugged. "It's okay. Honestly, none of us really missed her. Okay, Lance probably did, since he was old enough to actually remember her when she left. But my dad's wonderful, and he did a great job raising us. I don't feel as if I missed out at all."

"That's how Rocky and I feel about our mom. She went out of her way to find us positive male role models after our dad died when we were around five. We participated in a ton of sports growing up, along with scouting. Every single one of our coaches and scout leaders was a good influence on us. A tornado went through our town when we were around twelve or thirteen, and our house was spared—thank God, because I don't think Mom would've been able to afford to fix it up—but a lot of neighbors weren't as lucky. When she saw how interested Rocky and I were in what the construction guys were doing as they worked to rebuild houses, Mom talked to them to see if it was all right if we hung around while they worked. They agreed, and my brother and I spent almost every hour we weren't in school hanging out, watching the men work."

"Is that how you got interested in doing what you do now?"

"Yeah. One of the contractors realized we were genuinely interested, and not just scoping the place to rob it later. He put us to work. We earned some extra money to help our mom out, stayed busy, and fell in love with working with our hands."

"That's great," Lilly said.

"Yeah."

They both looked up when a bell sounded over the entrance to the diner, and Lilly saw three of Ethan's friends enter. Raiden was easy to recognize, as the only redhead, and because he was so freaking tall. He literally had to duck to make it through the door without hitting his head. Not to mention the friendly-looking bloodhound at his side.

Talon was the second tallest man of the group, sporting a neatly trimmed brown beard and blue eyes that focused on her with such intensity, Lilly had to look away. She had no idea what he did before he found his way to Fallport, but he was definitely intense.

Zeke, in comparison, looked like the friendly one of the bunch. Lilly remembered Ethan telling her that he owned the bar they'd yet to tour...which meant he was probably used to putting people at ease.

The trio headed for the table and Ethan stood up to greet them. Lilly started to do the same, but Zeke quickly said, "No, don't get up, Lilly."

She eased back into her seat as the men got settled around the table. The bloodhound sat next to Raiden, then, with a hand signal from his master, lay down with a loud groan.

Lilly was somewhat surprised the dog was allowed inside the restaurant, but then again, this wasn't a huge city. The rules were different in small towns, as she knew firsthand.

"So, Lilly, it's nice to officially meet you," Zeke said with a warm smile.

As Lilly returned his smile, she noted that while the man might look friendly and easygoing, there was an underlying vibe that warned her to tread carefully.

"Same," she said, making eye contact with all three men to make sure they knew she was talking to them all.

"So," Tal said, leaning forward with his elbows on the table. "What's your story?"

For the first time, Lilly realized he was British. His accent was super sexy, but she wasn't sure how to answer his question.

"No," Ethan said curtly.

Lilly glanced at him in confusion. But his attention was on his friend.

"We aren't doing this," he said firmly.

"Doing what?" Tal asked, sitting back in his chair.

Ethan gave him a look.

Lilly put her hand over his for a second and squeezed. Then she sat up straight. She had nothing to hide. Besides, soon she'd be gone and would never see these guys again.

Ignoring the pang of disappointment at that thought, she said, "I'm Lilly Ray. I grew up in West Virginia. I have four older brothers. I went to college on the East Coast, moved to California because that's where I heard all the good jobs were in the industry. Which was correct. I worked my ass off and did my best to ignore all the sexual harassment flung my way. I'm good at my job—damn good. But the place wore me down. So I started taking jobs that were out of California. They don't pay as well, but I'm trying to save up enough money to settle down somewhere, hopefully close to my brothers so I can be more present in their lives, and in their children's lives.

"I took the job with the paranormal show because it seemed like it would be interesting. We've got, I think, one more shoot to do after this one, then I'll find another gig—I'm a contract worker, so I get hired one job at a time. Do I believe in the paranormal? Yes. Do I believe in *every* paranormal phenomenon out there? No. Yes, we'll be filming in the forest, but I truly don't think anyone will get lost. Those guys aren't outdoors people, but we'll just be going far enough away from the town so any mischievous teenagers won't get it in their heads to come out and mess with the investigation. We aren't going to be hiking twenty miles to find Bigfoot.

"I'm not sure what else you want to know, but I'm happy to answer any questions you have. I've signed an NDA though, so there might be some things I *can't* answer, and I hope that doesn't upset you. I'm not trying to be sneaky or anything, but I can literally be sued for a million bucks or more if I talk about the show."

She could've continued, but she just lifted her chin and stared at Tal, praying her honest response was enough to reassure him of... whatever. Lilly wasn't sure *what* he was looking for, or why he'd agreed to come eat with them if he didn't trust her, but she'd learned growing up with four brothers not to back down when men attempted to intimidate her.

Tal stared at her for a beat, then smiled.

And good Lord, the smile changed everything about his countenance. He went from downright scary to jaw-dropping sexy in a heartbeat.

"Okay," he said.

Lilly glanced at Raiden, who nodded at her.

One more to go. Taking a breath, she turned her attention to Zeke.

"You guys order yet?" he asked.

Lilly blinked. "Yes. I mean, I'm not sure Sandra actually gave us a choice, but since chicken-fried steak, garlic-parmesan pretzels, and chocolate lava cakes sounded delicious, I think I'm glad I *wasn't* given a choice," she said honestly.

"You're getting the same thing," Ethan told his friends. "Didn't think you'd mind."

"Nope, sounds good," Zeke said.

Lilly let out the breath she hadn't realized she was holding. For some reason, she really wanted these men to like her. It wasn't rational, as they'd probably forget about her the second she was gone, but she was relieved she'd managed to get over the first hurdle of meeting them.

"I talked to Rocky before coming over here, and he wanted me to ask you something," Raid said.

Turning her attention to the somewhat nerdy-looking man, who was still handsome in his own way, Lilly said, "Shoot."

"Have you ever worked on one of those home shows?"

Lilly grinned. It was such a normal question. She was expecting something more along the lines of wanting to know something about Tucker or the paranormal show. "Well, as a matter of fact, yes. The job before this one."

"A renovation show?" Ethan asked, the interest easy to hear in his voice.

Lilly shook her head. She shouldn't be surprised he was as interested as his twin, with their construction background and all. "No, sorry. It was one of those real estate shows. You know, where the couple has to decide between three houses to buy."

"And? Are they real?" Raid asked. "I mean, it sounds as if their jobs are always made up. The wife will be like, 'I work with rescued animals,' and the husband will say, 'And I work from home making origami animals and selling them on the internet.' Then their budget is like two point five million."

Lilly chuckled. "Right? I've noticed that too. And to answer your question...no, they aren't real."

She swore all four men leaned forward, eager to hear more.

"So, the couple on every episode has already bought their house. Anywhere from a week to months before the show is taped. The producer goes through the current houses in the area that are for sale and picks two others for the couple to 'choose from.'" She used air quotes around the last two words, then continued. "They—the producers—actually choose the wish list for the couple. If a gas stove is on the list, they make sure two of the houses have it and one doesn't. If they list open concept, again, two might have it, but not the third, and so on. For the viewer, it feels as if the choice is a hard one because no house has everything they want.

"Everything is also taped the same weekend, so the little snippets at the end, when they say it's a month or two later and the couple has settled in? That's all a lie. If you look closely, many times the furniture is the same as it was when they were touring the house...because it was *their* furniture, already moved in. If the house was empty during the show, the snippet about how they're doing is often filmed outside, so the viewer doesn't realize there still aren't any furnishings in the house."

All four men were staring at her in disbelief.

Tal finally broke the silence. "Man, now I won't be able to watch any of those shows again."

"You watch them a lot?" Zeke asked.

"Well, yeah," Tal said with a shrug. "I love looking at all the houses."

"I'm not sure I want to tell Rocky," Raid said. "He loves those reno shows. I'm guessing they're probably as fake as the real estate ones."

Lilly hadn't worked on any of them, but she knew others who had, and Raid was right. But she kept her mouth shut.

"Incoming," Karen said as she approached the table with a huge tray on her shoulder. It took two trips for her to drop off all the plates, but when she was done, there wasn't an inch of leftover room on the table.

The smell of everything was incredible, and Lilly had a feeling if she lived here, she'd probably gain fifty pounds simply because she wouldn't be able to resist the amazing food. From the huge brunch Whitney had made, to the cinnamon roll she'd had earlier as a snack, to the mouthwatering chicken-fried steak that came with sides of mashed potatoes and fried okra—not to mention the pretzels and the dessert, which Lilly had no doubt would be as good as the rest of the meal—she'd have to hike miles and miles every day to stay the same size she was right now.

As if Ethan could read her mind, he leaned in, his breath tickling her ear as he said, "We don't eat like this all the time. Sandra likes to test people."

"Like the woman you brought here who got a salad?" She couldn't help but ask.

Ethan winced, but nodded. "Yeah. Like her."

"He wasn't dating her," Zeke said after swallowing a piece of okra. "She was looking into buying a house here in Fallport, and she got a quote from Rocky and Ethan to gut the place and re-do it. Rocky bailed as soon as he looked at the house, telling her he wouldn't take the job."

"She wanted to make it ultra-modern, and Rocky refused on principle," Tal chimed in.

"It was perfect the way it was," Ethan muttered. "It just needed a little touch-up. Not a gut and re-do."

"Anyway, Ethan was being polite, taking her to lunch to break the news that neither of them were interested in the project," Zeke continued. "It wasn't a date," he finished, repeating himself.

Lilly couldn't help but be secretly pleased, though she did her best to keep that from her tone as she asked, "So did she buy the house?"

"Nope," Raid said. "She stuck around for another couple days, but when she got the cold shoulder from just about everyone, she decided she didn't want to live here after all."

Lilly couldn't help but laugh. She shouldn't. It wasn't very cool of the locals to be so judgmental, but again, that was kind of how small towns worked sometimes.

The rest of the lunch went well, as far as Lilly was concerned. Ethan's friends were funny, once they relaxed a bit. They talked more about her job—she admitted she had no idea what she'd do once the filming of the show was over—she heard a few stories about the people Raid's bloodhound, Duke, had found over the years, and it made more sense why the residents of Fallport had no problem with the hound going wherever his master did.

Lilly liked the loyalty the town showed toward the good people who lived there. She had no doubt they were standoffish and suspicious of newcomers, but it seemed as if once someone proved their worth, the townspeople embraced them with open arms.

By the time Lilly had eaten half her giant piece of chocolate lava cake, she was so full, she didn't think she'd be able to stand. She flopped back in her chair, put a hand on her belly, and moaned.

The men around her laughed.

"This isn't funny," she complained. "How the hell am I going to hike around the woods for hours with a camera on my shoulder when I feel as if I'm gonna pop?"

"Sounds like you're gonna need the energy," Zeke said as he pushed back from the table.

The others followed his lead and stood as well. To her surprise, Duke came over to her chair and snuffled her hand. The dog hadn't shown any interest in her whatsoever throughout the meal, but he seemed eager to befriend her now.

She pretended not to see the raised brow Raid shot to the others as she bent over Duke's head.

"Aren't you a smooshy boy?" she asked as she petted him. She smiled up at Raid. "He's so sweet."

"Actually, he's really not," Raid said with a shrug, sounding a little confused. "He's pretty much a grump. He loves food and being out in the woods. He merely tolerates everything else."

Mentally shrugging, Lilly stood. "Well, he seems like an easy-going boy to me."

The group all walked toward the front of the diner, and Sandra appeared as if out of nowhere.

"How was your meal?" she asked.

"Amazing, as you well know," Ethan told her.

"Delicious."

"Hit the spot."

"Those pretzels were the shit."

The men praised the meal, and Lilly did the same. "If I wasn't scheduled to work tonight, I'd go back to the B&B and immediately fall into a food coma...which, by the way, is a huge compliment," she told Sandra with a smile.

The owner beamed. "Good."

Lilly took out her phone and pulled her credit card out of the silicone pocket she'd attached to the back. She hated carrying a purse and the small pocket easily held her driver's license and a couple credit cards. It was perfect for her needs.

To her surprise, Sandra actually took a step back as she held out the card.

"Oh, no," she said, with a shake of her head.

At the same time, Ethan gently pushed her forearm down. "I've got it," he told her.

"But—" Lilly started.

"Nope," he interrupted. "Eagle Point SAR has a tab here. We pay it off at the end of every month. It's fine."

"And they tip twenty percent, which makes my servers very happy," Sandra said. She winked at Ethan and added, "But it's sweet that she wants to pay."

"That was subtle," Tal said under his breath. "Not."

Lilly blushed as she put her credit card back into the pocket. It seemed as if the owner of the diner had definitely given her stamp of approval. But things weren't like that between her and Ethan.

Were they?

Zeke held the door open as they all filed out into the beautiful spring afternoon. It wasn't so hot that the sun made her feel as if she was melting, but it also wouldn't be freezing at night when they were hiking through the woods, which was good. Most of the trees had leaves on the branches, which made for good Bigfoot hunting —or so Tucker had proclaimed the night before.

Lilly had wanted to say that it would be easier to see an eight-foot-tall, hairy humanoid creature tromping through the woods in the winter, when there weren't any leaves, but she didn't think the producer would be amused.

She stood somewhat awkwardly as Ethan said his goodbyes to

his friends. Duke once again stuffed his snout into her hand, so Lilly busied herself with saying farewell to the slobbery hound.

Once again, Raid simply shook his head as he watched the dog with her. Then he gave his friends a chin lift and headed in the direction of the library.

Tal shook her hand before he headed back to the barber shop, but Zeke reached out and pulled her in for a hug.

"Zeke," Ethan warned.

"What?" the other man said with a grin. "Just sayin' goodbye."

Lilly couldn't help but chuckle. "It was nice to meet you."

"Same," Zeke said. Then he got serious. "Be careful out there. It'd be better if you all had a guide, but your producer declined our offer."

"You offered to be our guide?" she asked in surprise.

"Yeah. He laughed and said you didn't need an outsider trying to take pictures and leak info about the show."

Lilly rolled her eyes. Yeah, that sounded like something Tucker would say.

"The *last* thing you need to worry about out there is fucking Bigfoot," Zeke said.

Lilly tilted her head. "Meaning?"

"There are bears. And bobcats. And moonshiners."

"Moonshiners? Ethan mentioned that yesterday."

"Yeah. The forest is a great place to hide their stills. And they can get very cranky if someone accidentally stumbles across their stash. If that happens, I recommend you back up and get the hell out of the area."

"Do you know where they are?" Lilly couldn't help but ask.

"A lot of them, yeah. But the old timers know we won't say anything. Our job is to find lost people, not illegal alcohol," Zeke said.

"I'll mention it to Tucker," Lilly told him.

Zeke nodded, then he smiled, and the easygoing bar owner was back. But again, Lilly felt as if she'd gotten a glimpse of the real man under the façade. She hadn't met the other three members of the SAR team, but she had a feeling they'd be just as complex as the four she'd had lunch with.

"Haven't seen you in On the Rocks for a while, Chaos...it'd be nice to see your ugly mug on the other side of my bar soon."

Ethan nodded. "Maybe I'll stop in tonight. Rocky's finishing a big job and he'll probably be up for a beer or two."

"Great. See you guys tonight then." With that, Zeke turned and strode down the sidewalk and back toward his bar.

Lilly turned to Ethan. "Chaos?" she asked.

He grinned. "That was my nickname when I was a SEAL."

"Wait—you were a SEAL?" Lilly asked with wide eyes.

"Yup. As was my brother. Zeke was a Green Beret, Tal was in special forces in the UK, Raid was in the Coast Guard, Brock—otherwise known as Bones—was US Customs and Border protection, and Drew—who we sometimes call Koop, because his last name is Koopman—was a member of the Virginia State Police."

"Wow. I'm impressed," Lilly said honestly. "Whitney mentioned you all had some sort of military background, but that's just...wow."

Ethan shrugged off her admiration. "We're just men who served our countries in one way or another, and now all we want is to live a simple life."

Lilly nodded. She got that. "Well, I think Fallport is a lovely place to live that simple life."

"Sometimes less simple than others," Ethan said, looking at his watch. He frowned. "I had hoped to show you the library and Zeke's bar, but it's getting late."

Lilly checked her own watch, surprised to see how much time had passed. They'd been eating and talking for longer than she'd thought. "Yeah, if I'm going to get a nap in, I should probably get going," she said regretfully.

Ethan nodded and they walked back toward his car at the post office in a companionable silence. As they approached, Silas, Otto, and Art were still sitting in the same place they'd been earlier.

"So? What'd you think?" Silas asked as they neared.

"About the town? I love it," Lilly said.

"No, about Ethan," Otto corrected.

Lilly blushed and glanced at him. He was shaking his head at the older man. "Don't embarrass her," he said.

"She's not embarrassed. Are you?" Otto asked.

"It's good to court a lady," Art threw in. "Too many men these days skip that and go straight to smoochin'."

Lilly couldn't help but laugh. She *was* a little embarrassed, but these men were so genuine, there was no way she could be offended. "So far, so good," she told Otto.

"Word is Sandra likes her," Silas told Ethan.

"And I saw Duke took a liking to her too," Art said. "That dog don't like nobody."

"You better be careful," Otto warned, "or Raid'll steal her away."

"Nobody's stealing anyone," Ethan said with another shake of his head. "Now if you'll excuse us, Lilly needs to grab some z's before she has to work tonight."

"Supposed to be a full moon," Otto said. "That's when the beasts change, you know."

Silas smacked the back of Otto's head as he said, "That's werewolves, you idiot. Not Bigfoot."

"Hey! All animals get hinky with the full moon," Otto argued.

Lilly was still grinning when Ethan held open her door. He waited until she was settled, then shut her door and jogged around the back to his own side. He waved at the three men and pulled out of the space. As he did, he said, "Remind me not to park in front of the post office the next time we come to town."

Lilly burst out laughing.

Ethan glanced at her, and she loved the easy smile on his face.

"They were funny."

"I hope they didn't make you too uncomfortable. Actually, I hope no one did today. Fallport's great, but people tend to like to get up in everyone else's business."

"No, everyone was nice," she told him before resting her head back on the seat. She turned her head to smile at Ethan. "I had a good time today. I spent so much time in Hollywood, where everyone ignores everyone else and you don't even know the name of your neighbor who's lived there for five years, that I'd almost forgotten how great small towns could be."

"Yeah," Ethan agreed. "Although they're not always great. Keeping a secret is nearly impossible. It's so bad that if I buy a bottle of aspirin at Grogan's store, by the time I get home, I've gotten three or more phone calls from residents asking if I'm all right."

"So I guess buying condoms is out then, huh?" Lilly asked—then blushed. "Sorry, don't answer that."

But Ethan just laughed. "Exactly. Same with pregnancy tests."

"I can imagine," she said.

It wasn't far to the B&B, and before Lilly was ready, Ethan was pulling up in front of the stately old home. He turned to her. "Be careful tonight. Zeke's right, there's a lot of things that could hurt you out there in the woods."

"Besides Bigfoot?" Lilly joked.

But he didn't even crack a smile. "Yeah."

"I will. But seriously, if Roger, Trent, Chris, and Michelle last more than a few hours wandering around in the dark making Bigfoot mating calls—or what they assume are mating calls—and whacking trees with sticks, I'd be surprised."

"What do you think they'd do if one of those calls actually worked?" Ethan asked. "If a horny, eight-foot-tall Bigfoot came charging through the trees with a raging hard-on, ready to answer the call of love?"

Lilly giggled. "Oh my God, I'd pay good money to see that." When she had herself under control, she looked back at Ethan. "Thanks again for a great day. I needed this."

"Me too," he said. Then he turned off the engine. "I'll help you get the stuff you bought inside."

"Oh, that's okay. I can get it," she said quickly.

"I'm sure you can, but there's no way I'm sitting here on my ass while you lug that crap inside."

She should've known he'd say that. "All right. But instead of bringing it inside, maybe we should just put it in my car. That'll keep me from having to move it twice, and since I have to bring it to Tucker and Trent, it makes more sense."

"Sounds good."

It took only a couple minutes to move the tent and other stuff she'd bought into her rental. Then Lilly stood there, suddenly feeling a little awkward. "Well...thanks again, Ethan."

"You're welcome. I know you're going to be working every night, and probably sleeping during the day, and I have to get some work done myself...but if you wake up and get bored, I'm happy to entertain you again. I'd love for you to meet Rocky, and I bet Drew and Brock'll want to hang out too, after hearing the others talk about our lunch today."

He sounded almost nervous—which surprised the hell out of Lilly. But if there was any way she could swing it, she definitely wanted to hang out with Ethan some more. "I'd like that," she said shyly.

"Great. Text me anytime. Day or night. I mean it. I know the phones don't work that well in the woods, but if you need anything, just give me a shout and I'll do what I can to help."

"Okay."

They stared at each other for a long moment before Ethan took a step forward and pulled her into his arms. It was a quick hug, and Lilly didn't want to let go. But she forced herself to drop her arms, then smiled up at him.

"See you around," he said.

"See ya," Lilly said, watching as he strode back to his car. He waved once, and she returned the gesture before turning and heading inside.

Whitney wasn't around, which Lilly was grateful for. She wanted to keep the memories of the day to herself and cherish them for a while. Everything about her time with Ethan made her miss her family. They were close, as he seemed to be with his friends. The town made her think of home.

And then there was the way Ethan made her feel...as if she was the most important person in the world. He didn't look through her. Didn't dismiss her as if she was nobody, as many producers and talent had throughout the years. She'd also laughed more today than she had in ages, which felt awesome.

Lilly kicked off her shoes, set her alarm, and climbed into bed. She closed her eyes and sighed. She hadn't been looking forward to this shoot for many reasons, but suddenly she hoped it lasted longer than the week or so it was scheduled for. The thought of leaving Fallport, and Ethan, was actually a little painful.

She pushed that thought away. There was no telling what the upcoming shoot would bring. Hoping like hell she was right when she'd told Ethan that they'd probably not be filming all night, and she'd have another chance to hang out with him, Lilly let herself drift to sleep.

CHAPTER SEVEN

"So, what'd you find out about the shoot?" Rocky asked Ethan that night at the bar. They'd met up after Rocky finished the inspection of the renovations he'd done on another one of the older houses in town. Drew and Brock had joined them too.

"Yeah, Ethan," Zeke teased with a grin. "What'd you find out about the shoot?"

"Shut up," Ethan said, throwing a balled-up napkin at him.

Zeke laughed and headed down the bar to make a drink for one of the regulars who'd just arrived.

"I'm guessing lunch went well?" Rocky asked with a grin.

"Yeah."

"You still think she's nice?"

Ethan nodded. Nice wasn't exactly the word he'd use, but it'd do for now.

"Wait, I thought you were hanging out with—what's her name again? Just to find out more information about where the show's filming in the forest?" Drew asked.

"He likes her," Rocky practically singsonged.

"Oh, for God's sake, shut up," Ethan grumbled, shoving his

brother's shoulder so hard he almost fell off the barstool. Then he turned to Drew. "Her name is Lilly. I gave her a tour because she seemed genuinely interested in seeing the town, but also to get more information about the shoot."

"And?" Brock asked.

"And she said there wasn't a set plan for tracking down Bigfoot. They would just go into the woods and see what they could find."

"Fuck," Drew sighed, bringing his beer to his lips.

"She did seem to think they wouldn't go far though," Ethan said. "Just far enough in so any of the local kids wouldn't feel the urge to try to interfere with the show. She thinks they'll be done by midnight or a little later."

"Well, at least that's somethin'," Rocky said.

"She also has a GPS, which makes me feel better," Ethan told his friends. "The producer doesn't, but at least one of them will be able to backtrack to whatever parking lot they're using."

The other three men nodded.

"So...what did the good townspeople think of Lilly?" Rocky asked with a grin.

"Well, I think Otto, Silas, and Art liked her. And she impressed Sandra by not ordering a salad and eating the chicken-fried steak she had on special," Ethan said. "But I'm guessin' most people are gonna need a bit more time to get to know her before they decide."

"Which they aren't going to get, since she's only here to film the show, then she'll be gone," Drew said.

His friend wasn't trying to be a dick, but Ethan didn't like hearing him confirm so bluntly what he already knew in his head. He took a sip of his own beer to hide his irritation. But he should've known he couldn't hide *anything* from his friends. They'd been through a lot together, and all of them were more observant than the average person.

"Wait...you really *do* like this chick, don't you?" Drew asked, his eyes narrowing.

Ethan sighed. "Yeah. There's just something about her that

sucks me in. She's down-to-earth. Funny. Smart. She doesn't take herself too seriously."

"Not to mention she's pretty," Brock threw in.

"Yeah, there's that too," Ethan said with a small grin.

"Duke loved her," Zeke said.

"*What*? Are you serious?" Drew asked.

"Yup. Went right up to her and slobbered all over her hand. Demanded she pet him."

"Wow," Brock said. "That dog doesn't like anyone but Raid. And he only tolerates us."

"I know. I was shocked too. But obviously the dog has good taste," Zeke said, before ambling toward a customer at the opposite end of the bar.

Ethan couldn't argue with that part, though Duke's behavior *was* surprising.

Raid had rescued the dog when he was just a puppy. He'd been driving in the north part of the state, coming back from a librarian conference—whatever that was—when he saw a man stop along the side of the road and throw something out. Raid had been curious enough to turn around to see what he'd dumped. Turned out to be a bloodhound puppy. It had been in bad shape, obviously abused and neglected.

Raid couldn't leave the poor thing on the side of the road, so he'd picked him up and brought him home...and the rest was history. He'd trained the bloodhound to search for human scent, and the two were devoted to each other. However, the bloodhound was very standoffish. Didn't like too many people, probably because of the abuse he'd suffered as a puppy. But given the dog's reaction to Lilly, he'd been as enamored as Ethan himself.

"Sucks that she's gonna leave," Drew said after a moment.

"What if she doesn't?" Rocky asked.

Everyone turned to look at him.

"You know something we don't?" Ethan asked. He couldn't help the surge of longing that went through him.

"Don't get too excited," Rocky warned, quickly dashing Ethan's hopes. "I haven't heard any gossip about her or anything. But, Ethan, when you put your mind to it, you can convince someone of just about anything. Remember that time we were in Africa and had gotten separated from our teams?"

"What happened?" Drew asked, leaning his elbow on the bar.

Ethan rolled his eyes. His brother loved to tell this story. He was surprised Drew and Brock hadn't already heard it. Rocky was slipping for sure.

"We were screwed. Half a dozen extremely unfriendly locals surrounded us and began to close in. We were in hostile territory and about two minutes from getting beaten to within an inch of our lives and dragged through the streets by our ankles. Then Ethan somehow made them think an air raid was imminent. He kept frantically pointing to the sky and pointing to his watch. I'd swear he even squeezed out a couple of tears. He was acting completely freaked out, so much so, even *I* began to believe him. The men around us backed off, running in six different directions, trying to get away from the bombing they were sure was coming."

Drew and Brock laughed.

"Yeah, that sounds like our fearless leader," Brock said.

"All I'm saying is, if you like her...why not see if you can't convince her to stay in Fallport?" Rocky asked.

"Right. So she stays, then things don't work out. That would suck because this town's tiny, and her living here if things go bad wouldn't be good. Not at all," Ethan said.

"But what if they *didn't* go bad?" Rocky asked.

Ethan took a deep breath. His brother had a point.

"Look, you're a hell of a catch, bro. I know you better than just about anyone on this planet. You work hard, you don't do drugs, you've got a good amount of money in your bank account, you treat women well when you *do* date. If you're interested in Lilly, then I know she's something special, even without actually knowing much about her. And I know *you*—if you don't at least try to see where things could go between you, you'll regret it."

His brother wasn't wrong. That was the good *and* bad thing about being so close to his twin. He knew him too well. "So I'm just supposed to tell her she should quit her job and move here and do... what? It's not like there's a big need for professional camera operators in Fallport."

"So, she can find something else to do," Rocky said with a shrug, not sounding concerned in the least.

"If someone told you to quit SAR and 'find something else to do,' you wouldn't be upset about it?" Ethan asked.

"Yeah, I see your point. But here's the thing...do you think Lilly loves what she does as much as we do? Is it in her blood and soul?"

"I don't know her well enough to answer that," Ethan said.

"Then *get* to know her," Rocky insisted.

Ethan wanted to pound his head on the bar top. Rocky was making it sound like the easiest thing in the world to get to know Lilly, convince her to quit her job and move to Fallport, where they'd live happily ever after. That wasn't how the world worked.

"What do you have to lose?" Drew asked.

"The worst that can happen is she blows you off," Brock threw in.

"Why are you guys pushing so hard?" Ethan asked. "Seriously, I spent a few hours with her today, and that's it."

"Because we've never seen you show this much interest in someone," Rocky said. "She's clearly different. That's obvious by your reaction to her. When was the last time you went out of your way to show someone around town? It's not like Fallport is that big. She could've taken a walk around the square without your help."

Again, his brother had a point.

"I think we all know our chances of being in serious relationships are pretty damn low," Brock said. "Time in the service hasn't done any of us any favors in that regard. And it doesn't help that we live in the middle of nowhere, and are more comfortable spending time in the forest than in any kind of social setting. If you truly feel a connection with this woman, you should explore that. No one's saying you have to marry her tomorrow. But there's nothing wrong with wanting a long-term relationship and doing whatever's necessary to give it the best chance of succeeding."

"What if we told you right now that she was leaving tomorrow? That you'd never see her again. Never have a chance to get to know her better. What would your honest reaction be?" Rocky asked.

Ethan frowned, and the beer he'd swallowed a moment ago churned in his belly.

"That's what I thought. She's made an impression on you," Rocky said. "The brother I know wouldn't dismiss that oh-shit feeling when we're in the middle of an op, and this is the same damn thing."

"Not exactly," Ethan said dryly. "I'm guessing Lilly isn't gonna pop up from behind a car in the parking lot with an RPG on her shoulder and threaten to blow my head off...along with half the block."

"You know what I mean," Rocky told him.

He did. Ethan sighed. "She's going to be working nights for the foreseeable future. She needs to rest during the day."

"Excuses," Rocky said in disgust.

His brother was right. Ethan *was* just making excuses. Today was one of the best days he'd had in a very long time. He enjoyed spending time with Lilly and got a kick out of seeing her interact with the men and women of Fallport. Almost everyone had been friendly, if not completely welcoming, but he had a feeling that they'd all come around with time. Lilly wasn't stuck up. She'd said often enough that Fallport reminded her of her own hometown. And she'd also said she was looking for a place to settle near her family.

"I'll send her a text tomorrow. Ask if she wants to get together again before she goes to work," Ethan said.

All three men beamed, genuinely happy for him.

"What's everyone so excited about?" Zeke asked as he rejoined them, wiping his hands on a towel.

"Ethan's gonna officially ask Lilly out. Then he's gonna get her to quit her job and move to Fallport so they can get married and have babies," Rocky said helpfully.

Zeke's brow shot up in question.

"That's not exactly what I said," Ethan argued, shaking his head.

"Well, I think it's great. Good luck," Zeke said with a nod. "Anyone want another drink?"

It was so like his friend to just go with the flow. Zeke was the most easygoing member of the SAR team...but when provoked, he never hesitated to let the deadly Green Beret loose.

It also didn't surprise Ethan that Zeke was all for him pursuing Lilly. He hadn't missed the glances his friend had been throwing at Elsie, one of the waitresses, all night. He clearly liked her...but seemed to be keeping his distance for some reason.

Drew was the first to call it quits a little while later. He was working long days, since tax season was upon them, keeping him extremely busy. Brock left next, but not before getting a promise from Ethan to let him meet Lilly sooner rather than later.

Rocky nudged Ethan with his shoulder. "You aren't mad at me, are you?" he asked when it was just the two of them.

"About what?"

"Pushing you about Lilly."

"No. I'm still not sure trying to pursue anything with her is a good idea. There's a larger-than-average chance she's not going to want to go out with me, like on a legit date."

Rocky shrugged. "Then it's her loss. But from what I've heard from Raid and Tal, she's into you."

His brother's words made Ethan relax when he didn't even realize he was tense. "Yeah?"

"Yeah," Rocky confirmed.

Ethan liked the thought Lilly was just as interested. He'd thought the same thing, but it was nice to get confirmation.

"You gonna be around to help me tomorrow?" Rocky asked.

"Of course. What time?"

"I was thinking around ten. I'll get there at eight and get started. I should be ready for wiring by ten. I'll text you the address when I get home."

"Sounds good. You about ready to go?"

Rocky lifted his beer and chugged the last bit, then stood. "Yup."

Ethan left forty bucks under his glass for his and Rocky's beers, plus a healthy tip. The two brothers walked out of the bar side by side, giving Zeke a chin lift as they went.

It was less than a mile to their apartment from the bar, and both men enjoyed the fresh air as they walked home.

"See you tomorrow," Ethan told his brother when they arrived back at their complex. It wasn't a large building. Only two stories, with a total of eight apartments.

"Ethan?" Rocky asked.

"Yeah?"

"Happy for you."

Ethan chuckled. "Don't be happy yet. She may not agree to see me, between her shifts and trying to catch some sleep."

"She will," Rocky said confidently.

Ethan simply smiled at his brother, then unlocked his door and headed inside. He turned on the overhead light and threw his keys onto the table just inside the front door. The apartment was small, but Ethan had never needed a ton of space. He had a leather couch, no dining table, a large TV, and an oversized easy chair. The galley-style kitchen was out of date but functional, which was all Ethan required.

As he looked around his living space with fresh eyes, he wondered what Lilly would think. Was she the kind of woman who expected stainless steel appliances, granite countertops, and cloth napkins on a perfectly set table? He didn't think so, but then again, he didn't really know her. And it wasn't as if Ethan wouldn't like those things for himself, it was more that they just hadn't seemed important. He'd been in the poorest communities in the world, and had seen people living happy and fulfilling lives. On the other hand, he'd also seen the most obscene displays of wealth from miserable human beings not satisfied with what they had and wanting more.

He'd vowed to never fall into the latter category. As long as he had his brother and friends, food to eat, and a roof over his head, he'd be happy. And he was. But Ethan couldn't help but worry just a bit about the future. He didn't want to be lonely forever. Didn't want to come home to an empty house or apartment for the rest of his life.

Lilly might not be the woman meant for him...but what if she was?

Rocky was right, he'd totally regret not taking a chance that things might work out between them.

Ethan headed for his bedroom. The queen-size bed had always been adequate, since it was just him. He'd never brought a woman here, and hadn't really thought much about sharing his bed with anyone. Regardless, he didn't want a huge bed. If he loved someone, he'd want her close. He imagined he'd enjoy holding a woman all night. He'd never done so. Ever.

But now all he could think about was Lilly, sleeping in his arms.

Shaking his head, knowing he was getting way ahead of himself, Ethan wandered into the bathroom. It was attached to the bedroom but tiny. The shower/bath combo wasn't exactly a designer's dream, but the water was hot and there was plenty of it.

He got ready for bed, then threw his dirty clothes into the hamper along one wall of the bedroom. He climbed under the sheet on his bed in nothing but a pair of boxers and reached for his phone. It was late, and Lilly would probably be out of cell phone range, but he wanted her to know he was thinking about her and hoped to see her when she got off work. Make it clear he was interested in getting to know her better.

. . .

Ethan: Hi. I know you probably won't get this until you're out of the deep dark woods, but I wanted to let you know that I had a good time today. I'd like to see you again. Maybe after you get some sleep, we could hang out? If you're interested, shoot me a text. I'll be helping Rocky tomorrow morning, but should be free in the afternoon. If not...I'm sure I'll see you around.

He would definitely see her around. Ethan wasn't going to let a lack of response deter him. He'd arrange to accidentally run into her, if necessary, and see if the connection he felt was still there. Of course, if she honestly didn't seem interested, he'd back off. Ethan had never pushed himself on a woman and wasn't about to start now...even if the woman in question had intrigued him more than anyone had in years. Maybe ever.

Satisfied that he'd done what he could to make the next move, Ethan lay in the dark and stared at the ceiling. He wondered where Lilly was and what was going on with the show. Maybe they'd found Bigfoot already, and the cast and crew would be packing things up and heading out tomorrow.

He shook his head. No, the one guy was going to spend a night or two in the woods for a solo investigation, whatever that was. Lilly, and the rest of the people working on the show, would be around for at least a few more days.

Ethan realized he was smiling at the thought.

He rolled onto his side and closed his eyes. He felt like a boy excited for Christmas. He was looking forward to hearing how tonight's filming had gone. But more than that, he was simply excited to see Lilly again.

CHAPTER EIGHT

Lilly wanted to scream. The shoot wasn't going well. Not at all. Trent and Roger had been sniping at each other all night. Trying to talk over each other and come up with the best ideas for finding Bigfoot. Michelle screeched every time she walked into the many spiderwebs woven across the trails and between trees, and Chris looked hungover as hell.

Not to mention, Brodie wasn't happy with the sound. Kate and Andre were obviously having some sort of issue with each other—and neither was happy with Tucker, since they'd already worked today, and he'd made them come in tonight as well. And Joey was simply in a piss-poor mood and refused to talk to anyone for whatever reason.

On top of all that, Tucker was ignoring everyone's crankiness and trying to pretend that everything was fine. That walking through the woods at night, off trail at that, was perfectly normal.

Lilly wasn't exactly having the time of her life. But at least she didn't have to pretend to be interested in what she was doing and smile for the camera.

After walking through another spiderweb, Michelle screamed,

then turned to Tucker and shouted, "Seriously, this is bullshit!" as she frantically tried to swipe the web off her face.

"What do you want me to do about them?" Tucker asked. "It's not as if I can order the bugs and spiders in the forest to go away until we're done filming."

"I know, but what are we even *doing?*" she whined. "We're walking in circles! This is boring as hell. We need to *do* something. When are we gonna get to do those yells and stuff? And who's gonna go and yell back? And I want to whack some trees already!"

It took everything in Lilly not to roll her eyes.

"All right. I think we have enough footage of everyone stumbling around in the dark," Tucker said magnanimously.

Lilly had a feeling if Michelle hadn't stopped to pull her hissy fit, they would've continued wandering around the forest until the sun came up. At least she'd been assigned to walk behind the hosts. Poor Trent and Joey had to be in front of them so they could get some head-on shots, which meant they were constantly tripping over their own feet and trying to climb over tree limbs and other debris to stay far enough ahead of the foursome.

"Trent and Michelle, I think we'll start with the two of you. We'll head back to that hill we passed a while ago. You can talk about how it's the perfect place to hear Bigfoot respond to your calls. Chris, you and Roger go up to the ridge on the other side, the one we saw yesterday, and you can respond to their calls and pound on some trees."

"Wait, why do we have to go all the way up to that other ridge?" Chris complained.

"Because I said so," Tucker said belligerently.

"This sucks," Roger said under his breath.

"Tomorrow, you guys will get to be center stage," Tucker reassured Chris and Roger. "Wear the same thing you are tonight, and we'll just pretend tomorrow is an extension of the same evening. I'm guessing we aren't going to have time to do both shots before it gets light."

Lilly's heart sunk at Tucker's pronouncement. She'd hoped they'd be done around one or two. By the way it sounded, they were going to be out here all night.

"No can do," Trent said. "Tomorrow I'm starting my solo investigation."

Tucker muttered under his breath. Then louder, said, "Whatever. Michelle and Andre can head into the woods to play Bigfoot."

Now Lilly heard *Andre* bitching under his breath. It wasn't the first time the camera operators had been asked to fake an encounter with whatever paranormal entity they were searching for, but this *was* the first time it involved a good deal of exertion... namely hiking through the woods to get to a point where it sounded like Bigfoot was far away.

"This is boring as shit," Chris complained.

Tucker whipped his head around. "What did you just say?" he bit out.

Lilly held her breath. It was never good to piss off Tucker, but apparently Chris was tired enough not to care.

"This episode is boring as shit! We aren't doing anything new. We need to actually *find* something. Not just hear noises in the dark. It's all well and good to pound on a tree and to let out a bunch of yells, but we need to actually see evidence of fucking Bigfoot if we want to get any kind of ratings. We need to be different from the other shows."

"What do you want to do, have someone dress up as Bigfoot and tromp through the trees?" Trent asked with a laugh.

"Maybe," Chris said. "At least it'd be different. We could film them far enough away, and blur the footage, so no one can be sure of what we saw. We just have to make it look realistic enough that it *could* be Bigfoot."

"That's dumb," Joey said.

Lilly looked at him, her eyes widened exaggeratingly, trying to tell him to shut up. Tucker hated it when the camera operators involved themselves in any ideas about the show. He tolerated it from the talent, but when someone he deemed beneath him dared to speak up, he didn't take it well.

But Joey ignored her nonverbal warning. Or maybe he didn't see it, since they were in a dark forest. Whatever the case, he kept talking.

"Seriously, viewers today can pause the show. Zoom in. Digitally repair shit. I don't know. But if we attempt to bullshit them with an actual Bigfoot sighting, they're gonna call BS. That's why all the other shows work. They give just enough tantalizing evidence that they *might* have seen or heard something. It keeps the viewers coming back for more, in the hopes that the next show will have something more concrete. If we flat-out film Bigfoot on our first attempt, we'll be laughed off the airwaves."

He wasn't wrong. And Lilly had a feeling Tucker knew it. But he was too conceited and stubborn to admit it. Especially since it was Joey who'd pointed it out.

"You don't know what you're talking about," Tucker said, dismissing Joey altogether. "Tomorrow, I'll make some calls. Get us some better equipment. In the meantime, we just need to shut the hell up and film some good shots. The last thing we want is to have to weed through a bunch of shit and come up with nothing usable. Joey, you and Lilly go with Chris and Roger. Maybe you can get some shots of them walking and talking about tree knocks and doing some calls we can use."

Well, shit. Why was *she* being punished along with Joey? She hadn't said a word. But Lilly knew better than to refuse.

Brodie fussed with the cast members' audio for a bit before they all started walking toward their next assigned placements. It took a good two hours for the four of them to get to the top of the ridge they'd seen the day before. It wouldn't have taken that long, but Chris and Roger argued about where exactly they were supposed to go.

Joey was apparently pissed enough to keep his mouth shut and let the two men argue amongst themselves. Lilly didn't dare put in her two cents, as she knew she'd be dismissed entirely. Even though she was the most experienced outdoorsperson in the group, no one thought about asking for her opinion.

Whatever. Lilly didn't care. She'd been growing discontent with the show for a while now. Even the home search show hadn't been nearly as bad as this one was. No, it wasn't as if the homeowners were actually making a decision between three houses, but it was all harmless fun in her eyes, and they did actually buy a new home.

This? This was flat-out lying, and Lilly didn't like it. She also felt trapped. She didn't know what she'd do if she wasn't a camera operator. But she was getting to the point that going back to her dad's place with her proverbial tail between her legs was preferable to this...hiking in the woods, in the dark, in the middle of the night, to film some spoiled wannabe TV stars pretending to be the legendary Bigfoot.

When they finally arrived where Chris and Roger thought they were supposed to be, it took another twenty minutes to get the radios working well enough so they could communicate with Tucker and the others.

Lilly's camera was on her shoulder, as it had been for the entire two-hour trek. God forbid one of the talent fell or hurt themselves, and she didn't get it on film. Tucker would fire her on the spot.

So she was ready and filming when Trent asked via radio, "You ready? We're going to do some knocks."

"We're ready," Roger said, talking over Chris.

Twenty seconds or so later, the sound of a muted thump sounded through the woods.

Lilly sighed, happy she'd gotten it and no one had been talking at the time. It was stupid to be proud that she'd managed to catch the knock when her footage was going to be used to dupe people, but she still was.

Chris gripped the thick branch he'd found earlier and walked toward a large tree. He reared back and hit it as hard as he could.

The crack of the branch against the wood was loud, and Lilly filmed as it reverberated through the empty forest.

Chris and Roger grinned at each other, their bickering seemingly done for now.

"Let's do that again," Tucker said over the radio. "That sounded perfect from here. Could you hear our knock?"

"Loud and clear," Roger reassured him.

And so it went. Grown men and women spent the next hour or so hitting trees, pretending the answering knocks from their co-workers miles away were actually from Bigfoot communicating with them.

Lilly figured if there was Bigfoot in the woods, his communication would probably be something closer to asking them to shut the hell up already.

"Do we want to try a yell?" Trent asked across the radio.

"Yes," Chris and Roger said at the same time.

But Tucker disagreed. "No, we need to finish up this knocking business first."

There was silence on the radio for a few minutes, and Lilly had a feeling Tucker was arguing with Trent. Finally, the producer came back on and said, "I'm thinking you guys need to go a little farther away. Brodie says that he thinks the knocks are too loud. Too perfect."

"Fucking hell," Chris said, his good mood vanishing in an instant. "I don't want to fucking walk another step deeper into this forest. It'd serve him right if we *did* get lost."

Lilly sighed. She didn't want to walk anymore either. Her shoulder was getting sore from the camera. It had been a long time since she'd had to lug it around for hours. Even with the mandatory breaks, she was still sore. She had a feeling Tucker wouldn't be sympathetic in the least, so she sucked it up.

By the time Tucker was satisfied with the night's shots and the footage they'd gotten, it was almost four in the morning. Roger and

Chris were barely talking to each other, and they weren't saying more than a few curt words at a time to Tucker over the radio.

When the four of them—Lilly, Chris, Roger, and Joey—met back up with the rest of the group, it was obvious no one was in a chatty mood.

For the first time in her career, Lilly turned off her camera while still on location. The battery was almost dead anyway. She'd already changed it out three times and had hours and hours of footage from tonight. Anything that happened on the way back to the parking lot wasn't going to be caught on film. At least not by her.

She and Joey were walking at the end of the line as they trudged back to their cars. He looked at her and asked quietly, "What do you think he'd do if we all up and quit at the same time?"

Lilly wasn't sure what to say to that. Joey had never been all that chummy with her. Hell, none of them had. They said hello, good-bye, and sometimes talked about the best angles and stuff, but no one ever really got personal.

"All of us camera operators, or the cast too?"

"Everyone," Joey said. "I'd like to see him try to have a show without us."

She gave him a commiserative smile. It was a silly question, because yeah, without all of them, there wouldn't *be* a show. Now, if just the staff quit, he could probably have replacements there within a day. It would be harder to replace the talent.

Kate was walking in front of Joey and obviously overheard his question. She turned and said, "Jobs are a lot easier for *you* to find than for me and Lilly. Anyone who says discrimination isn't alive and well today hasn't stood in our shoes."

She wasn't wrong. Lilly had been passed over for countless jobs in her career. She couldn't prove it was because she was female, but she had her suspicions.

"Just once I'd like to be on a show with a producer who actually listens to us," Joey bitched. "I mean, it's not like we don't know what we're talking about."

"I heard this show was partly your idea," Kate replied.

"It was. Trent and I came up with it one night, and even came up with the different things we'd investigate."

"Isn't it a one-season kind of show though?" Kate pressed. "I mean, there are only so many paranormal things to investigate."

"Maybe, but we can always go to different countries to investigate the same things. And there are plenty of things we haven't done yet. Crop circles. The Marfa Lights in Texas. Besides, there have been Bigfoot sightings all over the world, and there are ghosts in every fucking building and cemetery, it seems like. There are still other things we can look into."

"Like what?" Kate pressed.

"I don't know. I'm tired, my feet hurt, and my arm muscles are sore as fuck from carrying this camera," Joey complained.

"Right," Kate said, rolling her eyes. Lilly caught the movement right before the other woman turned to look where she was walking.

"I'm sick of being treated like shit," Joey mumbled.

Lilly didn't particularly like it either, but honestly, tonight's shoot could've been worse. Yes, it had been long. And more difficult since everyone was as cranky as a toddler who hadn't gotten a nap. But it wasn't raining. It wasn't too hot or cold. This part of Virginia was beautiful, and they'd gotten some good footage. She was more upset about all the fakery and bad behavior than the actual act of filming.

Just then, Roger tripped over a tree root in the middle of the path and went down hard on his hands and knees.

Tucker immediately turned to the camera operators. "Did you get that?" he barked.

Lilly shook her head, and Kate and Joey also answered negatively.

"I got it," Andre said.

"Thank God *one* of you is doing your job," Tucker said in disgust. But he didn't order them to start filming, so Lilly simply shrugged and continued trudging along. She couldn't get any good footage anyway, since Chris, Michelle, Trent, and Roger were all walking at the front of the line and she was toward the back.

"I'm waiting for him to order one of them to get lost so he can get it on film," Kate muttered as she turned back toward Lilly and Joey once more. "I mean, what would be more exciting than one of the talent getting lost in the woods and encountering Bigfoot? Especially if we weren't there to record it. Think of the stories he, or she, could tell when they were finally found."

"I think he'd get a hard-on if one of them got hurt too," Joey said. "There's nothing he'd like better than if one of the four fell and broke their damn leg."

"If that happened to one of us," Kate said, obviously agreeing with Joey, "he'd tell us to get our asses up and keep filming. But if one of the talent fell, he'd want them to milk their injury for all it's worth. Call in a helicopter and all that shit to 'rescue' them. Anything for a rating."

Lilly couldn't disagree. But she wasn't comfortable talking about this when Tucker was literally fifteen feet in front of them.

The rest of the hike to the parking lot was done in silence, and when they neared the entrance of the trail, Michelle said, "Oh, thank God we're finally here."

Lilly thought her words summarized what everyone was thinking fairly nicely. No one said much as they walked through the parking lot. No one said goodbye as they climbed into their vehicles and headed for the hotel.

It took Lilly a bit of time to put away her camera and extra batteries from her pockets. By the time she looked up, she was the only one in the lot. She wasn't afraid of the dark, but still thought it was rude for them to just leave her there alone. Sighing, she got behind the wheel and turned the key.

For just a second, she wondered what she'd do if it didn't start. With no cell phone service, and no way to contact anyone to help her, she'd either have to walk back to town—which was at least eight to ten miles—or wait until it got light and someone came to hike.

Luckily, that wasn't something she had to worry about at the moment. The rental started up without any issues and Lilly headed for the B&B. The second she parked, her phone began to vibrate with notifications as it connected with a cell tower.

Loving the silence, and being off her feet, Lilly took the time to see what she'd missed while in the woods.

She had a weather alert notice for California, which she kept forgetting to turn off, since she no longer lived there; an amber alert for a child missing out of Roanoke, Virginia; a couple news items from the local station back home in West Virginia.

And a text from Ethan.

Lilly quickly unlocked her phone and clicked on the text.

Ethan: Hi. I know you probably won't get this until you're out of the deep dark woods, but I wanted to let you know that I had a good time today. I'd like to see you again. Maybe after you get some sleep, we could hang out? If you're interested, shoot me a text. I'll be helping Rocky tomorrow morning, but should be free in the afternoon. If not...I'm sure I'll see you around.

She beamed. Butterflies swam in her stomach when she thought about the man. She was positively giddy to have heard from him, to know he wanted to see her again. She still wasn't sure it was a good idea to encourage him when she was only here for a short time, but her thumbs were moving over the screen before she could stop herself.

Lilly: I had a good time too. I have to be back at work by seven tonight. Maybe we can meet up around one or so? That will give me some time to get some sleep.

She hit enter, then winced. Shit, she hadn't even thought about what time it was. She hoped Ethan had his phone on silent so she didn't wake him.

Lilly: Sorry it's so late. Or early. My hope that we'd be done by midnight or one didn't exactly pan out.

She slapped herself in the forehead once more after she hit

enter. Shoot, he probably couldn't have his phone on silent because if he got called out for the search and rescue thing, he'd need to be accessible. Muttering an apology, she sent one more text.

Lilly: Sorry about the third text. You're probably ready to throw your phone by now. My only excuse is that I'm tired and cranky from being around other tired and cranky people all night. We didn't see Bigfoot, and we didn't get lost...I'm thinking both are wins. I wanted to say that I'd love to see you again, and that I really enjoyed meeting your friends today. Or yesterday. Whatever. If you aren't too mad that I sent three texts when I should've stopped at one, I'll talk to you later.

This time, Lilly knew she was done. She always got a little punchy when she was tired. She definitely should've stopped after the first text. Didn't people say that you shouldn't look too eager to go out with someone? She didn't know who the "people" were who said that, but it was silly advice anyway. Since she wasn't allowed to speak or show much emotion while on the job, she tended to go overboard in her personal life. It turned some people off, but whatever. She was who she was, and that wasn't going to change now.

Lilly got out of the car and stuffed her phone in her pocket, grabbing the camera before heading into the house. By the time she got her batteries charging, then had changed, showered, gone to the bathroom, brushed her teeth, and climbed into bed, Lilly was half asleep.

But that didn't stop her from reaching for her phone and reading the text from Ethan one more time. She fell asleep with a huge smile on her face.

CHAPTER NINE

Two days later, Lilly was no closer to figuring out what the hell she was doing than when she'd first accepted Ethan's offer to show her the town. Because with every minute she spent with him, the more she liked him. She'd always been independent, her dad and brothers had made sure of that. She'd never needed someone in her life. She was perfectly happy by herself.

But she found herself thinking about Ethan while she was tromping around the forest. When she was driving. When she was settling down to sleep. It was somewhat surprising...and disconcerting.

She was also enjoying her time in Fallport. She could just picture how the square would look decked out for the holidays with a light layer of snow over everything. Ethan had told her all about the fish fry the volunteer fire department puts on in the fall to raise funds for the upcoming year.

He'd brought her to Caboose Park for a picnic dinner last night, before she'd headed off to work. He'd called Whitney ahead of time and she'd made a bunch of finger foods, and they'd watched a group of kids run around and play while they ate and talked. It was called

Caboose Park because there was a big ol' caboose smack-dab in the middle of the grassy area. Ethan didn't know who had put it there, but the children Lilly had seen loved playing in and on it. Someone had even affixed a slide coming out one side.

All in all, Fallport was peaceful and, for the most part, people were friendly. She had a feeling when the show aired on TV, the town was going to be inundated with Bigfoot hunters. Which would bring in some tourist dollars, but probably be a pain in the ass at the same time. Especially for Ethan and his friends, who would have to go out and rescue people when they got lost searching for the legendary creature themselves.

Lilly could tell a few locals weren't all that fired up to meet her, including a few women she'd met when Ethan brought her into A Cut Above, during their first outing. They were nice enough, but reserved. She got the distinct feeling they didn't think she was good enough for Ethan. She couldn't exactly disagree. The more she learned about the man, the more intimidated she got. Oh, he never said or did anything to make her feel that way; it was more the things she'd learned from Whitney and others in town when he was out of earshot.

He was the de facto leader of the Eagle Point Search and Rescue Team. He'd once climbed down a thirty-foot drop-off on the mountain without a safety line to grab hold of a child who'd fallen and landed on an unstable ledge. He played Santa Claus one year when the guy who usually did had gotten sick. He volunteered for all sorts of committees, always over-tipped, didn't drink to excess, and generally was a damn good man to have around. And all that was without anyone knowing what accolades he may have gotten as a Navy SEAL.

Yeah, it was safe to say Lilly's accomplishments in life fell way short of the things Ethan Watson had done. And one of the things she liked most about the man was that you'd never know by looking at him or meeting him that he was so revered in the area. You'd never know he struggled with PTSD—he'd admitted as much to her the night before. He was an easygoing guy who went out of his way to be kind to everyone he came in contact with.

But the fact remained, no matter how much she enjoyed spending time with Ethan, her time here in Fallport was limited. With each day that passed, she became more worried about how much it would hurt to leave. She found herself wanting to *stay*. To get to know Ethan and his friends more. To become a part of this close-knit town.

Which was crazy. Wasn't it? If she was going to pick a new place to live, shouldn't it be a larger city where there were more opportunities to find a job? Meet people?

Her thoughts in turmoil, Lilly pulled into the parking lot of the Rock Creek trailhead they'd be using for filming tonight. Tucker had decided to film a little farther out from Fallport, so they were about fifteen miles from the center of town on a new trail they hadn't used before. She turned off her engine and got out, heading over to where Tucker was standing with the others. Trent was the only one not there, as he'd started his individual investigation the day before. Tonight was his last by himself, then tomorrow, he should be back with the others. In the meantime, they'd continue filming. When Trent returned, they'd get some more footage of the entire team in the forest together, before moving on to the next investigation.

Ignoring the pang of sorrow that thought caused, Lilly walked up to the group. "Hey."

Everyone greeted her, but the enthusiasm the team had in the beginning of the series had definitely waned.

"Glad you're here. I need you to go to Roanoke and pick up a package for me," Tucker said nonchalantly.

Lilly blinked. "What?"

"I ordered some night-vision cameras. The ones with the heat tracker things on them. They came in this afternoon, and I need you to go get them so we can get some footage with them tonight. I'm thinking that's the angle we should go with. That we see something big on the heat tracker. It'll be really far away, so no one will be able to tell what it is, but we'll say we're certain it's Bigfoot."

Lilly shook her head. "It's already seven. Roanoke is two hours away. Where did you have these things delivered and why can't we wait until tomorrow?"

"They were sent to one of those delivery locker things in a twenty-four-hour pharmacy. It was the closest I could get them to this godforsaken town. I'll text you the address. And we need them as soon as possible. I'm thinking you can leave now and be back by midnight, if you don't fuck around and drive like a granny. We can get a few shots tonight, then get the main footage we need of Andre walking around in the distance tomorrow, when Trent's back with us."

"How come I have to go?" Lilly asked.

"Because you were the last to show up," Tucker snapped. "Make sure to plug in the cameras on your way back here, so they're charged and ready to go by the time you arrive."

Lilly couldn't believe what an ass Tucker was being. "How am I going to find you guys when I get back?" she asked.

"Just start down the trail. I'm sure you'll figure it out," Tucker replied, then turned his back on her to talk to Roger, Chris, and Michelle.

She stared at her boss for a moment with her mouth open in disbelief. On one hand, she was impressed that he didn't think she needed to be coddled or couldn't be trusted with the errand. He treated her just as badly as he did everyone else, regardless of her gender. But sending her to a city she wasn't familiar with, to some random pharmacy that was two hours away, didn't seem safe.

She couldn't help but wonder when the stupid cameras were delivered. Probably that afternoon, which meant he could've driven himself to Roanoke to pick them up...but he was either too lazy or just didn't want to make the trip.

"Sorry he's being an ass," Joey whispered as he came up beside her. "If it makes you feel better, he didn't say anything about ordering the cameras to any of us."

His words didn't help.

"I'm thinking you could probably drive slow, take your time when you get to Roanoke, then claim there was a really bad wreck on the interstate or something...and it was too late to go out into the woods to find us when you got back."

Lilly glanced at the cameraman. He was grinning, and she couldn't help but return his smile. "Yeah. I've heard I-81 is a bitch between Blacksburg and Roanoke."

"Besides, I think you're getting the better end of this deal," Joey said. "You won't have to be tromping around the woods. I think it's supposed to rain tonight."

"Ugh," Lilly said.

"Come on, Joey. We want to find a good spot to set up before it gets completely dark," Tucker called out.

"Drive safe," Joey said with an apologetic shrug.

"Yeah."

Lilly watched the group head out single file down the well-marked trail. She didn't wait until they were out of sight before heading back to her car. She hadn't planned on driving over two hundred miles tonight, so she needed to get gas, which she'd be sure to expense back to the show.

Deciding that Joey was right, and she needed to look at this as a nice change of pace and enjoy her time away from the shoot, she settled into her car and put the key in the ignition. She took a moment to find an oldies radio station—that was playing eighties music; it was just wrong that they considered that to be oldies—before pulling out of the parking lot.

* * *

Six hours later, Lilly was tired and grumpy. She'd totally planned to lie about the wreck on the interstate, as Joey had suggested, but unfortunately for her—maybe it was karma—she didn't have to make up a story. There really *had* been an accident, and she'd ended up sitting for an hour on I-81, waiting for a jackknifed tractor trailer to be righted and towed away.

Then she'd gotten lost looking for the pharmacy, and had held her breath until she was back in her car and driving away, as it definitely wasn't in a safe area of town. Lilly had seen at least two drug deals going down as she'd searched for the place, and she'd never been so glad to be back on the interstate. She hadn't plugged the two cameras into her portable charger because she hadn't wanted to take the time while at the pharmacy. So she stopped at the first rest area and took care of that, glaring at the blinking yellow indicator.

It was ridiculous to resent an inanimate object, but at that moment, Lilly hated that the cameras meant more to Tucker than her safety.

For the first time that night, her thoughts turned to Ethan. She'd bet everything she owned—which wasn't all that much, just enough to fit in the basement of her dad's house back home—that he never would've suggested sending her out in the middle of the night to pick up stupid cameras.

Lilly was never more relieved to see the exit for the highway that led to Fallport. Only thirty more minutes and she'd be back in the small town. It was one-thirty in the morning, and there was no way she was heading into the woods when she got back to the trailhead parking area. She'd sit her happy ass in her car and wait for Tucker and the others to get back to *her*.

She'd been driving for ten minutes after taking the exit when flashing lights down the road caught her attention. She hadn't passed any other cars since pulling off the interstate, and they were literally in the middle of nowhere. Checking her phone, Lilly saw she only had one bar of service as well.

Stories her brothers and dad had told her about serial killers lying in wait for naïve victims to fall into their trap swirled in her mind. She shouldn't stop, she knew that...but what if that was her? What if her car broke down and she had no way of contacting anyone and was stuck on the side of the road? She'd want someone to stop and check on her.

Her foot was already coming off the accelerator before Lilly had truly decided what she was going to do. As she approached the car on the side of the road with its hazards flashing, she could see that one of the back tires was completely flat. The car was listing to the right. There still weren't any vehicles behind her, only pitch dark-ness. There wasn't even a moon out tonight because it was too cloudy with the rain that had been predicted.

Lilly came to a stop literally in the middle of the road, her car still in drive, ready to floor it if someone came out of nowhere and tried to kidnap her. She rolled down the passenger-side window a couple inches and watched as the person in the disabled car did the same.

A wave of relief came over Lilly when she saw the driver was a woman. On the heels of that feeling was her father's voice, telling her to be careful, that it could still be a trap. There could be someone waiting nearby, and the woman was only a lure.

"Are you all right?" Lilly called.

Her words seemed to break whatever restraint the woman had, because tears spilled down her cheeks and she shook her head. Then, to Lilly's surprise, a little boy popped up from beside the woman. He couldn't be more than seven or eight, the same age as a few of her nephews.

"We're stuck!" the boy said.

"Shhhh," the woman said, then turned to Lilly. "Are you going to Fallport? My phone doesn't have any service and it's too dark to walk anywhere to see if I can get a signal down the road. Maybe you can call someone for me when you get there?"

Lilly was horrified that the woman would even *think* about walking along a highway at this time of night. First, it was pitch dark. Second, it was supposed to start raining anytime now. Third, she had a kid. Fourth, there was no telling how far she'd have to walk before her phone worked.

She could keep thinking of reasons, but there were enough horrible things going through her head about what could happen to the duo, so she merely said, "Stay put. I'm gonna pull in front of you and come back to help."

"Oh, but—"

Lilly didn't wait to hear what the woman was going to say. She could no sooner leave her on the side of the road than kick an innocent puppy.

She quickly pulled her car out of the middle of the road and climbed out. It looked like she was going to be even later getting back to town, but at the moment, she didn't care.

Still slightly wary that this could be a trap—though the woman's tears and the fear in her voice sounded genuine—Lilly walked back to the car.

The woman and her son had gotten out, and she had a powerful flashlight in her hand. Lilly approved. It would make changing the tire easier, and she hoped the woman was prepared to use it as a weapon if she had to. By the grip she had on it, Lilly thought she was.

"I ran over something in the road. I think it was a four-by-four. I didn't even see it until it was too late," the woman said. "The tire immediately went flat."

Lilly stared at the tire and nodded. "Do you have a spare?"

"I think so."

"Right. So how about we get this changed and we can get you on your way."

The woman stared at her for a moment. Then asked, "You know how?"

"To change a tire?" Lilly asked. "Yeah. I have four brothers...I would've been kicked out of the family if I didn't learn how," she joked.

She was aware of the little boy's eyes on hers as he clung to his mom's hand. He was scared, but trying not to show it. She gave the pair some space and walked to the back of the car. "Pop the trunk and we'll see what we have to work with."

The woman leaned into the driver's side and pulled the lever releasing the trunk. Lilly grinned when she saw the empty space. "Thank goodness this isn't full, so we don't have to remove everything to get to the spare," she said with a smile.

"I just cleaned it out yesterday," the woman said.

"I'm Lilly," she said, realizing she hadn't introduced herself.

"I know. You're in Fallport for that TV show," she replied.

Lilly wrinkled her nose. She wasn't all that surprised the woman knew who she was. "That's me."

"I'm Elsie. Elsie Ireland. This is Tony."

"I'm eight. But my birthday's like, really soon, so I might as well be nine. Did you find Bigfoot yet?" the boy asked.

Lilly smiled. "We're workin' on it. You're in, what, the third or fourth grade?"

"Third. How'd you know?"

"I have a couple nephews your age," Lilly told him.

The boy nodded, then he looked at her skeptically. "Do you really know how to change a tire?"

"Yup," Lilly said as she reached into the trunk for the spare.

"But you're a girl."

"I am," Lilly agreed as she stood with the tire in her hand. She propped it against the side of the car, then turned back to Tony. "Gender doesn't have anything to do with knowing how to change a tire. You're a boy—do *you* know how to do it?" She knew the answer to her question already, but asked anyway.

"I'm too young."

"Who says?" she asked. "I was five the first time I helped my dad change a tire."

His eyes got wide. "You were?"

"Yup. You want to learn how? Help me?"

"Yes!" he answered right away.

"Thank you," Elsie said quietly.

"Of course," Lilly told her with a smile.

She grabbed the small bag of tools she'd found with the spare and knelt by the flat tire. Elsie stood over them and pointed the flashlight, giving them the light they needed in order to get the job done.

Lilly patiently explained everything she was doing. She let Tony try to remove the lug nuts, and when they wouldn't budge, helped him stand on the lug wrench to give it enough torque in order to get them off. Tony was very serious throughout the process, paying close attention. Lilly let him do as much as he could. She had to lift the flat tire off and put the new one on, but Tony did practically everything else.

When he'd cranked the jack, his eyes got big as he realized he was actually lifting the car off the ground. He lay down to peer underneath, to see what the jacking point looked like, and Lilly explained why that reinforced part of the car was where the jack had to go. His tongue came out as he concentrated on tightening the lug nuts on the spare tire. Lilly made sure they were tightened all the way, so the tire wouldn't fly off as they continued down the road.

Then he smiled in delight as he cranked the jack down, lowering the car onto the tire once more. He turned to his mom and said, "I did it!"

"I see that, baby," Elsie said with a small smile.

"We don't need Dad. We're fine on our own," he said fiercely.

Elsie took a deep breath but kept her composure. "Yes, we are," she agreed.

The boy went to get back in the car, but Lilly said, "Wait a second, what about all this stuff?"

Tony looked confused.

"You don't think the tools are going to clean themselves up, do you? They aren't going to hop back in their bag and climb back into the trunk. You have to take care of them, so they'll be exactly where you need them the next time. You can't change a tire without them."

Comprehension set in and Tony nodded. He immediately knelt on the ground and began to clean up.

"Thank you," Elsie whispered as she sidled closer to Lilly. "I seriously didn't know what I was going to do before you stopped."

"It's okay."

"I need to learn more about this kind of thing. I just don't have a lot of time since I work a lot, and with trying to keep up with Tony's activities."

Lilly nodded. "Being a single parent is hard."

"Do you have kids?" Elsie asked.

"No, but one of my brothers is raising his two kids by himself. Well, not really by himself, since he lives in the same town as my dad. But he doesn't like to ask for help too often, even though there are lots of people willing to lend him a hand when he needs it."

Elsie's lips twitched. "Are you telling me I should ask for help?"

"No!" Lilly said, somewhat chagrined that's what Elsie had gotten out of what she said. "I would never presume to know anything about your situation. I'm just saying that I know how hard it can be to be a single parent."

"Thanks. It *is* difficult. But I'll do anything for Tony," Elsie said firmly.

Lilly liked this woman. It was obvious she was struggling, but she wasn't giving in.

"Where do they go?" Tony asked, standing with the tools in his arms.

"I'll show you," Lilly said. Elsie followed them around the car, pointing the light into the trunk as Lilly lifted the compartment where the spare tire usually sat. "There, see that little cubby? Yeah, right there. Good. Now, can you hold this up for me while I put the tire back in?"

"Why not leave it there?" Tony asked, his little nose scrunching up.

"On the side of the road?" Lilly asked in surprise.

"Yeah. I see 'em there all the time."

"Well, because hopefully it can be fixed, and it'll save your mom money if she doesn't have to buy a new tire. And if we left it here, that would be littering. It's also dangerous. What if your mom pulled off the side of the road and hit one? And it's bad for the environment. And water can build up inside it after it rains and mosquitos can lay their eggs in there." She struggled to come up with something else to make her point, but Tony seemed to understand.

"You're right. Sorry. Here, I'll hold this for you."

Lilly smiled at him and picked up the flat tire. When it was stowed inside the compartment in the trunk, Tony closed the lid and headed for the car.

"Thank you again," Elsie said.

"No problem. You'll want to get that tire fixed as soon as you can. It's not safe to ride on the spare for too long. I'll follow you to Fallport to make sure you're good."

"You don't have to do that," Elsie protested.

"Yes, I do," Lilly said firmly. "Besides, we're going to the same place, it's not a big deal. Don't go over fifty though; again, it's not safe."

"All right. I appreciate this so much. I work at On the Rocks. If you have time, I'd love to treat you to dinner or something. It's bar food, not like Sunny Side Up, but it's still good."

"That's the bar that Zeke owns, right?" Lilly asked in surprise.

Elsie nodded. "You've met him?"

"Yeah, I had lunch with Ethan, Tal, Raid, and Zeke one day. I really liked him."

"He's a good guy," Elsie said.

Lilly thought she heard a note of wistfulness in her tone, but since she didn't really know the woman, she wasn't sure. "I'll probably not be in town for much longer, but if I can, I'll definitely stop by. I've heard a lot about the bar and I'm curious."

"Cool."

"Go ahead and pull out ahead of me and I'll follow you," Lilly said.

Elsie nodded and held out her hand. "Thank you again."

Lilly shook the other woman's hand.

"You made Tony's night. I feel bad that I can't teach him stuff like that."

"I'm sure you teach him lots of other things," Lilly said easily. "Come on, let's get out of here. It's really late and I bet you're tired."

"I am. Tony had an appointment with a specialist in Roanoke and it ran late. I didn't want to spend the money on a hotel and decided to go ahead and head home." She laughed, but it wasn't a humorous sound. "I probably should've just stayed."

"Is he all right?" Lilly asked.

"Yeah. He had heart surgery when he was a baby and this was just a checkup. He's doing great."

"I'm glad," Lilly said. "But if you'd gotten a hotel room, I wouldn't have met you," she said with a grin.

"True. Hopefully I'll see you at the bar before you leave."

"I'll do what I can to make that happen," Lilly told her, knowing there was no way she was going to leave town without doing just that.

The two women smiled at each other for a beat, then Lilly headed for her car as Elsie climbed into her own.

The remaining twenty-minute trip back to Fallport was uneventful, and Lilly waved out the window as Elsie pulled into a small parking area in front of the Mangree Motel and RV Park on the outskirts of town. It was a rundown-looking building, but there were plenty of lights in the parking lot and a small but well-maintained pool in the front, surrounded by a fence.

Lilly wasn't going to judge. Elsie seemed as if she was doing the best job she could, and Tony looked happy and healthy.

It was two-thirty in the morning before she arrived back at the parking area for Rock Creek Trail. She'd just turned off the engine, planning on staying right where she was and not tromping off into the woods by herself, when she caught movement out of the corner of her eye.

For a second, visions of killers coming for her swam in her mind —then just as ridiculously, Lilly had a flash of fear that Bigfoot had decided to show himself. But it was only Roger coming out of the woods. He was quickly followed by everyone else.

Somewhat surprised they were back already, when the last couple nights they'd stayed out until at least four, Lilly got out of her car to meet them.

"What took you so damn long?" Tucker barked.

Lilly stopped at hearing the venom in his tone. Tucker frequently got cranky, but not usually like this. "There was an accident on the interstate. Then I got lost trying to find the pharmacy with the lockers. I had to stop at a rest area to pee and to plug in the cameras, then a lady had a flat tire and I stopped to help her change it."

"You knew that I wanted to use them tonight," Tucker said, clearly not pleased.

"I'm sorry. I can't control the traffic."

"Whatever," the producer muttered. "Where are they? I'll take them with me so we can get familiar with how they operate at the hotel. And we'll have to work all night to get the shots we need tomorrow." With that, he stomped toward her car, wrenching open the back hatch to grab the now fully charged cameras.

"Ignore him," Andre said as he came up beside her. "He's just cranky because everyone else is. Michelle pitched a fit tonight and Roger flat-out refused to walk three miles to another ridge to do more fucking Squatch calls." He chuckled. "It was kind of awesome to see everyone standing up to Tucker for once. Everyone collectively refused to do any more filming tonight, since the rain's moving in. We've got more than enough footage of everyone walking through the woods, banging on trees and doing those ridiculous mating calls, or whatever they're supposed to be."

Just then, it began to rain, as Andre predicted. Small drops at first, but within seconds, a deluge started, soaking everyone to the bone before they could get to cover.

Everyone ran for their cars, leaving Lilly standing in the parking lot by herself. Again. The back hatch of her rental was still open... and all she could do was laugh.

The night had been weird, but also good. It had felt nice to help Elsie and her son, and to know they weren't still sitting by the side of the road, stressed out about what to do, or worse, walking through the now pouring rain.

Lilly jogged to her car, shut the hatch that Tucker hadn't bothered to close, then jumped behind the wheel. Her hair was dripping wet and she was tired, but at least she hadn't had to hike miles through the woods. She was still annoyed that she'd had to drive all the way to Roanoke to pick up the cameras, but she couldn't deny it had been a nice break from the show.

And that was the thought that rattled around in her head as she drove back to the B&B. She'd never dreaded her job before. It was just a job. Something that paid the bills. Sometimes it was even fun. But she realized that she'd actually come to dread being around Tucker, the cast, and even the other crew. They used to be friendly, at least, laughing and joking during their breaks and between shots. But now they all did their own thing, ignoring everyone else. It seemed the more time they spent together, the grumpier they got... and the atmosphere was beginning to suck the life out of her.

It was definitely time for a change. She didn't want to spend the rest of her life hating what she did for a living. She had no idea what else she might do, but filming fake "reality" television wasn't it.

Feeling as if she'd made a major decision, even if she hadn't actually decided anything, Lilly's heart seemed lighter than it had when she'd set out for Roanoke earlier that evening.

She pulled up behind the bed and breakfast and pulled out her phone. It had become a habit over the last couple of days to check her messages and notifications when she got home at the end of the night. She'd heard her phone dinging earlier, but hadn't gotten a chance to check it. More concerned about getting out of the scary neighborhood safely, then driving, then helping Elsie fix her flat tire.

As usual, she had a text from Ethan. She was smiling even before she read it.

Ethan: I can't believe you like pineapple on pizza. I'm not sure we can be friends any longer. :) Drew and Brock enjoyed meeting you today. My favorite part of the day was when Brock was explaining some of the tools he used on the cars in his shop, and you corrected him. I've never seen him speechless before. That was awesome. I hope work went all right tonight. Text me when you wake up tomorrow and I'll come pick you up...that is, if you still want to see the house Rocky and I are working on. Sleep well.

Lilly smiled. She loved surprising people. No one expected her to know things about cars. Or construction. Or plumbing. Anything that was stereotypically a "man's job." Just like she'd surprised Tony and his mom tonight. Brock *had* been surprised when she'd corrected him, then he'd laughed and said if Ethan didn't marry her, he would.

She'd blushed, and even Ethan had looked a little uncomfortable, but he'd shaken it off and told his friend to keep his hands to himself—then hooked an arm around Lilly's shoulders and pulled her against his side.

It had felt great to be held by Ethan, even if he'd let go way before she was ready. It was also hard to tell if he just saw her as a friend, or if he wanted more.

Lilly knew where *she* stood. With each day that passed, she definitely wanted more. But there was the whole "I'm only here for a job" thing hanging over both their heads. It was smarter to keep things on a friendly level, but that was getting harder and harder the more she got to know him.

She clicked on the box under Ethan's text to respond.

Lilly: I can't believe you put jalapenos on everything. That's weirder than pineapple on pizza. :) Yes, I still want to go with you tomorrow. I'll actually be ready earlier than usual too. Long story, but I didn't have to walk miles through the forest tonight and I'm actually home before four. I'll tell you about it when I see you. Tomorrow will be another long night, but I'm celebrating the fact that I can probably be human before noon. See you soon. Good night.

Ethan had said he didn't mind her texting him when she got home, so she tried not to feel guilty about sending him notes so late—or early. She got out of her car, grabbed her camera, and headed inside to get ready for bed.

It took a while for her to actually fall asleep, since she wasn't as exhausted as she usually was. The day had turned out pretty good. From hanging out with Ethan and his friends, to meeting Elsie, to getting closer to some sort of decision about her job...Lilly felt relaxed for the first time in a long, long while.

* * *

Anticipation raced through his veins. Tonight had *sucked*. Nothing had gone right. But soon, very soon, things would get exciting. The show was about to get a huge kick in the pants—and he couldn't *wait* to see how everyone reacted.

He hadn't planned what happened, but now that it was done, he realized it was perfect. He felt stupid for not thinking of doing it before now.

He *should* feel guilty. Should feel remorse. But he didn't.

It was all for the good of the show.

Hiking around the woods, yelling and banging on trees, was stupid. *This* was the thing that would earn the show an Emmy nomination. Nothing could top it. Hell, the inevitable rumors alone that Bigfoot was upset to be discovered—and had done something about it—were as good as gold.

Sighing, he lay on his bed and smiled up at the ceiling. The excitement rolling through him made him almost giddy.

Yeah, this show was nothing without him. He was going to single-handedly make *Paranormal Investigations* a success. Even if no one else knew what he'd done.

He fell asleep with a smile on his face and a clear conscience. He'd done what he had to do. Everything else would now fall into place.

CHAPTER TEN

The next morning when Ethan stopped into Grinders to grab a coffee and a muffin, he ran into Clara Wooten. She was part of a group of ladies who lived to gossip...but unlike Silas, Otto, and Art, her group was somewhat vicious about it. The ladies—Dorothea, Cora, Ruth, and, of course, Clara—didn't even try to hide it when they were digging for information. The more scandalous, the better.

Clara greeted him with a smile, then proceeded to talk Ethan's ear off as he waited for his coffee to be made. It wasn't until she said Lilly's name that he paid attention.

"I'm sorry, I'm still half asleep. What was that?" he asked.

"I said that I hoped you'd bring Miss Lilly around to our book chat this afternoon at the library," Clara said.

Ethan stared at her in surprise. He'd gotten the distinct impression Clara and her friends hadn't cared much for Lilly, or anyone connected to the TV show. Though they'd been at the town hall meeting, of course, scowling at the cast and crew.

He had no idea what had changed between then and now to make Clara be all sweetness toward Lilly, eager to spend time with her. Especially at one of her precious book club meetings. The four women were the only ones in their "club," and they talked about books all the time anyway, so Ethan had no idea why they also had a specific time and place set up to officially discuss them. He hadn't really cared enough to ask.

And now they wanted Lilly to join them? Something was up.

"I don't know what her schedule is like," he told Clara.

The older woman just shrugged. Even though it was early, her hair was perfectly done in the beehive hairdo she preferred. Ethan had always been fascinated by her hair; it never moved. Even when it was windy out. She must use a shit-ton of hairspray to get it to stay so perfect. He'd never seen her with her hair mussed. Clara was the shortest of her posse at around five-four, but her hair made her seem a lot taller. At sixty-eight, she was in fairly good shape, even though she had a cinnamon roll from Grinders every morning with her sugary coffee.

"It seems as if she's been off in the afternoons lately, so she should be free around three for our meeting," Clara informed him.

Ethan wasn't about to confirm or deny that Lilly would be there. "I'll talk to her," he settled on saying. Then he couldn't help but add, "I thought you guys didn't care much for her."

Clara hemmed and hawed and finally shrugged. "It wouldn't be Christian of me to say I didn't like someone without getting to know them," she said after a moment. "It's no secret that I'm not a fan of people exploiting our town with that Bigfoot nonsense, and it's not like she'll be staying. But after hearing what happened last night, I can't help but change my view of her."

Ethan frowned. "What happened last night?"

Clara looked positively gleeful that she could pass on gossip to someone who hadn't heard the latest yet. "Oh, well, that woman who works at On the Rocks—the one with the boy, who lives at the Mangree—she had a flat tire and was stranded on her way back to town. It was dark, she was scared, and Miss Lilly stopped and helped her."

Ethan shook his head. "That can't be right. Lilly was working last night."

Clara beamed. "No, she wasn't. I heard it from my gardener this morning, who heard it from her cousin, who's friends with one of the maids at the Mangree Motel, who was called in early this morning to clean a room after a few of the high school boys had a party. She talked to the night clerk, who said that the woman... what's her name again?"

"Elsie?" Ethan asked.

"Yes! That's her. Anyway, the clerk talked to Elsie after she got home—well after midnight, mind you—because she had to come to the front desk to exchange the coffee maker in her room that wasn't working, and everyone knows how much she's addicted to coffee. But since she doesn't go on shift until noon, and she can't afford to come in here to get her fix every morning, she has to use the coffee maker Mangree supplies in their rooms."

Ethan resisted the urge to roll his eyes and tell Clara to get on with it. He knew from experience that she couldn't be rushed when she was on a roll.

"And Elsie told her the whole story. How she hit something in the road and almost lost control of her car. She managed to get it to the side of the road, but she had no cell service, because those dang phone companies refuse to put up a tower between the interstate and Fallport. It's ridiculous because it's just not safe, but of course they don't care, because they're a highfalutin company with more money than sense. Anyway, so there she was, broken down on the side of the road, easy prey for rapists and serial killers, and she even had her son with her. She was scared to death when lights came up behind her.

"She was so relieved that it was that camera lady she'd seen in town. Elsie was flabbergasted when the little lady offered to change her tire for her! Heard she did a fine job of it too. Then she followed her all the way back to the Mangree to make sure she got there safely. Yes, sir, Miss Lilly's good people. I knew it from the first time I met her, but you know, she's leaving and all, so it didn't make sense to get too close."

Ethan's head was spinning. He'd had no idea Lilly hadn't worked last night and immediately wondered what she was doing on the road so late. He wasn't all that surprised she'd stopped to check on a disabled car, even if the thought of what might've happened if it hadn't been Elsie and her son, and instead, someone who was lying in wait for someone to stop so they could be robbed—

Ethan halted that train of thought. He was as bad as Clara with his overactive imagination right now. "She's still leaving," he couldn't help but say.

Clara waved her hand in the air, dismissing his words. "I know, but she's such a sweetheart for stopping to help Elsie, that we wanted to do something to show her we appreciate her kindness."

Ethan hadn't missed the 'we' pronoun, meaning Clara had already talked to her posse that morning. "I'm sure a simple thank you would be more than enough for Lilly."

Clara ignored him. "We're getting to the good part in our book. It's where the bad guy is gonna get what's coming to him. Then the sex chapter."

"Here's your coffee, Ethan," the young woman behind the counter said as she handed him his coffee and a small bag with his muffin. She was grinning, obviously enjoying his discomfort with the direction Clara's conversation had taken. It was well known that the books the ladies discussed were always romances. He didn't have anything against them, but didn't exactly want to stand in the middle of the coffee shop and listen to Clara talk about sex.

"Thanks," he said, stuffing a five dollar bill into the tip jar. He nodded at Clara. "It was good seeing you this morning. I need to get going if I want to be on time meeting my brother."

Clara nodded with a smile. "Don't forget to tell Miss Lilly about our book club!"

"I won't," Ethan told her, then quickly turned and headed for the door before she could come up with something else to talk about.

He resisted the urge to send Lilly a message to ask about what happened the night before. When he'd read her text upon waking, he hadn't thought much about what she'd been doing that didn't involve hiking in the woods; he'd just been happy that he'd get to see her earlier than usual. But of course now, he couldn't *stop* thinking about it. It made no sense that she was on 480, the road that ran between Fallport and I-81.

But he really did need to get moving if he was going to finish the wiring Rocky needed done, so Ethan could meet Lilly. Not that Rocky would give him shit for bailing early if he wanted to.

Doing his best to push his curiosity to the back of his mind, Ethan climbed into his Outback and headed for the worksite.

Two hours later, his phone rang. Pulling it out of his pocket, he saw Zeke was calling.

"Hey, what's up?" he asked as he answered.

"Not much. Just talked to Elsie and she told me what happened last night," Zeke said. "You hear?"

"I ran into Clara at Grinders this morning," Ethan told him.

"Oh, yeah. You heard," Zeke said. "Brock's taking care of Elsie's car as we speak, including getting her four new tires. I can't believe she drove all the way to Roanoke on those pieces of shit. They were practically bald. It's a miracle she didn't roll over when that tire blew."

"She okay with that?" Ethan asked. Elsie was a proud woman. She'd arrived in town about a year and a half ago, very close-lipped about where she came from and how she'd ended up in Fallport. And much to Zeke's frustration, she didn't accept help easily. Ethan had a feeling Zeke would have a fight on his hands to get her to let him pay for new tires.

"She doesn't know," Zeke said.

Ethan burst out laughing. "Good luck with that," he told his friend.

"She'll accept them, if nothing else because having good tires will keep Tony safe," Zeke said.

Ethan had a feeling his friend was right. And if she still tried to turn down his help, he'd work something out where she could pay for the tires in installments...and probably lie about how much they cost in the process.

"Anyway, I was calling to see if you knew why Lilly was even out that way so late."

Ethan wasn't surprised he was asking. His friend was very sensitive to women's safety, honed by his years as a bar owner. The last thing he wanted was someone getting assaulted leaving On the Rocks. He'd implemented several different safety measures, including women being walked to their cars when they left. He also had signs in the women's bathroom explaining that if anyone felt unsafe—with a date or a patron—they could order specific drinks to alert the bartenders to the issue, and they'd call the police or otherwise get them safely out of the building without fanfare.

So Zeke learning that one of his employees had been stranded wouldn't make him happy—especially someone Ethan suspected he was attracted to. Finding out Lilly had also been there would have him doubly worried.

"I don't know. I'm supposed to see her later."

"Well, when you do, tell her I appreciate what she did for Elsie."

"I will."

"And for the record...Fallport could use more people like her. People willing to stop and help when it's needed. Too many people would've just driven right by Elsie without a second thought."

"I agree."

"Then do something about it," Zeke said.

Ethan rolled his eyes. His friends were pushing him hard to get Lilly to stay, but he couldn't be upset about it. She was nice. Considerate. Easy on the eyes. And it wasn't lost on his teammates that he'd been in a damn good mood lately, which they correctly attributed to him spending time with Lilly.

But asking her to stay after knowing her such a short period of time seemed more than a little crazy. He knew if the roles were reversed, he'd probably run like hell if a woman asked him to quit his job and stay in a random town after less than a week.

That didn't mean he wasn't trying to figure out how things between them could work. How they could keep seeing each other.

"If something's up, let us know and we'll do what we can to help," Zeke said, as if he knew Ethan wasn't going to acknowledge his previous statement.

Zeke didn't need to offer his help, or the team's. Ethan already knew he could count on them anytime, day or night, to have his back. "I will. I'll talk to you later."

"Bye."

Ethan hung up and stuffed his phone back in his pocket. When he turned, Rocky was standing there.

"Zeke?" he asked.

"Yeah."

"Not surprised." Ethan had told his brother all about what Clara had told him that morning. "He's got a soft spot for his waitress," Rocky said.

"Yup," Ethan agreed. They all knew Zeke liked Elsie, but the one time someone had brought it up, Zeke had shut down the conversation, insisting she had too much baggage. And he wasn't talking about her son. Zeke liked kids. A lot. So Tony wasn't the issue. No one actually knew what her baggage was, but it was obvious she had her fair share.

"You heard from Lilly yet?" Rocky asked.

Ethan was shaking his head when his phone vibrated. He pulled it out and smiled.

"Guess that's my answer," Rocky said, laughing.

Ethan read Lilly's text and did his best to ignore the butterflies in his stomach. It was crazy how excited he got when he heard from her, let alone when he was with her.

. . .

Lilly: I'm up! I resisted the urge to stuff myself with Whitney's amazing brunch. If I keep eating like I have been, I'm not going to fit into my clothes much longer. And I also kind of want to go by On the Rocks this afternoon, if you don't mind.

Ethan: You want to see Elsie.

Lilly: I see the gossip network of Fallport has kept up its stellar reputation. :)

Ethan: Nothing's a secret around here. I'm interested to hear the story from you though.

Lilly: It's not a big deal.

Ethan: I'm thinking Elsie disagrees.

Ethan looked up to see his brother staring at him with a goofy grin on his face. "What?" he asked.

Rocky shrugged. "Haven't seen you this giddy to talk to a girl since we were thirteen and Missy Buckmeyer caught your eye."

Ethan chuckled. Missy had been two years older than them, and had been his first sexual experience. Yeah, he'd been pretty besotted over her back them. What he felt for Lilly, of course, was far different. Deeper. Which was crazy, since he'd just met her, but whatever.

"And for the record, the rest of the wiring can wait until tomorrow, so if you want to head out, that's cool. I can work on the floors in the other rooms the rest of the day."

"Appreciate it," Ethan said. Then he turned back to the phone.

Ethan: I'm done here with Rocky. You free?

Lilly: Absolutely. Do you have any specific plans for us today? Other than On the Rocks, of course.

Ethan: Bowling?

Lilly: Oh, I'd love that! It's been forever since I've bowled.

Ethan: Great. I'll see you in about ten minutes or so.

Lilly: I'll be here.

Ethan shoved the phone back in his pocket and immediately turned to the door. He was grateful the work he'd done that morning hadn't been strenuous and he didn't have to make a detour to go back to his apartment and shower before meeting with Lilly. Even taking five extra minutes to get to her seemed too long.

* * *

They'd stopped by On the Rocks for lunch, but it had been so packed they didn't get a chance to talk to Elsie much at all, but Ethan had no doubt they'd be able to connect sooner or later. Ethan managed to tamp down his curiosity about her side of what he'd heard about what happened the night before long enough for them to get to the bowling alley, grab their shoes, help Lilly find a ball she liked, and even through an entire game. But when she begged him to play another, to give her a chance to beat him, even though he'd won by over a hundred points, he said, "I'll give you a rematch if you tell me what the hell happened last night."

Lilly tilted her head as she stared at him. "I thought you already heard the story?"

"Clara informed me of how you changed Elsie's tire, and while I was getting our shoes, I heard all about how you charmed little Tony and now he wants to be a mechanic when he grows up. I also haven't missed how a couple people we saw earlier were all smiles and super friendly when just yesterday, those same people weren't sure about you."

Lilly frowned. "And you're upset about that?" she asked.

"No," Ethan said. "I'm fucking thrilled. I knew they'd loosen up once they got to know you. Coming to the rescue of one of our own just sped that along."

"Then why do you sound kind of mad?" Lilly asked.

"Because I don't know why you were on that road in the first place. At one-thirty in the morning. By yourself."

Lilly sighed. "Right. Shall we sit while I tell you the story? It won't take long, but you look stressed, and the last thing I want is rumors going around that you and I are fighting."

"Shit, sorry. You're right. I'm just worried."

"And you've been wondering what the hell I was doing last night all morning, haven't you?" she asked with a small smile.

He nodded. "Got it in one."

"Well, then, I admire your restraint. My brothers would've jumped down my throat the second I got in the car with them."

"I definitely wanted to ask, but didn't want you to think I was overstepping."

They sat on the small bench behind the bowling lane. Lilly studied him silently for a long moment. "What are we doing?" she asked quietly.

Ethan snorted. "I have no idea."

Amazingly, she grinned. "Glad I'm not the only one."

"I like you, Lilly. And believe me, I've never gone out of my way to spend every day with a woman who I knew was leaving in a few days."

Her smile dimmed.

"You've gotten under my skin. But I'll be dammed if I can make myself tell you it's not a good idea to hang out, or make up some excuse to avoid you. Hell, I find myself re-reading the texts you've sent me just to feel closer to you when you're working."

"Me too."

"So...I'd like to keep in touch when you leave. Maybe after you film the last episode, between this and your next job, you might consider coming back here and hanging out for a while?"

Lilly's cheeks pinkened a bit. "I'd like that."

Ethan let out the breath he hadn't realized he'd been holding. "Great."

"Yeah," she agreed, smiling again.

"Now...you want to tell me the whole story about last night?" he asked.

Lilly sighed. "It's not a big deal. When I got to the Rock Creek Trail parking area, Tucker told us he'd ordered some thermal cameras that were delivered to some pharmacy in Roanoke. He ordered me to go pick them up." She shrugged. "So I did."

"By yourself?" Ethan asked.

"Yeah. The other camera operators were needed for the show, the cast obviously couldn't go, Brodie needed to be there for sound, and Trent was still off doing his solo thing."

Ethan stared at her for a long moment, trying not to be offended. Finally, he asked, "You didn't even think about calling *me*?"

Lilly frowned. "I... No."

"Why not? I'd like to think I've made it pretty obvious that I like spending time with you. And we not only could've had more time to get to know each other, but it would've been safer than you being out that late by yourself."

"Jeez. I'm so sorry. You're right. I totally should've. It was just... Tucker asked me to go out of the blue, and I wasn't happy about it. He wanted me to get back as soon as I could so we could use the thermal cameras last night. It was a work thing, and it didn't even cross my mind that you might want to go with me."

"I'm trying really hard not to take offense to that," Ethan said honestly.

Lilly reached for his hand and squeezed it tightly. "I guess I'm just used to doing things on my own," she said gently. "You're right, I totally would've loved to have you with me. The traffic sucked and I was bored out of my mind. Not to mention, the pharmacy wasn't in the best part of town and I got lost trying to find it."

Ethan hated hearing that. It made his skin crawl to think about Lilly in any kind of dangerous situation. But she was a grown woman who'd been looking after herself for a long time. He didn't like that her asshole of a boss had sent her all the way to Roanoke by herself, but he felt better knowing she hadn't purposely tried to avoid spending time with him. He did his best to lighten the mood by saying, "And I could've held the flashlight while you changed Elsie's tire."

She smiled shyly at him. "You mean change it for her, right?"

"Nope. I suck at anything having to do with cars. Just ask Brock. He thinks I'm hopeless. I'll leave the automotive stuff to you."

She stared at him.

"What?"

"I just...I can't believe you admitted that."

"Why not? I'm not perfect, so I'm willing to admit when I can't do something."

"Well, you're different than most guys I've met then. Most think it's their duty to be all macho and take charge of stuff like that, even when they don't know how to use a socket wrench."

"What's a socket wrench?" Ethan asked with a completely straight face.

Lilly opened her mouth to respond when he laughed.

She rolled her eyes and smacked his arm.

Ethan was still aware that she was holding his hand, but he wasn't sure *she* knew it. He wasn't going to do anything to make her let go. He liked the feel of his hand in hers.

"You are a grown-ass adult, Lilly," he said after a moment. "You're obviously very capable of looking after yourself. I'd never want to stifle that or make you feel as if you're less than I am, simply because of your gender. But that doesn't mean there aren't situations that are less safe for you because you're a woman. Driving around in the middle of the night is one of those situations. Nothing good happens between two and four in the morning."

"You sound like my brothers."

"That's because we're right," he said firmly. "You're a woman, a damn good-looking one. And you aren't as big or strong as a lot of men. They could easily overpower you no matter how much self-defense training you've had."

"I don't think that's true," she argued.

"I was a SEAL. I've seen women who've trained with men their entire lives get taken out by one punch to the face. These are women who I firmly believe could've passed SEAL training if they'd been allowed to try. Some people are bullies, Lilly. And the thought of some of them using their strength advantage to hurt you makes me feel a little crazy."

She squeezed his hand once more. "I should've called you," she said, conceding his point.

Ethan nodded. "Moving on. So...how much longer do you think you'll be here?"

"Well, tonight we'll film with the thermal cameras. Tomorrow will be long, as Tucker will expect us all to meet to discuss the shoot, and to see if anyone feels like we need to re-do anything or if we've missed something. We'll probably need to do some daylight shots of Trent talking about his solo investigation with the others and discussing what he found."

"So...if all that goes smoothly, you could be headed out the day after tomorrow at the earliest, two days from now at the latest?"

Lilly nodded.

"That stinks," Ethan muttered.

"Yeah. But...I like you too, Ethan," she said shyly. "And the best part of my night is when I pull up to the B&B and check my messages. I'm guessing that's not going to change when I'm some-where else, on some other shoot."

"It's a good thing we're here at the bowling alley right now," Ethan informed her.

"It is? Why?" she asked in confusion.

"Because I don't want you to be the center of any more gossip—and laying you out on this bench and kissing the daylights out of you right now would definitely make for good conversation among the busybodies who live here."

She laughed. "Can you imagine how fast word would spread? We'd probably be hearing comments in the morning about how we were going at it right here on the bowling alley floor!"

He chuckled. "You are not wrong."

They stared at each other for a charged moment before Lilly grinned. "Right, so...you gonna let me kick your butt or what?"

"You want me to throw the game?" he asked.

"What? No. Why?"

"Because that's the only way you'll kick my butt at bowling."

"Whatever," she said with another roll of her eyes. She stood up and walked over to the ball return, grabbing the bright pink monstrosity she'd picked out. "One strike, coming right up," she declared before turning to the lane. She concentrated on the pins at the far end, took a deep breath, dropped her arm, and let the ball go.

She turned and wrinkled her nose sheepishly when it immediately landed in the gutter. "Okay, that was just my warm-up throw. I'm totally gonna kick your butt now."

Ethan stood and met her as she stepped off the lane. Without thinking, he wrapped his arms around her and hugged her tightly. He rarely initiated any kind of intimacy like this with women, not wanting any of his actions to be misconstrued, but it simply felt right. Even more so when her arms tightened around him in return. He buried his nose in her hair and inhaled deeply. She smelled sweet. He had no idea what it was, but he had a feeling from this moment on, he'd always associate the smell with Lilly.

Cognizant of the watchful eyes of the few people bowling around them, he let her go much sooner than he wanted and headed to the ball drop. He knew Lilly would be pissed if he didn't try his hardest, so when he let his ball fly, he wasn't surprised when he knocked all ten pins down.

"Well, crap," Lilly muttered, then smiled at him. "Good job."

Yeah, it was safe to say this woman had definitely gotten under his skin. Even though she'd be leaving soon, they'd agreed to keep in touch. He'd have to be all right with that. Maybe down the line things between them would work out. In the meantime, he'd live for the moment. He'd learned from his time as a SEAL that life wasn't guaranteed. So he was determined to do whatever he could now to be the kind of man Lilly couldn't forget.

CHAPTER ELEVEN

The next morning, while he was eating the fried eggs he'd made himself for breakfast, Ethan's phone rang. He assumed it was Rocky calling to tell him when he'd be heading out to the house, since they'd agreed to carpool today. So he was surprised and excited when he saw Lilly was calling.

She'd told him the day before that she expected filming last night to go late, since they'd be using the thermal cameras she'd had to pick up. They had a lot of footage to record, and she'd bitched about how long it would probably take.

"Hey, Lil," he said as he answered.

"Hi. Um...we have a situation."

Ethan straightened, hearing the stress in her voice. "What's wrong?"

"Trent's missing."

It took a second for her words to sink in. "What?"

"Trent. He was doing his solo investigation camping thing, and last night, we all expected him to show up for the last bit of filming. He was supposed to talk to the others about what he'd seen and show them any evidence he had, as well as join the group for the search with the thermal cameras. But he never showed. We all assumed maybe he'd decided to stay out there an extra night, or perhaps was exhausted and had gone to the hotel to sleep off his adventure. Anyway, this morning, I got a call from Kate. She told me that he wasn't at the hotel."

"When was he last seen?" Ethan asked, all business.

"The day he went out for his solo investigation."

"Do you know where he was camping?"

"Well, we knew where he was *supposed* to be, but when he still didn't show this morning, some of us went out to where he was going to set up, and he wasn't there. We looked around for a while but didn't find any trace of him, nothing to indicate a tent had been pitched or anything. So we aren't sure where he actually decided to camp."

"Idiot," Ethan muttered. The first rule of outdoor activities was to always let someone know where you were going. "Has anyone called the police?"

"Tucker was going to."

"All right. I'll see what I can find out and warn the guys that we might be headed into the mountains."

"Um, there's something else," Lilly said tentatively.

He braced himself. "What?"

"Tucker wants to film the search for him."

Shaking his head, Ethan sighed. "Of course he does." He couldn't stop Tucker from sending a camera crew to follow him and the other members of Eagle Point Search and Rescue, he'd need release forms from his team if he wanted to use the footage. He wasn't all fired up to sign the stupid thing...though Ethan had a feeling the mayor would pressure them all to cooperate, in the name of bringing more tourists to Fallport.

"I told him that you guys could search faster without a bunch of us tromping behind you, but he ignored me."

Ethan wasn't surprised. Lilly had hinted several times that her boss thought someone getting hurt made for good TV. "We'll deal with that if and when the time comes," he told her diplomatically. "Where are you now?"

"I'm back at the B&B, but in a few minutes, everyone is meeting back at the Fallport Creek Trail, that first trail we filmed on."

"Where's Trent's car?"

"At the Fallport Creek parking area, so we're all hoping he's somewhere near there."

"All right. Don't panic. I'm sure he's close by. Especially if he doesn't care much for camping and being outside."

"I hope so. There's one more thing you should probably know."

"What?"

"Tucker's already planning on saying he was taken by Bigfoot."

"Fuck," Ethan said.

"I know. It's ridiculous, but since we're here trying to find Bigfoot, he thinks it'll be a great addition to the show. That Bigfoot got mad we were close to proving his existence and decided to do something to stop the evidence from getting out. Or that Trent actually got him on camera, and Bigfoot had to get rid of him as a result."

"Well, hopefully that'll get nipped in the bud when we find him and he's fine," Ethan said.

"I'm sorry," Lilly said.

"For what?"

"That you and your friends have to come out and look for him. You warned Tucker when we first got here that this might happen, and you wouldn't be happy if you had to take time away from your jobs to find us."

"It's fine," Ethan soothed. "I'm sure we'll find him soon and we'll be back at our boring jobs before the end of the day."

"I hope so. I can't say I'm close to any of the cast on the show, but I hate to think of him out in the woods hurting or scared. I guess I'll see you soon?"

"Yeah, Lil. You will. Wish it was under better circumstances. But I'm still happy I'll get to see you."

"Me too," she whispered. "Drive safe."

Ethan smiled. "I will."

"Okay. Bye."

"Bye."

Ethan ate the rest of his breakfast in three big bites, then placed his plate into the sink and turned to head to his bedroom. He needed to change and call the others. Looked like Eagle Point Search and Rescue was once more on the case.

* * *

Thirty minutes later, Ethan stood in the crowded parking lot with his team, listening to the scant details about Trent Morrison's missing person case. His phone was going straight to voice mail, which either meant it was turned off, the battery had died, or he was out of cell range. Requesting his cell phone carrier to do a trace wouldn't help, since the forest was dense and, once out of Fallport, there weren't any towers to ping off of.

The chief of police, Simon Hill, was there, as was one of the two detectives Fallport employed, all the members of the investigative show, and a few onlookers.

As Lilly had warned, Tucker was almost giddy with excitement over everything that was happening. He was flitting here and there, ordering his camera operators to make sure to get everything on film. He was absolutely no help in actually pinpointing where his missing actor was, and Ethan wondered if he'd orchestrated this entire thing in order to try to get ratings. Trent was probably sitting warm and dry somewhere, having a good laugh at all the hubbub. In a day or so, he'd wander back out into the woods and pretend to stumble into the path of the SAR team.

Ethan didn't like being so cynical, but he couldn't help it. He'd met men like Tucker in the past and had no doubt the producer would do whatever it took to make sure his show was a success, thus ensuring he had a job in the future.

Luckily, Simon Hill was a good man who mostly let Ethan and his team do their thing. He didn't try to insinuate himself into any of the searches they conducted. One of his staff ventured into the woods only if something criminal was found. He left the searching to the experts, which Ethan appreciated. The last thing they needed was to have someone else go missing.

"All right, I'm thinking we break into three teams," Ethan told his friends. "Rocky, you, Drew, and Brock head west toward Eagle Point. Zeke and I will take the Barker Mill Trail where it branches off from the Fallport Creek Trail to the east. Raid, you and Tal go where Duke leads you."

As always, Raid was there with his bloodhound. The dog had a better recovery rate than the men did. Duke had been trained to search based on scent. All he needed was a piece of the missing person's clothing or something he or she had touched recently, and his nose would go to the ground and he'd be off. He could follow a trail from miles away...if he could catch a scent.

The only issue was that Duke wasn't a cadaver dog. If a person was deceased, their scent changed and couldn't be tracked by Raid's dog. And in these woods, a person's body decayed very quickly. Not to mention, animals usually found the body before anyone else, and nature took over.

If Trent was alive, Duke would find him. If not...well, it could take a very long time, if ever, before his body was found in the vast wilderness of the Appalachians.

Tucker was standing near where Ethan was talking to his crew, and obviously overheard, because he turned to his own staff and began handing out assignments.

"Kate, you and Roger go with the dog. Chris, you and Joey follow the guys headed west. Lilly, you and Michelle go east."

"No," Michelle said with a shake of her head. "I'm tired. We were up all night, and there's no way I'm tromping through the woods again."

"Especially when there's no guarantee they're gonna find anything," Chris added.

"And I'm sorry, but by the look of these guys," Roger said, using his thumb to gesture to Ethan and his team, "they'll easily outpace us. There's no way I can keep up with a dog."

Tucker glared at the cast of his show.

Ethan saw Lilly duck her head as her lips twitched. The situation wasn't humorous in the least, but he couldn't blame her for being amused over a mutiny by the stars of the show.

"All right. But I'm gonna insist on you guys going," Tucker said, glaring at his camera operators.

"If Roger doesn't think he can keep up with a dog, I'm not sure how you think *I'll* be able to, lugging this camera around," Kate said.

"Fine!" Tucker said, sounding pissed now. "You and Andre can stay here and get footage of the cast. Lilly, you and Joey will follow the search and rescue teams." He shot daggers at the two of them, as if his threatening look could make them agree.

"Maybe we should just let Ethan and the others do their thing without having to worry about us slowing them down," Lilly said.

"No fucking way. Get your shit together and don't let them out of your sight."

Ethan didn't like how Tucker talked down to his employees. But he didn't want to stand there listening to them argue, not when they had a missing man to find.

"Sorry about this," Lilly said softly as she walked up next to him.

"You *did* warn me. It's okay," he said. Then he turned to his team. "Everyone stay on channel eight." They didn't need the reminder, but he wanted to make sure, just in case. They always used the same channel to communicate when they were on a search. If anyone spotted anything that indicated their target had been nearby, they'd let the others know and everyone would pivot in their search area, slowly closing in on the most likely location where the missing person might be.

"How come their radios work and ours sound like crap?" Roger asked as the SAR team headed out. Raid and Tal had to wait until someone went back to the hotel and got into Trent's room to find a piece of clothing Duke could use as a scent marker, but the others got to work right away. With any luck, they'd find something before Raid, Duke, and Tal headed out.

Ethan took point as he and Zeke started down the Fallport Creek Trail. Even though Lilly and some of the others had already searched for Trent on this trail, it was possible they'd missed a sign of where he could be.

The Fallport Creek Trail was more of a beginner's hike, and he genuinely thought this would be the route Trent would've taken, from everything he'd learned about the man from Lilly. He also had a specific destination in mind. A semi-clear plot of land about three miles from the parking area that would be perfect to pitch a tent. It was at the intersection of the Barker Mill Trail, and he hoped like hell that was where Trent would be found.

He and Zeke didn't speak as they walked, used to working together and keeping their eyes peeled for any sign of the missing man. It wasn't until they'd reached the clearing where he'd hoped to find Trent that Ethan even remembered it hadn't been just the two of them on the trail.

Feeling awful that he'd forgotten about Lilly, too focused on the search, he turned to see how far behind she was. To his surprise, she was right on Zeke's heels. Her camera was on her shoulder, her T-shirt had sweat stains around the neck and armpits, and he could hear her panting slightly from exertion.

He was impressed. Not many people would've been able to keep up with the punishing pace he'd set.

"It doesn't look like he camped here," Zeke said, turning Ethan's attention away from Lilly.

"Nope. Not even one night. I was hoping that even if he

wasn't here now, he might've at least stayed here before deciding to move to another spot." The grass wasn't tamped down and there was no sign anyone had spent any significant amount of time here.

He unclipped his radio and pushed the button on the side to speak to the others. "This is Chaos. Anyone see any signs?" he asked. For some reason when they were on the search, they all used their nicknames. He figured the habit went back to their time in the military. When they were searching, they were in professional mode, and using their nicknames just came naturally.

"Nothing yet," Koop, aka, Drew, replied.

"We're just leaving the parking area now," Raid said. "Duke seems to be on the trail."

"Bones here. Which direction is he headed?" Bones was Brock.

"Hard to tell as of yet. He's zigzagging a lot, which means the scent isn't very strong and is mostly airborne," Raid said. "Will update as soon as we've got something."

Ethan sighed and turned to Zeke. "What are you thinking?"

Instead of answering, his friend turned to Lilly. "How far did you all come down this trail the first night when Trent was with you?"

She made eye contact with Zeke. "Honestly? I'm not sure. Everything looks very different in the light than it did when we were wandering around at night."

"You have your GPS with you?" Ethan asked.

Lilly looked surprised, then she grimaced. "Shoot. No. Sorry. I took it off last night when I got home, and didn't think to grab it when Tucker called and told me what was going on. I think I was still partially asleep. I just hightailed it out to the parking area."

"It's okay," Ethan told her. "If we still need to, we can look at it later." Then he reached for the water bottle he always carried in the pack he wore on the job. "Here. You do look tired."

She reached for it without hesitation. And even though they were in the middle of a job, Ethan couldn't help but feel a jolt when her lips closed around the nozzle. She swallowed several times before handing it back.

"Yeah, Michelle wasn't lying. We were up almost all night. I got to Whitney's just after four in the morning, and got about two hours of sleep before Tucker woke me with his call."

"Go ahead and take a break while we look at the map and try to figure out where Trent might have gone," Ethan told her.

But instead of putting down her camera, Lilly shrugged. "Looking at a map would be a good shot."

He wanted to protest, preferring she take care of herself, but he couldn't. She was right. And she was just doing her job. So she stood over him and Zeke as they pulled out the topographical map of the area and spread it on the ground. They discussed possible routes and places that were appropriate to pitch a tent.

After a moment, Lilly put down her camera and pointed at a ridge on the map. "I think that's where we were the first night. Well, half of us. We separated so we could do the knocking on trees thing and the stupid mating calls. The ones on the far ridge would respond and the cast all pretended what they heard was Bigfoot."

Ethan was somewhat surprised she admitted to the trickery, but this wasn't exactly the time to hold anything back. Not when someone was missing.

"All right, we'll head in that direction then. It's possible he wanted to get as far away as he could from anyone who might be hiking so they didn't interfere with what he was doing," Ethan said. Then he turned to Lilly. "You good to keep going?"

"Yeah."

Ethan reached for her camera as he stood—and grimaced at how heavy it was. "Good God, this thing has to weigh at least ten pounds."

Lilly smiled. "More like thirteen," she said, reaching for it.

Ethan felt even more guilty for the punishing pace he'd set earlier.

As if she could read his mind, Lilly said, "It's fine. I'm used to it."

His respect for Lilly and her fellow camera operators rose a notch. Remembering Michelle's complaint that she was tired seemed ridiculous now, since she hadn't hiked around the woods all night with a thirteen-pound camera on her shoulder. Lilly had been up just as late as Michelle and the others, but she wasn't complaining.

"For the record...you're amazing," Ethan blurted.

Lilly tilted her head away from the camera viewfinder and smiled at him.

"Have to say, I'm glad *you* were assigned to us, and not any of the others," Zeke said. "You're quiet, we haven't had to wait for you to catch up, and you're dressed for what we're doing. It's appreciated."

"Thanks, guys. As I've said many times, my family did their best to make sure I was prepared for anything when it came to outdoorsy stuff. They didn't care that my legs were shorter than theirs and I was younger, they took me along on ten-mile hikes as if it was nothing. Although, I have to admit, I've lost some of my stamina over the years. Being a camera operator isn't always the most active job."

"You're doing fine. Come on, let's see if we can't find Trent so we can all get out of the woods, huh?" Ethan said. There was more he wanted to say. Like he wanted to meet the men who'd raised such an amazing woman. That he admired the hell out of her. That he'd take her to some of his favorite places in the forest if she stayed. But he kept his mouth shut and did his best to turn his attention back to the job at hand.

* * *

Three hours later, the trio walked out of the woods into the parking lot having not seen any evidence of the missing man or his campsite.

The rest of the team was waiting for them when they arrived. They'd kept in close contact and none of the others had any luck either. Even Duke had lost Trent's scent about a mile from the parking area. It was as if the man had disappeared into thin air, which everyone knew was impossible.

Tucker and the rest of the cast were no longer there. They'd obviously gone back to their hotel to await news of their missing friend. Or maybe they'd gone to get some sleep. Ethan didn't know, and at the moment, they weren't his concern.

Simon *was* there though. Most likely waiting for information about what they did—or didn't—find.

Lilly stood back with Joey as Ethan and his team spoke with the police chief.

"Anything?" Simon asked.

"Nothing. The man either disappeared without a trace, or he was never here in the first place," Ethan said.

"I'm guessing the latter," Rocky said. "The farther west we went, the less signs we saw that *anyone* had been that way recently."

"And I'm thinking the scent Duke picked up must not have been recent, was from the first night, when Trent filmed with the others," Raid said.

Looking down, Ethan saw Duke lying on his side next to Raid's feet. His jowls were filled with slobber, but his eyes were shut as he napped. The dog looked lazy as hell, but Ethan knew from experience, he was bred to be able to follow a scent trail for miles. He would walk until he fell over from exhaustion if he wasn't kept in check. And if he ever got off his lead, he could literally end up in West Virginia. But overall, he was a laid-back dog who loved his master and lived for any kind of food. He and Raid were extremely close, and Ethan had no doubt they'd each give their lives for the other.

"Did anyone have anything else to say about where they thought he might be?" Tal asked Simon.

"No. Although that reminds me..." The police chief turned to where Lilly and Joey were standing. "I'm going to need to interview the two of you. I spoke with everyone else while you were with the search teams."

Lilly nodded, and Joey said, "Of course," softly.

The chief turned his back on the two crew members and said in a tone that couldn't be overheard, "Something's fishy here, and since you guys found nothing, I'm thinking today was a wild goose chase."

"Agreed," Koop said.

"There's little chance a man who doesn't like the outdoors, who had nothing but a generic Walmart tent and sleeping bag, went any farther out than we searched," Rocky added.

"Someone knows something," Simon said. "And I'm going to find out what it is." Then he straightened and said louder. "I'll be in touch. Appreciate your time and service today."

When the police chief walked away, Ethan turned to his team. "What are you all thinking? Should we try somewhere else?"

"Where?" Raid asked. "We need a starting place. You know as well as I do that we can't blindly search thousands of acres and expect to get lucky. There's just too much ground to cover."

"It would be a waste of our time," Koop agreed.

"Anyone think that maybe Bigfoot got him after all?" Tal asked. Everyone turned to glare at him. He chuckled. "Kidding!"

"I'll check in with Simon later today," Ethan told everyone. "If he's gotten any more information out of anyone, I'll let you know and we can regroup."

"Sounds good. I've got taxes to do, so if that's all, I'm gonna get going," Drew said.

"You don't feel even the smallest urge to do some investigating yourself?" Rocky asked.

"None whatsoever," Drew said. "I put all that behind me when I left the State Police. I'll gladly let Simon deal with interrogating people and trying to figure out who's lying about what. I'll take my numbers and the solitude of the forest any day, over going back to that world." And with that, he turned and headed for his car.

After Simon spoke with Joey and Lilly, most likely making arrangements for them to go in to be interviewed, he too headed for his cruiser. The others followed suit, and soon, Ethan was standing in the parking lot alone with Lilly.

"Wow, was it something I said?" she joked.

Ethan's lips quirked up. "You tired?"

"Exhausted," she said without hesitation. "But I'm not sure I can sleep. I can't help thinking about where Trent might be and what happened to him."

"Well, hopefully nothing happened to him," Ethan said. "I'm sure he just got turned around and is lost. We'll find him," he said confidently.

"I hope so. What are you going to do the rest of the day?" she asked.

"Well, I was going to go work on the house Rocky is remodeling, but I'm thinking it might be more useful if I looked at some maps and tried to figure out where the hell Trent thought would be a good place to camp by himself for three days."

"Somewhere near a shower and fast food," Lilly quipped.

But Ethan didn't smile.

"What?"

"You have a good point."

Lilly shook her head. "No, I was kidding."

"But like you said, Trent isn't an outdoor kind of guy. He might go out in the dark and do some filming, but what if he did that, left his camping gear, and went somewhere warm and dry for the rest of the night?"

"Like maybe he came back to the hotel each night? But what about his car? Wouldn't one of the others have seen it?"

"I don't know. Nothing is making much sense so far, but we'll figure it out. You think you'd be able to sleep if you came back to my place with me?" The offer popped out without thought, but Ethan wasn't sorry he'd made it.

Lilly looked surprised.

"I'd just like to keep you with me. I'm guessing you're probably sore from being up all night, then carting around that rock on your shoulder for hours today. Everyone else is probably back at the hotel sleeping. You should be too. There's no telling when Tucker will call you to come to work. You know as well as I do that he's going to milk this as much as he can. He's going to want some footage of everyone being concerned and freaking out. I promise that my bed is comfortable, even if my apartment complex is a piece of crap. You'll be safe. I give you my word."

Having Lilly in his bed wasn't something Ethan even dreamed would happen during her short visit to town...but now he couldn't get the image out of his head.

"I trust you. It's just that I don't want to be a nuisance."

Ethan couldn't help but chuckle. "You won't be. And I'm assuming you need to go to the station and talk to Simon later? I can feed you when you wake up and take you over there." It was a lame argument. She could easily get to the police station herself and Whitney would most certainly have no problem finding something for her to eat.

But Ethan hadn't lied; he *did* want to keep her close. He didn't know what happened to Trent, was hoping he was just an inexperienced wannabe TV star lost in the woods—or even "lost" on purpose, for the cameras—but what if he wasn't?

"I'd like that," Lilly said with a small smile. "I need to stop by the B&B and grab my camera chargers though. And maybe change clothes."

"No problem. I'll follow you back and chat with Whitney while you do what you need to. Then we can go to my place and we'll play things by ear from there."

"Okay."

"Okay," Ethan echoed. He couldn't stop himself from reaching for her. "You were great today," he said quietly as he curled his hand around the side of her neck. Her skin was soft and slightly damp from the exertion of all the hiking they'd done. She leaned into his touch...and Ethan was a goner. That small bit of trust almost undid him.

She closed her eyes and sighed.

They stood like that for a full minute before Ethan forced himself to let go. Her eyes came open and he could see how tired she was.

"Come on. Let's go before you fall asleep standing up," he said.

Lilly nodded. "Ethan?"

"Yeah?"

"Thanks."

"For what?" he asked.

"For looking for Trent and taking his disappearance seriously. For inviting me over. For not bitching about me having to tail you this morning. For being so good at what you do. I watched you today, and I'm impressed. Very impressed. You don't miss much, and it makes me think that you and your team really will find Trent. Just...thanks for everything."

"You don't have to thank me for any of that. And we *will* find him. I can promise you that."

"I hope so."

He put his hand on the small of her back and led her to her car. He took her camera, shaking his head again at the weight of it, and placed it on the floor behind the driver's seat. She rolled down her window after she shut her door, and Ethan said, "Drive safe."

She smiled. "Ethan, I only passed like one car on my way out here this morning. I'm not sure I have to worry too much about rogue crazy drivers."

"Don't care. You never know when Bigfoot will step out in front of you and make you lose control," he said.

"Oh, Bigfoot jokes. Nice," she teased.

Ethan grinned, forcing himself not to lean down and kiss her through the window, and stepped back. "See you at the B&B."

Lilly nodded and reached for the ignition. Ethan jogged over to his own car and pulled out of the parking lot behind her. He had no idea what the next few days would bring, but he had a bad feeling about whatever was happening. He was confident he and his team *would* find Trent...he just had no idea what shape he'd be in when they did.

* * *

He grinned. Huge.

Today had been awesome!

Exactly the reaction he'd hoped for.

Everyone was freaking out, and it would make for awesome television.

The search for Trent was going to be edge-of-your-seat TV, and he could just envision the episode ending on a cliffhanger. Where was Trent? Would he be found?

And then when his body was discovered...

The man shivered in delight. Yeah, this was definitely going to be *the* most talked-about show. Ever.

He just had to be patient. Not give anything away. The police chief was being incredibly thorough and the last thing he wanted was to make himself look like a suspect. No, he just had to keep his cool and ride things out. Not say anything that would give away what he'd done. If that meant Trent had to stay missing a while longer, so be it.

Those search and rescue guys thought they were so good. Well, if they were...they'd eventually find him. Then the real fun could start.

CHAPTER TWELVE

Lilly rolled over and smiled as she inhaled. The second she woke up, she knew she wasn't in the comfortable bed at the bed and breakfast. She was at Ethan's apartment. In his bed. His more-comfortable-than-the-bed-at-Whitney's-place bed.

Though, he hadn't exaggerated. The apartment complex he and his brother lived in was...not so appealing. It wasn't in a bad area or anything, but the apartment itself was rundown, the appliances old, the fixtures probably from the eighties or earlier. Yet, it still felt homey. Probably because of all the books Ethan had on shelves around the living room, along with pictures of his brother and friends. Including one of him and Rocky standing with someone who had to be their mom between them. There was a throw blanket and pillows on the sofa. He even had some scented candles strategically placed around the space.

The bed, though... He clearly hadn't spared any expense, and whatever mattress he had seemed to cradle her body. All the aches and pains from her long night and morning in the woods seemed to dissipate the moment she lay down. Not to mention, the linens smelled like Ethan, which was heavenly.

Lilly fell asleep almost as soon as her head hit the pillow. Looking at the clock, she saw that she'd slept for four hours straight. She could do with another couple hours, but there were things she needed to get done. First and foremost, she wanted to see if Trent had shown up yet, sheepish about the hubbub he'd caused. If not, she had to go talk to the police chief, even though she had literally nothing to tell him. Since she wasn't staying at the same hotel as the others, there was nothing she could contribute to the investigation.

As she was psyching herself up to get out of bed, the door opened. Lilly looked over and saw Ethan standing in the doorway.

"Hey," he said quietly.

"I'm up," she told him.

"I see. I was just coming in to check on you. You said you'd meet with Simon in about an hour, and I thought you might want to eat something before we left."

"Thanks. I could eat," she said, sitting up.

"You sleep okay?" he asked.

"Like a rock."

They stared at each other for a heartbeat—and suddenly Lilly felt tongue-tied. It was crazy because she'd spent a lot of time with this man in the last week or so. And she'd never felt as off-kilter as she did right now. Maybe it was because she'd taken off her cargo pants to sleep and she was in his bed in nothing but a T-shirt and her underwear. Maybe it was because of the look in his eyes. A look she had a feeling was reflected in her own.

She wanted this man. And she might be out of practice when it came to dating and the opposite sex, but she was fairly certain he wanted her too.

As if he could read her mind, Ethan pushed off the doorjamb and walked closer. He sat on the edge of the bed and reached for her, his fingers sliding into the hair at the nape of her neck, and Lilly shivered. She'd been able to control herself and not jump him when he'd done the same thing in the parking lot earlier, but now...

the room was dim since he'd closed the shades, she was half naked, her skin was covered in his scent, and her heart was beating a million miles an hour.

He didn't say a word. Didn't ask permission. Simply leaned toward her.

Lilly met him halfway, reaching out to grab hold of his shirt as she did.

Their lips met as if they'd done it a thousand times before. Her eyes closed and she did her best to memorize the moment. Ethan's lips were soft and warm, and for a brief second, he did nothing but press a soft kiss against her own. Then his hand tightened on her neck and he tilted his head. His tongue licked along the seam of her lips, and Lilly opened for him.

The kiss went from gentle and exploratory to carnal in a heartbeat.

The next thing she knew, she was on her back and clutching at Ethan's shirt as he devoured her. They kissed for several long minutes, learning the taste and feel of one another. Their tongues dueled, their teeth nipped, their hands roamed. And every second felt as natural as if she'd known this man her entire life.

A small whimper escaped her throat when Ethan pulled back. He hovered over her, his eyes probing as he studied her face.

Lilly licked her lips, loving that his gaze immediately was drawn to her mouth.

"That was..." she said, hesitating as she tried to find the best word to describe their kiss.

"Fucking perfect," Ethan said, completing her sentence.

Lilly smiled. "Yeah."

His hand came up and he smoothed her hair away from her cheek, but he didn't move to let her up. So Lilly let her hands roam up and down his muscular arms, loving the feel of him as he held himself above her.

"I knew this was going to happen," he said after a moment.

"What?" she whispered.

"That if I got you in my bed, I wouldn't want to let you out."

She smiled shyly. "It's a very comfortable mattress."

"Told you," he told her. Then he took a deep breath and exhaled before shaking his head and sitting up.

Lilly scooted up so her back was against the simple headboard.

"I put the bag you packed over there," he said, gesturing to the side of the room without taking his eyes from hers.

"Thanks." Lilly had packed her toothbrush and toothpaste and a set of clean hiking clothes, just in case the team went back out to search for Trent and she was ordered to go with them once more. She wanted to be prepared and not have to waste time by going back to the B&B. It wasn't that far away, nothing in Fallport was, but still.

Ethan opened his mouth as if he was going to ask her something, but he shut it and stood. "Tomato soup and grilled cheese sandwiches all right for lunch? Or whatever meal comes between lunch and dinner? Linner? Dunch?"

Lilly really wanted to ask him what he was about to say, but was honest enough to admit that maybe she didn't want to know. That kiss had been amazing. Life changing. And she wasn't completely certain she was at a point yet where she was ready to change her life. So she smiled at him and said, "That sounds great."

He gazed wistfully at her once more, before walking out the door and closing it behind him.

Lilly closed her eyes and touched her slightly swollen lips for a moment, before taking a deep breath and throwing her legs over the edge of the bed. She headed for the small en suite bathroom, grabbing her bag along the way. She hadn't expected to fall for a guy when she'd arrived in Fallport, and even though this wasn't the most convenient time to do so...when Trent was missing, and she had no idea what she was going to do when the show was over...she wasn't sorry.

For the time being, all Lilly could do was take one day at a time.

First, they had to find Trent. Then she could try to figure out what her next steps would be.

* * *

Ethan watched Lilly carefully later that night. She'd had a hard day, but was trying to pretend everything was perfectly normal. They'd just eaten a delicious meal Whitney had prepared, and since there were now two other guests staying at the B&B, he hadn't been able to talk to her about everything that had happened as they ate.

Her meeting with the detective assigned to Trent's missing person case had gone on way longer than Ethan had expected it to. She'd been grilled for two hours at the station earlier that afternoon. By the time she'd been free to go, Ethan wasn't happy. He'd been with Lilly practically every minute of the time she hadn't been working, and he knew for a fact that she hadn't had anything to do with the disappearance of her co-worker. Despite that, the detective had put a ton of pressure on her to try to find out what was going on.

Since Ethan hadn't been with her twenty-four seven, the detective speculated that she could've snuck out of the B&B and done something to Trent. Which was ridiculous, but the small police force was doing its due diligence.

There had been a lot of questions about why no one had been concerned when they hadn't heard from Trent while he was out by himself for two days. Uncomfortable questions that no one on the show had been able to answer very satisfactorily. The man was a part of their crew; someone should've noticed he was missing way before they had.

After the interrogation, Ethan had taken Lilly to Grinders to get a rejuvenating cup of coffee, and one of the customers had said something snarky under his breath. Ethan hadn't heard it clearly, but it was something about Bigfoot and interlopers. He'd immediately stepped toward the man, telling him in no uncertain terms that he needed to keep his mouth shut, or the next time he needed assistance from his team, or anyone else in town, he'd not find it readily available.

Shortly after, Tucker had called Lilly and she'd had to go film an impromptu news conference that he'd set up for Roger, Chris, and Michelle to plead for information about their friend. When they were in front of the cameras, everyone looked subdued and concerned, but Lilly had admitted to Ethan that afterward, when they thought no one was listening, she'd overheard them talking about what a genius Trent was, that he was probably laughing his ass off wherever he was holed up. They'd even discussed where they would put their Emmy awards when the show won.

To top off her crappy day, the couple who was staying at the B&B had come to Fallport specifically because they'd heard there had been Bigfoot sightings, and they wanted to see what they could find themselves. Ethan knew Lilly felt guilty about her part in what might eventually be a rush of tourists. It would be a boon for business owners like Whitney, but would probably change the vibe of the town.

All in all, Lilly was doing her best to remain professional and stoic, but Ethan could see she was having a hard time with everything. As much as he wanted to take her back to his apartment—he couldn't get over how much he liked seeing her in his bed that morning—it was too soon for that.

The kiss they'd shared had been better than anything he'd imagined—and he'd thought about kissing her *a lot* in the last couple of days. It hadn't been awkward in the least, and one of the hardest things he'd ever done was pull back and leave her in his bed.

"Thank you for another wonderful meal," Lilly told Whitney.

"Of course. I love cooking for others," the older woman said. "One of the reasons I started this B&B was because I was bored. And being able to make meals not just for one is a bonus."

"All I can say is that it's a good thing my job here involves hiking miles at a time."

Whitney smiled at her, then she sobered. "What do you think happened to your friend?"

Ethan wanted to shut the conversation down, but didn't want to embarrass either Whitney or Lilly. So he stayed quiet, vowing to step in if it looked like Lilly was getting more stressed than she already was. The other two guests had already gone up to their room, planning to get an early start in the morning.

"I have no idea," Lilly said. "Trent's not exactly an outdoorsy kind of guy. I keep hoping he got sick of the assignment and maybe left town or something. That he'll call Tucker—that's the producer —from some five-star hotel and say that he quit."

"Do you think..." Whitney's voice lowered. "Not that I'm all that convinced, but maybe there's some truth to this Bigfoot stuff?"

"No," Lilly said firmly. "Whit, you've lived here a long time. And in all those years, have you heard of anyone seeing *any* sign of Bigfoot?"

"Well, no."

"Exactly. Bears, yes. Bobcats, sure. But eight-foot humanoid creatures who are so smart that no one has *ever* found concrete evidence of their existence?"

"When you put it that way, it does sound kind of silly," Whitney said.

"Exactly."

"So if you don't believe in Bigfoot, what are you doing working on this show?"

Lilly hesitated, and Ethan couldn't deny he was as interested in her answer as Whitney.

"A girl has to eat," she said with a small smile, after a long pause.

"I get the sense that you're a smart woman," Whitney said. "I'm thinking that you could probably find a job that you actually enjoy."

"I don't hate what I do," Lilly argued.

"Right, but you don't love it either," Whitney said with certainty. "You're an adult and can do what you want, but it seems to me there could be other things you can do to put food on the table that you actually enjoy doing. For instance, we sometimes get people in town for weddings, and I've heard them complaining that there aren't any videographers in the area. And just the other day, the principal of the high school was looking for someone to film the football games next year, because the coach wants to be able to review the plays to make the team better."

"Whitney—" Lilly began, but the other woman was on a roll.

"And I'm guessing that you're no slouch when it comes to taking pictures either. I know filming isn't the same thing, but there are a ton of people in this town who would love to have a professional photographer in our midst. School pictures, recitals, the July 4th parade, the festivals...I could go on and on about situations where people would pay a lot of money for good pictures of their kids and families. Not the crap shots that people take on their phones these days."

"I'm not sure—"

"And Fallport isn't exactly as exciting as Hollywood, but it's a lot less expensive, I'm sure. It wouldn't take as much money to live here as it would somewhere else, so—"

"I think she gets the point, Whit," Ethan said, interrupting before she made Lilly even more uncomfortable than she already was. Lilly's entire body was tense, and he couldn't tell if it was because she hated what her host was saying...or she liked it. But on top of everything else that had already happened that day, including the stressful trip to the police station, it was obvious Lilly had reached the end of her rope.

As much as Ethan liked Whitney's suggestions and would love it if Lilly moved to Fallport permanently, she had a career she'd worked hard to get, and things were definitely still up in the air as far as the show was concerned. Until Trent was found, they'd probably continue to be that way.

Lilly shot him a small, grateful smile before turning to Whitney. "I appreciate the vote of confidence. I love it here, most of the people I've met have been very friendly."

Ethan wanted to snort at that. She hadn't missed the standoff-ishness of a few residents. At least until she'd come to Elsie's aid. That had changed the general opinion of her quickly.

Whitney sighed and scooted her chair back from the table and stood. She grabbed her plate and started toward the kitchen, before turning and pinning Lilly with a look and a kind smile. "Life's too short to do something you aren't passionate about. Money's all well and good, but at the end of the day, it's the relationships you form, the people you meet, and how often you laugh that matter."

With that, she turned and disappeared into the kitchen.

Lilly stared after her for a moment, then sighed herself.

"She means well," Ethan said softly.

"I know." Then she turned to him and said, "I wanted to thank you for standing up for me with that guy at the coffee shop. It wasn't necessary. I mean, I've heard a lot worse things said about me by people who haven't liked whatever show I'm working on, but I still appreciate it."

"I told you that I'd never let anyone disparage you when I was around, and I meant it."

Lilly stared at him for a heartbeat, then she closed her eyes. "It's...My own boyfriends didn't do that for me, and you...me...we aren't even dating."

"Aren't we?" he asked, raising a brow. "Maybe not in the conventional sense, but, Lilly, I've been with you every spare minute you have. Trust me, I don't do that."

Her ocean-blue eyes were huge as she stared at him. Not wanting to hear her deny they were dating again, Ethan stood and held out his hand. "Come on."

Lilly looked up at him in question but didn't hesitate to put her hand in his and let him pull her upright. "Where are we going?"

He didn't respond, but led her toward the stairs. He didn't stop when he stepped into her room, heading straight for the bathroom. He dropped her hand and crouched to look under the sink.

"What are you doing?"

"Whitney's always bragging about how she has everything a weary traveler might want...ah, here we go," he said, grabbing a bottle of bubble bath. Then he turned to the tub and turned on the hot water. It wasn't a fancy bathroom, but he didn't think that would matter much to Lilly right now.

"Seriously, Ethan, what's happening?" she asked.

He turned to her and put his hands on her shoulders. "You've had a long, emotional day. We have no idea what tomorrow might bring, so for right now, you need to relax. I figure a hot bubble bath will help you do that."

She stared up at him.

"What?" he asked. "Don't tell me you don't like baths. I mean, I know some people don't, but when I get to my breaking point, soaking in the tub helps *me*." He hadn't meant to admit that, but now that he had, he wasn't sorry.

"I love baths," she said, her voice cracking.

Realizing she was on the verge of crying, Ethan turned to feel the temperature of the water to give her time to compose herself. When he faced her again, she was smiling.

"I'm proud of you," he said.

She wrinkled her brow. "Why?"

"Because of the way you've handled everything thrown at you recently. You never complained when you worked all night, then had to hike another six miles with that rock you call a camera on your shoulder. You stayed strong even when the cops tried to make you admit to something you didn't do. You have to be worried about Trent, and yet you've stayed positive. And tonight, when you could've told Whitney she was an interfering busybody who didn't know what she was talking about, you let her say what was on her mind. I think you're pretty amazing, Lilly."

She closed her eyes and took a deep breath before opening them again. "You ever feel as if all it'll take is one more thing and you'll shatter into a million pieces?"

"Yes," he said simply.

She raised a brow in question.

"There's a saying in the SEALs...the only easy day was yesterday...and it's very true. All we can do is roll with the punches thrown our way and keep going. But that doesn't mean we can't take a time-out now and then."

"Did you like being a SEAL?" she asked.

Ethan thought about her question for a moment, then shrugged. "Sometimes, yes. It was the best job in the world. I felt as if I was making a difference. Then there were the days that made me wonder what the hell I was doing. No matter what I or my squad did, the next day there would be more terrorists, more assholes trying to kill anyone who didn't believe the exact same thing they did. Living in a world where there are more people trying to kill you than wanting to be your friend finally got to me. Not to mention the fucking politics."

"Is that why you got out?" she asked, stepping closer to him.

Rocky was the only person in the world who knew the *real* reason he'd called it quits, but telling Lilly felt right. "It was a factor, yes," he told her. "But it was my last mission that tipped the scales for me. We were hunting for a Taliban general. A guy way up on the totem pole. A man who was worse than Osama Bin Laden ever was. We'd narrowed down his location to one of his hideouts, and were moving in when we heard a baby crying. The kid was screaming so loud and was obviously in major distress. It was heartbreaking.

"We turned a corner in the house we were searching...and there she was. Lying in the middle of the floor, surrounded by dirty clothes and other household odds and ends. She had black hair, was probably around six months old. She was swaddled so tightly, she couldn't move her arms or anything. Her face was bright red because of her screaming, and my heart immediately fell.

"I was the last man in line to enter the room, and even as I opened my mouth to warn my teammate who was at point to not go near the baby, I knew I was too late. His wife had just had their third kid while we were deployed, and there wasn't a chance in hell he would've been able to ignore that kid. The second he picked her up, the bomb she was lying on top of was triggered.

"It killed the baby, my friend, and two others in my squad instantly. I was blown backward and had a severe concussion and a broken vertebrae in my back. My other team members had damages ranging from severed limbs to traumatic brain injuries. The only reason we got out of there was because another SEAL team was coming up on our six, and they were far enough away to not be caught in the blast. They got us back to base and the hospital."

Lilly didn't hesitate to wrap her arms around him, and nothing had ever felt as good as her body against his. Her touch gave Ethan the ability to continue.

"When I healed, I knew I couldn't go back. Not to a world where someone thought it was perfectly all right to use a defenseless baby as a weapon. I was done. I needed something different."

Lilly's hands gently caressed his back. "You liked helping others, but needed to do it in a way that didn't involve the violence."

Ethan nodded. "Exactly. My brother and I weren't in the same squad, but when he heard what happened, nothing would've kept him from my side. He was there while I was in the hospital and browbeat me all throughout physical therapy. I was lucky, and we both knew it. So when I got out, he didn't hesitate to do the same. We came here, formed the Eagle Point Search and Rescue team, recruited the others...and here we are."

"Fallport's lucky to have all of you. And Whitney's right," she said softly, resting her cheek on his chest.

"Yeah?" he asked, encouraging her to keep talking.

"I don't love my job. But I've been doing it so long, going from one project to the next, that I have no idea what I'd do if I quit."

"I felt the same way about the SEALs. I'd been in the Navy for so long, I couldn't imagine doing anything else. It was scary to make that decision, but I knew in my heart it was the right thing for me.

CHAPTER THIRTEEN

The last week had been a series of highs and lows. Highs when Lilly got to spend time with Ethan. Lows when each day passed with no sign of where Trent had gone or what had happened to him.

This morning, Tucker had called a meeting at the hotel where he and the others had been staying. They'd all gathered in the parking lot —where the producer informed them all that it was time to move on.

The schedule for the next episode had been pushed back a week, but it couldn't be put off any longer. They had to get to Lake Memphremagog to try to get a glimpse of Memphre, the monster said to inhabit the freshwater glacial lake between Newport, Vermont, and Magog, Quebec, Canada.

"But the Bigfoot episode is going to be the one that puts us on the radar," he went on, as Lilly and everyone else stared at him in shock. "We have to leave, but we also need to get the moment Trent is found on film. Lilly, you'll stay here and stick to the SAR team like glue. I'll send you a list of people to interview about what they think happened to Trent. We need opinions that he was taken by Bigfoot, so those are the only people I'm interested in talking to.

I'm negotiating with a few locals now. Once they receive payment, I'll get you their info."

Lilly couldn't believe what she was hearing. They were *leaving*? Without Trent? And he was paying people to say Trent had been attacked by Bigfoot? She shouldn't be surprised—and yet, she was. Tucker had already proven he didn't care about anyone or anything but ratings, and all the paranormal stuff they'd caught on camera had been manufactured by one of the cast or crew, but still. This was...abhorrent.

For just a moment, she wondered if the producer was in on whatever had happened to Trent. Like, maybe he'd driven him to Roanoke and put him on a plane or something, just to get a story like this for the show.

"You contact me the second anything happens. If a scrap of his clothing appears, you better be there to get it on film," Tucker warned.

Lilly stiffened. She didn't like his threatening tone. But he didn't give her time to comment before he continued.

"I envision this episode being at least two hours long. Maybe we'll split it up into two, three, or even four separate episodes. We've got a ton of footage already, and with whatever is found after we leave, I'm sure we can string it out. Hopefully when we find Trent's campsite, his handheld camera will be there and will have some good stuff on it. And of course, the others can blame not finding the Memphre in Canada on their sorrow and stress over what happened to poor Trent. Mark my words, this is gonna be *the* hit show. I guarantee it!"

Lilly looked around at her fellow camera operators and the cast, and was dismayed to see that instead of being horrified by what Tucker was saying, they merely seemed bored. As if one of their friends hadn't disappeared off the face of the planet without a trace. And as if he wasn't going to be used as a ratings ploy. She had a feeling they all still believed Trent was playing some sort of game, that he was alive and well somewhere, and that he or Tucker had planned the entire thing.

"Right, so everyone get your stuff packed up and we'll head out around eleven or so. I need to speak with the police chief, give him my contact info so he can keep in touch about what's happening here. He said that we were free to leave, since there was no evidence any of us had anything to do with Trent being missing."

He laughed, as did most of the others, but their chuckles were a little more uneasy than the producer's.

"Let's get moving. Lilly, hang on a sec, I want to talk to you."

Lilly didn't really want to hear what he had to say—but this was her chance to tell him what she thought about him using Trent's disappearance as a gimmick to get viewers. She stayed where she was while the others all headed back toward the lobby of the hotel. It was telling that not one of them bothered to say goodbye to her. She didn't register on their radar unless they needed something from her. Lilly realized that was partly her fault. Not staying at the same hotels had put distance between them, but she'd been hoping that Trent going missing might make them more of a team. She'd obviously been wrong.

"Right, so I'm counting on you to get some good footage while we're all gone," Tucker said. "I know you can't be everywhere at once, but it's important for you to be on hand when Trent's body is found."

Lilly gaped at him. "Did you just say when his *body* is found?" she asked incredulously.

"Well, yeah. You aren't so naïve to believe that he's still alive after all this time, are you?" Tucker asked with a snort.

"Plenty of people have survived lost in the woods for longer than a week," she argued.

"Yeah, but those people aren't Trent. We both know he's hopeless in the wilderness. I'm just saying that we need that footage for the show. So don't fuck it up. I picked you to stay because I've noticed how buddy-buddy you are with that search guy. You can use that to your advantage. If you can, get him to talk to you about the search and what's going on. I'm sure he'll be more willing to talk if he doesn't know you're recording. Video footage would be best, but if you don't think you can get that, I can make do with audio. We can dub it over footage we've already got of him walking through the woods."

"I'm not going to secretly record him," Lilly seethed.

Tucker stepped closer, getting in her personal space. He spoke in a tone Lilly had never heard him use before. At least not aimed at her. "You'll do whatever I tell you to do, or I'll have you fired so fast your head will spin. I forget who said it, but they were right. This show is exactly like all the others. We're doing the same shit, investigating the same things others have before us. But no one's *ever* had someone lost or killed as a result of the thing they're investigating. People are gonna eat this shit up.

"This is my chance to break out of fucking small-time shit like this and get a shot at shows and films with *real* stars. So keep the damn camera running at all times. Upload your videos every day to the server so I can look them over. Don't fuck this up, Lilly. If you have to spread your legs for that search guy, *do it*. Just get me this story."

With that, Tucker turned his back on her as he headed for the lobby doors.

Lilly was literally speechless. She wouldn't have been able to get words out even if she wanted to. And all she *really* wanted to do was take a shower. She couldn't believe he'd just told her to sleep with Ethan to get good footage for his show. That was...

She didn't know what that was. Besides gross and outrageous.

For the second time in less than twenty minutes, Lilly wondered if Tucker was behind Trent's disappearance. It made sense...and the idea made her sick to her stomach.

On autopilot, she went back to her car and climbed behind the wheel, still shocked by the things Tucker had said to her.

She headed back toward Fallport with no real destination in

mind. For the first time in a week, no one wasn't dictating where she needed to be, and when. After lunch, Ethan and Brock were heading to a part of the forest they hadn't searched before, and she'd accompany them, but right now, she had nowhere she needed to be.

And it was a good thing. Lilly's head was spinning. She was disgusted with Tucker, her co-workers, and the entire entertainment industry. Working on a show that investigated paranormal activity seemed harmless enough. But that was before she knew exactly what went on behind the scenes. The trickery and outright lies that were being fed to the viewers. It was all bullshit, which made Lilly feel as if her *job* was bullshit.

No job was worth feeling this way. She wanted to quit. It was her first instinct the moment Tucker had told her to secretly film Ethan.

The only thing holding her back was Trent. She felt as if she was the only one who genuinely cared about him being missing. If she quit, Tucker would just leave one of the other camera operators in Fallport, and who knows what they'd do to get the footage the producer so desperately wanted?

But could she stay on when it went against everything she thought was right?

When she got back to the B&B, instead of going inside, she headed for the hammock in the backyard. It was strung between two trees, their branches creating a canopy, so guests could use it in the summer and not sweat to death in the hot sun.

Lilly climbed in and pulled out her phone, clicking on the number of the one person she knew could make her feel better.

As usual, her dad answered within two rings.

"Hey, baby girl," he said in greeting.

Just his voice was enough to make Lilly tear up. "Daddy," she said tremulously.

"Whose ass do I need to kick?" he growled, obviously hearing the upset tone of her voice.

"No one's. You have time to talk?"

"I always have time to talk to you," he said, the love easy through the connection. "What's up?"

"It's so good to hear your voice."

As if her dad knew she needed some time before jumping right into what was bothering her, he began to update her on all the hometown gossip. Listening to his stories made her realize all over again that Fallport was exactly like the place she'd grown up. Her dad sounded a lot like Otto, Silas, and Art. Grumbling about the newcomers to town and telling her about who'd been sick and who was getting married.

"I miss you," she told him when he stopped to take a breath.

"And I miss you. Now, you ready to tell me what's going on?"

Lilly couldn't help but chuckle. "You know me well."

"Of course I do. Now spill."

So she did. She told him all about Fallport and the quirky residents she was coming to enjoy. About how Whitney was doing her best to stuff her like a Thanksgiving turkey. About how beautiful the area was, and even though she'd been hiking through the forest for her job, how much she enjoyed every second of being out in nature.

She must've said Ethan's name a few times too many, because when she finally trailed off, her dad said, "So...you like this Ethan guy?"

"He's different," Lilly said.

"How so?"

That was another thing Lilly loved about her dad. While he was protective and always wanted only the best for her, he wasn't the kind of dad who hated every guy she was interested in on principle. He always preached that actions spoke louder than words, and he based his opinions on what people did, not what they said they were *going* to do.

"He makes me laugh. And he's intense, but in a good way."

"I have no idea what that means," her dad deadpanned.

Lilly chuckled. "I don't know that I can explain it."

"Try."

"Right, well, he's former military. He was a Navy SEAL. He's insanely observant. He can tell you the names of everyone who was in a room, even if we were only there for ten seconds. If I'm hungry, he seems to know it. If I'm tired, he has no problem changing whatever plans we might have so I can get some sleep. And I know you'll love this—he even stood up for me when a guy said something derogatory about the show being in town."

"He sounds like a good man," her dad said.

"He is," Lilly said quietly.

"If the town is so great, and you're hanging out with this Ethan guy, who you really seem to like...it must be the job that's stressing you out."

Lilly wasn't surprised her dad had figured it out. It wasn't a secret that she'd been less and less enamored with her work. Part of the reason she took the job on this show was because it got her out of Hollywood. She'd hoped that would rejuvenate her love for what she thought was her dream career.

"Yeah. Things are...they're not good, Daddy."

"Talk to me, baby girl."

"One of the hosts of the show is missing."

"What? How? What the fuck?"

Lilly could just imagine her dad sitting up straight and glaring as he bit out the questions. "He decided he wanted to do a solo investigation. I bought him a tent, sleeping bag, and some other basic camping supplies, and the plan was for him to stay out in the woods somewhere for a few days. He'd film his search for Bigfoot, then meet back up with the rest of the cast. We'd wrap up the shoot and go to Canada. But he never returned from the woods. Ethan and his search and rescue team have been looking for a week, but haven't been able to find him, or even where he camped."

"Holy shit."

"Yeah. We've delayed the next shoot as long as we can, but we can't anymore. So Tucker and the rest of the cast and crew are heading up to Canada, and I'm staying here to film the continued search."

"And he's practically salivating to get the moment he's found on film, isn't he?" her dad asked.

"Yeah. He talked about getting his *body* on film, Daddy. And told me to secretly tape Ethan talking about the search too. I'm just so disgusted with him, the show...everything. It's all bullshit. Tucker actually had Andre tromping around the forest wearing big ol' fake Bigfoot feet. It's just..." Her voice trailed off.

"You hate it."

"Yeah."

"Then quit," he said succinctly.

"I've seriously thought about it."

"And?"

"I feel as if I bail now, I'm leaving Trent to the wolves, so to speak. Right now, I'm practically his only advocate on the show. If I'm not here, who knows what someone else will do to get a good story, whether it's true or not?"

"You think he's really missing? Or is this a ratings ploy?" her dad asked.

"I honestly don't know, but I don't feel right just leaving."

"And you've worked hard to get this job," her dad said.

Lilly felt awful even thinking about herself when Trent was missing, but she said, "Yeah."

"You can always find another job, baby girl. You're damn good at what you do. Look, it hasn't escaped my notice that you've been feeling out of sorts lately."

Lilly snorted. Out of sorts. That seemed like the understatement of the century.

"I see the way you look at your nieces and nephews. You want that for yourself. Kids. A permanent home. Someone to love. And you aren't going to be able to find what you want if you're constantly moving around from location to location on those shoots."

He wasn't wrong. Lilly had come to the same conclusion last Thanksgiving. She'd missed being around her family so much, and it had been so hard to leave on Friday to head back to work instead of spending the entire weekend with everyone. She'd been questioning what she was doing with her life ever since.

"All I'm sayin' is that maybe this is a blessing. Not your friend being missing or your asshole of a boss...but having an excuse to quit. I can hear in your voice how much you love that little town you're in. Not to mention, your young man is there."

"He's not *my* young man," Lilly protested.

"But you want him to be."

She did. Just like she wanted to quit her job. Like she wanted to stay in Fallport. But she had no idea how to make any of that work.

"One day at a time," her dad said, as if he could read her mind. "You don't have to solve all your problems right this second."

"I know."

"Good. Once Trent is found, you can reevaluate. And for the record...you'd kick ass in anything you decided to do. From the time you were a baby, you were always determined to succeed. You started walking way before most babies your age, simply because you wanted to keep up with your brothers."

"Thanks, Daddy."

"Not blowing smoke up your butt, just sayin' it like it is. And always remember, if this Ethan guy doesn't continue to treat you like a princess, you kick him to the curb. Don't settle, baby girl. You deserve a man who sees your worth. And if Ethan is smart, he'll realize how amazing you are and will hang on with both hands."

"Whatever, Dad," Lilly said with a roll of her eyes.

"I might be biased, but I think you're the bestest daughter in the whole world," he said.

"And I think you're the bestest daddy in the whole world," Lilly returned. They'd started telling each other that back when she was in elementary school. She found comfort in the familiar words.

"I love you, baby girl."

"Love you too, Daddy."

"Call me and let me know how things are going. I hope they find Trent soon."

"I will, and me too. Thanks for the pep talk."

"Anytime."

"Talk to you soon."

"Yes, you will. Bye."

"Bye, Dad."

Lilly clicked off the connection and stared up at the leaves over her head with a small smile. Her dad always made her feel better.

"Hey."

Lilly jerked in surprise and nearly fell out of the hammock. She looked toward the house and saw Ethan leaning against a tree not too far away from where she was lying. "Jeez, Ethan, you scared me to death," she said, putting a hand on her chest.

"Sorry," he said, pushing off the tree and coming toward her. "Whit said you were back here, and I didn't want to interrupt your phone call. Everything okay?"

"Yeah." She desperately wanted to talk to him about everything that was going on.

"Heard the others are headed out," he said.

Lilly blinked at him. Then she looked at her watch and shook her head. "Man, Fallport's gossip network is way better than back home. It only took about thirty minutes for word to get around."

Ethan chuckled. "Well, first, people aren't exactly sad to see everyone go. I think the blush of being the focal point of a TV show about Bigfoot has worn off."

"Wait until it airs. They'll really hate it then."

"I know. And secondly, when everyone checked out at the same time, it set off the informational superhighway in town. My phone's been going off nonstop with people informing me the 'TV people' are leaving. I came straight here to try to catch you before you left. But Whitney said you hadn't told her you were checking out...and I don't see you frantically packing."

Lilly sat up and swung her legs over the side of the hammock. "I've been assigned to stay here and film the search for Trent," she told him. "And I wouldn't leave without talking to you."

Ethan nodded. "Glad to hear that, Lil. I admit, a part of me was afraid that this had been one-sided." He gestured between them with his hand as he said that last part.

"It's not," Lilly said softly. Then, because she couldn't stand keeping anything from him, she blurted, "Tucker wants me to secretly record conversations between you and your team about searching for Trent."

"What?" Ethan asked, a furrow forming in his brow.

"He's convinced this episode is going to be epic and a smash in the ratings, because he can't remember a time a main host of a show was hurt or killed before. He wants to make it look like Bigfoot might've carted poor Trent off, and he's planning on milking his disappearance for all its worth. I've been ordered to get as much juicy footage as I can, and he told me if I could get some secret footage or audio of you and your team discussing anything about the search that might be scandalous, it would only make the show that much better."

Lilly knew she was talking too fast, but she couldn't help it. She hated even the thought of deceiving Ethan. And being a part of Tucker's plan, capitalizing on whatever happened to Trent, made her feel slimy and sick inside.

Ethan stepped forward, closing the space between them. He crouched down so he was eye level with her, since she was still sitting in the hammock. He reached out and put a hand on her waist, steadying her as he met her gaze head on.

"I was a little pissed when I heard everyone was leaving. I had it in my head to storm over here and throw a mini tantrum about you not telling me you were headed out. But the second I saw you lying out here, obviously not leaving, I realized how irritational I was being." He heaved a big sigh. "You also have a job to do, and I'd be an asshole to stop you from doing it. Even though Tucker's methods suck, I'm not upset you're staying. Far from it. I'm relieved. Excited. Fucking ecstatic."

"Are you mad?"

"That you were told to record me in secret?"

"Yeah."

"Furious," Ethan said.

Lilly's stomach dropped.

"But not at you. Lil, you didn't even wait three minutes before blurting everything out. I think that bodes well for our relationship."

She liked that he used that word. She *wanted* to be in a relationship with this man. Was thrilled that he seemed to feel the same.

"I love that you're too honest to do that to me."

Despite his words, Lilly felt awful. Because she didn't feel all that honest. Not after standing by and filming the shit she already had without saying anything in protest.

Ethan put his finger under her chin, and she looked up to meet his concerned gaze. "What's going on behind those pretty eyes of yours?" he asked.

"I'm not as honest as you think. This entire episode has been nothing but deception. I already mentioned the return yells and wood knocks were manufactured by crew members. Tucker also got ahold of these huge Bigfoot shoes, and Andre walked all over the place with them so the cast could 'find' them. He even planted some swaths of hair for the cast to find. And don't get me started on how much money Tucker has used to pay people for their 'stories' about whatever paranormal thing we're investigating. From aliens, to the Chupacabra, to Bigfoot. It's all been a bunch of lies. And I've been silent about it all," Lilly told him.

But instead of getting mad, Ethan just shrugged. "It's all harmless fun for TV," he said.

"But Trent is missing! That's not harmless."

"You're right. It's not. It sucks. But you're doing your job."

"I don't like my job much," Lilly told him. "I want to tell Tucker to go fuck himself and quit."

"Then do it."

"It's so messed up that everyone is just leaving and going to the next shoot, as if nothing's wrong. Trent is *missing*. If I quit, I somehow feel as if I'm letting him down. That no one will care about what happened to him. And Tucker will just send someone else here to get the sensational story he's after. At least if it's me... maybe I can film the truth behind his disappearance."

His eyes searched hers, and she couldn't tell what he was thinking. Then he knelt and brought his other hand up to her face. He didn't comment on her job, or try to convince her to stay, as Whitney had. At least not with words. He used his lips to make his argument for him.

And he made a hell of a case.

Lilly lost herself in his touch. In the way his lips moved over hers. In how his tongue made goose bumps break out on her skin. She inhaled his subtle scent—probably from the soap he used, because Ethan wasn't a man to wear cologne—and it reminded her of the day she'd napped in his bed.

He continued to slay her when he finally pulled back. "Thank you for telling me what Tucker wanted you to do. I trust you, Lilly. I want the best for you. And not quitting on the spot, for Trent's sake, says a lot about the person you are. Everything about this case stinks to high heaven. I don't have to be in law enforcement to suspect foul play. If that turns out to be the case, I'd rather not have you running around Canada with Tucker and the others...who knows what else they'll plan in order to get good ratings? You're safer here."

Lilly had thought about that too. "So you think I should do what Tucker wants me to?"

"I think you should stay here in Fallport. Stick close to me. Film my team and I looking for Trent. You'll be doing your job, just without the subterfuge."

"He knows I like you. He actually told me to fuck you to get better footage," she blurted. Lilly decided that Ethan's kisses had short-circuited her brain somehow.

"He's an asshole," he replied. "I'm surprised he hasn't been reported for sexual harassment by now. Once we find Trent, you can tell Tucker to fuck off and quit with a clear conscience, if that's still what you want to do."

Lilly thought about that for a long moment. She still struggled with staying on at all, because it felt so wrong to use Trent's disappearance as a gimmick to gain viewers.

But she *could* placate Tucker and make him believe she was doing exactly what he wanted, while actually being an advocate for Trent...and preventing anyone else on the cast from returning to make the show even more sensationalized.

"For the record...when everything is said and done? I'd like you to stay in Fallport. I know it's a lot to ask, especially considering your job pretty much demands you travel all over. But I've never been drawn to someone like I am to you. If I let you go without at least *attempting* to convince you to stay, I have a feeling I'll be kicking myself for the rest of my life. I don't know that you'd be able to continue doing what you are now if you stayed, but I have a feeling anything you decide to do, you'd excel at."

Lilly couldn't believe what she was hearing. This man was...

Fuck, he was *everything* she'd always wanted in a partner. Someone who would support her no matter what she did.

She threw herself at him, and he caught her with a small *oof*. He lost his balance, falling back onto the grass in the process. Lilly ended up straddling his stomach. His hands had clamped onto her waist to keep her from hurting herself, and she could feel him laughing under her.

"So...you're staying on to keep filming?" he asked.

Lilly nodded. "I'll stay. But I'm not secretly filming anyone."

"Good. Now that we're on the same page...Brock and I are heading out to search again in an hour. You still want to come?"

"I do. Do you have a lead?"

"No. We're just methodically searching all the places we think Trent might've gone. The places it would be conceivable to get to without too much trouble. He might've gotten a recommendation from someone local, about somewhere that was off the beaten path, and gone there."

"Why wouldn't someone have come forward to say that they'd talked to him then?" Lilly asked.

"No clue."

"Hey! You two all right?" Whitney called out from the door to the house.

Ethan chuckled, then tilted his head back and yelled, "Maybe we're just taking a nap!"

"On the ground? Whatever," she said. "Since you're headed out to search again, I've made a snack to tide you over. Come on in and eat before you go!"

"Wanna bet she's got enough dishes to cover the table as her 'snack?'" Lilly said under her breath.

"Not taking that bet," Ethan said, sitting up.

Lilly clutched his arms so she didn't fly off his lap, but she needn't have worried. Ethan kept his firm grip on her waist. She stared into his eyes.

"I'm happy you're staying," he said softly. "Not thrilled with the circumstances, that it's because Trent is missing, but pleased all the same."

"Me too," Lilly said.

He stared at her for another beat before taking a deep breath and moving to get up. He took her hand in his and headed for the house without another word.

"My dad approves of you," Lilly said.

Ethan's lips twitched. "Yeah?"

"Uh-huh. I was talking to him when you arrived. I told him about you."

"Things work out with us...I'm looking forward to meeting him."

"You are? I thought most men were scared to meet a woman's dad."

"Anyone who raised someone as amazing as you isn't someone I'm scared of," Ethan said. "I already respect and admire him. And hope he'll feel the same."

They'd reached the house by that point, and Lilly didn't get a chance to reply before Whitney was ushering them into the kitchen, where she'd laid out a spread of both leftovers and a casserole she'd just "whipped up" at the spur of the moment. But Lilly was thinking there was no doubt her dad would respect and admire Ethan right back.

* * *

He hadn't expected to leave before Trent was found.

But maybe that was for the best.

Lilly was staying, and she'd get the footage the show needed to succeed.

Yeah, it was better that he wasn't there. Wasn't involved in any way. The stupid police chief didn't suspect him, so he was in the clear. All they needed was the final footage of Trent being found and the emotional backlash that would cause.

Trent shouldn't have dismissed him. Should've treated him better. If he had...then maybe he'd still be alive.

They could've worked together to make the show a success, but Trent wanted the fame all to himself. He'd have never shared it. He'd never even admitted how the show came about in the first place.

Never admitted that *everything* had been Joey's idea.

He sat in the back of the van, silently seething. He'd thought he and Trent were friends. But when push came to shove, Trent treated him just as badly as everyone else. Joey and Trent were supposed to be co-hosts of the show they'd created. Instead, Trent hadn't so much as protested when Tucker was brought on board and immediately nixed the idea, instead hiring Michelle for her boobs and the others for their looks.

So what if Joey wasn't drop-dead handsome? Most of the other hosts of similar shows weren't models either. They could've made it work. But Trent had gone along with anything Tucker wanted, reassuring Joey that even if he wasn't one of the faces of the show, he'd still profit from it.

Trent had ensured Joey was hired as one of the camera operators, but as time went on, Joey had seen the writing on the wall. Trent began to treat him differently. Like he wasn't as important. And when Joey made suggestions about the show, Trent had blown him off in front of everyone.

Well, Joey bet he regretted that now.

He kept his face carefully blank, but inside, his anger turned to glee. Trent was right, the show *was* going to be a success.

All because of Joey.

If he hadn't done what he'd done, the show would've failed from the get-go. It was boring and cheesy and unoriginal. But this? A man disappearing and being mauled by Bigfoot? Instant fame for everyone involved.

He'd do what he could to worm his way into Trent's spot in the limelight. Season two was going to be Joey's chance to prove that he had what it took to be a television star.

He wished he could be there when Trent was finally found, but he'd revel in watching the tapes. Patience was key—and Joey had that in spades.

CHAPTER FOURTEEN

The past week had been long. Lilly was happy to spend more time with Ethan, getting to know him better, but her enjoyment was overshadowed by Trent still being missing. She wanted to sink into the joy of her budding relationship with Ethan, but knowing the reason she was still in town was because there'd still been no sign of Trent was disheartening.

She'd been hiking every day with the Eagle Point Search and Rescue team. The men were taking turns going out and looking for any sign of the missing paranormal investigator. The day Lilly followed Raid and Duke was one of the toughest. The bloodhound kept his nose to the ground for the entire five hours they were on the trails, and it felt as if she'd run the whole time.

But no matter how hard they looked or where they searched, no one had any luck. At the end of the week, Ethan and the team had a meeting with the police chief, and they all agreed that either Trent had left the area and camped elsewhere, or he hadn't actually spent a night in the woods at all.

Or someone had packed up his campsite, so as not to leave any trace of the man.

And if discovering where he might've camped had been difficult, finding a person, or body, in the vast Appalachian Mountains without any starting point was almost impossible. There were just too many places to look. Not to mention, the damage scavenging animals could do to a dead body.

But until Trent was found—either in the woods, or safe and sound somewhere—Eagle Point SAR wasn't going to give up.

The only time Lilly felt any kind of contentment was in the evenings. Because she was no longer working nights, they were able to spend them together. They had dinner, watched movies, and simply got to know each other without her job or anything else hanging over them.

Of course, the second Trent was found, dead or alive, she'd be expected to join the rest of the cast and crew. But with every day that passed, they were closer to finishing their filming in Canada and wrapping up the series without her, which didn't exactly upset Lilly. Not when things were going so well between her and Ethan.

Though she had to admit, for the last several days...she'd been a little confused by the mixed messages he was sending.

Ethan never failed to look out for her when they were in the woods searching. He made sure she was eating, taking breaks, didn't have any blisters, and was forever sending her glances that made her feel downright giddy. But at night, after they'd eaten, watched TV, then cuddled and made out on his couch...he would pull away from her, announce that it was getting late, and offer to take her home.

Lilly wanted to insist she didn't have to go home. That she'd prefer to continue kissing and touching him...in his bedroom. But she was too chicken.

It was increasingly obvious that something was bothering him, and she was scared to death it was *her*. That he didn't *want* to make love with her. Had changed his mind about wanting a relationship once she left.

She supposed if that was the case, him stopping things before they got too far was better than Ethan using her for sex, then cheerfully waving goodbye when the time came.

Lilly was an adult. She shouldn't have a problem talking to him about what she wanted. But she was worried he'd decided he just wasn't that into her. Which was ridiculous, considering they'd spent every moment of their spare time with each other for weeks now. If Ethan didn't like her, he wouldn't continue to do that...would he?

She was confused, and she hated it. Relationships had always been hard for her, which sucked. It was more difficult for her to be honest and just talk to guys than it should be.

She vowed that tonight would be the night she'd just flat-out ask Ethan why he didn't seem to want to move their relationship to the next level.

It was telling for Lilly that she was categorizing what they had as a relationship. Things had moved quickly between them, but being with Ethan felt right. More so than with anyone she'd ever dated.

Which was why him going from kissing her with his hand up her shirt, to standing on the other side of the room, putting his shoes on to take her home, was so confusing.

Tonight, she was going to get up the nerve to ask him what was wrong.

But she had the rest of the day to get through first. She'd gotten home from another search with Tal and Brock, showered, sent off the footage to the server for Tucker to review, and Ethan would be arriving to pick her up before too long. Then she was finally going to get to spend time with Elsie and Tony. She'd stopped by On the Rocks to see her earlier in the week, but the place had been packed and the waitress didn't have time to chat.

Today was Tony's birthday, and he was having a birthday party at the Mangree Motel and RV Park's swimming pool. Elsie had invited both her and Ethan, and Lilly was looking forward to it. The motel's pool wasn't very big, and it was in the middle of the parking lot surrounded by concrete and a flimsy fence, but Tony was still excited and looking forward to hanging out with his friends from school.

She was chatting with Whitney in the large living room of the B&B, waiting on Ethan, when they heard the sound of rushing water above their heads.

"What's that?" Whitney asked, looking up at the ceiling in alarm.

But Lilly was already moving. She had a feeling whatever she was hearing, it wasn't good, especially since they were the only two people in the house at the moment. She took the stairs two at a time and headed toward the sound of the water, coming from the bedroom next to the one she was staying in.

She stepped inside the room—and saw a geyser of water spewing from beneath the toilet. Water was pooling in the room and quickly making its way toward the bedroom carpet.

"Oh my goodness!" Whitney exclaimed. "What do we do?" she asked, panic making her voice high-pitched.

Luckily—or unluckily—Lilly had seen the same thing happen at her dad's house. She rushed into the bathroom and quickly turned the knob behind the toilet, stopping the flow of water. "Do you have some old towels?" she asked Whitney. "We can try to soak up some of this water before it gets under the tile."

Without a word, Whitney turned and rushed out of the room.

Moving quickly, Lilly lifted the wet bathroom rug and put it in the tub. She took the soaking toilet paper, which had been on a cute TP holder next to the toilet, and tossed it in the tub as well. Whitney returned by then, and they both worked on soaking up as much water as they could from the floor.

"Where's the water turn-off valve for the house?" Lilly asked after they'd piled all the soaking-wet towels together. She wasn't an expert on flooring, but it looked as if they'd gotten the water taken care of before too much damage had been done.

"Um..." Whitney said blankly.

"It's okay. I'll find it," Lilly assured her, smiling. She didn't want to take apart the toilet to check the rubber seals without making sure she wouldn't inadvertently cause another flood. Typically, turning the water off at the toilet was enough, but again, she didn't want to take a chance.

It took ten minutes to find the master water valve to the house, but once the water was off, Lilly got to work trying to discover the cause of the leak.

The simple job of checking the rubber seals inside the tank turned into her removing the entire toilet and discovering it had shifted on its pedestal, and had been leaking water under the tiles for far longer than just that morning.

She was wiping her brow and making a mental list of what she needed to purchase from the hardware store to fix the toilet—and wondering how she was going to break it to Whitney that the entire floor of the bathroom was likely going to have to be replaced because of the leak—when Ethan appeared in the doorway.

"Um..." he said with a small smile. "What did that toilet ever do to you?" he joked.

Lilly grinned. "We had a small water issue earlier."

"That's what Whitney said. She also told me that you didn't even hesitate to wade in, no pun intended. That you got the water turned off and knew just what to do to get control of the situation."

"Four brothers, remember?" Lilly said with a shrug.

Ethan quickly glanced over his shoulder, then stepped into the bathroom. He crowded her back against the counter. "Is it wrong that seeing you in here, a wrench in your hand, the toilet removed from its pedestal, is a huge turn-on?" he asked.

Lilly rolled her eyes. "Yes," she told him.

"Whatever," he said, lowering his head.

Lilly immediately met him halfway. If Ethan was turned on by her rudimentary plumbing skills, she wasn't going to complain. They made out like teenagers in Whitney's bathroom until they heard her coming down the hall.

Ethan pulled back and studied her with a look Lilly couldn't interpret. She didn't get a chance to ask him what he was thinking before Whitney appeared.

"Oh, my," she said, shaking her head at the state of the room.

"The good news is that we kept the geyser of water from reaching the bedroom carpet," Lilly told her. She was hyper-aware of Ethan's hand on her waist as he stood next to her. "The bad news is that there was a leak coming from where the toilet was attached to the floor. I don't know how long it's been there, but the wood under the toilet, and probably here in the bathroom in general, is waterlogged and rotted. It'll need to be replaced."

"Mold?" Ethan asked.

"I didn't see much, but I'm not an expert," Lilly said.

"I don't know what I would've done if you weren't here," Whitney said. "I would've had to call someone, and that water would've kept on spurting the entire time."

"Whoever you called would've told you about the valve on the back of the toilet," Lilly assured her.

"Still. I'm so glad you were here."

"Rocky can help you fix this up," Ethan told Whitney.

"Thank goodness," she said with a sigh.

"I'll call him on our way to Mangree," Ethan said.

"Oh, I'd forgotten! You guys need to get going!" Whitney exclaimed. "You're going to be late."

"It'll be fine," Ethan soothed. "I'm sure the party will start without us. You know how nine year olds can be."

"We need to turn her water back on before we go," Lilly said, stepping away from Ethan.

"I've got it. You can change while I take care of that."

Lilly looked down at herself and wrinkled her nose. Her jeans were soaked from the knees down from kneeling on the floor and her T-shirt hadn't fared much better. She was kind of scared to look at her hair. It was probably a frizzy mess.

"Will it be okay to turn back on?" Whitney asked in concern.

"It'll be fine," Ethan reassured her. "Lilly's got the water turned off in here. Is this room rented sometime in the next week?"

"I'll have to check," Whitney said. "But I think I can move people around."

"If you need my room, I can figure something out," Lilly offered.

Whitney looked appalled. "If you think I'm gonna kick you out after your help today, you're crazy," she said. "You've been a model guest. I wish everyone who rented a room was like you. No, *I'll* figure it out."

"All right. I'll go get the water sorted. Lilly, I'll meet you down-stairs?" Ethan asked.

"Yeah. I'll be right there."

She headed for her room and managed not to laugh when she saw herself in the mirror. The humidity in the small bathroom and the exertion from taking apart the toilet had made her hair look like she'd just slept on it for fourteen hours straight. She quickly brushed it out, deciding to go ahead and put it up in a messy bun. She was about to stand outside for a few hours; leaving it down hadn't been a good choice in the first place. But she always wore it up, so she'd wanted to look pretty for Ethan.

She changed into another pair of jeans and put on a T-shirt she'd picked up in New Mexico that had a picture of a cow being sucked up into an alien ship. Then she hurried down the stairs. She picked up the box she'd wrapped for Tony the day before and turned to Ethan. "I'm ready."

He was staring at her and smiling.

"What?" she asked when he didn't move toward the door or say anything.

"You're going to continue to surprise me, aren't you?" he asked.

Lilly frowned in confusion. "What do you mean?"

"Is there anything you can't do?"

"Plenty," she said without hesitation. "If you're referring to the toilet, I've helped my dad plenty of times change out a toilet that had a bad seal. My brothers usually ask for my help when they're doing things around their houses too. But if you want me to decorate or make any kind of gourmet meal, you're out of luck."

"Come here," he said gruffly, pulling her into him.

He hugged her tightly and Lilly hung on, inhaling deeply, loving how Ethan smelled.

They were still standing like that when Whitney appeared in the doorway. "Enough of that canoodling," she scolded. "You're already late."

Lilly and Ethan shared a look and a smile at the word canoodling, but obediently stepped away from each other.

"Will you be back for dinner?" she asked.

Lilly glanced at Ethan for confirmation.

He reached for the present and shook his head. "I don't think so, Whit. I'm sure we'll have cake and stuff at the party and then we'll head back to my place. I've got some steaks I picked up earlier that I thought I'd grill up."

"All right. I'll see you in the morning then. Will you let me know what Rocky says?"

"Of course," Ethan said. "But I'm sure he'll be here tomorrow to see what the damage is and what supplies he needs. He'll get you fixed right up."

"I appreciate it."

"Of course. You ready?" Ethan asked, turning to Lilly.

She nodded, then Ethan took her hand and led her out the door.

* * *

Three hours later, Ethan watched from a chair next to the Mangree Motel and RV Park's small outdoor pool as eight little boys shrieked and screamed, trying to see who could make the biggest splash.

The water in the pool was freezing, but that didn't seem to

matter to Tony and his friends. What made Ethan smile, however, was Lilly. Elsie had been flustered and almost overwhelmed when they'd arrived, and Lilly had immediately taken charge. She was so good with the kids. She'd told him on the way to the party that she loved hanging out with her nieces and nephews, and it was obvious she had experience coming up with ways to entertain them.

Tony had introduced her to his friends as the lady who'd taught him to change a tire, and when they didn't believe he could actually do it, Lilly had somehow convinced Ethan to let him take a tire off his car and put it back on...with her supervision, of course.

Then Tony had opened presents, they'd all eaten cake and ice cream, and it had been Lilly's idea to have the cannonball contest. She'd even managed some time to chat with Elsie and a few other moms who'd stuck around. Elsie had taken a few pictures throughout the party, but somehow Lilly had ended up with the camera, and she was now capturing every second of the fun and games of the afternoon.

It didn't escape Ethan's attention that she made sure to get plenty of shots of Elsie with her son, which the single mother would surely treasure later. It was hard to get pictures of yourself with your kid when you were the one always taking the photos.

"She looks like she's fitting in just fine," Rocky said. Ethan's twin had shown up to talk about the repairs he was going to do at Whitney's place, and had ended up staying.

"Yeah," Ethan agreed.

"Heard from Simon today," Rocky said.

Ethan forced his attention from Lilly and the laughter coming from the other end of the pool, where the boys were still trying to outdo each other. "Yeah?"

"Yup. He went out to talk to Clyde this morning. As you know, his moonshine still is fairly close to that first trail we checked out."

"And?" Ethan asked when his brother didn't immediately continue.

"And Clyde said he 'didn't know nothin' 'bout no missin' man.'

That's a direct quote, by the way. Mom would kill me if I used a double negative. Anyway, when Simon was leaving, he saw a bunch of stuff sticking out of a dumpster Clyde has on the property. When he looked closer, it was a tent, sleeping bag, and a cooler."

Ethan stared at Rocky in dismay. "Seriously?"

"Uh-huh. He's getting a search warrant now, but it looks like it's our missing guy's stuff."

"What the fuck? Why did Clyde have it?"

"He told Simon something about the guy making all kinds of racket in the woods, and how pissed off Clyde was about it. He swears he didn't do anything to Trent. When he heard Trent was missing, he went and checked where the noises had been coming from two nights before and found the campsite. Picked everything up because he didn't want anyone nosing around too close to his operation."

"Dammit," Ethan swore.

"Yeah. Any chance Duke might've had to pick up a scent is long gone by now."

"Not to mention, any forensic evidence that Simon and his people might've found in the campsite has been contaminated."

"They're going to pull the tent and the other stuff and see what they can get, but yeah, the chance is low that there will be anything useful."

"You think Clyde killed him?" Ethan asked his brother.

Rocky shrugged. "It's possible. If he was annoyed enough while Trent was out there, maybe. And Clyde is a paranoid son-of-a-bitch. Everyone knows he has stills out there in the woods, so that's not a secret. But he likes to think he's flying under the radar, and doesn't want anyone to spy on him and find out his secret recipe for that rotgut shit he brews."

"So we go back to Fallport Creek Trail tomorrow and start looking again?" Ethan asked.

"I'm guessing that's probably our best bet," Rocky agreed.

"Damn. We've wasted weeks looking in the wrong place."

"Maybe. Maybe not. Trent could've decided to go somewhere else to look for Bigfoot."

"Possible, since no one has found his rental car," Ethan replied.

"You want to know what I think?" Rocky asked.

"You know I do."

"Someone from the show's involved. Trent Morrison didn't disappear into thin air. I think one of the cast or crew knows exactly what happened but isn't talking."

Ethan nodded, having already expressed the same thought to Lilly. He looked over at her as she burst out laughing. She was so full of life, so trusting. He didn't like the thought of anyone near her being involved in whatever the hell was going on.

"Be careful, bro," Rocky said quietly.

Ethan turned his attention back to his brother. "You warning me away from her?"

"Fuck no. I think she's probably the best thing that's happened to you in ages. You've seemed more...energized...than I've seen you in a long time. But I have a feeling that when Trent is found, the shit's gonna hit the fan. And if someone on that show is involved, things could get ugly for your girl."

Ethan couldn't help but look back over at Lilly. "That's not good," he said, suddenly even more concerned for her safety.

"Nope. But you know we'll all have her back. All we have to do is spread the word to watch for anything out of the ordinary and the gossip network will mobilize. She won't be able to sneeze without it being reported."

Ethan nodded. He hated being the focus of the town's attention, and had a feeling Lilly would too, but in this case, if someone she knew had a hand in whatever had happened to Trent, he wouldn't complain about it.

"Come on, you two, we need more judges!" Lilly yelled over at them.

"Duty calls," Rocky said with a grin.

"Thanks for the head's up," Ethan said.

"Of course. You gonna tell Lilly that Trent's camping gear has been found?"

"Yeah. Later. Her boss is gonna be pissed if she doesn't get that shit on film for his fucking show."

"Not sure Simon is gonna approve that."

"Nope," Ethan said as he stood.

"I bet if you asked, he'd let her get some footage of the tent and stuff after it's been recovered," Rocky suggested.

"Fucking hate Hollywood," Ethan mumbled.

"You and me both, brother," Rocky agreed.

They headed over to where the kids were playing, and Ethan spent the next half hour watching the boys splash into the pool and doing his best to praise every kid...all the while keeping his eye on Lilly, who he'd never seen smile so much as she did as she took picture after picture.

Lilly snuggled against Ethan later that night. She was stuffed from the delicious dinner he'd prepared and still riding high after the fun afternoon. Elsie had been welcoming, as had the other mothers. Zeke had even shown up toward the end of the party—and she hadn't missed the looks he and Elsie shot at each other when they thought the other wasn't looking. There was something between those two, and she hoped one of them made the first move toward a relationship that was more than just boss and employee.

For the first time in years, Lilly felt as if she belonged somewhere. She had new friends, and having a camera in her hands, taking pictures of Tony and his buds, had been a blast. It had been a very long time since looking through a viewfinder had been anything more than a job.

She wanted to top off the first truly relaxing day since Trent's disappearance by progressing her physical relationship with Ethan... but he'd seemed tense all evening.

"You okay?" she asked.

He sighed—and Lilly braced.

"I need to tell you something I learned from Rocky today."

Lilly sat up straighter, but Ethan kept his arm around her waist. "What's wrong?"

"Simon found Trent's tent and other camping stuff."

"What?" she gasped. "Where?"

"There's a local guy, his name is Clyde Thomas. He makes moonshine. Prides himself on having some of the best hooch in the area. He's also paranoid and grumpy as shit. He's lived here in Fallport his entire life. Never been married. Lives by himself in a ramshackle trailer on the outskirts of town. Apparently, Trent was camping near one of the stills Clyde has hidden in the woods. It pissed him off and worried him, probably thinking maybe Trent would find his stash. When Trent went missing, Clyde found the campsite and took Trent's stuff. Threw it away on his property."

"Oh my God. Does he know where Trent is? Did he hurt him?" Lilly asked.

"The police chief is still working on finding that out."

"Where was he camping?" she asked.

"You know that trail we searched the first day?" Ethan asked.

Lilly nodded. "The Fallport Creek Trail."

"Yup. Trent set up his campsite about two miles down the way we'd searched. Off the trail about a hundred feet."

"So you would've found it that first day if this Clyde guy hadn't taken all the stuff," Lilly concluded.

"Possibly," Ethan said, nodding.

Lilly leaned against Ethan, her mind spinning.

"You okay?" he asked gently.

"I just can't believe that guy didn't say anything. It's not as if it's been a secret that Trent's missing, or that you and your team have been looking for him or his campsite."

"You heard me say he's paranoid, right?" Ethan asked.

"Yes. But still," Lilly said. Then she looked back up at him. "Now what?"

"Now we go back to where he was camping and expand our search from there."

Lilly nodded. She supposed if she really wanted to do as Tucker had ordered, she'd be trying to figure out how to get footage of the tent and stuff from Trent's campsite. Or seeing if she could interview the moonshiner guy. But since she cared more about finding Trent, she wasn't even going to ask Ethan about the possibility of talking to Clyde.

They sat in silence, each lost in their own thoughts, until she yawned, the day finally catching up with her.

"You're tired," Ethan said. It wasn't a question. He stood, and Lilly mentally sighed. She'd hoped to talk to him tonight. Wanted to sleep in his arms, in his bed. But it looked like that wasn't going to happen.

She let him pull her upright and felt a little better when he wrapped his arms around her. "We're going to find him," he said softly into her hair.

Lilly nodded. Guilt once more hit her. She wanted to find Trent, she did. But finding him meant her time here in Fallport would come to an end. Unless she was ready to make some major changes in her life, which was really scary, especially when she couldn't figure out what it was Ethan wanted, and when she was too chicken to freaking ask him.

The bed and breakfast was quiet when she let herself in. Ethan had walked her to the door tonight and kissed her with so much passion, Lilly was panting by the time he pulled back and abruptly turned to head back to his car. She'd felt his erection against her belly, and once again, confusion swamped her.

Men. They were so confounding sometimes.

Straightening her shoulders, Lilly headed up the stairs to her room. Tomorrow, she'd have to deal with Tucker, letting him know about Trent's camping equipment being found. Ethan and his teammates would be eager to head into the forest to search again, now that they had confirmation of where Trent had been, at least that first night. And she wanted to look at the pictures she'd taken today at the party and edit some of the better ones for Elsie and the other moms.

She needed some rest...but no matter how much she tried to put Ethan out of her mind, she couldn't do it. Lying in bed, in the dark, she couldn't help but close her eyes and snake a hand between her legs. She was horny. Being with Ethan, but not being *with* him, was getting more difficult every day. But she had a feeling he'd be worth the wait.

CHAPTER FIFTEEN

The days were going by quickly for Ethan. It had been a week since Lilly had calmly fixed the "exploding toilet," as she was calling it. A week since they'd found out where Trent had been camping.

In the morning, he either worked with Rocky or did odd jobs around town for people who needed electrical work. In the afternoons, the team continued their search for any sign of the still-missing Trent. He took turns searching with his teammates but they were honestly at an impasse. They knew where his campsite had been, at least initially, but they hadn't been able to find any sign of where he might have gone from there. The man had literally disappeared, leaving no trace behind, and it was as baffling as it was frustrating.

Ethan was beginning to think Trent really *had* left the area and was probably fat and happy somewhere, sipping a martini. He remembered Rocky's suspicion about someone from the show being involved—an idea that had already occurred to Ethan—and wondered once again if Trent had planned the entire thing with Tucker for ratings.

The producer had been livid that Lilly wasn't able to get any footage of the tent and other camping stuff in Clyde's dumpster. He'd been even more irritated that she hadn't interviewed the moonshiner. That part was Ethan's fault. When she'd told him what her boss wanted her to do, he'd put his foot down. Clyde wouldn't take kindly to her sashaying up to his door, and he'd like it even less if he ended up on a fucking TV show.

While the search for Trent was frustrating as hell, Ethan's relationship with Lilly was going well. He was impressed with her stamina, how she had no problem keeping up with him and his teammates as they searched the forest surrounding Fallport. They'd gone up and down canyons, and she followed along without any issue whatsoever.

Ever since she'd changed Elsie's tire on the side of the road, Lilly had become popular with the locals. When word got out about the pictures she'd taken at Tony's party, and edited for free, the few who *hadn't* come around had finally thawed. It probably helped that Rocky and the rest of the guys never hesitated to sing her praises.

She and Ethan continued their routine of going back to his apartment and spending the evening together. She'd upload any footage she'd taken each day to the server—with Tucker calling every other day or so to get updates on the search—then they'd spend the evening talking, cuddling, kissing.

Ethan was thrilled with the way his relationship with Lilly was progressing—save for one part.

He wanted to invite her to stay the night, had been on the verge of doing just that several times...but he always chickened out.

It wasn't that he didn't want her in his bed again. He did. More than he could remember wanting almost anything. Her scent had stayed on his sheets for days after she'd napped there. Just the thought of holding her all night, making love to her, had him hard in seconds.

But he was scared.

Him. A fucking former Navy SEAL. A man who had no problem

heading out into the wilderness at night, by himself, with nothing more than an old compass to show him the way, was scared.

Lately, his nightmares had gotten worse. He'd go to sleep feeling relaxed and happy, and wake up covered in sweat, choking the shit out of one of his pillows. He'd *literally* be on his knees with the damn pillow under him, his knuckles white with the amount of pressure he was using to squeeze the stuffing.

The dream was always the same. The baby was screaming. Ethan could somehow read the infant's mind. The girl knew she was about to die, and she was terrified. He'd look around in the dream and see a man, her father, standing in the room with a smirk on his face. He actually had no idea who the child's father was, but in his nightmare, he just knew.

Ethan would rush the man, always managing to catch him before he could flee. He'd tackle him and wrap his hands around his throat, doing his best to kill him before he could set off the explosives with a remote. But every time, the man was able to push a giant red button on the device in his hand, setting off the bomb.

Ethan would wake up as he was flying through the air, his hands still locked around the terrorist's throat.

With the baby's cries still echoing in his head.

It had been years since the incident. He'd talked to therapists, had thought the nightmares were gone for good. But shortly after meeting Lilly, they'd started again.

That hadn't happened with any other woman he'd dated...not that there'd been many. And in his latest nightmares, it wasn't just his fellow SEALs in the house, about to be blown up—Lilly was there too. Standing in a corner, a camera on her shoulder, filming the whole thing. He knew without a doubt that if he didn't stop the man from setting off the explosion, not only would his friends get hurt or killed, along with the innocent baby, but Lilly would die as well.

The nightmares were bad enough. But his *worst* fear was that he'd fall asleep with Lilly in his arms...and wake up with her throat in his hands, instead of a pillow.

So every night, he drove her back to the B&B, waiting until she was inside safe and sound before driving back to his apartment and going to sleep alone.

He knew he was hurting Lilly with his refusal to ask her to stay. She was confused, and he couldn't blame her. They'd make out on his couch, and just when things were getting almost to the point of no return, he'd offer her a drink or something to eat, or he'd get up to use the bathroom. Not long after that, not trusting himself to stop things before they went too far, he'd tell her it was getting late and use the next day's search as an excuse for them both to get some sleep.

He hated acting so wishy-washy and wanted to explain his fears to her, but something always stopped him.

Even now, in his apartment again, with Lilly waiting for him to sit down and cuddle with her after another dinner together, he was hesitating. He *desperately* wanted her to stay, but he was scared of what would happen if she did.

"We need to talk," Lilly said—and Ethan's heart nearly stopped. Those words were never good. The very last thing in the world he wanted to hear was that things between them weren't working out. Honestly, he wouldn't blame her if that was what she said. He was keeping her at a distance, and he hated it.

He'd been puttering around in the kitchen like a dick to avoid sitting on the couch. He knew he wouldn't be able to stop himself from reaching for her. And one thing would lead to another...and he'd have to take her home to keep from going too far, from asking her to stay. But he didn't want to take her home yet. He liked having her there. She was funny, smart, and they never ran out of things to talk about.

So, he was hiding in his kitchen like a fucking chump.

Taking a deep breath, he carried the bowl of popcorn he'd been fussing over into the small living area and put it on the coffee table someone had given him when he'd first moved to town. Taking a deep breath, he turned to look at Lilly.

He was relieved she didn't look angry. Just concerned.

"What's going on?" she asked.

"What do you mean?"

Her face fell at his question. As if she was disappointed in him. Hell, Ethan was disappointed in himself. This wasn't like him. He didn't like it when people played games, and he was doing just that right now.

"Talk to me, Ethan. Am I cramping your style? Are you sick of me hanging around? I mean, I wouldn't blame you, we've spent just about every minute with each other for the last few weeks. I can probably back off on going with you for every search. It's not like Tucker doesn't have a million hours of your back walking through the woods already."

"No!" Ethan almost shouted. "It's not that."

"Then what? You want to be just friends? I've noticed that you don't really get tense until we're back here in the evenings. If that's the case, just tell me. I don't want to force you to kiss me if your feelings have changed."

Ethan quickly shook his head, appalled that she thought that. But what else could she think? Just when things got heated between them, he was the one to stop. "I want you," he blurted almost desperately.

Lilly stared at him.

"I just don't want to hurt you."

She blew out a breath. "If that's your precursor to saying something like 'it's not you, it's me,' I don't want to hear it," she said. Ethan could hear the irritation in her tone, and the hurt.

"It's not!" he exclaimed. "Shit." He ran his hand through his hair and took a deep breath. "Lately...I've been struggling with my PTSD."

Her irritation immediately morphed into concern. It made him want her all the more. "What can I do to help?"

He shook his head. It was such a Lilly response. "Be patient with me," he replied. "As I said, I want you. There's *nothing* I want more than to take you to my bedroom and get you under me."

"But?" she asked.

"I'm having nightmares," he admitted. "I wake up with my fingers wrapped around my pillow, choking the shit out of it, because I think it's a man in my dreams who's about to blow up the bomb that hurt and killed my squad."

Lilly nodded slowly. "And you're scared you'll hurt me."

"Yes," Ethan said, relieved he didn't have to explain that part.

"What brought them on?" she asked with a tilt of her head.

"What?"

"Why now? I'm assuming you were doing all right before. So why have the dreams started, do you think?"

"I don't know." Then, he shook his head. "No, that's a lie. It's you."

She looked stricken. "Me?"

Ethan reached for her hand, not letting her pull away. "I didn't mean that like you took it. I mean...you're *there*, Lilly. In my nightmare. Standing in a corner with your camera on your shoulder. I'm desperate to stop the man from hitting the button on the detonator, not because it would hurt me or my friends, or even that baby. But because *you're* there. I care about you. Fuck, Lilly, you've slipped under my skin so easily, it's as if you were meant to be mine. But I don't want to hurt you. I would sooner cut off my own arm than do anything to harm you. And if I invite you to stay, and I have that dream, I could do just that. If I woke up with your neck in my hands, I wouldn't be able to handle it."

He appreciated that she didn't immediately say something like "you won't." Because she couldn't guarantee that, and as much as he didn't like it, he couldn't either.

"So, I'll ask again. What can I do to help you get through this? Have you talked about it with any of your friends? I'm sure they'd probably understand. Your brother especially."

"No. But I'm thinking I need to."

Lilly nodded. He didn't think she realized that her fingers were lightly stroking his arm. It was soothing, and he loved that she wanted that connection with him even if they were talking about a tough topic.

"I can't understand what you're going through, but I'm here for you, Ethan. I hate that you're struggling, but I admire you so much."

"Admire me?" he asked skeptically. "Because I wake up trying to murder someone from my dreams?"

"Yes. The alternative is that you aren't affected at all by what happened. That you don't care about your friends getting hurt or that baby dying. That you see me in your dreams and it doesn't matter that I'm going to get caught in the crossfire of that explosion.

"You're an amazing man, Ethan. I'll tell you that as many times as you need me to in order to start believing it. You aren't perfect. You make mistakes. You fail at stuff. I don't know what, but I'm sure there are things you aren't good at." She smiled, letting him know she was teasing. "And for the record, I want you too. I don't sleep around. Never have, never will. I like to feel a connection with someone before I get intimate with them. I think I felt that connection with you from the first day we met. It's weird, and it makes me somewhat uncomfortable, but as my dad tells me, life is too short to have regrets."

She took a deep breath as if bracing herself, then said, "I understand now why you've shuttled me out just when things are getting good. And I get why you don't want me to sleep in your bed...but we could still make love without me staying overnight. Just sayin'." She smiled shyly at him.

Ethan stared at her. He didn't deserve this woman. He didn't. "I don't ever want you to think I'm using you for sex," he said. "And kicking you out after we make love just feels abhorrent."

"So how about if you *don't* kick me out?" she asked. "Now that I understand where you're coming from, it wouldn't be a shock if you got up and slept somewhere else. Or I can sleep on the couch. I'm not saying that if we continue to see each other, I'll always want to leave your bed afterward, but I have faith that you'll overcome this. That you'll trust yourself as much as I trust you."

Ethan couldn't stop himself from reaching for her. He slid his fingers into her hair and held on as he leaned close. He rested his forehead against hers and did his best to get control over his emotions. "You'd do that for me? Let me love you, then give me the space I need so I don't hurt you?"

"I think I'd do just about anything for you, Ethan," Lilly said simply.

"Tonight? Now?" he asked, knowing he sounded way too eager, but he couldn't get the vision of a naked Lilly out of his head.

"Yes. Absolutely yes."

Ethan hadn't expected this. He'd wanted the first time they made love to be romantic and the night to be perfect. But there was no way he could turn down such a generous offer. Not when he'd thought about little else for weeks.

His free hand slid up and under the back of her shirt, flattening against her spine. She arched toward him and grabbed hold of his biceps as his lips took hers. He kissed her as if this was the last time he'd ever touch her. Poured all the love and relief he felt into the kiss. Relief that she hadn't told him he was being silly, or rejected him outright.

There weren't many women like Lilly out there, and he knew it. Ethan wasn't going to let her go without a fight. He even suspected that if she wanted to live somewhere else, he'd go without a second thought. He'd never wanted to leave Fallport and Eagle Point Search and Rescue, but at that moment, his devotion to this woman went deeper than his job.

But maybe he felt that way because he knew without a doubt, Lilly would never ask him to make that sacrifice. He wasn't a fortune teller, but he had a flash of the two of them standing near

The Circle downtown, watching a parade, holding hands as they waved at their two kids who were on a float going by. It was fanciful and Lifetime Movie-ish, but he didn't care.

"What's that grin for?" she asked.

Ethan hadn't realized he'd pulled back and was smiling at her like a lunatic. "I'm just happy," he told her. "And relieved that you're giving me a second chance. I was a dick, I'm sorry. I should've talked to you about what was going on in my head. I can't imagine what you thought when I hustled you out of here every night."

"I was thinking that something was wrong and that you'd tell me when you could," Lilly said. "You're not a man who plays games, so the thought that you were suddenly using me for some reason never crossed my mind."

That was it. Ethan needed her naked. Now.

He stood, grabbing her hand as he did and practically dragging her down the hall.

Lilly giggled behind him, and Ethan memorized the sound. It was sweet and sexy and happy, and he wanted to hear it every day for the rest of his life.

That should've scared him, but then again, he'd just envisioned them watching their two nonexistent children in Fallport's Fourth of July parade.

He stopped by his bed, mentally cringing that he hadn't made it that morning, but since she wasn't looking at his sheets in disgust, just staring as if she wanted to devour him, he put it out of his mind.

Then, as if they'd discussed it ahead of time, they both reached for their shirts. She got hers off first and reached behind her for the clasp of her bra.

Ethan couldn't keep his hands to himself, he palmed her tits when they were exposed by the bra falling to the floor.

Lilly hummed and arched her back, pressing herself into him. "They aren't huge," she said in an apologetic tone.

"You're perfect," Ethan said, not wanting her to disparage

herself in any way. Her tits weren't large, but they were propor-tioned to her tall frame. Her nipples were long, and as he stroked her, they began to harden, which in turn made his cock do the same.

He already knew this first time wasn't going to last as long as he wanted. It had been too long since he'd been inside a woman, and this was Lilly. The woman he'd wanted since the first moment he saw her. A woman he respected and admired. He *needed* to be inside her.

But before he could do that, he had to make sure she could easily take him. He gestured to the bed and she immediately climbed onto his mattress.

"Pants. Off." He was having trouble stringing a complete sentence together, but she didn't seem to care. She shucked her pants, underwear, and socks, and lay on his bed completely naked, wearing nothing but the smile on her face.

Ethan quickly kicked off the rest of his own clothes and joined her. The moment his skin touched hers, he inhaled deeply, reaching for his cock to squeeze the base. Hard. He was two seconds from exploding all over her belly, and he hadn't done more than feel her softness against his hardness.

Lilly giggled again.

Ethan smiled and reached between her legs.

Her laughter ended abruptly as she gasped at the first touch of his fingers to her folds.

"God, Lilly...you're already wet."

"I've pretty much been that way for weeks," she admitted.

Feeling humbled by this woman, and wanting to make their first time together memorable, he found her clit and brushed it lightly. She jumped in his arms.

"Sensitive," he murmured.

"Yeah."

"This is gonna be fun," he said with a smile, then got to work seeing if he could get his woman off with his fingers.

Ethan wasn't even freaked out at the "his woman" thought. As far as he was concerned, she *was* his. She fit him perfectly. Both physically and into his lifestyle. She liked Fallport, and the residents liked her back. She loved being out in the forest and didn't even bat an eyelash when he spent time with his brother or friends. Not like that had happened much lately. Ethan had spent as much of his spare time with Lilly as he could manage.

"Ethan!" she exclaimed, opening her legs wider and arching her back. He continued to stroke her clit, using his other hand to play with her folds. He entered her soaking-wet body with a finger and groaned as her muscles immediately clamped down on the digit.

"More," she whispered. "Faster."

Ethan didn't hesitate to obey her demands. He added another finger inside her as well, fucking her with them as he rubbed her clit harder and faster. She was riding his fingers within seconds, her eyes closed, fingers of one hand digging into his arm as the other gripped the sheet beneath her.

She was so damn beautiful. Ethan couldn't take his eyes off her. Her tits quivered and shook as she fucked his hand, and he loved the bloom of red that formed on her chest as she got closer to the edge.

Her thighs began to tremble, alerting him to her impending orgasm.

"That's it, Lil. Come for me."

She let out an adorable high-pitched grunt before she curled upward. Her thighs closed on the hand between her legs and she shook all over.

Nothing affected him as much as this woman's pleasure. His hand was soaked and he was so hard it hurt, but he couldn't move as Lilly continued to quake under him. When she finally lay back and looked up at him, demanding, "*Now*. I need you inside me," Ethan couldn't do anything but obey.

He removed his fingers from her wet sheath and brought them to his mouth. He licked them clean, moaning at her musky taste, even as he climbed over her, his cock in his other hand. He was about to sink into her when he forced himself to stop. He closed his eyes and clenched his teeth, fighting for control.

"Ethan?" she asked.

He felt her hands rubbing up and down his thighs, and a burst of precome leaked out of the tip of his cock.

"I don't have a condom," he muttered between clenched teeth. "I mean, I *do*. They're in the bathroom. Give me a second and—"

"I'm on the pill," she said, interrupting him.

Ethan's eyes popped open and he stared down at the woman beneath him. She was completely relaxed, didn't look upset or perturbed in the least.

"What?"

"I'm on the pill," she repeated. "My dad took me to the doctor when I was sixteen, and I've been on it ever since. I was so embarrassed, and so was he, but he didn't want me to get pregnant as a teen. He wanted me to get a degree and find myself before becoming a parent." She grinned. "I wasn't even having sex yet, but *he* didn't know that. Sorry—that's too much info for right this second. But I'm covered. And it's been a long time since I've had sex. I'm clean."

"I am too," Ethan said. "It's been over a year since I've been with anyone."

"I trust you," she said. "But I understand if you don't trust me. Women trick men all the time into getting pregnant, but I'd never do that to you. I'm not going anywhere if you want to get..."

Her voice trailed off as Ethan notched the tip of his cock between her legs and sank inside in one slow thrust.

CHAPTER SIXTEEN

Lilly inhaled sharply at the feel of Ethan filling her up, doing her best to stay relaxed. He was big, and it really *had* been a long time since she'd had anyone inside her.

When he was buried to the hilt, his balls pressed up against her ass, he leaned down and caged her with his arms. Staring into her eyes, he said, "I trust you."

His words shot straight to her heart. Lilly swallowed hard and nodded. She couldn't speak because her throat was clogged with tears she refused to shed. This wasn't a time to cry. Not when Ethan was inside her. Not after he'd just given her the most intense orgasm she'd had in ages, and he'd yet to fuck her properly.

His hips moved back, and she moaned at the loss of him inside her. But he immediately sank back inside her, making Lilly arch her back at the delicious friction. She'd never felt as full as she was right now. When he bottomed out, he brushed against her still extremely sensitive clit, and she shivered.

He grinned. "Like that?"

"Duh," she whispered.

His smile widened, and he moved his hips again. He fucked her so slowly. In and out. Never losing eye contact as he made love to her.

Lilly wouldn't ever forget this moment. She felt as if she'd been floundering through life, and being with Ethan, suddenly everything made sense. She put her feet flat against the mattress and the next time he eased inside her, she pushed her hips up to meet him. Their skin slapped together, sounding loud in the otherwise quiet room.

"Hold still," Ethan ordered.

"No," Lilly said with a shake of her head. "Go faster."

"I want this to last," he said.

"And I want to see you lose control," she countered.

"I don't want to hurt you."

"You won't."

"Seriously, Lil. You feel so good. You're soaking wet. Almost scalding my cock, and you're so damn—*God*, yeah...squeeze me just like that," he said on a groan as she tightened her inner muscles.

Lilly couldn't help but grin. Ethan might be on top, but she was in control.

Then, any thought that she was running the show flew out the window when Ethan pulled back once more and slammed inside her. *Hard.*

"Oh my God! Yes," she moaned. "Do that again."

He did. And it felt just as good the second time. He put a hand under her ass, tilting her pelvis up, and did it again. This time he rubbed against her clit in such a way that it made her twitch in pleasure.

Lilly did her best to meet his thrusts, but soon all she could do was lay there and take what he was giving her. And what he was giving her was the best sex she'd had in her life. It felt as if her entire body was tingling. Her tits shook, along with the mattress, with every one of Ethan's thrusts. He was sweating, his flesh slickly gliding over her own, which might've grossed her out if it was anyone but him.

Throughout it all, his gaze never left hers. It was intense. Almost *too* intense.

Lilly closed her eyes, needing a reprieve.

"No. Don't look away. Open your eyes, Lil."

She did, and swallowed hard at the passion she saw in his gaze.

"Never. Felt. This. Before," he said in time with his thrusts. "Not. Letting. You. Go."

"Good," Lilly breathed.

She watched as Ethan's orgasm overcame him. His jaw was tight and the veins in his neck were standing out as he pushed inside her once more and groaned.

Lilly tightened her legs around him and brought a hand to his face. She held on to him as he spilled himself inside of her, filling her to the brim.

But if she thought they were done, she was mistaken. He didn't pull out, merely shifted his weight to one arm and moved the other hand down their bodies. He gathered some of her wetness and his come from where they were joined and began to stroke her clit once more.

"Ethan!" she cried.

"Come on my cock," he growled.

Lilly was still extremely sensitive from her earlier orgasm, but couldn't seem to utter any words of complaint. Her legs flew open and she tried to thrust against him, but his body held her still. Her hips continued to undulate as best they could under him as she quickly flew toward a second orgasm.

"That's it, Lil. Let me feel it this time."

This orgasm felt different since he was still inside her, filling her up even though he was only half hard. She cried out and came as he continued to stroke her.

"Fuck, that's incredible," Ethan groaned, but Lilly was too far gone to reply. It was as if her brain had shrunk and all she could do was feel. Her nipples were tight and felt extra sensitive as they brushed against Ethan's chest when he lowered himself over her.

Sighing in relief when the intense feelings tapered, Lilly opened her eyes. Ethan was staring at her once more, his face mere inches from her own. She was breathing as if she'd just run a half marathon, and all she wanted to do was burrow into his skin.

As if he could read her mind, Ethan lowered himself even more, keeping some of his weight off of her while still pressing her lightly into the mattress. He buried his nose into the space between her shoulder and neck, and they lay like that for a long moment.

She loved feeling him from shoulders to thighs. Even having him still inside her felt right. Lilly kicked herself for not talking to him earlier. They could've been doing this for the last week.

Now that she was coming down from her sexual high, she couldn't help but think about what he'd told her earlier. She hated that Ethan was having nightmares. Hated even more that she was a part of them. She didn't know how to help him, and that sucked.

She caressed his hair, his back, even his ass. It wasn't until his cock finally slipped out of her body that he lifted his head. "Fucking hate that part," he muttered.

Lilly couldn't help but grin.

"Stay put," he ordered as he pushed himself up and off her.

Lilly wanted to protest, but since she was ogling his naked body, she didn't complain as he walked toward his bathroom. He was back a moment later with a washcloth.

"That had better be warm," she warned as he came toward her.

"Would I dare touch you with a cold washcloth?" he asked with a grin.

"Not if you ever want to get inside me again."

He didn't respond with words, but pressed the thankfully warm cloth between her legs. For some reason, this didn't feel weird, though she'd never had anyone tend to her like this before. Ever. She felt so comfortable with Ethan, all she could do was lay there and smile up at him. It helped that he seemed perfectly content being naked with her. And the tender look on his face reassured her that he liked what he was doing.

His free hand rested on her cheek, and he leaned down and kissed her. It was long, slow, and sweet, and before he pulled back, Lilly was squirming under him. His hand continued to move, cleaning his come from between her legs, and each time the cloth brushed against her clit, desire bloomed once more.

Before she could anticipate his next move, Ethan had scooted down between her legs and was spreading them wide.

"Ethan?" she asked, coming up on her elbows.

"Shhhh. My girl needs more."

Shocked by how horny she still felt, Lilly fell back with a sigh. He wasn't wrong. She'd never been this turned on before. She couldn't get enough of this man.

Luckily, he didn't tease her. His mouth immediately closed over her clit, and Lilly moaned at how good his tongue felt against the extremely sensitive bundle of nerves.

He licked, sucked, and used his fingers to bring her to the brink once more. Lilly was going to be sore tomorrow, but she didn't care. Not when Ethan's attentions felt as good as they did.

* * *

Ethan kicked himself for not sucking it up and talking to Lilly before tonight. He should've known she'd be understanding. He'd fucked up. He could've had her under him just like this for the last week. Maybe longer. Instead, he'd been too scared.

Lilly was as sensual as anyone he'd ever known. She'd already come twice, and when he'd cleaned her, it was obvious she needed more. He wasn't ready to fuck again, but he had no problem taking care of her. It was his pleasure. And honor.

The sheets under her ass were soaked with her pleasure, and his, and he couldn't get enough. He loved how slick she got, how she undulated under him, chasing her own pleasure. He put one hand on her belly to try to keep her still and used the other to slowly finger fuck her. His fingers made squelching sounds as they entered and retreated from her body, and he'd never heard anything so carnal in his life.

He latched onto her clit with his mouth and did his best to throw her over the edge once more. She bucked under him, and it was all he could do to keep his lips on her. But then she froze, and he knew she was seconds away from exploding. He sucked harder, smiling when she whimpered and began to shake.

He lifted his head to watch as she orgasmed once more. Fuck, she was gorgeous.

Another rush of her juices coated his fingers, and he smiled. All he could smell was her. Them. He wanted to roll around and bathe in their scent. His cock twitched, but when he looked up at Lilly's face, he could tell she was finally done.

Testing the washcloth, and realizing that it had cooled in the time it had taken to get her off again, Ethan stood and walked back to the bathroom. He ran the water until it was warm once more, then rinsed the cloth. When he returned to the bed, Lilly was lying just as he'd left her. Her limbs starfished out and her eyes closed.

Smiling, feeling proud of himself—and her—Ethan once more washed between her legs. She mumbled her thanks, but didn't completely rouse. He used the washcloth on himself, then threw it across the room, smiling when it landed with a plop on the tile floor just inside the bathroom. He'd deal with it in the morning.

Then he moved Lilly's body until she was under the sheet, avoiding the wet spot they'd made, and pulled her close. She melted against him, wrapping one leg around his and clinging to him as if she could meld herself into his skin.

It felt...amazing.

Ethan had never really loved this part of sex before. It always felt a bit awkward. But with Lilly, it felt as if this was where she was meant to be. Where *he* was meant to be.

"Let me enjoy this for ten minutes, then I'll get up and go," she mumbled against his throat.

Everything in Ethan rebelled at the thought of her leaving. But he couldn't help but feel touched that she offered. She hadn't ignored his fears. Hadn't blown them off. Was trying to do what was best for him.

"Stay," he said, turning to kiss her forehead.

"But—"

"I'll get up in a bit and go sleep on the couch."

His words roused her enough so she lifted her head. "Ethan, no. That's not fair."

"What's not fair is you having to get up and get dressed, and me taking you across town to sleep in a bed that's not mine. I want you here, Lilly. Want my bed to smell like you. Want you to smell like *me*. And I want to hold you until you fall asleep in my arms."

"I hate those motherfuckers," she said, sounding more pissed off than he'd ever heard her before.

"Who?" he asked, genuinely lost as to who she was talking about.

"The assholes who've made you hurt," she said, putting her head back on his chest. Her fingers brushed against the tattoo on his pec lazily. "But you'll beat them. I have no doubt."

Her confidence in him made Ethan's heart race. "I will," he said. He had extra incentive now. To sleep all night with Lilly in his arms. But the thought of hurting her was still too real. Too big to ignore.

She turned her head, kissed his chest, then settled against him once more with a sigh.

She fell asleep not too much later, and Ethan lay there under her for a long time. Feeling replete and thanking his lucky stars that this woman had somehow made her way to him. It was as unlikely as him surviving that bomb all those years ago, but here he was.

Here *they* were.

Finally, knowing he couldn't lie there any longer without falling asleep and risking the precious bundle in his arms, Ethan slid out from under Lilly. She grumbled when he moved, only settling down when he put his pillow in her arms. She turned her head, inhaled deeply, then promptly fell back to sleep.

Ethan leaned over, kissed her forehead, made sure she was covered with the sheet and comforter, then headed for his dresser. He grabbed a pair of sweats and left the bedroom. He didn't look back, knowing if he did, he wouldn't be able to leave her.

He got himself settled on his couch, one hand under his head, the other on his belly, and stared up at the ceiling, smiling. He fell asleep...and dreamed about his two kids, laughing and skipping along a forest trail, as he and Lilly followed along behind them, holding hands and smiling at each other.

CHAPTER SEVENTEEN

Lilly stood in the doorway to Ethan's living room and stared at the man sleeping soundly on the couch. It had been six days since their relationship had changed to a more physical one, though he still wasn't sleeping all night in his bed with her.

She understood his concerns. But she also hated not being able to wake up in his arms. Because she knew if falling asleep snuggled up to him was as amazing as it was, opening her eyes to a naked Ethan would be just as soul-satisfying.

He thought she slept through him leaving the bed, but she didn't. She hadn't. Not once. How could she when she was plastered against him, warm and sated from their lovemaking, then lost her human pillow?

She wasn't sleeping well at all, actually. Simply because she was worried about Ethan. But every morning, she asked if he'd had a nightmare, and every morning, he seemed surprised that he hadn't. Lilly decided to take a little credit for that. Being worn out by work, then hiking during the day, and having at least one monster orgasm in the evening seemed to be helping him rest, keeping the nightmares at bay.

But...was he having nightmares and just not telling her? Is that why he continued to sleep on the couch? She hadn't heard anything. And if she did, should she go out and wake him up? Should she ignore him? It killed her that she didn't know what to do to help.

This morning, she decided she was going to try something. Ethan would probably be pissed at her, but she didn't care. Lilly knew without a shadow of a doubt this man wouldn't hurt her... even in his sleep.

She tiptoed closer, careful not to make a sound, and got down on her knees next to the couch. She wanted to show him what he was missing by not waking up next to her. Ethan was on his back, one arm thrown over his head, the other resting on his naked belly. The blanket he'd been using was on the floor, obviously having been kicked off at some point during the night. He was breathing deeply and evenly.

Lilly couldn't help but take a moment to admire how good-looking he was, the boxers he wore resting low on his hips, so low she could see the beginning of his pubic hair. His cock wasn't hard, but she could still clearly see the outline of it under the cotton of his underwear. Her mouth watered remembering how good he'd made her feel the night before with that cock.

Going down on a man wasn't something she'd done all that often. But she figured she owed Ethan after all the times he'd made her orgasm with his mouth. Taking a quiet breath, she eased the waistband of his boxers down and took hold of his cock at the same time, tilting it up and wrapping her lips around it.

Lilly was surprised at how quickly he got hard. She supposed it was because he already had the start of a morning woody, but before she'd even bobbed her head three times, he'd grown to twice his normal size.

She put everything she had into the morning blow job, using her hand to caress his length when she pulled upward, and sucking hard as she took him as deep as she could.

"Shit, Lil," he muttered.

She couldn't help but smile as she felt his hand tangle in her hair. He didn't push her down, forcing her to take more of him; he merely held on. Lilly knew her performance wouldn't win any awards, but Ethan didn't seem to mind in the least.

Way before she was ready, he suddenly sat up. He grabbed her around the waist and hauled her up onto the couch with him. His fingers went between her legs and they both groaned at how wet she was.

Without wasting any time, Ethan pulled the crotch of her sleep shorts to one side and notched the head of his cock at her opening.

"Fuck me," he ordered.

Lilly sank down on him without hesitation. Her head flew back at how good he felt in this position, and she braced herself on his chest. Still wearing his oversized T-shirt, she began riding him hard.

"That's it. You started this, so finish it," he growled.

The sex was fast and dirty. Neither had undressed, too lost in sensation. Lilly bounced almost frantically on his cock. But it wasn't until he used his thumb on her clit that she got close to coming.

She couldn't help but stop thrusting when her orgasm approached, grinding tightly on his cock as she teetered on the edge. When Ethan pinched her clit, she shook uncontrollably and came.

While she was still in the midst of her orgasm, he raised her a few inches off his hips and proceeded to fuck her from below, pumping his hips as he chased his own release. It came seconds later, and he held her down on his throbbing dick as a long moan rumbled in his throat.

Lilly fell against him, boneless and breathing as hard as if she'd just marched up and down one of the mountains outside town. When she had her breath back, she mumbled, "Morning."

"Good lord, Lilly," Ethan said, panting. "What brought that on?"

She lifted her head, loving the feel of him inside her. "What? I'm not allowed to make love to my man?"

He stared at her for a beat, then asked, "That's all it was?"

She shrugged. "I woke you up out of a deep sleep...and you didn't hurt me."

His gaze was unwavering, and she couldn't read his expression. So Lilly kept talking.

"See, the way I see it, I just need to prove to you that you'd *never* hurt me. You haven't had any nightmares in almost a week. I'm hoping maybe they were just a biproduct of you being horny. Now that you're getting sex on the regular, your hormones have evened out and your mind isn't so overactive."

"You have no idea what you're talking about, do you?" he said with a small smile.

"No. But it sounds good, right?" She grinned, then sobered. "Ethan, you aren't going to hurt me. I hate that you're coming out here to sleep. It sucks. For both of us. I trust you. Now I need you to trust yourself."

"If I ever hurt one hair on your head, I'd never forgive myself," Ethan told her.

Lilly palmed his cheek. It was scratchy, and she loved the way his facial hair felt against her skin when they kissed.

"Just give me a bit longer, Lil. I don't like leaving you either, but the alternative is unacceptable."

"All right. But for the record...I do trust you."

"That means the world to me."

"And I'm gonna have to keep on being creative to find ways to prove that you aren't going to subconsciously hurt me," she told him.

Ethan grinned. "I'm one hundred percent on board with you being creative, if this morning was any indication of what you have in mind."

"I'll get better at that in time," she said a little shyly.

He gaped at her for a second, before chuckling. "Lilly, if you get any better at sucking my cock, I won't last long enough to get inside you."

Lilly felt her cheeks heat, but she just smiled down at the man she'd fallen head over heels for.

"What's your plan for the day?" he asked.

She blinked at the abrupt change of topic. "Um, well, I guess that depends on you and your team. I'd planned to tag along while you guys do your search. Then later this afternoon, I promised Tony I'd show him how a toilet works. I know, I know," she said before Ethan could comment. "It's weird. But after he heard about the water explosion at Whitney's house, he asked if I could show him what to do if that ever happens in the room he and his mom are staying in. I tried to tell him it was a freak thing, but he was adamant. I think since he doesn't have a father figure around, he's super interested in learning anything he considers 'manly.'" Aware she was babbling, Lilly asked, "Why? What're your plans?"

"I was just wondering how long we had this morning before you were going to be off charming the residents of Fallport."

Lilly rolled her eyes. "Whatever."

"I'm serious. Everywhere I go, people are telling me how much they like you. And how charming you are. And Otto told me if he was twenty years younger, he'd give me a run for my money with you."

Lilly laughed. "Um, twenty years would make him sixty. That's still a bit old for me."

Ethan grimaced under her.

"What? What's wrong?" Lilly asked. "Am I too heavy?" She went to put some of her weight on her knees, but he grabbed her waist and held her in place on top of him.

"Nothing's wrong. When you laughed, I felt it around my dick," he said nonchalantly as if he was telling her what the weather would be that day.

"Oh."

"So, since I'm in charge of the search today—and when we're leaving—that means I've got you for a while longer this morning," he told her with a grin. Then he sat up, holding her against his chest and standing in one fluid motion.

Lilly resisted the urge to screech and held on tight as he headed for the bedroom. He'd already proven that he was strong enough to carry her one evening when he'd held her against the wall and taken her.

He carefully lowered her to her back in his bed, somehow managing to stay inside her the entire time. Amazingly, he'd gotten hard again.

"For the record...I loved waking up with your mouth on me, Lil."

She smiled.

"But I came too fast. Now that you took the edge off, I'm gonna last longer this time. Wanna see how many times I can make you come before you make me lose control?"

Lilly's smile slipped. "I'm not sure—"

"I am. This'll be fun."

Lilly liked orgasming as much as the next girl, but she knew from experience that when Ethan set his mind on something—like pleasuring her—he didn't stop until he was one hundred percent sure he'd succeeded.

It was a good thing neither of them had to be anywhere early that morning...because by the time Ethan was done proving his prowess in pleasuring her, and coming again himself, Lilly could barely move.

* * *

In the afternoon, Lilly followed Ethan and Tal through the woods on another dishearteningly unsuccessful search for Trent or his body. Afterward, she showed Tony how to turn off the water to the toilet in her room at the B&B, explaining the rudimentary physics of how it worked and installing a new one, all with the approval of

Whitney, who'd decided to change out all the toilets in the house just in case.

Now, Lilly was lounging in the living room, relaxing with the older woman after dinner.

Ethan was meeting with his team. They needed to take a different approach in their search for Trent. He was nowhere near where Clyde had claimed to find his camping gear and everyone was getting frustrated at their lack of progress. It was like looking for a needle in a haystack because they had no idea which direction the man might have gone. There were hundreds of thousands of acres to search, and without being able to narrow down where he might have gone, it would be nearly impossible to find him.

So tonight, Lilly had dinner with Whitney, and Ethan would be coming over after his meeting.

"You know, it's okay if Ethan stays here," Whitney told her.

Lilly almost choked on the tea she was drinking. "What?"

"There's no need to be embarrassed," she said with a small smile. "I was young once too, you know. And it's obvious Ethan's your beau."

Lilly did her best not to blush. It wasn't as if she was ashamed or embarrassed that she and Ethan were having sex, but it seemed wrong to do it in Whitney's house. Like she was her de facto mother or something. "I'm not sure what our plans are, but thanks," she said after a minute.

Whitney beamed.

Lilly was saved from any further comments on the subject by the ringing of her phone. It was Ethan.

"It's him," she told Whitney as she stood. "I'll just go take this in the other room."

"Okay, dear," the woman replied.

"Hey," Lilly said as she answered and walked to the other room. When she got there, she realized that it wasn't exactly private, so she headed for the door leading out to the backyard.

"Are you at the B&B?" Ethan asked.

Lilly frowned as she shut the door behind her. "Yeah, why?"
"Trent's been found."

The three words made Lilly's heart stop for a moment. Then it began beating overtime. "Really? That's awesome! Where was he? Is he okay? What happened? Can I talk to him?"

"He's dead, Lil," Ethan said gently. "I'm so sorry."

For a second, Lilly froze in confusion. She was shocked at Ethan's bluntness, but also appreciated it. She was of the opinion that bad news was always best delivered succinctly and quickly, not leaving any room for doubt. But her first thought at hearing Trent had been found was that he was alive. Despite how long he'd been missing, she'd still harbored hope he was alive and well and this was all a ratings prank.

"Oh my God," she whispered.

"A pair of tourists were hiking and camping along a section of the mountains about twenty-five miles outside Fallport. Deep in the woods. The trail's difficult and leads to Eagle Point...the peak we named our search and rescue team after. We hadn't expanded our search that far out yet, figuring that he'd be closer to town, but it was one of the things the team and I discussed tonight."

Lilly was still having a hard time wrapping her head around the fact that Trent was dead. "What happened?"

"We don't know. Won't know anything until an autopsy is done. That'll take some time. But...it wasn't good, Lil."

She swallowed hard. If Ethan thought Trent's condition wasn't good, that meant it *really* wasn't good.

"I'm not going to be able to get there to see you tonight. You gonna be all right?"

"Yeah," she whispered. "Can I do anything to help?"

"No. There's not much anyone can do. We're gonna go out to where he was found with Simon and the detective to help guard the scene. They'll take pictures in the morning when there's more light, and try to find any evidence that might still be there. The state crime scene team will arrive tomorrow, but we have to make sure the scene stays secure until then."

"Okay. Will you have cell service?" Lilly asked.

"Doubt it. But I'll get in touch as soon as I can."

"Thanks for calling," she said.

"Of course. Lil?"

"Yeah?"

"I'm sorry."

"Me too."

"Try to get some sleep tonight."

Yeah, right. She didn't see that happening. Not only had she gotten used to falling asleep with Ethan, now she was going to be thinking about poor Trent, and Ethan and his team being in the woods all night, guarding his dead body. Nothing about this situation boded well for sleeping. But instead of saying any of that, she simply replied, "I will."

"Fuck. Wish I could be there, sweetheart."

And just him saying that made Lilly feel a little bit better. "You have a job to do. I'll be okay."

"All right. If you need anything, reach out to Raid."

"He's not going out with you?"

"No. He's been working Duke extremely hard lately, and he needs a mental break. The dog, not Raid. But if you need *anything*, he'll be happy to help. And if he needs to, he can get word to me."

"I'll be fine, don't worry about me," Lilly told him.

"That ship's sailed, hon," he said wryly. "I'll talk to you tomorrow."

"All right. Be safe."

"Always. Bye."

"Bye."

Lilly hung up and stood in the yard for a few minutes. She felt awful for Trent's family. She wondered if anyone had told the rest of the cast and crew, and if so, how they were taking the news.

Sighing, Lilly went back into the house. She told Whitney the sad news, and they spent a couple hours talking about the show, and about a few good memories Lilly had of Trent.

Eventually Lilly went upstairs, wanting some time alone. She lay on her bed, and it wasn't until after a few hours spent staring up at the ceiling blankly that she thought about Tucker. She mentally cringed. He wasn't going to be happy that she hadn't been there when Trent was found. But he'd have to understand there was little she could have done, not when some random hikers had found his body instead of the search team.

On the heels of that thought was the certainty Tucker definitely wouldn't be happy that she wasn't out in the woods *now*. But even he had to understand that there was no way the police were going to let her get anywhere near the crime scene with a camera. Even if they *would* allow it, she wouldn't defile Trent's memory by putting him on film for everyone to see.

Tucker would just have to be all right with that. And if he wasn't? Tough shit.

CHAPTER EIGHTEEN

"You're fired."

Lilly stiffened. "No. I *quit*," she countered.

Three days had gone by since Trent's body had been found, and the discovery had so far led to more questions than answers. He was near a very advanced trail that Lilly admitted she didn't think he'd ever choose to hike voluntarily. Not to mention, it was miles from where his camping gear had been found. No one knew how he got to the area; his rental was still missing, and he certainly didn't walk the twenty-five miles.

Not only that, but Ethan had told her two nights ago, after Trent's body was removed and taken to Roanoke for an advanced autopsy and examination by crime techs, that the handheld camera he'd had with him was discovered under his body. It was not only badly damaged by decomposition, but it also looked as if it had been chewed on by some sort of animal.

Simon told Ethan that he had high hopes the computer guys at the state crime lab would be able to recover the footage. Lilly had reported everything she could back to Tucker, keeping him informed what was going on. She'd expected to hear from him the day after she'd sent him an email about Trent being found, but this was the first time since then he'd called.

"I can't believe you're being such an asshole over me not getting Trent's *dead body* on film. This is the real world, Tucker!" Lilly seethed. "Not some make-believe world where everyone goes home after the cameras turn off."

"I never should've left you there! You're too interested in spreading your legs for that SAR guy. I told you to be there when Trent was found. Not only did you fail, you didn't get *any* footage of the body. There was plenty of time for you to get out there while the state crime lab was traveling to that stupid town, yet you didn't bother. You've fucked the episode, and we're going to have to get creative in order to finish it! I just pray there's something juicy on his handheld camera."

"Good luck getting your hands on it. It's evidence, Tucker."

"That's no longer your problem. I'm sending Joey out there to take your place. Give him your camera and everything else the show's paid for. The stipend you've been getting ends today. You're on your own paying for your lodging."

Before Lilly could tell him what a bottom-feeding asshole he was, he continued speaking.

"Don't even think of fighting me on this, Lilly. I've got enough shit on you that you'll *never* get another job in Hollywood. The bottom line is that you fucked us. We had a setup for an amazing ending to this show, and thanks to you, we'll have to cobble shit together instead of using firsthand footage. And don't give Joey any shit either. He'll be reporting back to me if you do anything else to sabotage the show. And I guarantee I've got better lawyers at my disposal than you could *ever* hire."

Lilly was done with Tucker's threats. "Listen, asshole, first, you have *no* shit on me because I'm a damn good employee and we both know it. But I'm sure SAG would be extremely interested to hear all about the personal errands you make the camera operators do for you. That kind of shit is not in our contract. Furthermore, if it comes down to comparing my reputation in the industry to yours, we *both* know who will come out on top—that's *me*, in case you're confused. After a decade, I have a stellar reputation. Directors ask for me by name. You've got what...nepotism? Your grandfather's reputation? Don't kid yourself, Tucker. If pushed, more people will stand by *me* than you.

"I can't believe you even *asked* me to get footage of a dead man. That's low, even for you. And you can't sue me for giving Joey shit—which I would never do anyway. Talking to someone isn't illegal. And refusing to take pictures of a freaking dead body or to record someone without their knowledge isn't sabotage, it's called being a decent human being! You have no legal ground to stand on, and we both know it.

"I'm done with your abuse, Tucker. I quit, as of right this second. I wish you and the others luck with the show, but I'm done. And if you do *anything* to try to damage my career, remember that I know an awful lot about how this entire series has been falsely portrayed. All I have to do is give a tell-all interview about the fabrications that were done to make the shows more interesting and your career will be finished before it even started. Don't mess with me, Tucker. It's not in your best interest."

With that, Lilly hung up. She didn't want to hear any more empty threats from Tucker. She was so done with him and his damn show.

"Bravo," Ethan said quietly from the doorway.

Lilly turned. She hadn't heard or sensed him standing there.

They were at Ethan's apartment. He'd gotten about ten hours of sleep in the last three days combined, and he definitely wasn't in a good mood. The fact that there was a press conference later that morning wasn't helping. As the founder of the Eagle Point Search and Rescue team, it was up to him to explain the details about their search. Simon would be there to answer questions and share what he could in regard to the investigation into Trent's death, but Lilly knew Ethan wasn't looking forward to the press conference.

"That was Tucker," she told him, sighing. "He tried to fire me because I didn't get him any footage of Trent's body in the woods and because I wasn't there when he was found."

"That's bullshit," Ethan said tightly.

"I know," Lilly said. She shrugged and took a deep breath. "So I told him I quit instead. And you know what? It's fine. More than fine."

"That asshole," Ethan raged. "Are you a part of a union? He can't fire you for not being there when *no one* was fucking there except for those two hikers. And they're probably scarred for life. The fact that he wanted you to film that shit so he could put it on TV is so fucking wrong, it's not even funny. How would *his* family feel if his dead body was used as a damn ratings ploy?"

Lilly stepped into Ethan's personal space and put her hands on his chest. He stopped ranting and took a deep breath.

"I'm so pissed on your behalf that I can't see straight," he said between clenched teeth.

"It's okay, Ethan. Honestly, I'm relieved. I hated what I was doing. Not the time I've spent with you and your friends, or the hiking, but lying to everyone who was going to watch that show. I stood back and let Tucker and the others lie their asses off, and I didn't say a word. I watched Tucker manipulate people, pay them to say what he thought the viewers would want to hear. I filmed the fake interviews, stood by as the cast lied through their teeth about hearing and seeing things. Even had to participate in some of the 'evidence' that was fabricated. Knowing he was milking Trent's disappearance was the last straw.

"I have no idea what I'm going to do now. I'm sure Tucker will try to blackball me in the industry, like he threatened, but he's an idiot if he thinks it'll work. I have a stellar reputation among my peers and with directors. No one is going to listen to him.

"The more immediate concern I have right now is that I don't have a place to live, since he's going to stop paying Whitney for my room at her B&B. I don't really want to go back to West Virginia to my dad's place, though I will if I need to. But all in all, I feel as if a huge weight has been lifted off my shoulders. I should've quit long before now, and it feels good to finally do what's right."

"Come 'ere," Ethan said, pulling her into him.

Lilly went willingly, snuggling into his embrace.

"Stay here. In Fallport. Everyone already loves you."

"I'm not sure about *everybody*," Lilly mumbled, remembering some of the glances she'd gotten when she was out and about during her first couple weeks here. Yes, people seemed to have thawed toward her after she'd helped Elsie and her son, but still.

"The people who count do," Ethan said. "Like me."

Lilly stopped breathing. Did that mean what she *thought* it meant? She lifted her head and looked up at him.

"I love you," he confirmed quietly. "I don't know how it happened, but it did. You snuck under my radar, Lil. I've loved spending time with you these last several weeks. I've smiled more than I have in years. I actually look forward to coming back to this shitty apartment of mine, when in the past I've found excuses to stay away. To keep from being alone." He paused. "You know the house Rocky is currently working on?"

Lilly nodded, overwhelmed with everything he'd just said.

"The owner's getting it fixed up to sell...and I want to buy it. For us, Lilly. It's not too far from town or my brother. I can't imagine not living near him. The house won't be ready for a few months but if you think you can stand it, you can stay with me here, at the apartment, until it's a done deal. I need to talk to the owner, see if he'd be willing to let me purchase it without putting it on the market—the last thing I want is to get into a bidding war with someone—and if you want to go see it sometime, to make sure you like it, we can definitely do that."

"Are you actually asking me to move in with you? And telling me you're going to buy a *house* for us to live in?" she asked in shock.

"Yes. I love you, Lilly. I want to spend the rest of my life with you. Here in Fallport. My job is flexible. I don't make a ton, but the money from my medical retirement from the Navy is fairly substantial. I'll never be a millionaire, but I've got enough for us to live on."

Lilly was having a hard time wrapping her mind around what was happening. She'd gone from being outraged, to relieved, to flabbergasted.

"Lilly?" he asked, sounding unsure.

"I love you too!" she blurted.

Ethan smiled. "That's good," he said softly.

"We haven't been dating that long. Maybe before I move in and you buy a house, we should make sure this relationship is going to last."

"It will," Ethan said immediately.

"You don't know that," she said with a shake of her head. "Ethan, you haven't even spent the entire night with me. And you haven't seen me eat cereal yet."

He chuckled. "Eat cereal?"

"Yeah. Or soup. I'm a slurper. I can't help it. It drives my dad and brothers crazy. Then I get impatient with the spoon and usually end up drinking the milk or broth straight from the bowl. It's kind of gross."

At that, Ethan laughed outright. When he had himself under control, he shook his head. "I don't give a shit if you slurp, Lil. I'm guessing I'll find it cute as shit. Your brothers hate it because they're your *brothers*. It's in their DNA to be annoyed by you. And if being a slurper is the worst thing you can think of about yourself, then I'm luckier than I thought I was...and trust me, I've thought plenty about how I'm a lucky son-of-a-bitch that you're with me."

"I don't want to be a burden," she said.

"You could never be a burden," he replied, framing her face with his hands and tipping it up to his. "Tucker's an asshole. He has no idea what a good employee he's lost. You're gonna find something to do here, I know it. This town needs you, Lil. *I* need you. Will you stay? If it makes you uncomfortable to move in with me—and I wouldn't blame you; this apartment's a piece of shit. It's a roof over my head and I don't have any issues with the other tenants, but I swear I wake up feeling as if I'm back in the eighties or something. Anyway, I'm guessing Whitney would love to have you at the B&B until the house I want to buy is done and mine."

She loved when Ethan had his hands on her. It made her feel cherished and close to him. She gripped his wrists and held on as his thumbs stroked her cheeks. "I can't afford what the show's paying her for the room," Lilly said honestly. "I mean, I have some money saved up, but not enough to pay for a room at the B&B for an extended period."

"Whitney would probably let you stay there for next to nothing," he told her. "She's lonely. She'd never admit it, but she doesn't get a ton of renters. It's not like Fallport is a tourist hotspot, and a lot of the hikers who come through stay at the chain hotel the cast and crew were in. She's loved having you there. She seems happier, and she'd even told me how much she loves having someone in the house to hang out with and to feed. Talk to her. I bet she'd charge you a reduced monthly rate that you can afford."

"I love her. She feels like the mom I've never had," Lilly admitted.

"So you'll stay? See where things might go between us? Think about moving in with me if I buy that house?"

Lilly's heart began to race in her chest. She wanted this. Wanted Ethan. Wanted to live in the house he and his brother were fixing up. Wanted to make Fallport her home.

She smiled. "Yes."

"Thank fuck!" Ethan said, letting his breath out with a whoosh.

Lilly giggled. "Were you that worried?" she asked.

"I've been dreading you leaving since I realized how much you mean to me," he admitted. "And I'm gonna deal with this nightmare thing. Although, I still haven't had one bad dream since you've been staying here."

"I hate that you leave me in the middle of the night."

"I hate it too," Ethan said. "There's nothing I want more than to wake up with you in my arms. And for the record, even if you don't officially move in, I don't want things to change between us. You have a free-standing invite to sleep in my bed whenever you want. I'll get you a key to the apartment later today. You've already got some of your stuff in my bathroom, and if you want to start keeping more clothes over here, that's cool too."

Lilly chuckled. "Isn't that kind of like moving in?" she asked.

Ethan shifted, sliding one hand behind her head and the other to the small of her back, slipping under her shirt and pressing her even closer. Lilly could feel his cock against her belly as she tightened her own arms around him.

"Well, this *is* a southern town. It's probably best we wait until you have my ring on your finger before we do that officially."

Lilly almost choked at his casual reference to marrying her. A vision of the two of them years down the line, mock arguing over who was going to get up and deal with their crying baby, flashed in her mind. She forced herself to concentrate on the conversation at hand. "So moving in would be frowned upon, but sleeping in the same bed every night wouldn't be? What's the difference?"

Ethan smiled. "No clue. But whatever. Don't care. As long as I get to hold you, I'm happy."

"This has been the weirdest day, and it's not even ten o'clock yet," Lilly said.

"I woke up dreading the day, not gonna lie. I'm not looking forward to this fucking press conference and dealing with stupid-ass questions about why we didn't find Trent. As if finding a person in hundreds of thousands of acres is easy." He rolled his eyes. Then his hand on the back of her head tightened. "But hearing my girl tell me she loves me and agreeing to stay in Fallport has me thinking *nothing* those reporters might throw at me will penetrate."

"And *I'm* thinking maybe some pre-press-conference penetration would help," Lilly said. The suggestion was corny as hell, but it achieved her goal. His cock twitched against her.

"Oh, yeah," he murmured. He rested his forehead on hers. "You really okay with what happened with Tucker?"

"It sucks, but yeah."

"Trent?"

"Again, I hate what happened to him, but I'm glad he was found and everyone can get some closure."

"Simon's determined to figure out what happened, who killed him. Fallport doesn't have any unsolved cases on the books. Nothing. All the robberies have been solved, and the very few murders that have happened, the killers were all put behind bars. There's no way Simon's going to let Trent's death go unsolved for long."

"Good," Lilly said.

"And I hate to bring this up...but the possibility that it was someone on the cast or crew is fairly high," Ethan warned.

"I know. I've already been grilled by the detective on the case, as you know. But it wasn't me," she said firmly. "So I have no problem with them taking my DNA and asking questions. I'll help in whatever way I can. Tell them whatever they want to know."

"I love you," Ethan said again.

Lilly grinned. She'd never get tired of hearing that. "And I love you."

"How about we forget about murders and reporters and producers for a little while and celebrate the fact that you're staying?"

"Deal," Lilly said softly.

Ethan shifted, then he was kissing her. Several minutes later, without taking his lips from hers, he picked her up and carried her toward the bedroom. Lilly's legs bumped against his, but she barely noticed. All she cared about was the possessive feel of his lips. When he put her down next to the bed she hadn't made that morning, it was a race to see who could get undressed first. Then they were naked and on the mattress.

Their lovemaking was fast and intense, but no less satisfying than the long and leisurely sessions they'd had in the past. As usual,

Ethan made sure she came before he took his own pleasure. Afterward, they lay together in a sweaty heap, and Lilly couldn't stop smiling.

"So...what are you going to do today, now that you don't have to film the press conference?" Ethan asked.

Lilly frowned. She hadn't even thought about that. "Would you mind if I still came? I'd like to support you."

"Mind?" he asked with a shake of his head. "I'd fucking love to have you there because you *want* to be, not because you have to be."

"Then I'm there. I do need to meet up with Joey at some point. I have no idea when he'll arrive. For all I know, he's already here. And if he *is* here, and knows about the meeting, I'm sure he'll be there with his camera."

"Why do you have to meet with him?" Ethan asked as he stroked her back with his fingers.

She was lying with her head on his chest and one leg hitched up over his. Her index finger traced patterns on his chest as they spoke. "I have to give him my camera and other things the show purchased. The computer I've been using to upload the footage, the battery chargers, things like that. That reminds me, I need to return the rental car too."

"Right. I can arrange that for you. I think I heard Drew bitching that he needed to head to Christiansburg to meet with a client. He wouldn't normally do that, but the person in question is wealthy and wants to meet in person to go over his taxes. I'm sure he wouldn't have an issue driving your car and turning it into a rental place there."

"How will he get back to Fallport?" Lilly asked in concern.

"I'll ask Rocky to pick him up."

"That's too much," Lilly said with a shake of her head.

"It's fine. Rocky won't mind. Especially because it's for you."

Lilly looked up at Ethan. "Really?"

"He knows how happy you've made me, Lil. And he hasn't hesitated to let me know I'd be an idiot to let you slip away. So he'll be over the moon that you're staying."

"I feel bad. Maybe I should drive it up there and come back with Drew after his meeting."

"Nope, Rocky'll take care of it."

"It's not like I'm doing anything," Lilly protested.

"Are we seriously arguing about this?" Ethan asked. But he was smiling as he said it.

"Apparently, yes."

"I can think of better things we can do when we're naked and in bed," he told her.

"You're such a guy." Lilly grinned and tried to slide off him to go shower.

But Ethan grabbed her around the waist and pulled her back. "Here's the truth—Rocky's becoming more and more of a loner, and I don't like it. He doesn't talk to many people besides the team, just sticks to himself. I'm worried about him. I figure him doing you a favor and getting out, even if it's only to Christiansburg, will be good for him. Maybe Drew can have a chat with him while they're on their way back and find out if something's wrong, or if Rocky's just going through a phase and will bounce back to the more friendly guy he's always been."

And just like that, Lilly's irritation bled away. "Did something happen? Is your brother okay?"

"Not that I know of, but I've noticed a slow change in him over the last year or so. I've tried talking to him about it but he always tells me he's fine, that nothing's wrong."

"Okay. He can return my car for me," Lilly said immediately.

"Thanks."

She chuckled. "This is just weird. You're thanking me for *you* doing me a huge favor." She shook her head. "This doesn't bode well for any future arguments we might have."

"I think it's awesome," Ethan said.

"You would," Lilly told him with an eye roll. "Now, as much as

258

I'd love to lie around naked with you for the rest of the day, we have places to go and people to see."

"Yeah. Sucks."

"Would it give you any incentive to get up if I said we could share a shower?"

"Yes. And just so you know, I'm going to convince the guy who owns the house Rocky's renovating to put in a kick-ass master bathroom. Complete with one of those huge car-wash-type showers. You know, the ones where you step in and there's a large shower-head coming out of the ceiling and jets on either side of the wall. That way, neither of us will have to be cold when we're showering together."

"Awesome," Lilly said. And it was. As much as she loved Ethan and sleeping at his place, the bathroom left a lot to be desired. The shower/tub combo wasn't meant for two and wasn't conducive to sexy times.

"And because I know you offered to shower with me out of the goodness of your heart, and not because you actually enjoy freezing your butt off while I'm under the spray, I'll let you go first."

"You really *do* love me," she blurted, laughing.

"Yeah, I do," he said with a completely straight face.

Lilly kissed him. How could she not? One kiss led to another, but before things could go too far, she reluctantly pulled away. "We really do need to get ready."

"I know," he said with a sigh. "You go on. I'll start us a fresh pot of coffee. I have a feeling we're gonna need it."

"Well, *you* will. You haven't gotten much sleep in the last three days. Are you doing okay?"

"I've gone with less when I was a SEAL," he said.

"But that's not what I asked. And you aren't a SEAL anymore."

"I can't decide if that was a dig about my age or how I'm not as in shape as I was when I was in my twenties," he said with a grin.

"It wasn't a dig and you know you're in amazing shape," Lilly told him. "I'm just saying that you aren't used to doing that stuff anymore. And you aren't superhuman. You need sleep just as much as the next person."

"I know. I was teasing you," Ethan said. "You're right. I *am* tired, and I'm nearing the end of my rope. But after this press conference, I'm planning on coming back here and getting some sleep. Happy?"

"Yes."

"Lil?"

"Yeah?"

"I'm just so very glad I met you. I realize that things between us have moved fast, and that there's still a lot we have to learn about each other, but my feelings for you aren't going to change. You've gotten under my skin, and I like you there. A hell of a lot."

"Same," Lilly said. She couldn't have said it better.

"Go on. Take your shower. I'll jump in when you're done, so don't bother turning off the water."

"Okay. You're going to be great today. I know it."

"Thanks for the vote of confidence."

Lilly scooted out of the bed and only felt a small twinge of self-consciousness as she walked naked toward the bathroom. It was hard to feel bad about her body not being perfect when Ethan had spent so much time up close and personal with every part she thought was flawed...and had praised every inch.

* * *

Joey couldn't decide if he was happy or pissed he was being sent back to Fallport. A part of him really wanted to find out what information the cops had on Trent. But he also knew it wasn't smart to be around, considering he was the one who'd killed the man.

Trent *deserved* what happened to him.

He never should've asked Joey for help that night. He was all ego when he was the center of attention and people were kissing his ass—and when he was passing off Joey's ideas about the show as his own. But when he was alone in the woods and had to come up with shit to entertain viewers, he was helpless.

He hadn't hesitated to call Joey. Needed someone to bail him out, as usual.

Well, Trent had gotten what he wanted. He'd be famous for sure...except he wouldn't be around to enjoy the notoriety.

Now, all he had to do was make sure nothing got in the way of the show succeeding. Joey would do *anything* to make it a hit.

He decided it was a good thing Tucker had sent him to Fallport to salvage what he could. He wasn't afraid to record people without their knowledge, unlike Lilly.

Just thinking about her made Joey's blood boil. She was fucking useless. She hadn't gotten *any* footage of Trent's body. Even a body bag shot would've been better than nothing. She'd claimed it was out of respect for his family that she'd stayed away from the trail while Trent's body was taken away.

Fuck that. And fuck Lilly. Joey was ten times the cameraman she was.

This show was *his* baby, even if no one acknowledged that fact. And Lilly may have ruined the whole thing because she was too busy screwing some local redneck!

But Joey would see this to the end, and next season, he'd be on the other side of the camera...

An idea hit him suddenly.

An awful, wonderful idea.

Everyone knew Lilly and Tucker didn't get along. That she'd quit. What if people thought Tucker was so enraged Lilly hadn't gotten any footage of Trent, so pissed that she'd quit...that he'd gone off the deep end?

What if *two* people ended up dead?

The brilliant idea swam in Joey's head, vivid images and plans forming.

The show would become even *more* famous. Not only would people be desperate to watch *Paranormal Investigations* to see what the hell happened, it could be featured on one of those crime shows at some point.

They'd *all* get famous. He'd be set for life! And that asshole Tucker would get what he deserved.

Lilly should've done what was asked of her. If she had, maybe she wouldn't be ending up the same as Trent.

It had been easy enough to get rid of his friend; it'd be even easier to take out that bitch.

CHAPTER NINETEEN

Two days later, Ethan sat across from Simon Hill as the other man updated him on the Trent Morrison case.

They were still waiting on the forensic report to come back from the state crime lab, which unfortunately could take months. There was a huge backlog of cases, and while the lab was working as expediently as possible, there was simply too much evidence from too many cases, and not enough manpower to process it all quickly.

But the autopsy had just been returned. Ethan wasn't a police officer, but he and Simon had worked on enough missing persons cases together that they'd become fairly close. At least professionally. He was grateful the chief was willing to share details with him, especially because what had happened to Trent was a little too close to the woman he loved.

Even though Lilly wasn't working for the show anymore, Ethan was still cautious. Someone had killed Trent, and there was no way he wanted that person's attention turning to someone else on the show...say a camera operator. Or a former camera operator.

"We were right. Morrison was definitely murdered," Simon said.

Ethan nodded. They'd already assumed as much.

"It was hard to tell specifics from the autopsy because of decomp, but his hyoid was fractured."

Now *that* surprised Ethan. "He was strangled?"

"Looks that way. There was no evidence of bruising, but mostly because the skin was too damaged to be able to see anything like that. He also had a broken fibula on his right leg. It's difficult to tell if that happened from a fall or something else."

"What are you thinking?" Ethan asked.

"It's hard to know for sure. I'm hoping that camera he had will tell us more. But I'm thinking he either fell or was hit extremely hard with something to disable him. It's difficult to fight someone off with a broken leg. The pain would've been immense, and would've made him fairly easy to subdue, I'm guessing."

"How'd he end up where he did then? He didn't walk all the way out there on a broken leg," Ethan said.

"No, he didn't. He was here to find evidence of Bigfoot, right?" Simon asked.

Ethan nodded.

"Maybe he had a run-in with Clyde near his campsite. He still hasn't admitted he even met Trent, but I'm not sure how he couldn't have. Maybe he wandered over because Trent was making a ruckus with his yelling and shit, trying to call Bigfoot. They had words, Clyde threatened Trent, and we both know it's not a good thing to get on Clyde's bad side.

"Or...maybe he called one of the TV people for assistance while camping. They had words, the killer got pissed at Trent, and walloped him with a tree branch. Then strangled him."

"So how do we figure out who it was?" Ethan asked.

"We wait for the forensics guys to come up with something. And hope the tech gurus working on the camera get done soon. I want this son-of-a-bitch," Simon said fiercely. "No one comes into my town and does something like this and gets away with it."

Ethan nodded. He wasn't especially pleased about what had happened either. "You think he's done it before? Or will do it again?" he asked.

Simon shrugged. "I figure there's a fifty-fifty chance of either one. He either had it planned or it was an act of passion and something in him snapped."

"He?" Ethan asked, already knowing what the other man was going to say, but wanting to make sure.

"Yeah. From everything I've heard about Morrison, I can't see him calling a woman for help. Not only that, but it takes a lot of strength to strangle someone. And even injured, I have a feeling he could've fought off someone smaller and lighter than he was."

"The person could've used something to strangle him. A belt. A rope. It wouldn't take as much strength then," Ethan said, playing devil's advocate.

"Yeah, but the killer would've still had to get something around his throat. And again, I think Trent would've fought like hell to keep that from happening. The other woman on the show, Michelle, she's only five foot six. And doesn't weigh much over one-twenty. There's no way she could've overpowered Morrison. Kate, the camera operator, is a bit taller and heavier, but it's still unlikely."

"And Lilly?" Ethan hated to ask, but needed to.

"We've already talked to Whitney, who vouched for the exact times she arrived back at the B&B, and confirmed she never left each day until you picked her up. So she's not a suspect."

"You narrowed down the time he was killed?" Ethan asked, surprised again. The last he knew, there was still a two-day window between the last time anyone had heard from the man and when he was discovered missing.

"No. We don't know yet which night he was killed, but you know Whitney. She doesn't sleep well. Between the floorboards that squeak, the parking area right below her window, and the sound of the water rushing through those old pipes of hers when someone flushes the toilet or uses the sink...nothing escapes her notice.

"Not to mention, she took my advice a few months ago and installed security cameras on the perimeter of her home, just in case. They're cheap, and the video isn't the greatest. Hell, it's grainy as hell. But still clear enough to see Lilly pulling in, then sitting in her car, messing with her phone for a few minutes before going inside. Your woman's in the clear, Ethan, so you can relax."

He hadn't realized just how tense he'd become. Ethan forced himself to lower his shoulders and took a deep breath. "So you think it's one of the others then?"

Simon pressed his lips together and nodded. "I'm working on reverifying alibis, and there are hours and hours of security footage from the hotel. The cast and crew were constantly coming and going, literally at all hours due to their odd shooting schedule. But anytime they weren't in the hotel, it's extremely hard to verify where they might have been. Some slept in late, others had morning or daytime shoots. We've got sightings of them here and there as they ate out, got gas, that kind of thing. Bottom line is, there was plenty of time for any of them to have driven out to meet Morrison and kill him. We haven't been able to rule out anyone. Roger, Chris, Brodie, Tucker, Joey, and Andre are all still persons of interest."

"Joey's in town," Ethan said, sure the police chief already knew.

"No shit," Simon said in disgust. "Fucker's been begging me for an interview. No matter how many times I tell him no, he won't back off. Heard he's been talking to everyone in town. Being inappropriate as hell too. Wish he'd just leave already. Why is he still here?"

"Probably for the exact reason you just said," Ethan said. "He's trying to get reactions from the locals about what happened."

"He also wants to know where Morrison was found," Simon said. "Wants one of my deputies to take him out there so he can get footage of the area."

"Not surprised," Ethan said. "Tucker wasn't happy when Lilly didn't get video of where his body was discovered. Probably threatened Joey that if he didn't get the location on film, he'd be fired too."

"Almost feel sorry for the bastard," Simon muttered. "But it doesn't matter if he finds it or not. We picked the area clean. Anything that looked even remotely like evidence was sent off to the crime lab."

"I'm sure he knows the trail he was found on, but not exactly where," Ethan said with a shrug. "He could go out to any plot of land in the woods and claim that's where it happened. Viewers wouldn't know any different. I'm guessing that's what he'll end up doing. It's not as if anyone on that show is a stickler for facts."

Simon chuckled for the first time. "Fucking Bigfoot. Give me a break. Even if I thought the legends and stories were true, I'd root for the ape. If the species is that good at staying under the radar and not being caught, more power to 'em. I hope it stays that way."

Ethan nodded. "Are you leaning toward *anyone* as the killer? I'm asking as the man who loves Lilly and wants to make sure she's safe."

"I can understand that. And between you and me, I think it's that asshole producer. He's slimy enough to want to do anything to make that show a success. Can't deny that one of his stars ending up dead while filming would be a hell of a ratings boost. I'm sure he'll spin it so it looks like fucking Bigfoot killed Morrison. But we all know it was no legendary creature that strangled him. It was a flesh-and-blood man, and I'm gonna nail his ass to the wall."

"Good. You need anything from me or my team, all you have to do is say the word."

"'Preciate that. Thank you for all the hours you spent looking for him. I don't say it enough, but Fallport is damn lucky to have you guys here. I'm working with the city council to allocate more funds for you next year. I know other cities would steal you away in a heartbeat if they could. The last thing I want is you guys being swayed because of a lack of funding."

"We aren't going anywhere," Ethan reassured him.

"Good."

Talk turned to other topics, and after another ten minutes or so, Ethan stood. He shook Simon's hand. "Thanks for keeping me in the loop."

"Of course. If Lilly hears anything concerning from her former co-workers, or that asshole boss of hers, you'll bring her in to talk to me?"

"Absolutely."

"Not that I expect trouble, but keep your eye on her," Simon warned.

"Plan on it. At the moment, she's over at On the Rocks. She's gotten pretty close with Elsie and they're havin' lunch on her break. Zeke's keeping an eye on her for me. She said after lunch, she's going to go over and play a round of chess with Otto, Silas, and Art."

"Lord help us all," Simon said with an eye roll.

Ethan chuckled. "They'll pump her for info while dishing out the latest gossip in return, which Lilly loves but won't admit. She's gonna go back to Whit's afterward and help her with some odds and ends around the house. She feels guilty for the tiny amount she's being charged for her room, even though she spends most nights with me, so she's offered to be a handyman around the house. Today she's dusting the tops of the ceiling fans and changing some of the light bulbs that are too high for Whitney. Not thrilled she'll be on a ladder, but since she's staying, I'll deal."

Simon smiled. "You've got yourself a good one."

"Believe me, I know. But anyway, she'll have eyes on her all day, and I'll make sure it stays that way until you nail the bastard who killed Morrison."

"Good. I'm doing all I can to try to get the evidence reviewed faster. Hopefully we'll know something soon. The DNA evidence will take a while, but I'm keeping my fingers crossed that we'll have that camera data today."

"If you get a chance, I wouldn't mind hearing what you find."

"Consider it done."

"Thanks. Later." Ethan gave the chief of police a chin lift and headed for the door. He wasn't terribly surprised by anything he'd learned.

Ethan pulled out his phone and dialed Lilly's number, needing to hear her voice after all the talk about someone she knew likely being the killer. She answered after the first ring.

"Hi!" she said happily.

Ethan immediately relaxed, her cheerful voice reassuring him that she was fine. "Hey," he said.

"How was your meeting with the chief?"

"Not bad. I'll tell you about it later. How's Elsie?"

"Busy," Lilly said with a laugh. "But it's obvious how much everyone likes her around here. We hadn't sat down for three seconds before someone was interrupting to say hello...and looking disappointed she was on break and wouldn't be waiting on them."

Ethan chuckled. "Yeah, she's one of Zeke's best hires. Anyway, I just wanted to call and touch base. Make sure everything was good."

"Is there a reason why it wouldn't be?" she asked.

"No. Not really. I just worry about you, considering whoever killed Trent is still out there."

"I'm fine. Promise."

"Stay that way, okay?"

She laughed. "Okay. Anything you want me to ask Art and the others?" she asked.

"Um...no?"

He'd never get enough of her giggle. "All right. I'll bring you up to date on all of Fallport's gossip tonight when you pick me up. Speaking of which...will you go with me to buy a car? Not a fancy or expensive one, but I need *something* so you don't have to constantly drive me everywhere."

"I don't mind," he replied.

"I know, and I appreciate it, but I'd still like to have my own set of wheels."

"I'm happy to go with you."

"Thanks. Oh, and I talked to my dad this morning...and I think he's planning a trip here."

"Yeah?"

"Uh-huh. I hope that doesn't freak you out."

"Not at all. I told you once that I'm looking forward to meeting him. That hasn't changed."

"I think he wants to make sure you're as great as I've told him you are. It's annoying, but he's my dad, so I understand."

"I do too. It's fine, Lil."

"Okay. But if my brothers say they're coming, I'm putting my foot down. I don't want to subject you to them yet."

Ethan chuckled. "You sure Whitney's all right with picking you up later?"

"Yeah. She's making a list of all the things she hasn't been able to get done around the house...but she isn't happy about it. I told her not to leave anything out, or else. I don't actually know what I'd have done if she didn't, but my threat worked," Lilly said happily. "She's doing me a huge favor by charging me pennies for my room. She also said she's happy to drive me wherever I want to go and pick me up. Which is another reason why I need my own car."

"Makes sense. I'm headed over to the house. If something happens and your ride falls through, give me a yell. I can take a break to come get you."

"Okay."

"I'll let you go so you can enjoy the rest of your lunch with Elsie. Tell her I said hello."

"I will."

"Love you, Lil."

"Love you too. I'll see you later."

"Bye."

"Bye."

Ethan hung up, satisfied that Lilly was good to go for the afternoon. Despite that, he pressed his lips together, hoping against hope that Simon would be able to figure out who killed Trent before too much longer. He needed to be sure his Lilly was safe. And in order to do that, the murderer needed to be caught. The sooner the better.

CHAPTER TWENTY

"It was so good to spend some time with you," Lilly told Elsie.

"Same. While I love living here, there aren't a lot of women my age who I've gotten to know." Her gaze lowered. "Or feel like it's worth befriending because of my situation."

Lilly reached out and grabbed the other woman's hand. "Your situation? What, because you're a single mom, working your ass off, and doing the best you can for your son?" she asked.

Elsie shrugged a little self-consciously. "I live in a motel, I'm a waitress, and I'm considered a newbie in town."

"You've got a roof over your head and work really hard. There's nothing wrong with that, Elsie."

She shrugged. "I want better for Tony."

"From where I'm sitting, he's happy, smart, and kind. I'm not sure what else you could want for him."

"Thanks," she said.

Lilly nodded and squeezed her new friend's hand.

"I appreciate you taking the time to show him stuff I know nothing about. He really needs a male figure in his life, but I'm not ready to date."

Lilly didn't take offense. She could show Tony how to do things like change a tire and do basic maintenance, but she was no substitute for a positive male role model.

She looked over at the bar and saw that Zeke was staring in their direction once more. And she knew it wasn't because *she* was there. She'd quickly noticed that he *always* kept one eye on Elsie. "You know," she said as nonchalantly as she could. "Zeke's a good guy. I'm sure he wouldn't mind spending time with Tony."

Elsie blushed and shook her head. "Oh, no, I couldn't ask him to do that. He's already been so good with my schedule."

"It doesn't seem to me that he'd mind in the least," Lilly said.

Elsie glanced over at the bar, the pink in her cheeks deepening when she saw Zeke looking her way.

"Thanks for coming to eat with me," she said, desperately trying to change the subject.

Lilly chuckled. "Okay, I'll drop it. But you know, I've hung out with him and his friends a lot over the last month or so, and I'll tell you right now that they're all amazing. Considerate, funny, and gentlemanly."

"You forgot intense," Elsie said wryly.

"Yeah, that too," Lilly agreed. "But they've all seen a lot with their previous jobs, so it's to be expected."

"Zeke was a Green Beret," Elsie said, the awe easy to hear in her tone.

Lilly already knew that because of her talks with Ethan, but she said, "Really?"

"Uh-huh. He doesn't really mention his time in the Army, but I overheard him talking with Tal once. They were comparing stories." Elsie shivered. "He saw some pretty awful stuff."

"Ethan did too. He still has bad dreams sometimes." The two women stared at each other for a beat before Lilly added, "I'm thinking spending time with Tony might be good for Zeke. Help him forget some of those bad things he saw and did."

She could tell Elsie was thinking about it. Knowing she'd

pushed enough for today, Lilly stood, Elsie joining her, and she hugged her new friend. "Don't work too hard today," she said.

"I won't. I really am glad you're staying," Elsie said.

"Me too. And I might be asking Zeke for a job if I can't figure out something soon," Lilly quipped.

"I'd love that, but I'm guessing you wouldn't enjoy it much. The pictures you took of Tony are awesome. You should pursue that."

Lilly nodded. She'd been thinking about doing just that. Whitney had mentioned it a while ago, and the more she thought about it, the more it appealed to her. She'd loved being in the thick of things at Tony's birthday party, and there wasn't another professional photographer or videographer in Fallport. She might not become a millionaire doing it, but she'd like it a hell of a lot better than what she'd been doing lately, that was for sure. "I'm thinking about it."

"Say hi to Otto and the others for me," Elsie said as she walked Lilly to the door.

"I will. See you later!" Lilly gave Elsie one more hug, then walked out into the beautiful spring day.

She walked around the square toward the post office, enjoying the weather and saying hello to everyone she saw along the way. It felt good to have been accepted as quickly as she was by most locals...especially since the reason she came to Fallport wasn't very popular.

There were some people, like Harry Grogan, who fully embraced the show. He was busy getting all sorts of merchandise made up in preparation for the throngs of people he expected to visit once the Bigfoot episode aired. For his sake, Lilly hoped he'd eventually make lots of money. But the more popular opinion was that the show was a pain in the ass, and they dreaded a possible influx of people coming to search for Bigfoot.

She waved at Davis, who was sitting in the grassy area in the middle of the square, happy when he waved back. Ruth and Clara were at A Cut Above, as usual, and while they didn't wave, they did smile through the window as she walked by. Lilly was taking that as a win. The route she took kept her away from the pool hall Ethan had warned her against, and she was glad, since she could see a few scruffy-looking men standing outside the front doors.

She smiled upon hearing Silas, Otto, and Art arguing about something in their usual spots outside the post office.

"Hi," she said as she approached.

"'Bout time you got here," Art grumbled.

Lilly didn't take offense. Art was always grumpy about something. She leaned down and kissed his cheek. He complained about that too, but it was obvious he didn't really mind.

She greeted Otto the same way, and when she went to kiss Silas on the cheek, he turned his head at the last second, so she pecked his lips instead.

He grinned and put a hand over his heart. "Did you see that, boys? She kissed me!"

Lilly could only laugh at his antics. If it had been anyone else, she would've been pissed. But she couldn't be mad at an almost-seventy-year-old balding man who spent his days gossiping and hanging out with his buds.

"That was rude," Otto scolded.

"Not cool," Art said.

Silas frowned and turned to Lilly. "I didn't mean nothin' by it."

"I know, it's okay," Lilly said. "But if Ethan comes by and challenges you to a duel, don't come cryin' to me."

They all laughed. Silas reached out and squeezed her hand. "Won't happen again."

She smiled at him. "So...who's gonna teach me how to play?" she asked. She knew she was opening up a can of worms, asking for chess lessons from the three men, but if nothing else, it should be entertaining.

Thirty minutes into their instruction, Lilly was as lost as when they'd started. As soon as Art told her one thing, Otto or Silas

275

would contradict him. Then the trio would argue over the rules of the game. It was hilarious—and Lilly was having a great time.

Between trying to explain which moves were legal and how to score points, the men told her the latest gossip. Everything they shared was pretty harmless, and Lilly was surprised to realize she actually knew some of the people they were talking about.

When the topic turned to Davis, Fallport's one and only home-less person, Lilly asked quietly, "Isn't there anything we can do to help him?"

"Won't accept help," Silas said.

"I wish he would," she said on a sigh.

"Me too. He says he's too messed up in the head to live inside. Says he feels claustrophobic. The shop owners all make sure to leave him food, so he doesn't go hungry, and there's a lean-to behind the police station that he uses when the weather's bad."

She'd known about the food from a conversation she'd had with Ethan, but not about the lean-to. "What about in the winter when it's cold?" Lilly asked in concern.

"Old Town Auto lets him stay in the bays," Otto chimed in.

"Oh, well, that's good," Lilly said. She was still concerned about the veteran, but was glad the locals were doing what they could to take care of him.

"I heard that other camera guy was talking to him yesterday. Offering him money to talk about Bigfoot and claim he saw him in town," Otto said.

Lilly turned to stare at the older man. "Seriously? Joey offered him cash to talk to him?"

Otto shrugged. "That's what I heard."

"Me too," Silas added. "And he's been hanging out near the high school, trying to talk to kids when they get out of class as well. The camera guy, not Davis, that is."

Lilly saw red. It was one thing for Tucker to be an asshole, and she suspected Joey was just doing as he was ordered, but that was too much. They had way more than enough footage to make the damn episode; Joey was just being a nuisance.

"If you'll forgive me, gentlemen, I forgot there's something I need to do," she apologized as she stood.

"All right, missy," Art said. Lilly had a feeling he wouldn't mind getting back to his normal routine.

"You all right?" Otto asked.

"I'm good," Lilly said, doing her best not to look as pissed off as she felt. "Thanks for the lesson. We'll do it again soon. Okay?"

"Sure," Silas said, turning his attention back to the board. "Otto, it's your turn."

Lilly waved once more, then she fast-walked down the street. She dialed Joey's number as she turned the corner, putting her back to the brick behind her, making sure she was out of sight of the prying eyes of the patrons and owners of the businesses in the square.

"Hello?"

"Joey, it's Lilly. We need to talk." She didn't beat around the bush and didn't even try to hide her irritation.

"What's wrong?"

"You need to stop harassing people for information about Trent and Bigfoot. Tucker has more than enough film for the stupid episode. I gave you my camera the other day. Why are you still here?"

"Tucker wants more," Joey said somewhat apologetically.

"Well, stalking the high schoolers and poor Davis isn't cool. What's next, seeing if you can get a third grader to talk to you about how he saw Bigfoot eat the family pet?"

"It's not like that," Joey protested.

His tone grated on Lilly's nerves. "Then what's it like, Joey?"

"You know how Tucker is. He's obsessed."

"I *do* know," Lilly said, some of her anger leaking out, now that Joey had confirmed what she'd suspected—this was all Tucker's doing.

"I shouldn't be here too much longer. And I'm sorry if I've upset anyone, but I don't know who I should talk to and who I shouldn't. Will you meet with me and give me some ideas? You know this town and the people much better than I do."

Lilly sighed. She didn't want to be involved in the show any longer. But if she could prevent him from harassing everyone, and help him get what he needed so he'd leave sooner, shouldn't she do it? "Fine."

"Thank you so much!" Joey said. "Now?"

"What?"

"Can you meet me now? I'd like to get this done. Tucker's already talking about the second season of the show, and I want to be in on those talks. So the faster I can get footage to appease him, the sooner I can get back to California and make sure I'm included on the team for the next season."

Lilly looked at her watch. She had about an hour before Whitney was supposed to pick her up. "All right," she said. "But I don't have all afternoon. I've got plans."

"Really?"

She straightened at the disbelief in his tone. "Yeah, Joey. I have a life outside of filming."

"Sorry, I didn't mean that like it sounded. I'm just surprised. It sounds like you've decided to stick around. Anyway, I don't think it'll take long at all. Where are you? Can I pick you up? Have you gotten another rental yet?"

"No. And yes, you can pick me up. How about outside the dog park behind the buildings on Main Street?"

"That'll work. I know where that is. Behind the bakery and coffee shop. Thank you so much, Lilly. Seriously. I'm on my way now."

"See you soon," Lilly said.

"Bye."

She clicked off the phone and shook her head. She didn't want to hang out with Joey. First, she was completely over everything having to do with the paranormal investigative crap. Second...it kind of hurt to see him. Up until this last gig, she'd put everything into her career. But maybe this would be a kind of closure. A way to put her life as a camera operator behind her once and for all. And in the process, she could try to honor Trent's memory. They weren't close, but she hated that his death was being used as a marketing ploy.

Maybe if she could convince Joey to talk to people about their thoughts on *Trent*, she'd feel better. It shouldn't be too hard. Trent wasn't a local, but he'd known how to charm strangers. There had to be *some* people he'd interacted with who might have nice things to say about him on film. She'd encourage Joey to talk to the workers at the hotel and the restaurants in the area.

Satisfied with her plan, she headed for the dog park. It wasn't too far away, but still, Lilly was looking forward to getting a car. She hated car shopping but with Ethan helping, maybe it wouldn't be so bad.

Thoughts of Ethan made her realize she should tell him about her change of plans. She clicked on his name on her cell and waited for him to answer, but the phone just rang before going to voice mail. She left him a short message about meeting Joey, promising to call him when she was done. She shoved her phone back in her pocket and waited.

Joey pulled up minutes later in a nondescript black rental sedan. She got into the passenger seat and smiled at her former co-worker. "Hey."

"Thanks again for helping me out, Lilly. I appreciate it," Joey said with a huge smile.

"Of course."

He pulled away from the dog park and turned right. Then took another right down Main Street and headed west, out of town.

"Where are we going?" Lilly asked.

"I thought we'd go somewhere more private. I'm guessing by your reaction I'm not a very popular person around here right about now. I can drop you off wherever you want when we're done talking."

Uneasiness shot through Lilly. "Okay. There's a pull-off not too far down the road we can use."

But when they neared the spot Lilly was thinking of, Joey didn't slow down.

"Joey? You missed it."

"I know." This time, his voice was flat.

The uneasiness she'd felt a moment ago flared into something bigger. "Pull over," she ordered. "Right now."

"No."

"Joey. I'm not kidding. I didn't agree to leave town." He was headed away from civilization. In fact, he was headed for the mountain trailheads where they'd done most of their filming.

He didn't respond, simply stared straight ahead as he drove.

Lilly was genuinely scared now, not sure what was going on, but knowing it wasn't good. She thought of the conversation she'd had with Ethan about how Trent's killer was likely one of the guys she'd worked with on the show. She wasn't sure she completely believed it at the time—but now she couldn't stop thinking about the idea.

She quickly pulled her phone out of her pocket, but before she could click on Ethan's name, the phone was slapped out of her hand.

Glancing over at Joey, she saw a look on his face she'd never seen before. Gone was the affable camera operator she'd gotten to know over the last few months.

He looked absolutely furious.

"I don't think so," he sneered.

Lilly opened her mouth to say something—what, she didn't know. She just instinctively knew she had to placate this man so he didn't do something crazy.

She didn't get a chance. His fist barreled toward her face and he hit her. Hard.

Her head flew to the side and slammed against the window next to her, the car swerving a bit at Joey's movement.

Lilly saw stars and blackness threatened to overtake her. She fought it. There was no telling what Joey would do if she was unconscious.

Before she could regain her equilibrium, he hit her again.

This time when her head hit the window, she blacked out immediately.

CHAPTER TWENTY-ONE

Ethan wiped his brow. He and Rocky had just spent the last twenty minutes wrestling with a heavy support beam in the house. The old one hadn't been installed correctly and it was a miracle the house hadn't fallen in on itself. He'd heard his phone ring a few times, but hadn't been able to answer it.

When he pulled out his cell, he saw that both Lilly and Simon had called. Neither had left a message, so he clicked on Simon's name first, hoping for more news on the case. The police chief answered after only one ring.

"What's up?" Ethan asked.

"The state lab sent us the video they were able to recover from Morrison's camera," Simon said without beating around the bush. "It's mostly him wandering around in the woods near his campsite. Then the video cuts out and when it comes back on, he's in the part of the forest where he was found by the hikers. He's walking, seemingly talking to himself about seeing signs of Bigfoot and how he thinks he's getting close, when he suddenly screams and falls. As you know, the camera was under him, so there's no video...but there's audio."

"Of?" Ethan asked when Simon paused.

"His death. The sound is muffled, probably because Trent had fallen on the camera, but you can hear him asking why and begging someone to stop. Then there's a lot of gurgling and struggling."

"And?" Ethan asked impatiently. He knew Simon wouldn't have called to tell him if he didn't have something else.

"The killer isn't on film, of course. But he says, 'Thanks for the Emmy,' before walking off. I can only assume he was in a hurry to get out of there and forgot about Trent's handheld, but even though the camera was under him, the voice is clear. Morrison had the volume turned all the way up. Probably to make sure he caught Bigfoot walking through the woods or some such shit."

"Who was it?" Ethan asked.

"You aren't going to like this," Simon warned.

"*Who?*"

"Joey Richards. I sent voice samples of all the people working on the show to the state from the interviews we'd done. They matched. They're ninety-five percent sure it was him."

"Fuck," Ethan swore. "I need to call Lilly."

"Yeah, that's why I called. I've sent some guys to track down Richards. They haven't had any luck so far."

"I appreciate the head's up. Lilly met with him a couple days ago to give him her camera and stuff. I was there. I didn't even sense anything off about him."

"We're still looking into him, but apparently he and Morrison went back a long way. They came up with the idea for the show together. Did you know Richards started his career in Hollywood in front of the camera?"

"No."

"He did. He was in a few soap operas, had a couple bit parts in movies. But when nothing came of it, he fell back on the camera operator thing. Apparently he did that in college before he decided he wanted to be a star. I'm guessing jealousy about the show's possible success overtook him. Morrison was one of the stars, and if anyone was going to be famous, it'd probably be him. Maybe it pissed Richards off."

Ethan was only half listening. He needed to talk to Lilly. Now. Tell her under no circumstances was she to go anywhere near Joey until he was in custody. "I have to go."

"Right."

"Keep me updated."

"Will do."

Ethan clicked off the phone and immediately touched Lilly's name on the screen.

"What's up?" Rocky asked.

"It's Joey," he said succinctly.

"Shit," Rocky said.

Ethan's tension rose when Lilly's phone went immediately to voice mail. She always kept her phone on. Always. He left a short message telling her to call him as soon as she could, then clicked on Zeke's name.

"Yo. What's up?" Zeke said as he answered.

"Is Lilly there?"

"No. Why?" All lightness disappeared from his friend's tone.

"Simon believes Joey is Trent's killer. And I can't get a hold of Lilly," Ethan said.

"She was here earlier. Had lunch with Elsie. Left a little after one-thirty. Hang on..."

Ethan could hear his friend walking and the bell over the entrance to the bar tinkling as he opened the door.

"Elsie said she was going to hang out with the guys at the post office, but I don't see her over there. You want me to go ask them if they saw her?"

"Yes."

Ethan heard Zeke jogging across the square. In less than thirty seconds, he could hear his conversation with the three older men.

"You guys seen Lilly today?" Zeke asked.

"She was here earlier," Otto told him.

"When did she leave? And why?" Zeke asked.

"Probably about half an hour ago," Art said.

"She said she had something to do," Silas volunteered.

"What?" Zeke asked.

"She didn't say," Silas said.

"Think. It's really important," Zeke said harshly. "Did she get a phone call or something?"

There was silence for a moment, and Ethan held his breath.

"No, no phone call," Otto said. "But we were talking about Davis. And she was really concerned about him. I told her that when it got cold, he stayed at Old Town Auto."

"That's right, and that got us talking about the TV guy. And how he was asking Davis questions," Silas threw in. "And I told her that he'd been hanging around the high school trying to talk to some of the kids too."

"That's when she remembered something she had to do," Art said. "That happens to me too. I can be in the middle of doing something else, like brushing my teeth, and suddenly it occurs to me that I forgot to put the milk carton back in the fridge."

"Right. Thanks, guys," Zeke said. "You hear that, Ethan?"

"Yeah, I heard. I don't feel good about this."

"Me either." A few seconds went by, then Zeke said, "She's not anywhere I can see."

Just then, Ethan's phone vibrated in his hand. He pulled it away from his ear long enough to see that a voice mail had come through on his phone.

"Hang on, Zeke, I've got a message."

"Call me back," Zeke ordered.

"I will." Ethan hung up and immediately clicked on the message icon. Looking at his watch, he realized the message was actually left almost forty minutes ago. He pressed his lips together in annoyance. He *hated* how spotty the service could be anywhere outside of downtown.

He heard Lilly's voice, and relief washed over him—until her message sank in. She'd been planning to meet with Joey. The one person in the world she needed to avoid right now.

"Fuck!" he cursed as he called Zeke back.

He didn't mince words when his friend answered. "He's got her," Ethan said.

"We don't know that."

"Actually, I do. The message on my phone was from *her*, telling me she was meeting with Joey and she'd call me when she was done. The damn thing didn't come through until now. Where would they go?"

Ethan was already on the move toward his car, his brother right at his side. His twin might not know what was going on, but he would support Ethan no matter what.

"To the hotel? Or headed to Roanoke?" Zeke suggested.

Ethan turned to Rocky once they were in his car. He connected the phone to the car's Bluetooth so all three could talk. "Where would Joey take Lilly if he wanted to harm her?"

Rocky thought about it for a moment. "The mountains."

Ethan's stomach dropped. That's what he thought too. "But where?"

"Do you think he'd be stupid enough to take her to the place he killed Trent?" Rocky asked.

"Maybe," Zeke said. "If he wants people to think the same person killed both Trent and Lilly...he might bring her to the same area."

Pressing his lips together, Ethan started his car and quickly backed out of the driveway of the old home. For a second, Ethan was living in his nightmare. He envisioned the baby screaming his head off, knowing something bad was about to happen.

As soon as the picture formed, he pushed it away.

No. They'd get to Lilly in time. They had to.

But if they were wrong about their assumption of where Joey would take her, it could literally mean Lilly's life.

"We're on our way," Rocky told Zeke.

"I'll call the others. And Simon. We'll meet you there. Don't wait for us," Zeke said.

"Ten-four," Rocky said, then reached over and ended the connection.

They drove without speaking. There was nothing to say. Both men were lost in their heads. Ethan was thinking about Lilly. Her sweet smile. Her laugh. How she felt in his arms. He couldn't lose her after just finding her. He couldn't.

Determination rose within him. This wasn't the day Lilly died. No way. He'd do whatever it took to make sure of that.

* * *

Lilly came to slowly, not sure where she was or why her head hurt so badly. She lifted a hand toward her head—and something around her neck tightened to the point she couldn't breathe.

"Don't touch the rope," a voice said from above her, just as the pressure around her throat lessened.

Opening her eyes, Lilly saw Joey's face. He was straddling her hips, smirking at her, holding a rope in his hands.

"Joey? What's going on?"

He stood. "Get up," he ordered, instead of answering her question.

When she didn't move fast enough, he pulled on the rope.

It was then Lilly realized the rope in his hands was connected to a loop around her neck.

No. Not a loop. A fucking noose.

She was in deep shit here.

Having no choice, she shifted to her knees and then to her feet. She swayed a bit, staring at Joey in dismay as her memories came back.

The conversation with the Gossip Guys. The call to Joey. How she'd agreed to help him, if only to get him out of Fallport faster. How he'd hit her in the face.

287

Reflexively, she reached for her pocket, only to find it empty.

Joey noticed. Of course he did. "If you're looking for your phone, it's lying shattered in a hundred pieces on the side of the road. You didn't think I'd give you a chance to call anyone, did you? Or let someone track the signal? Besides, your phone won't work out here anyway. Now start walking."

He jerked on the rope again, making her gasp as it tightened around her neck once more. Lilly couldn't help but reach for it, trying to loosen the rough material around her throat. But Joey yanked on his end so hard, she went to her knees once more.

"I said, *don't touch it!*" he yelled, his voice echoing through the trees. They were in a gravel parking lot at what looked like one of the many trailheads in the area around Fallport, and there were no other cars. She was on her own. "Every time you touch the rope, you'll regret it. Get up and fucking *walk!*"

Lilly did as ordered. She didn't know where they were, but she definitely knew why he'd brought her to the woods—Joey had killed Trent. She wasn't sure why, but it didn't matter at the moment. The big question now...why was he doing this to *her*? Was he actually planning on killing her too? It made no sense.

But Lilly kept her questions to herself and began to walk in the direction Joey directed. The trail was narrow and overgrown, and the farther they walked, the more scared she got.

Joey stayed behind her, and she realized he wasn't kidding about making her regret touching the rope when she reached up to feel the side of her head, where she'd smacked against the passenger window when he'd hit her.

He must've thought she was trying to remove the rope, because he yanked it from behind. She went flying backward, landing on her ass and doing her best to get air in her lungs because of how tight the noose had become.

"I warned you," he hissed. "Now walk faster. We have a ways to go."

His words didn't make her feel any better, but she'd learned her lesson. She wasn't going to put her hands anywhere near her head or the rope. Joey was going to break her neck if he pulled too hard.

What she *could* do was make as clear a path as possible for Ethan and his friends to follow. She'd watched them at work often enough to know what they looked for when they searched for a missing person. Scuff marks on the forest floor. Broken vegetation. So she shuffled her feet as much as possible, pretending to stumble. Made sure to brush aside leaves and branches as she passed. She wanted to leave her scent on as many objects as possible so Duke would be able to follow her trail.

She had no doubt the Eagle Point Search and Rescue team would be looking for her. But when? That was the million dollar question. Thankfully, she'd told Ethan exactly where she was supposed to be, and when, and they never went long without checking in on each other.

She'd also left him a message about meeting Joey. But would he figure out where he'd brought her?

She didn't know, but it was unlikely she'd be able to get away, so she had to believe Ethan would figure it out. Her life literally depended on it.

As they walked through the peaceful and serene forest, Joey began talking.

"I bet you're wondering what this is all about, huh?" he asked, without giving Lilly time to respond. "I killed Trent. He deserved it. Did you know the show was *my* idea? Trent and I were talking one night and making fun of all the paranormal shows on TV. I mentioned how profitable they probably were, how it seemed most concentrated on one thing or another. Either Ghosts or Bigfoot or aliens. We started talking about a show that investigated *everything*. Even planned all the episodes. The two of us would be the hosts, and we'd be different from all the others because we'd actually *find* something on each show. Not just a bunch of nothing, leaving the viewers disappointed. We'd see more than just glimpses of shadows or hear faint voices. We'd see actual *apparitions*. Get them on film.

Get interviews from people who'd experienced the paranormal firsthand.

"When we found an investor, it was supposed to be our big break. Then *Tucker* was hired, and instead of Trent and I being the stars, Tucker decided we needed a woman for diversity and to draw in female viewers. Suddenly I found myself on the outs—and Trent didn't have the balls to stick up for me! For our ideas. I was relegated to being behind the camera. *Again.*

"At first I didn't even care, was just happy the show was going forward. Until I realized it's gonna be a huge hit. And instead of Trent doing his best to get me in front of the camera, he treated me like shit! Like any other crew member. He *betrayed* me," Joey seethed, sounding unhinged.

"I didn't plan on killing him," he said almost nonchalantly. "But he called me after the first night he'd camped by himself, begging for help. He hated being out there alone and couldn't think of anything interesting to do for the cameras. So I went out, tromped around, let him film the bushes moving and the sounds I was making. He was so fucking excited." Joey snorted derisively. "It was his idea to come way out here. That moonshiner gave him shit about filming near his place, so Trent wanted to head farther out, make sure we could film without being interrupted.

"I drove him out here that second night. As we walked this trail, looking for a good spot, I told him I wanted to be a guest star on the show up in Canada. I wanted to be in front of the camera, like we'd planned from the start. He laughed at me. Actually fucking *laughed*," Joey hissed. "Said I wasn't star material. I got so mad! I picked up a branch and hit him as hard as I could. Got his leg. Broke it. Heard it snap. But I didn't care. He went down, and I had my hands around his neck before he knew what was happening. Do you know how long it takes to strangle someone?"

Lilly felt sick. She couldn't answer.

"I *said*, do you know how long it takes to strangle someone?" Joey repeated, tugging on the rope.

Lilly managed to keep herself from reaching for her neck. "No," she whispered.

"Four to five minutes. Oh, he went unconscious way before that, but it was a good long while of me squeezing his throat before he actually died."

Lilly was horrified all over again.

"It felt *so good!*" Joey exclaimed, laughing as they continued walking. "If I can't make it big on the show that *I'd* thought up, he doesn't get to either."

Lilly couldn't believe what she was hearing.

"But now *you're* trying to undermine the show," Joey said darkly. "And I can't have that. Tucker knows what he's doing. This is going to be the most talked-about show in the country. Poor Trent was attacked by Bigfoot and killed. Everyone's so upset, and we've got a whole memorial episode planned. But *you* fucked up and didn't get the shots we needed for the dramatic ending! The moment Trent's body was found. Mangled and eaten by Bigfoot in the mountains. You fucked my show! But now...with *two* people ending up dead... everyone's going to be talking about it. We'll be on every news station and all the talk shows. I'll finally get the recognition I deserve, that Trent *stole* from me."

This wasn't the person Lilly thought she knew. Joey had gone off the deep end, was completely delusional. He was a *monster.* And if she was going to survive, she had to think fast. Had to figure something out.

While Joey continued berating her for somehow not knowing the exact time and place some random hikers were going to find Trent's body, Lilly frantically tried to think of ways she could escape. If she could jerk the rope out of Joey's hands, she could run into the forest. She was in better shape than Joey, although he was bigger and stronger. But the second she lifted a hand toward the rope, he'd jerk on it and possibly break her neck.

No, she needed to wait and do her best to make a run for it when Joey let down his guard. All she needed was one opportune moment, and she was gone. For now, she'd do her best to remain compliant and not cause Joey to do anything rash.

She had no idea how long they'd walked when he finally jerked her to a stop. She held her breath, ready to fight for her life if Joey tried to strangle her like he did Trent.

But he merely smiled. A look so sinister, it made Lilly's skin crawl.

"Now comes the fun part."

"Joey, don't do this," she begged, scared out of her mind.

"I'm not going to do anything," he said calmly. "You're so distraught over the loss of your career and because the show is going to be a smash hit without you, you can't cope. You came out here to kill yourself."

Lilly stared at him in disbelief. Was he kidding?

No, he definitely wasn't.

"Of course, if Tucker doesn't let me take Trent's place, he'll need to be taught a lesson too. So maybe the police will get a tip that he killed you in a fit of rage for screwing his show. Either way...we're gonna have some fun. Turn around."

She stared at him in dread. She didn't want to turn her back on Joey. This wasn't the man she'd laughed with over something stupid Tucker wanted to do on the show. Not the guy she'd shared dinner with. Bitched with about having to hike for miles and miles, or sweat for hours in the New Mexico sun. This was a stranger. Someone she didn't know.

"I *said*. Turn. Around," Joey growled, his voice low and harsh.

Not knowing what else to do, Lilly turned. She was shaking so hard, she was amazed she could still stand. She heard Joey shuffling around behind her, but she squeezed her eyes shut, wondering if dying was going to hurt.

Lilly hated herself right then. She should be fighting. Running. Attacking Joey. Literally *anything*. But she was frozen in fear. Her family had taught her to fight, but they'd never been in a situation like this. Swallowing bile, she waited.

292

"All right. Time to start," Joey finally said, his tone friendly and light.

Lilly opened her eyes, but she didn't have a chance to turn around before the rope tightened. She was wrenched back a few steps.

Then, to her horror, her feet began to lift from the ground.

Frantically twisting her head to the side, she saw Joey laughing as he pulled on the rope. He'd thrown it over a thick branch and was hoisting her body upward.

Her hands flew up without thought, frantically tugged at the strands around her throat, but they were too tight. Her air was completely cut off. She couldn't breathe.

For a moment, Lilly panicked. This was it—she was going to die.

Then instinctively, she reached above her head and grasped the rope. She pulled herself up, taking her weight off the rope around her neck. She gasped for air, coughing and inhaling deeply.

A strange sound echoed through the trees. It took her a moment to realize it was Joey, laughing maniacally as he watched.

"Yeah, that's right. You can save yourself for a while. But how long can you manage to hold your own weight? Not forever, I'm guessing. You'll eventually lose your grip, and the rope will cut off your air. Then you'll pull yourself up again...but each time, you'll get weaker and weaker, until you can't do it anymore. Poor Lilly, killing herself because she's a failure."

Flooded with fear, Lilly realized he was right. She was in good shape, and because he hadn't tied her arms, she could pull herself up on the rope, but she wasn't strong enough to do it indefinitely. The rope was too long for her to climb up to the branch. She was too far away from the base of the tree to use it for any kind of leverage.

All she could do was swing at the end of the rope and try to hold herself up as long as possible so she didn't strangle herself.

She was going to die—and Joey was going to sit below her and watch.

She wanted to cry. Wanted to scream that this wasn't fair. But neither of those things would help her. And Lilly wasn't going to give up. No way. The longer she drew this out, the better chance Ethan had to find her.

Joey tied the end of the rope around the base of another tree, then stared up at her with his arms crossed, a huge grin on his face.

Lilly's arms burned as she held her weight. The only possible good thing about this situation was that no one in their right mind would ever believe she'd managed to rig all this up by herself. No one would think she'd killed herself. Ethan would *know* she hadn't.

It seemed almost silly to hope Ethan would somehow know where she was and come to her rescue, but Lilly had faith in him. Whitney was supposed to pick her up. When she didn't find Lilly waiting, she'd have called Ethan. He'd figure out something was wrong and call in his friends. They were all badass former military types. They could track her phone's signal far enough to know which direction she'd gone. And Joey's car was in the parking lot. They'd see it and come looking.

She just had to hold on. Literally.

Ethan would find her. The alternative was unacceptable.

CHAPTER TWENTY-TWO

Ethan held his breath as they pulled into the parking area at the head of the Eagle Rock Trail.

"Thank God," he said as Joey's rental car came into view.

"He's here," Rocky added in satisfaction.

Ethan threw his vehicle in park and jumped out. He ran toward the rental—and swore when he saw blood on the passenger-side window. Joey had hurt Lilly. He was going to pay for that.

"Look," Rocky said, gesturing toward the ground not too far from the entrance to the trail. There were scuff marks in the dirt, as if there had been a fight of some sort. But there was no blood, and no sign of either Joey or Lilly.

Ethan wanted to call out, but knew that was the absolute worst thing he could do. He and Rocky needed the advantage of silence to sneak up on Joey. They also needed to move fast. If Lilly was hurt, that might slow down Joey's progress, but they didn't have any time to waste. The man could be hurting Lilly right this second.

Without having to stop and talk about a plan, Ethan and Rocky started down the path at a fast jog. They'd done this plenty of times as Navy SEALs, but this time they weren't weighed down with heavy packs on their backs. They were both more than capable of killing with their bare hands, so a lack of weapons didn't make them hesitate for a moment.

They ran quietly and carefully for at least two miles before the sound of something other than the birds and the wind through the trees met their ears. Ethan stopped short, not even breathing hard. He held up his hand to his brother, but Rocky had already come to a halt as well.

Ethan tilted his head, trying to figure out what he'd heard. Then the sound came again.

Laughter.

A man was laughing hysterically somewhere just ahead of them. They weren't far from the spot where Trent's body was found, but they weren't quite there yet. Joey had either gotten impatient or he'd planned something different for Lilly. By the sounds of his glee, it was the latter.

"Easy," he said as Rocky began to move forward. He'd lost enough friends and colleagues who'd acted before assessing a situation, he wasn't going to lose his brother. It was two against one, but neither he nor Rocky knew what Joey had up his sleeve.

They crept forward, keeping away from the trail and hopefully out of sight. Rocky broke off, circling wide so they could surround Joey. Ethan strained to hear Lilly's voice, but all he heard was continued laughter.

When he finally got close enough to glimpse the scene, he froze in horror.

His Lilly was hanging from a noose about ten feet above the ground. She was doing all she could to hold herself up so she wasn't strangled, but it was obvious she was struggling.

His first thought was to run to her.

He closed his eyes for a breath to gain control. If he rushed in there without a plan, Joey could kill her. At the moment, Lilly was alive. As much as he hated seeing her suffering, it was better than the alternative.

Looking across the small clearing under the tree, Ethan spotted Rocky, his brother's shocked gaze matching his own. They had to move quickly. They had no idea how long Lilly had been strung up, but they would both clearly see her arms shaking and hear the distress in her cries.

They communicated via hand signals, then Ethan nodded.

He took a deep breath—and stepped out from behind the trees.

"Let her down!" he shouted.

As predicted, Joey spun toward him, taking his eyes off Lilly.

That's what they needed. All of the man's attention centered on Ethan.

"Get back!" Joey yelled, his face a mask of rage. He swiftly bent to grab a large branch near his feet, but Rocky tackled him before he could even touch the makeshift weapon.

Joey went down hard, landing on the ground with an audible *oof*.

Ethan's attention immediately swung to Lilly. He didn't give a shit what happened to Joey. His brother would take care of him.

Lilly's legs were swinging, and Ethan thought he heard his name fall from her lips in desperation as he sprinted toward her. He instinctively knew the woman he loved more than life itself was literally seconds away from dying right in front of his eyes.

"Get off me!" Joey screamed. "I was screwed out of something that should've been mine! Everything was *my idea* and I was demoted to the background! A fucking line in the credits! It's not fair! And she fucked the show! She should've been there when Trent was found! I thought you guys were supposed to be *good*. You should've found him that first week! The footage would've been fucking epic! Now the finale is gonna suck because of *her*. *She has to pay!*"

Ethan had no idea what the hell Joey was yelling about, but he didn't spare him a glance. All that mattered was getting Lilly out of that fucking noose. As he approached, he realized he couldn't get to her from below. Joey had pulled her so high, her feet dangled about eight feet off the ground. She couldn't reach his shoulders to take the weight off the rope. The only way to get her down was to untie the rope where it was fastened around the base of a tree.

"Hang on, Lil! I'll have you down in a second."

Ethan could see how close she was to losing her battle to hold her weight. Even as he watched, her hands slid and she dangled frantically at the end of the noose.

She made a strangled noise before reaching up once more.

Fuck. He had to get her down.

Running to where Joey had tied off the rope, he tried to undo the knot. But Lilly's weight on the other end had tightened it so much, no matter what he did, he couldn't get it loosened. Every second he wasted was another second Lilly suffered.

"Shit! Rocky, I can't get it. I need a knife!" he called out.

He looked up and saw his brother tightening plastic zip-ties onto Joey's wrists—and recognized the look of regret on his twin's face.

"I don't have one. I used it at the house for something and then I left so quickly, I didn't even think to pick it up."

Ethan looked around the forest floor for something, anything, he could use to sever the rope. Seeing nothing, his panic increased —something that had never happened before in a life-or-death situation. Ethan couldn't control the cry of anguish that escaped his lips.

Rocky appeared at his side and roughly pulled him over to stand below Lilly. "Get on my shoulders," he ordered. "That'll give you enough height so she can prop herself on your shoulders, get the weight off her neck and arms so she can loosen the noose."

For a split second, Ethan looked at Joey. He was lying on the ground, his arms secured behind his back, but his legs were free. Rocky hadn't finished making sure he couldn't go anywhere.

As if Joey realized at the same time that this was his chance to get away, he rolled to his knees, then managed to get to his feet without using his hands, since they were still secured behind his back. He stumbled and ran toward the trail that would lead back to the parking area.

Ethan didn't care. All that mattered was Lilly.

Rocky got down on his knees and Ethan didn't hesitate to climb on his shoulders. When he was settled, Rocky stood. He wobbled for a moment, getting his balance, but Ethan didn't have a moment of doubt that his brother would drop him.

Rocky was right. Sitting on his shoulders gave Ethan enough height to be able to reach Lilly's legs. He grabbed her knees and placed them on his own shoulders.

"Kneel on me, Lilly," he ordered. "Take the weight off your arms."

She immediately did, and Ethan heard Rocky grunt as he shifted, doing his best to stay still as the pressure on his shoulders and legs increased.

Ethan grabbed hold of Lilly's thighs and did his best to reassure her. "I've got you, Lil. You're good now. Take a deep breath. That's it. Another. You're safe now."

"Joey—" she choked out.

"Don't worry about him. Your only job is to breathe," Ethan told her.

But it hit him that they could be in deep shit. Joey could get out of the flex cuffs and come back, killing them all if he had a weapon in his car. They hadn't figured out a way to get Lilly down, and Rocky couldn't stand there with both his and Lilly's weight on his shoulders indefinitely.

Yet, for this moment, this very second, all he cared about was Lilly breathing and not being strangled.

A minute or two passed before Lilly said, "Now what?"

He'd never been as proud of someone as he was of her right this second. She'd be perfectly within her rights to freak the hell out. But she was staying calm. "Can you loosen the noose?" Ethan asked.

He felt her shifting above him for precious seconds before she said, "No. The knot isn't loosening!"

Looking up, Ethan realized Joey hadn't used a normal running knot to create the noose. He had no idea *how* it was rigged, but it was moot if Lilly couldn't get the rope to loosen. "Okay, what if I put your feet under my hands and lifted you upward. Can you reach the branch above your head and climb onto it?"

He heard her take a deep breath. Ethan tipped his head back just as she looked down at him. When their gazes met, strength seemed to flow through him. He'd come so close to losing her. He still could, if something went wrong. They weren't out of danger yet, but he was going to do whatever it took to get her out of this.

"Maybe," she said.

That was enough for him.

"Rocky? How're you holding up?"

"Do it," his brother said. "I'm good."

Ethan didn't know if that was true or not, but he was going to have to take his word for it at the moment. They literally didn't have any other options. The last thing Ethan wanted to do was leave Lilly hanging so he could get down and climb the fucking tree or something.

He brought his hands up to his shoulders and said, "Okay, lift your right leg and put your foot in my hand. Good. Now the other one." When he had Lilly's feet in his hands, he took a deep breath. "All right. On the count of three, I'm going to lift you up. Ready?"

"No. But yes," Lilly said in a shaky voice.

"You can do this, Lil. Okay. One, two—"

His counting was cut off abruptly when they heard a shout coming from the forest trail.

For the first time since he'd realized Lilly was missing, Ethan's spirits soared. He opened his mouth to yell, but Rocky beat him to it.

"We're here!"

"Hang on, Lil, the cavalry is almost here," Ethan said.

He heard her sniff above him, and he felt like crying himself.

Within a minute, the small clearing was suddenly filled with the best sight Ethan had ever seen in his life. Zeke, Drew, Raid, and a slobbering Duke, who immediately began baying when he smelled Lilly.

"Where are Tal and Brock?" Rocky asked, even as Zeke took in the scene and immediately moved to the tree where the rope was tied. He pulled a large K-BAR knife from the sheath on his side and began sawing through it.

"They're taking care of Richards. Asshole saw us, ran off the trail and almost immediately hit a fucking tree. Knocked himself out cold," Drew said as he and Raid both grabbed Rocky, holding him steady.

"You got her?" Zeke asked.

"Yes," Ethan said, helping Lilly put her feet back on his shoulders, then grabbing her calves. "Hang on, Lilly. Zeke's gonna cut you loose. I've got you. Stay strong for another few seconds."

"Piece of cake," she muttered.

Ethan wanted to smile, but he couldn't. Not yet. Not until she'd seen a doctor and he had her home, safe in his bed and in his arms.

The rope was quickly cut and Drew and Raid helped Rocky to his knees. Then they reached for Ethan's arms, making sure he didn't fall as he climbed off his brother's shoulders.

His teammates finally put their hands on Lilly, lifting her off him.

The whole process took just seconds, but it felt like hours.

Drew and Raid set her gently on the ground—then Ethan was on his knees, his hands grasping her face, staring into her eyes.

"*Fuck*," he said. Then cursed again. He couldn't seem to form other words. Sentences were *completely* beyond his abilities.

He crushed her to his chest, and Lilly melted into him. He wrapped his arms around her tightly and closed his eyes as he buried his face in her hair.

He'd almost lost her. It had been too close. Way too fucking close. If he hadn't called Simon when he did... If they hadn't figured out where Joey might've taken her... If he'd jogged a little slower...

There were too many variables that could've meant she was dead by the time he got into that clearing. He'd been lucky. They'd *both* been lucky.

He realized Lilly was shaking. From head to toe, her body was vibrating in his arms. Ethan didn't want to let her go, but he needed to make sure she was all right. Was she having a seizure? Had she lost too much air to her brain?

Ethan pulled back. "Lil?"

"I-I'm o-okay," she stuttered. "D-Delayed reaction I th-think."

"Let me get that rope off her," Zeke said gently.

"Careful," Ethan warned. "Don't cut her."

"Never," Zeke promised as he quickly loosened, then removed the noose.

Both Lilly and Ethan sighed once it was off. Her neck was bright red, chafed and raw from the rope, there was a bit of blood in her hair, near her temple, and she'd obviously been struck in the face. She was going to have some hellacious bruises—and just the sight of her made Ethan want to hunt Joey down and fucking kill him.

"We need to get her looked at," Raid said. "We can take turns carrying her."

"I'm okay," Lilly protested.

Everyone ignored her.

"Any chance we can call in air support?" Ethan asked.

"I can run back to the parking area and see if I can get a signal," Drew volunteered.

"No!" Lilly said in a stronger voice. It was a little raspy, and again, the reason for it made Ethan want to go back in time ten minutes to kill Joey. "I can walk. I'm good."

"No," all five men said at the same time.

Lilly wasn't intimidated. "Look, that sucked. All right? I admit it. I thought this was it. I wasn't going to ever see any of you again. But he didn't win. My throat hurts. I'm gonna be sore as hell for the next week or so, at least. But my legs aren't broken. I can walk. Joey marched me in here to my death, but he lost. I'll be damned if I'm carried out."

"Your call," Rocky told Ethan.

Ethan pressed his lips together and stared at Lilly. He wanted to get her to a hospital right this second to make sure she was all right. But he also understood her need to gain control after a situation in which she'd had *none*.

"I didn't fight," she whispered, staring into Ethan's eyes. "I wanted to, but I was so scared. I froze. I shouldn't even have let him near me. He hit me in the car and when I woke up, he had the rope around my neck. He kept yanking on it, and I was afraid he'd break my neck if I didn't do what he said. When we got here, he told me to turn around...and I..." She faltered for a moment, and it took everything Ethan had not to break down as he watched her struggle.

But his Lilly took a deep breath and straightened her spine. "I'll go to the doctor. My throat hurts, but I can breathe. And swallow. I'm okay. Please, Ethan. I need to walk out on my own two feet."

He leaned forward and kissed her forehead. He studied the angry red marks around her throat again. Then he picked up a hand and gently kissed the red skin of her palm. She'd literally held her own life in her hands. He nodded. "Okay. But we'll be taking lots of breaks."

She nodded, then winced.

"And we're going straight to the clinic when we get back to Fallport."

"Okay."

"She's gonna need to talk to Simon too. I'm guessing he's caught up to Tal and Brock on the trail by now," Zeke said.

"He didn't come with you?" Rocky asked, clearly surprised.

"He did," Raid said. "But he told us to go ahead when it was obvious we were moving faster than he and his deputy could."

Ethan looked into Lilly's eyes again. "I love you," he said softly.

"I love you too. And I *knew* you were coming," she told him. "I just had to hold on, literally, long enough for you to get here."

Her belief in him made Ethan want to cry.

"You did a good job of scenting the trail," Raid said. "Duke took off like a shot and didn't slow down once."

Lilly looked up at him. "I watched you two work enough. I did my best to brush against all the leaves and stuff that I could."

"It worked," Raid said, smiling.

Duke chose that moment to step closer to Lilly and give her a long, slobbery lick on the cheek. She giggled, and Ethan knew he'd never hear a better sound in his life.

"I don't know about you guys, but I'm ready to get the hell out of here," Rocky said. Then he turned to his brother. "And you need to lose some weight."

"Shut up," Ethan said, rolling his eyes, though he appreciated his twin trying to lighten the mood. He stood, then reached for Lilly. As soon as she was on her feet, he wrapped an arm around her waist and pulled her against him. "We're taking this slow. And if you feel faint or if anything hurts, you tell me."

"I will," she promised, wrapping her own arm around his waist and giving him a bit of her weight.

She might've been determined to walk back to the parking area on her own, but it was obvious she wasn't exactly steady on her feet. Gritting his teeth, determined to give her what she needed, Ethan stepped toward the trail. He looked back once. Saw the end of the rope still tied around the tree as Zeke picked up the noose and started to gather the rest of the rope. Simon might need it in order to prosecute Joey. Ethan knew Zeke would take care of getting the evidence to the authorities.

The feel of Lilly against his side went a long way toward calming him. They'd fought evil today and had come out victorious. And the events of the last hour had made him even more sure of his love for Lilly. He'd never been so scared. Ever.

It was funny how a life-or-death situation could narrow down what was truly important. And Lilly was definitely his number one priority. He didn't want to live without her, and he'd spend the rest of his life making sure she understood how much she was loved. She was his, just as he was hers.

The tension Ethan had been carrying since the moment he'd failed to reach her earlier finally lifted from his shoulders, and he felt as if he could breathe once more. He leaned down and kissed Lilly's temple as they walked. He'd never been prouder of anyone. She hadn't fought back, but there was no telling what Joey would've done if she had. He might've killed her in the parking lot before Ethan could get to her.

The bottom line was that when death was staring her in the face, she hadn't given up. She'd fought like hell to stay alive.

"Ethan?" she said quietly.

"Yeah?"

"I didn't get a chance to change Whitney's light bulbs, and she's probably going to try to climb that ladder to do it herself."

Figured his Lilly was more worried about someone else right now.

"We'll take care of it," Rocky said from behind them.

Yeah, he'd lucked out when Lilly had come to town. Ethan knew it. Rocky knew it. Hell, everyone on the team knew it. She'd not only gained a boyfriend, but an entire team of men who'd always have her back.

The day had started out great, then gone to shit, but was ending on a good note. Ethan couldn't ask for anything more.

EPILOGUE

Lilly was surprised at the fuss everyone was making over her. It wasn't every day a killer came to Fallport, but she didn't think she'd done anything that anyone else wouldn't have, if they'd been in her same situation.

And she'd been lucky. So very lucky. The doctor had agreed.

Lilly had been released to go home that same evening, and for the first time, Ethan hadn't gotten up in the middle of the night to sleep on the couch. And every night since, he'd held her tightly, almost afraid to let go. She saw the agony in his eyes every time he glanced at her bruised neck, and she knew it hurt him almost as much as it hurt her.

But a month had passed since that awful day, and Lilly was more than ready to move on. She'd been the topic of gossip in Fallport for weeks and it was finally subsiding. Thanks to the scandal of the high school principal having an affair with not one, not two, but three of the teachers at the same time.

Joey was in jail awaiting trial, and Lilly was more than ready to testify against him. Nothing would keep her from the courtroom.

The murder trial would more than likely take precedence over her kidnapping and attempted murder, but either way, Lilly was more than ready to stand against him.

As far as the show went...it would probably go forward as planned. Which sucked. But Tucker hadn't broken the law, even if he was morally bankrupt. Lilly had no doubt he was going to milk what happened for all it was worth. It would make living in Fallport hell when the episode aired and the town was overrun by the curious and the Bigfoot hunters, but she—and the town—would deal with whatever happened.

One afternoon, she'd been sitting with Otto, Silas, and Art while Ethan worked on their future house, when Harry Grogan had walked up. He'd looked nervous and asked to speak with her. Lilly couldn't figure out what he'd wanted...but then he'd shown her the Bigfoot design he'd planned to emblazon on merchandise in his store. When he asked if she'd prefer he didn't go through with his plans, Lilly had melted.

She'd ended up spending thirty minutes talking marketing with him and tweaking his design. She was actually excited to get some T-shirts, hats, and mugs for herself when they were ready. And she was one hundred percent in support of milking the tourists for all they were worth. Merchandise, Bigfoot walks along the Fallport Creek Trail, naming food and drinks after the famous creature...she almost couldn't wait.

The town might not be able to prevent the show from airing, but everyone could certainly benefit from it if they tried hard enough.

She'd pretty much officially moved into Ethan's apartment, even though that hadn't been the plan. Neither could bear to be apart from the other, and since they were sleeping in his bed every night anyway, it just made more sense to bite the bullet and move her stuff in.

Ethan had talked to the owner of the house Rocky was renovating and reached an agreement to buy it before it was finished. So that paperwork was in motion. It wouldn't be long before they'd be moving into the house and officially starting their lives together.

But before that could happen, Ethan had to meet her family. All her brothers and her dad had wanted to come down to Fallport after Joey kidnapped her, but the last thing Lilly wanted was them losing their shit when they saw her injuries. Somehow, she'd managed to put them off for a month, but today was the day they were all scheduled to arrive.

Whitney's B&B was going to be full to the brim, because not only were her brothers coming, but their wives and families were too. Lilly had tried to talk all of her brothers out of visiting at the same time, but once the Rays got an idea in their heads, there was no changing their minds.

Even though she was nervous for them to meet her new friends —because she wanted them to love Fallport as much as she did— she was more worked up over the fact Ethan hadn't made love to her since she'd been kidnapped.

At first she was happy to simply be held. She'd been extremely sore; so much so, it hurt to put any weight on her arms or even lift them over her head. But she'd been fine for weeks now, yet Ethan was still treating her like she was made out of glass.

Lilly was done with that nonsense.

It was still early, the sun was just peeking over the mountaintops surrounding Fallport, and Lilly knew they had a few hours before her family would arrive. The next week or so was going to be full of laughter, reassuring her loved ones that she was truly all right, introducing them to her friends, and showing them the charm of Fallport. But for now, it was just her and Ethan, and she was determined to show him just how much she loved him.

Moving slowly so as not to wake him up, Lilly rose to her knees and lifted her shirt over her head. She was bare beneath it, her nipples immediately hardening as she moved to straddle Ethan's thighs. He shifted under her, and Lilly knew she had about three seconds before he was fully awake and doing his best to coddle her.

So she grabbed his waistband and pulled it down, taking hold of his semi-hard cock with her other hand. She'd done this before, woken him up just like this, and it had worked really well, so she went with what she knew.

Lilly lowered her head and took him between her lips.

She heard him groan but didn't stop what she was doing. She took pride and satisfaction in how he immediately began to grow in her mouth.

"Lilly...what are you doing?" Ethan asked as he shoved his hand in her hair.

Afraid he was going to pull her off him, Lilly sucked harder.

He didn't try to stop her, simply moaned once more.

Lilly put her best effort into the blow job, loving his taste. She'd missed this. Yes, she liked cuddling with him, but knowing she was the only one who had the right to do this turned her on. Big time.

In the past, Ethan had always stopped her before she could get him off, but this morning, he didn't seem to have any control. Small bursts of precome were continually leaking from his cock, and Lilly slurped them up, ravenous.

"I'm gonna come!" he gasped.

Lilly didn't pull away, simply took more of him, sucking harder.

Ten seconds later, he grunted as spurts of come filled her mouth. Lilly never let go of him, holding him steady with one hand while moaning and swallowing as he took his pleasure. It felt damn good that she could do that for him.

She'd just lifted her head after one last lick when Ethan moved. He grabbed her arms and turned, throwing her onto her back. Then he scooted down her body and dove between her legs. All Lilly could do was hold on as he practically devoured her.

Every lick, every suck, was meant to drive her crazy. And it did. Lilly couldn't remember him ever being this insatiable before, and he was definitely a man who loved going down on her.

"Ethan!" she cried out when he fastened his mouth on her clit and began to suck at the same time his tongue flicked against her.

He didn't stop. His sexy gaze came up to meet hers, but he kept his mouth where it was.

The sensations were too much. She'd been primed by going down on him and because it had been so long since he'd made love to her. His aggressive attention between her legs was such a turn-on. Curling up into him and practically crushing his head between her thighs, Lilly came. Hard.

When she finally came down, she realized Ethan was on his knees, palming his hard cock, poised to enter her. He didn't always get hard right away after coming, but she supposed, just like her, he was primed. He hesitated, waiting for her permission.

"Please, Ethan. Come inside me."

That was all it took. He slid inside her soaking-wet folds with one hard thrust.

They both groaned in ecstasy.

"Am I hurting you?" he asked between clenched teeth.

"You could *never* hurt me," she retorted. "Now shut up and fuck me."

Ethan grinned and did just that.

Afterward, when they were both sweaty and panting, Ethan lay with his head on *her* shoulder for once. One hand covering her breast and the other arm under her neck, holding her against him. Or holding himself against *her*. It didn't matter. Lilly had never felt closer to him.

"I love you," he said quietly.

"Love you too," Lilly reassured him.

Ethan lifted his head. "You're going to marry me, right?"

Lilly blinked at him. "What?"

"I'm planning on asking your dad sometime this week, after he gets to know me, if he'll give me permission to make you my wife."

"And if he says no?" Lilly asked, knowing there was no way in hell her dad would say no. He'd be ready to give her to Ethan after being around him for five minutes, she had no doubt.

Ethan shrugged and smiled against her skin. "I'm still marrying you," he said simply.

"All right," she said.

He lifted his head at that. "All right? That's all? No squealing? No kissing? No attacking my body in glee?"

Lilly giggled. "I'm saving all that for when I see the ring."

He grinned at her, then sobered. "I haven't had that dream in a month."

"I know," she said solemnly.

"I'm still worried about it coming back, but I'm not concerned about hurting you anymore."

"Why?"

"Because seeing you hanging there at the end of that rope has cured my consciousness of *ever* wanting to see you hurting. Just a warning, if you stub your toe in the future, I'm probably going to lose my shit."

That was as sweet as it was ridiculous. She told him so.

Ethan merely shrugged. "I love you. I can't stand to see you in pain," he told her.

"What are you going to do when I have our kids?" she asked with a frown. "I'm not going through pregnancy without you by my side every second. If I have to suffer through that, so do you."

Ethan's face blanched, but he didn't look away from her. "I'm torn," he said strangely.

"What?"

"I'm torn between being thrilled beyond belief that you're talking about our future kids, and wanting to insist that we don't have children just to save you from going through that pain."

That was sweet, but Lilly wasn't having it. "I'm not saying I want to hurt like I did that day, ever again. But I'm not going to be locked away in a padded room either. Shit happens, Ethan. But when it does, I know you'll be there to get me through it, just as I will be for you. I won't lie, having kids scares me, but when I think of a son with your eyes, and a daughter wrapping you around her little finger with just a look, I'm willing to do whatever it takes to get that. Wait—do you not want kids?"

"I want them. I've dreamed about them, in fact," Ethan told her. "I love you, Lilly. I'm not sure I deserve someone like you, but I'm not giving you back. No way."

She laughed. "Good, because I'm not going anywhere. You're stuck with me."

"No one I'd rather be stuck with," he reassured her. Then his expression softened and he leaned down and kissed her. It was a long, slow, intense kiss. By the time he pulled back, Lilly was practically squirming under him. "So, we've decided that we're getting married, having at least two kids, and that my new favorite way to wake up is with your mouth around my cock. Yeah?"

She smiled up at him. "Pretty much, yeah."

"Just making sure. We've got some time before we have to get ready to meet your family at Whitney's place, right?"

"Yeah, why?"

"Because I don't think my girl's quite satisfied yet." With that, Ethan's hand snaked down her body and between her lips.

Lilly let out a small squeak, but immediately widened her legs to give him room.

Yes, it was safe to say, Lilly was as happy as she'd ever been in her life.

* * *

Zeke stood behind the bar and smiled. The weather had warmed up outside—and inside On the Rocks, it was even warmer. Lilly was there with her entire family, and the vibe in the bar was a happy one. Brothers, sisters-in-law, nieces, and nephews. Her father as well. From what Ethan had said, they'd all wanted to come to Fallport as soon as they heard what happened to Lilly, but she'd somehow managed to talk them out of it and planned a family reunion of sorts this week instead.

The six other men on the Eagle Point Search and Rescue team were also there, laughing with Lilly's family and generally having a good time. Zeke loved seeing Ethan so happy. He deserved it. He didn't know the details of the missions he'd been on, which had obviously affected him...but he didn't need to hear them to understand. He'd been on plenty of missions that went sideways while in the Green Berets. It was nice to be living a more relaxed and normal life here in Fallport.

The bar was also full of local residents who wanted a front row seat to the rowdiness so they could gossip about it later. It was all a part of the charm of living in a small town. Everyone knew everyone else and felt as if it was their right to talk about them.

Reina, Tiana, Elsie, and Valerie, the bar's waitresses, were working their butts off to keep up with everyone's needs. He'd lucked out when he'd hired the women. They didn't complain and did their best to serve everyone with a smile, both because they enjoyed what they did and because they wanted good tips. Overall, everyone was in a festive mood, despite what had happened to Lilly.

Everyone in Fallport had kind of taken her kidnapping personally, finding it hard to believe that someone had snatched one of their own from right beneath their noses. And even though Lilly hadn't been in town that long, she was definitely one of their own.

Zeke's gaze inevitably went to Elsie again and again, as it did whenever she had a shift with him. She was one of the hardest-working employees he'd ever had. So much so, Zeke had to actually force her to leave sometimes. He knew she wanted and needed the money, but he worried that she'd get burned out if she didn't ease up.

She'd been in town for a year and a half, and she'd slowly grown on him. Zeke was aware that she worked so hard because of her son, Tony. She was determined to give him the best life she could, even if, at the moment, that was a home at the Mangree Motel and RV Park on the outskirts of town. It didn't bother Zeke that she lived there, but it was obvious it bothered Elsie.

He watched as she smiled kindly at one of the men at the table where she was taking an order, and jealousy hit him so hard, it was all Zeke could do not to storm over and kiss the hell out of her—so everyone would know she was off limits.

He'd been having more and more of those kinds of thoughts lately. His attraction to her had bothered him at first; he wasn't a good bet when it came to relationships. His ex-wife was a good reminder of that. But the more Zeke got to know Elsie, the harder it was to stay away. To not tell her how he felt.

He didn't know a lot about her, but what he did know, he liked. She loved her son more than anything on the planet and would do anything for him. She didn't drink. Didn't socialize all that much. Didn't gossip about everyone in town. And she had the best laugh.

They also had a bad relationship in common, so Zeke had a feeling she'd be on the same page when it came to anything serious.

He also saw something in her that she hid from others. A pain in her eyes. He recognized it because he had the same pain within himself.

She wore a façade she showed to the world. She kept up the pretense around her son so he wouldn't worry. But he had a feeling that late at night, when she was in bed, the past threatened to overwhelm her...just as it did him.

Zeke longed to soothe those hurts. To help her beat back her demons. But another, larger part of himself was afraid of her.

It was crazy. At six-two, he towered over her five-foot-five frame, but he suspected she could hurt him worse than any bullets or fists ever could.

He heard a burst of male laughter coming from the table Elsie was waiting on, and Zeke turned just in time to see one of the men reach around her and firmly grab her butt.

Elsie stumbled forward, hitting her hip against the corner of the table.

Zeke saw red. *No one* put their hands on his waitresses without their permission. And it was obvious Elsie was uncomfortable and didn't want the guy's attention.

He was halfway to the table before he even realized he'd moved.

He stopped behind Elsie and put his arm around her waist, pulling her away from the table—and the man who was touching her. She stumbled again, but didn't tense in his arms. If she had, Zeke would've released her immediately. If anything, she seemed to melt against him, placing her warm palm on his forearm.

"Keep your hands to yourself if you want to stay," Zeke growled. He honest-to-God-growled. He had no idea what had come over him, but he felt possessive and overprotective of Elsie.

"She wasn't complaining," the man said with a smirk.

It took everything in Zeke not to put his fist through the man's face. He opened his mouth to tell him to get the fuck out of his bar, but Rocky appeared as if out of nowhere.

"I got this," he told Zeke, gesturing to the back hallway and office with his head.

Zeke had never backed down from a fight, or from making sure someone knew they weren't welcome in On the Rocks ever again, but at the moment, all his attention shifted to the woman in his arms. He turned with Elsie and steered her toward his office.

He gave Reina a chin lift and was relieved when she nodded. She'd make sure the bar was covered until he returned.

Elsie didn't say a word as he headed down the hallway and ushered her into his office. He closed the door behind them and took a deep breath. He should've calmed down by now, but he wasn't calm in the least. He kept seeing that man's fingers squeezing Elsie's ass—and the look of alarm on her face.

He brought his hands to her cheeks and tilted her face up to his.

As usual, she wore no makeup. Her face was smooth and blemish free, strands of brown hair had escaped the ponytail she usually wore, and her deep brown gaze studied him with absolutely no fear. He hated the circles under her eyes, indicating she didn't get enough sleep, but he understood her need to do whatever she could to make a good life for her son.

It hit Zeke then. Like a freight train.

He was done keeping his distance.

Watching Ethan make things work with Lilly made Zeke want what his friend had. Proved maybe he could have it.

"Zeke?" Elsie asked cautiously.

She wasn't pulling away from him. Was standing there calmly, her hands clutching his wrists, not pulling away...just staring up at him.

"You okay?" Zeke asked.

She nodded. "Um...are you?"

"I am now. *No one* touches you, Elsie."

Her lips twitched. "*You're* touching me," she joked.

"Sorry. I should clarify—no one touches you but me."

She blinked at that, staring at him for a long moment. "What's happening?" she whispered, the humor gone from her tone.

"*We're* happening," he informed her, before slowly lowering his head.

Zeke gave her a chance to pull back. To protest. To scream. Something. But she did none of those things. Instead, her eyes closed and she sighed even as she lifted her chin.

Oh, yeah. Elsie Ireland's life had just changed...for the better. She might not realize what he'd meant, but she would.

Zeke had vowed never to become involved in a serious relationship again, not after the disastrous experience with his ex-wife. But as he claimed Elsie's lips with his own, for the first time in years, he had a good feeling about what he was getting himself into.

* * *

I hope you've LOVED meeting the new gang and getting to know life in Fallport. Elsie and her son Tony gained a protector in Zeke... and they're gonna need it! Find out why in *Searching for Elsie!*

Want to talk to other Susan Stoker fans? Join my reader group, Susan Stoker's Stalkers, on Facebook!

Also by Susan Stoker

Eagle Point Search & Rescue
Searching for Lilly
Searching for Elsie (Jun 2022)
Searching for Bristol (Nov 2022)
Searching for Caryn (TBA)
Searching for Finley (TBA)
Searching for Heather (TBA)
Searching for Khloe (TBA)

SEAL Team Hawaii Series
Finding Elodie
Finding Lexie (Aug 2021)
Finding Kenna (Oct 2021)
Finding Monica (May 2022)
Finding Carly (TBA)
Finding Ashlyn (TBA)
Finding Jodelle (TBA)

The Refuge Series
Deserving Alaska (Aug 2022)
Deserving Henley (Jan 2023)
Deserving Reese (TBA)
Deserving Cora (TBA)
Deserving Lara (TBA)
Deserving Maisy (TBA)
Deserving Ryleigh (TBA)

SEAL of Protection Series
Protecting Caroline
Protecting Alabama

Protecting Fiona
Marrying Caroline (novella)
Protecting Summer
Protecting Cheyenne
Protecting Jessyka
Protecting Julie (novella)
Protecting Melody
Protecting the Future
Protecting Kiera (novella)
Protecting Alabama's Kids (novella)
Protecting Dakota

SEAL of Protection: Legacy Series
Securing Caite
Securing Brenae (novella)
Securing Sidney
Securing Piper
Securing Zoey
Securing Avery
Securing Kalee
Securing Jane

Delta Force Heroes Series
Rescuing Rayne
Rescuing Aimee (novella)
Rescuing Emily
Rescuing Harley
Marrying Emily (novella)
Rescuing Kassie
Rescuing Bryn
Rescuing Casey
Rescuing Sadie (novella)
Rescuing Wendy

Rescuing Mary
Rescuing Macie (novella)
Rescuing Annie (Feb 2022)

Delta Team Two Series
Shielding Gillian
Shielding Kinley
Shielding Aspen
Shielding Jayme (novella)
Shielding Riley
Shielding Devyn
Shielding Ember (Sep 2021)
Shielding Sierra (Jan 2022)

Badge of Honor: Texas Heroes Series
Justice for Mackenzie
Justice for Mickie
Justice for Corrie
Justice for Laine (novella)
Shelter for Elizabeth
Justice for Boone
Shelter for Adeline
Shelter for Sophie
Justice for Erin
Justice for Milena
Shelter for Blythe
Justice for Hope
Shelter for Quinn
Shelter for Koren
Shelter for Penelope

Ace Security Series
Claiming Grace

ALSO BY SUSAN STOKER

Claiming Alexis
Claiming Bailey
Claiming Felicity
Claiming Sarah

Mountain Mercenaries Series
Defending Allye
Defending Chloe
Defending Morgan
Defending Harlow
Defending Everly
Defending Zara
Defending Raven

Silverstone Series
Trusting Skylar
Trusting Taylor
Trusting Molly (July 2021)
Trusting Cassidy (Nov 2021)

Stand Alone
Falling for the Delta
The Guardian Mist
Nature's Rift
A Princess for Cale
A Moment in Time- A Collection of Short Stories
Another Moment in Time- A Collection of Short Stories
Lambert's Lady

Special Operations Fan Fiction
http://www.AcesPress.com

Beyond Reality Series

Outback Hearts
Flaming Hearts
Frozen Hearts

Writing as Annie George:
Stepbrother Virgin (erotic novella)

ABOUT THE AUTHOR

New York Times, USA Today and *Wall Street Journal* Bestselling Author Susan Stoker has a heart as big as the state of Tennessee where she lives, but this all American girl has also spent the last fourteen years living in Missouri, California, Colorado, Indiana, and Texas. She's married to a retired Army man who now gets to follow *her* around the country.

She debuted her first series in 2014 and quickly followed that up with the SEAL of Protection Series, which solidified her love of writing and creating stories readers can get lost in.

If you enjoyed this book, or any book, please consider leaving a review. It's appreciated by authors more than you'll know.

www.stokeraces.com
www.AcesPress.com
susan@stokeraces.com

facebook.com/authorsusanstoker
twitter.com/Susan_Stoker
instagram.com/authorsusanstoker
goodreads.com/SusanStoker
bookbub.com/authors/susan-stoker
amazon.com/author/susanstoker

CPSIA information can be obtained
at www.ICGtesting.com
Printed in the USA
LVHW081918180322
713806LV00003B/178